SAVANNAH

THE CIVIL WAR BATTLE SERIES
by James Reasoner

Manassas
Shiloh
Antietam
Chancellorsville
Vicksburg
Gettysburg
Chickamauga
Shenandoah

SAVANNAH

James Reasoner

CUMBERLAND HOUSE
NASHVILLE, TENNESSEE

PUBLISHED BY
CUMBERLAND HOUSE PUBLISHING, INC.
431 Harding Industrial Drive
Nashville, Tennessee 37211

This novel is a work of fiction. Names, characters, places, and incidents either are the product of the author's imagination or are used fictitiously. Any resemblance to persons, living or dead, events, or locales is entirely coincidental.

Cover design by Bob Bubnis, Nashville, Tennessee.

Library of Congress Cataloging-in-Publication Data

Reasoner, James.
  Savannah / James Reasoner.
    p. cm. — (The Civil War battle series)
  ISBN 1-58182-328-2 (alk. paper)
    1. United States—History—Civil War, 1861–1865—Fiction. 2. Georgia—History—Civil War, 1861–1865—Fiction. 3. Savannah (Ga.)—History—Siege, 1864—Fiction. I. Title.
PS3568.E2685S28 2003
813'.54—dc21

2003000784

Printed in Canada

1 2 3 4 5 6 7 8 9 10—06 05 04 03

For the members of
the WesternPulps e-mail group,
especially the real Cap'n Jim

SAVANNAH

Chapter One

BLISTERING SUN. DUST THAT clogged the nose and throat. Rocks that gouged the flesh and hid venomous snakes. Pelting rain that was a relief from the heat but brought with it thick, clinging mud. And the memories that clung to a man's mind as tenaciously as the mud stuck to his feet . . .

With a ringing shout from thousands of throats, the Yankees surged up Missionary Ridge, and the ragged gray men of the South were forced before them. Surrounded by clouds of acrid powder smoke, with the wind-rip of bullets around their heads and the thunder of bursting shells pounding at their ears, the Confederates could stand no longer against the Northern horde. They broke and fled, and the Yankees howled and nipped at their heels like the ravening beasts they were, and what should have been a sorely needed victory was only another defeat, one more of a series that had torn the heart and soul out of the fledgling nation known as the Confederate States of America . . .

"Here, bust a tooth on this . . . Cory, you hear me? You all right?"

Cory Brannon blinked and shook his head. The recollections of Chattanooga faded. He looked over at Abner Strayhorn, who held out a piece of hardtack. Cory took the square of almost impossibly tough bread. "Thanks," he said and slipped it into his shirt pocket.

Tall, skinny, and sunburned, with a shock of unruly red hair, Strayhorn frowned. "Ain't you goin' to eat?"

"Not now," Cory said. "I'm not very hungry."

"Best to eat whilst you got the chance. Don't never know when them damnyanks'll show up again."

Strayhorn was right, but Cory didn't have any appetite. He shifted, trying to find a more comfortable position in the rocks among which the two men sat. That was impossible, of course. No place on Rocky Face Ridge was comfortable.

11

These days, no place in the whole Confederacy could make that claim, Cory thought.

Nearly six months had passed since the defeat at Chattanooga. May 1864 found the Army of Tennessee—now no longer commanded by the temperamental and irascible Braxton Bragg but rather guided by the genial and professional Joseph E. Johnston—ensconced at Dalton, Georgia, and across the broad valley surrounding the town. To the west was Rocky Face, eight hundred feet high and twenty miles long, where the Confederate line looked down upon the neighboring valley the Federal army would have to traverse before it could reach Johnston's men. The tracks of the Western and Atlantic Railroad angled across the valley and curved through a gap in Rocky Face on their way to Dalton, where they turned south toward Resaca and, ultimately, Atlanta.

After being forced to retreat from Missionary Ridge the previous November, the Southerners had pulled back into northwestern Georgia. Rumors flying among the dispirited soldiers had it that the retreat would not stop until they had run all the way to Atlanta. But Bragg, whose handling of the army had proven disastrous for the Confederacy yet again, called a halt at Dalton so the men could rest. Nearly everyone believed that the Yankees were right on their heels, but some scouting missions by the cavalry revealed that was not the case. For whatever reason, the Federals had held back. So Bragg stayed at Dalton, waiting to see what was going to happen next.

What happened was that he was replaced as the commander of the Army of Tennessee. Johnston assumed the command, and he immediately set out to get his army ready for a renewed assault by the Yankees. It was inconceivable that, having won Tennessee, the Northerners would stop now. To the south lay Atlanta, a rail and supply center that would surely be an irresistibly tempting target for the Federals.

Johnston began by reorganizing the army into three corps: two infantry corps under Gens. William J. Hardee and John Bell

Hood, and a cavalry corps commanded by Gen. Joseph Wheeler. Reorganizing a defeated army was one thing; raising its spirits was something entirely different. Johnston succeeded at the former and struggled with the latter, but although few were ready to give up, the tens of thousands of men who were arrayed atop Rocky Face knew that the odds were against them. The Yankees, it was said, had a hundred thousand men in Chattanooga now, and they were led by the fierce Gen. William Tecumseh Sherman. Ulysses S. Grant, who had won the victory at Chattanooga with Sherman's help, had gone to Washington to assume overall command of the Union forces and bedevil Gen. Robert E. Lee in Virginia. Grant would find wily old Marse Robert a tougher nut to crack than Bragg had been, the Confederate soldiers told themselves.

In the meantime, the Southerners would have to deal sooner or later with Sherman, so they kept a close eye on the valley west of Rocky Face. That was the way Sherman would come at them. Back in February there had been a minor battle in this spot as the Federals sent a small force against the ridge to probe the Confederate line then pull back. Since then, there had been only occasional sniping.

Cory used the sleeve of his shirt to wipe sweat from his forehead. Only a week into May, and already the weather was hot. Still, most of the men were glad summer was on the horizon. The winter had been wet, cold, and miserable. Threadbare blankets and ragged uniforms provided little protection against the chill. Many of the men no longer had shoes or boots and had to wrap rags around their feet in an attempt to keep their toes from freezing off. Cory was lucky in that respect. His shoes had a few small holes in them, but they were intact for the most part. At least he *had* shoes. That was more than most could say, including Abner Strayhorn, who stretched out his legs in front of him and wiggled his toes in the sunlight.

"Boy, that feels good," Abner said around a mouthful of hardtack. "I 'member when I was a boy runnin' barefoot through the grass and soakin' my feet in the crick. I never did like shoes much."

"You'll wish you had some when we go to marching again," Cory said.

Abner laughed. "Yeah, more'n likely. But I don't reckon we'll be pullin' out of here anytime soon. Ol' General, he likes to set, so we set. Make the damnyanks come to us."

That would happen, Cory thought, and probably sooner rather than later. Even now, it was easy to gaze off to the north and west from the heights of Rocky Face and imagine a haze of dust floating in the air, dust raised by wagon wheels and the hooves of the mules and horses pulling those vehicles and the feet of tens of thousands of blue-clad Yankee soldiers . . .

Only he was not imagining it, Cory realized as he sat up straighter and reached for his rifle lying on the rocky ground beside him. There really *was* a lot of dust over there, and that much dust could mean only one thing.

"They're coming," he said.

Abner wasn't paying any attention. He and Cory had been friends for several months, and Cory knew that the lanky Tennessean had a tendency to drift off into a world of his own, even when he was on guard duty and was supposed to be watching for the enemy.

"Yankees," Cory said, louder this time.

"Huh? What're you sayin', Cory?"

Leveling his arm and pointing, Cory said, "Look over there. The Yankees are coming."

Strayhorn's eyes widened in surprise as he looked where Cory was indicating. "Son of a bitch! There's so much dust, there must be a whole blamed army over there!"

Yes, the Union army, Cory thought, but he didn't say that. There was no point in making Abner feel foolish.

Picking up his rifle, Cory scrambled to his feet. He brushed rock dust off the seat of his trousers. "I'll go tell the lieutenant. He may know about it already."

Abner nodded. "I'll stay right here and keep an eye on those ol' boys. Y'all hurry back, Cory."

The two of them were posted atop a sheer cliff known as Buzzard's Roost that overlooked Mill Creek Gap, through which the railroad tracks ran. Confederate engineers had constructed dams to block the flow of the creek and flood much of the gap. The area that was left open was guarded by earthworks and overlooked by dozens of artillery batteries and a strong force on top of the flanking heights. Large boulders littered the ridge and provided good cover. If the Yankee infantry came, the gap's defenders would have plenty of shelter and a good place from which to fire back at the Northern invaders. If the Federals targeted the batteries on the gap instead, well, then, the rocks wouldn't help the men up above. The exploding shells would blow them to hell.

As he hurried across the broad, fairly level top of the ridge, Cory hoped that the Yankees sent the infantry first. He wanted to have a fighting chance. That was all the Confederacy had ever asked, he thought.

Lt. Edward Stockard was in charge of the detail manning Buzzard's Roost. He was in his midtwenties, not much older than Cory, but in this war, which had cost the lives of so many gallant soldiers, some men in their twenties were colonels or even generals. Stockard stood at the eastern crest of the ridge, balancing himself precariously on top of a boulder and squinting through a spyglass. He lowered the glass and looked down at Cory.

"I see them, Private Brannon," he said before Cory could speak. With a curt motion, he closed the spyglass into a short tube. "We knew the Yankees would come visiting sooner or later."

"Yes sir," Cory said. "What do you want us to do, lieutenant?"

Stockard smiled. "Give our guests a warm welcome, Mr. Brannon. A most warm welcome."

Cory nodded and turned to hurry back to the other side of the ridge. Stockard's response was just about what he had expected.

It still sounded odd sometimes, though, to hear somebody address him as Private Brannon. Cory had fought at Forts Henry and Donelson and at the little country church near Pittsburg Landing known as Shiloh, had raided into western Tennessee with the cavalry under the incomparable Nathan Bedford Forrest, had slipped into Memphis on a desperate, dangerous mission as a spy, and had taken part in the valiant but doomed defense of Vicksburg. But he had done those things as a civilian, not a real soldier. Not until the previous autumn had he sworn the oath and joined the Confederate army. A part of him still wished that he hadn't. Then he would have been free to go where he pleased, to pick his own fights. After the battle along Chickamauga Creek, he could have gone west with Forrest, who had befriended him what seemed a lifetime ago at Shiloh. The general was back in Tennessee now, Cory had heard, raising hell with the Yankee supply lines.

But even as those thoughts went through his head, Cory knew he couldn't have left, whether or not he was in the army officially. Col. Charles Thompson, one of his best friends and the uncle of Cory's beloved wife, Lucille, had been wounded at Chickamauga. Cory couldn't have ridden off and left him in the field hospital. Not that his staying behind with Bragg's army had done any good, he mused bitterly. The colonel had succumbed to his wounds anyway, dying as he and Cory stood looking over the hills of southeastern Tennessee.

There had been no way to get word of Thompson's death to his wife, Mildred. She and Lucille had fled from Yankee-occupied Vicksburg, heading west across Louisiana toward Texas. The understanding was that Cory and the colonel would join them when they could. But with tens of thousands of Yankees in their way, Cory and Thompson had been forced to go the other direction, to Chattanooga. Then had come the battles, the colonel's death, and the retreat to Dalton . . .

Cory didn't even know if Lucille was still alive. It was that simple—and that awful.

Abner crouched behind one of the boulders and poked the barrel of his rifle toward the oncoming Federals. "What'd the lieutenant say?" he asked as Cory came back to join him.

"To give them a warm welcome."

Abner spat. "We'll give 'em hell, that's what we'll give 'em."

Cory knelt beside his friend and nodded. He peered across the valley to the west of the ridge. The landscape was thickly wooded, like all the other valleys and ridges in this part of Georgia, but through gaps in the trees he could see movement. From time to time his keen eyes even caught flashes of blue. There was no doubt now. All along the crest of the ridge, men crowded forward, eager to catch a glimpse of the approaching foe. Gunnery crews loaded the heavy cannons that had been hauled up here with much sweating and cursing. Riflemen thumbed fresh percussion caps onto their weapons and wiped damp palms on the legs of their trousers.

Somewhere, far below the eminence, a bugle blew. Farther on, another bugler took up the call. The tinny notes floated up to the top of Rocky Face Ridge.

"Listen to 'em," Abner said. "Lettin' us know that they're comin', just as bold as brass. They ain't even tryin' to sneak up on us."

"There's no point in that," Cory said. "An army can't sneak up on anybody. Not one as big as what Sherman's got, anyway."

"Let 'em come. We'll send them damnyanks packin'."

Off to the north, a rattle of gunfire sounded as the Yankees launched an attack on that part of the ridge. Cory was not surprised when he saw a long line of blue-clad infantry emerge from the trees below and start toward the base of the ridge at a fast walk. Their enthusiasm got the best of them, and the Yankees broke into a run. They yelled as they came forward, just like they had at Missionary Ridge.

Cory rested the barrel of his rifle on one of the smaller rocks in front of him and aimed down at the charging Yankees. They were still a couple of hundred yards away and that much lower as well. Shooting accurately would be a tricky proposition. But there were so many of them, Cory thought. All he had to do was squeeze the trigger, and he could be pretty sure of hitting someone in that surging tide of blue.

He suddenly asked himself why they were doing this. The Yankees had to know that they were charging right into the guns of the Southerners. Did they really think that their enemies would let them just waltz through the gap? Were they that stupid?

He had ridden with Forrest, had overheard many discussions of strategy between the general and his subordinates. Colonel Thompson had also discussed tactics with him. Now, as he peered down at the running, shouting Federal troops, Cory realized what was going on. He knew a feint when he saw one. Somewhere, the Yankees were up to something. Somewhere, but not here, they were either launching a major assault or getting ready to do so.

But this knowledge did Cory no good. There was nothing he could do, no one he could tell who would believe him. The Yankees were right out there, attacking Rocky Face. A blind man would know that, because he didn't have to see them. He could hear them, could hear the rattle of musketry and the roar of artillery, could smell the powder smoke that now began to drift in thin streamers through the air. The sounds and smells of battle were unmistakable.

Cory pressed the trigger, felt the heavy kick of the rifle against his shoulder as he fired down into the Yankees. It was all he could do, all any of them could do as they knelt atop the ridge.

Volleys of rifle fire rang out all along the crest. The cannons began to thunder. Down below, in the valley, fierce shell bursts flung dirt and debris and pieces of Yankees high in the air. As Cory reloaded, he saw the Federals falling, tumbling forward as Confederate lead ripped through their bodies. Canister and grapeshot shredded many of them. They were dying by the dozens, Cory thought as he leveled his rifle again. He squinted over the barrel, no longer able to see very well because of the smoke, and pressed the trigger.

Little bits of flaming powder stung his right hand as the percussion cap snapped and set off the charge inside the barrel. Cory ignored the sensation. If the Yankees kept this up all day, by evening the back of his hand would be blistered by the powder and covered with scratches from the tiny shards of metal that flew out each time one of the caps exploded. His arms would be black and grimy to the elbows, and his face would be discolored from the smoke as well. His throat and nose would be raw from the acrid stench. That was part of the toll that combat extracted from a man.

Assuming, of course, that he survived.

Some of the Yankees stopped in the middle of their blind charge and dropped to their knees to fire up at the ridge. Cory heard a few rounds whine overhead, and others ricocheted off the rocks where he and Abner crouched. Shooting up at such a steep angle was even more difficult than shooting down, so the Yankees didn't do much damage. Cory wasn't particularly worried about being hit. He reloaded, aimed, squeezed off a shot, then did it all over again in the sort of routine that was all too familiar to him by now. Over the years, he had been haunted at times by the knowledge that he was taking the lives of his fellow men in battle, but he supposed he was numb to that now. He never even thought about it much anymore.

Time had little meaning under these circumstances, but when the Yankees broke off their charge and started to pull back, Cory could tell that they hadn't kept it up for very long. That went right along with what he had figured out earlier about this attack being nothing more than a distraction. The Yankees didn't retreat very far, though. They fell back to the thick stand of trees in the center of the valley and stayed there, showing themselves from time to time so that the Confederates atop the ridge would know they were still there. They were out of rifle range, but the Confederate artillery continued lobbing shells into the trees from time to time. The gunners couldn't keep up a constant barrage because they had a limited supply of powder and shot. That was one of the problems with the war effort. Everything was in short supply now.

Abner sat back and grinned in satisfaction. "Told you we'd lick 'em," he said. "You see 'em turn tail and run, Cory?"

"I saw them. I'm not sure we licked them, though."

"What do you mean by that?" Abner asked with a frown. "We're still up here and they're still down there, ain't they?"

"I think that's where they want to be," Cory said. He scooted back from the edge of the cliff so that he wouldn't present too tempting a target to any Union snipers, then stood up. "I'm going to go talk to the lieutenant again."

"See if you can get me a few more caps when you do," Abner said. "I'm startin' to run a mite low."

"I'll see what I can do." Moving in a crouch, Cory loped off across the ridge.

Lieutenant Stockard was talking to a captain. Cory didn't know all the officers, despite the months he had spent in this army. He knew he was in a corps commanded by Gen. William J. Hardee. None of that really mattered to him. He was never going to fit in as a soldier; that was one reason he had avoided enlisting for as long as he had. He could fight, and he really didn't mind taking orders, but inside he chafed at the military discipline and always would.

He supposed he had always chafed at discipline. Maybe that was why he had left the farm back in Virginia and headed west to make his own way in the world. His mother, Abigail, especially, had been a stern taskmaster, and he'd had three older brothers who liked to boss him around, too. His father had died when Cory was fairly young, but Cory remembered him as the most easygoing member of the family, a man who liked to laugh and had a tendency to dream too much, maybe. Cory had the same problem with dreams that were too big, but he came by it honestly, he supposed. It was part of John Brannon's legacy to him.

Cory waited until Stockard was dismissed by the captain. "Lieutenant, can I talk to you?"

"I'm a little busy, Brannon," Stockard said. "In case you haven't noticed, we're in the middle of a battle."

"No sir."

Stockard glared at him. "You hadn't noticed."

"No sir, I mean it's not a battle. Not a real one."

"What the hell is it, then?" Stockard flung a hand toward the western edge of the ridge, where rifles still barked and cannons blasted from time to time. "That doesn't sound like a fancy dress ball to me, Private."

"No sir, it's a real fight." Cory thought about giving up, but he was too stubborn for that. He continued, "What I mean is that the Yankees aren't really trying to take Rocky Face. They're just trying to keep us busy."

"What in the world makes you think that?"

"They've got to know they can't take this ridge with the small number of men they have out there. Then they broke off their attack too fast. It's a feint, sir. A diversion. They're going to hit us in force somewhere else."

For a second the lieutenant looked as if he were going to dismiss the idea out of hand, but then he frowned in thought and rubbed at his close-cropped beard. "Maybe you've got something there, Private. I know that General Johnston is convinced that the main force of the Yankee army is going to come at us through Crow Valley, to the north of Dalton. Perhaps Sherman is trying to draw more of our men up here to the ridge so as to weaken the town's defenses. It would make his job a lot easier if Dalton were only lightly defended."

"I wouldn't know about that, sir," Cory said with a shake of his head. "I just know that the attack didn't seem real to me."

"Men really died," Stockard pointed out. "Some of ours, but from what I saw, a great many of theirs."

"Generals sometimes spend the lives of soldiers like a man throws around coins in a dram shop."

Stockard's eyebrows lifted in surprise. "That sounds danger-ously close to insubordination. I'm going to forget I heard you say that, Private."

"Yes sir." Cory's jaw clenched tightly as he spoke.

"It doesn't matter whether the Yankee attack was a diversion or not. We've been ordered to remain here and hold this ridge, and hold it we shall. Not one Federal soldier shall be allowed to set foot atop the crest. Do you understand, Private Brannon?"

"Yes sir," Cory said again.

"Now return to your post and forget those foolish notions. We follow orders."

Cory nodded, saluted, and turned to go back to the rocks where Abner waited. He had forgotten to ask about getting more percussion caps, but he didn't want to bother Stockard with that now. The lieutenant was right about one thing: No Federal sol-dier would reach the crest of Rocky Face—because they didn't want to.

But somewhere else, Yankee boots would be trodding on Southern soil, and no one would be there to stop them.

Chapter Two

CORY'S INSTINCTS WERE CORRECT, although he didn't know it at the time. While infantry under Gen. George H. Thomas, nicknamed the "Rock of Chickamauga," made the assault on Rocky Face Ridge, the rest of Sherman's army was swinging south. In that direction, Rocky Face terminated in an undefended opening known as Snake Creek Gap. On the other side of the gap was the town of Resaca, which, like Dalton about twenty miles to the north, was an important stop on the Western and Atlantic Railroad. Sherman's plan was to pour through Snake Creek Gap, capture Resaca, and cut the railroad so that Johnston's Confederates would be stranded to the north. From there it would be a simple matter to encircle the Southern army and destroy it.

Unfortunately for Sherman, a sizable group of Confederate reinforcements was being led by Gen. James Cantey toward Dalton and had stopped to rest in Resaca. The Federals advanced through Snake Creek Gap as planned, but when Gen. James B. McPherson, in command of this part of the operation, called a halt and studied the town through his field glasses, he saw a lot more Rebel soldiers than he had expected to see. The hour was growing late in the day, too, so instead of pressing on to Resaca, McPherson ordered his men to fall back to Snake Creek Gap and bivouac there for the night.

Although McPherson tried to mask his movements, that evening Confederate scouts discovered his presence and galloped back to Dalton, bearing the news of this threat to Johnston's headquarters. The Confederate commander responded by shifting three divisions from John Bell Hood's corps to Resaca to reinforce the men under Cantey who were there already. Sherman's plan was ruined.

Yet even with the knowledge he now possessed, Johnston did not move sufficiently to counter the Federal thrust through Snake Creek Gap. Concluding that this was a feint like the attack on Rocky Face Ridge, the Confederate commander pulled back two divisions from the force he had sent to Resaca and positioned them halfway between the two railroad towns. Johnston was still convinced that the Yankees' main attack would come from the north, above Dalton.

Meanwhile, Sherman was furious when he learned that McPherson had failed to take Resaca. He moved even more of his army to the south, leaving only a small force in front of Rocky Face to keep up the desultory skirmishing.

Several days passed as Johnston grew more concerned about what Sherman might be up to—and with good reason. When a cavalry patrol around the northern end of Rocky Face encountered no Yankees whatsoever, Johnston realized his miscalculation. Sherman was trying to get around him to the south and west and cut off his army from supplies and reinforcements. Johnston would have to move fast to prevent that. The orders went out in the middle of the night: Get to Resaca, and don't waste any time doing it.

The Confederates could only hope that they would arrive in force before the enemy did.

"WHAT DID I tell you about shoes?" Cory asked as he and Abner Strayhorn marched through the slowly graying dawn along with thousands of other footsore and weary troops.

"Yeah, yeah, I know," the Tennessean said, wincing as his bare feet left little bloody spots in the dirt of the road from blisters that had burst. "Ol' General's sure had us movin' lickety-split since last night."

Indeed, the troops had marched all night down the road from Dalton to Resaca. They were on the outskirts of the town now, and as the shapes of the buildings began to be visible through the early morning mist, officers cantered along the column and called orders that had the soldiers swinging to the right.

Some followed narrow lanes while others cut through the yards that belonged to the houses of the settlement. Cory and Abner walked by one of these and saw a curtain twitch. The face of an elderly woman peered out, eyes wide with fear. Cory smiled at her, hoping that would reassure her. She would be protected against the marauding Yankees. He didn't know if her expression eased or not, because he and Abner had to press on hurriedly to keep up with the rest of their company.

What were the Yankees doing this far south, anyway? They should have been stopped farther north, in Virginia and Tennessee, Cory thought. The invaders never should have been allowed to get this far. After all, this was the Southern homeland. It had to be defended.

Even in his own head, the words rang hollow. He had started out hating the Yankees as much as anybody south of the Mason-Dixon Line, and he still thought they were morally and constitutionally wrong to have invaded the Confederacy. He would fight them on that basis, fight them as long as there was breath in his body. But somewhere, somehow, there should have been another way. The firebrands on both sides could have settled their differences without resorting to a war that had ripped the country apart and muddied the ground with lakes of blood and torn loved ones from each other's arms.

He had seen too much of it. Lord help him, he wanted to put his rifle down and just walk way. He wouldn't do that, of course. He was in the fight to the bitter end. The old Brannon stubbornness would permit nothing less. But he wanted it to be over. He felt disloyal to Colonel Thompson, to Lt. Hamilton Ryder, to all the other friends who had fallen in the service of the cause, but it was true. Enough was enough.

But not yet. The full price had not yet been paid. The Yankees were still out there, collecting the toll.

The troops moved onto high ground just west of Resaca that commanded a broad, swampy valley through which a little creek meandered. Cory looked north and south as the line was established. He couldn't see the end of the line in either direction. Hardee's corps held the center, with Hood to the north and Gen. Leonidas Polk, the Fighting Bishop, to the south. Polk had arrived with the rest of his corps a few days earlier to help with the defense of Resaca.

Cory peered across the valley and saw the Yankees over there, several hundred yards away. They weren't doing anything, just sort of milling around. Getting ready for battle, like their counterparts in gray and butternut on this side of the creek.

"When do you reckon they'll be comin'?" Abner asked as he rested the butt of his rifle on the ground and leaned on the barrel.

"When they're good and ready," Cory said.

That didn't happen right away. The sun rose fully, and the morning dragged by. Officers on both sides were busy supervising the preparations for battle, but in the frontlines, the foot soldiers stood or sat or squatted and waited. Some played cards, others talked, a few even sat down with their backs against tree trunks and fell asleep.

Cory surprised himself by dozing off. He had thought that he was too keyed up with anticipation to sleep. But as he leaned against a tree, his eyelids drooped and then closed, and he let himself go.

He came awake with a start as Abner jogged his shoulder. "They're comin', Cory," he said. "Better get up now."

Cory's muscles had stiffened from sitting on the ground. He used his rifle to brace himself as he pushed up to his feet. Peering across the valley, he saw the Union infantry advancing. They couldn't run across the brushy, swampy ground that was dotted with dead trees, but they advanced at a steady pace, striding forward toward the Confederate line.

Somewhere a cannon boomed, and a shell burst among the Yankees. That was all the signal the men needed, because the roar of artillery crescendoed until it seemed to fill the entire world. The bombardment swept viciously across the valley, scattering the blue-clad soldiers like tenpins. The ones who survived kept coming, though. They moved faster now, despite the rough terrain.

Cory and Abner dropped to one knee and lifted their rifles, two men in a line of thousands who all did the same thing. Cory cocked his weapon and sighted over the barrel at the attacking Yankees. They were close enough for him to make out individual figures, and the air was not yet so clogged with smoke that he couldn't see what he was looking at. He settled his sights on a barrel-chested man with a ginger-colored beard and pressed the trigger. The Yankee stumbled as Cory's shot struck him, but he stayed on his feet. Holding his rifle at a slant across his chest, the man trotted forward. Sunlight glinted on the bayonet fixed to the barrel of the rifle.

Cory started to reload, wondering what would happen if the wounded Yankee made it this far. Would the man come right to him, guided by some eerie, unknowable power to the man who had sent that chunk of lead ripping into his body? Would they settle things between them, bayonet against bayonet, hand to hand? Cory handled the chore of reloading automatically without taking his eyes off the ginger-bearded man. But finally he had to look down to place the percussion cap on the rifle's nipple, and when he looked up again, the Yankee was gone. Probably he had fallen, struck by more bullets, perhaps, and now he was just one of those huddled shapes lying face-down on the ground as his life ran out of him.

Cory found another target and fired again.

Surprisingly, some of the Yankees made it all the way across the valley and surged up the high ground into the middle of the Confederate line. Cory was vaguely aware of the heavy, hand-to-hand fighting going on a few hundred yards away, but with thousands of Federal troops in front of him, he was too busy to worry about what was happening elsewhere.

For several hours, until the middle of the afternoon, he and Abner knelt side by side and kept up a steady fire. Many of the Yankees were pinned down at the creek, taking shelter behind the near bank, and Cory wanted to keep them there. Every time one of them popped up and started forward, Confederate fire forced him back. Sometimes the Yankees didn't make it to the creek but fell short of it, riddled with lead. It was a grim, bloody business, but effective.

Late in the afternoon, the Yankees pulled back. "They're givin' up," Abner said. "They know they can't lick us."

His friend was full of boundless optimism, Cory thought. If everyone on the Southern side was still so convinced of victory, the Confederacy might stand a real chance. Cory couldn't summon up that much optimism anymore, though, no matter how hard he tried.

That night, a line of campfires stretched for miles to the north and south, marking the Confederate position. A similar array of fires across the valley showed where the Yankees were camped. Cory and Abner made a scanty, unsatisfying supper on hardtack and a small piece of jerky apiece, washed down with the bitter brew made from roasted grain that took the place of coffee. They slept for a while then went out to stand their turn on picket duty and stare at the winking yellow eyes that were the Yankee fires.

The night passed peacefully, and the next day got under way with only minor skirmishing in the center of the line where Cory and Abner were posted. To the north and south of Resaca, the action was much different, and sharp little battles sprang up and continued in both places. The Yankees were trying to cross the Oostanaula River. If they succeeded, they would be able to turn the Confederate flank on both sides. As Cory and Abner knelt behind the fallen trees they were using as makeshift breastworks and took occasional potshots across the valley at the enemy, they heard the rattle of rifle fire and the rumble of cannon in the distance.

Abner shook his head. "There's some pretty good scrappin' goin' on," he said, "and we ain't got any part in it. That's a pure-dee shame."

"I don't reckon the war's going to run out of fight anytime soon," Cory said. "Our turn will come again."

"I suppose. Still, I don't like sittin' here whilst our boys are doin' all the work somewhere else."

That evening, bad news filtered along the line. The Yankees had succeeded in crossing the Oostanaula north and south of Resaca. Once again, Johnston's army faced the distinct threat of being surrounded and wiped out. Orders came to withdraw quickly through Resaca and across the river. Cory and Abner were some of the last men to pull out. They stayed where they were, firing steadily at the Federal pickets in order to keep the Yankees from realizing that the Confederates were retreating. Finally, the time came for Cory, Abner, and the other sharpshooters to leave. They tramped across a pontoon bridge that crossed the Oostanaula. All of Johnston's men were east of the river now. They kept moving all night, sliding out of Sherman's trap before the jaws could close.

The army turned south, following the railroad, and two days of marching brought them to a fork in the road. Hoping to fool Sherman into falling into an ambush, Johnston split his army, sending Hardee's corps almost due south down the right-hand fork toward the town of Kingston, while Hood and Polk went southeast on the left-hand fork to Cassville. What Johnston knew and what he hoped Sherman didn't, was that a road ran between Kingston and Cassville that would allow Hardee's men to quickly rejoin the rest of the army. Johnston wanted Sherman to split his army, too, so that the reunited Confederate force could fall on a smaller group of the enemy at Cassville.

The plan almost worked. Sherman unwittingly cooperated by dividing his forces, but hesitation and miscommunication among the Confederate command led to the attack's being called off. That afternoon, Federal artillery fire struck hard at the defensive line Johnston had established south of Cassville. Not only that, but realizing what was going on, Sherman acted quickly to reunite his army. Once again, Johnston had no choice but to retreat. The long march through Georgia continued.

CORY STOOD leaning on his rifle as he looked across Allatoona Pass toward the Confederate fort on the other side of the gap in the thickly wooded mountains. The fort was built of stone and bristled with artillery. Down below, the railroad tracks snaked through the pass on their way to Marietta. Cory swung his gaze north along the tracks, wondering how far away the Yankees were. They were up there; he was sure of that. The Confederate army had retreated for several days before Johnston called a halt here at Allatoona. This was where they would stiffen and turn back Sherman, according to the talk Cory had heard. He hoped that proved to be the case. Already, Johnston had retreated more than half the distance between Dalton and Atlanta. If they kept this up, Cory thought, the Yankees would be in Atlanta by the time summer barely got started.

Stockard walked up to Cory. "Where's Strayhorn?" he asked.

"He's around here somewhere, sir. You know Abner. He wouldn't wander off from his duty."

Stockard looked as if he didn't know that at all. But before he could say anything else, Abner came strolling up out of the brush. A chicken dangled by its feet from his outstretched hand, and blood dripped from the fowl's neck where its head had been wrung off.

"Lookee what I got here!" Abner said. "We're gonna eat good tonight, Cory!" He stopped short as he saw Stockard. "Uh, howdy, Lieutenant."

Stockard frowned at him. "You're supposed to be standing guard duty here, Private. Did you desert your post to go chasing after some scrawny chicken?"

"Uh, no sir, not really. I heard some rustlin' around in the brush over yonder and thought . . . well, I thought it might be some damnyank spies. Yes sir, that's just what I thought when I heard all that rustlin'." Abner made a sweeping motion with the hand that wasn't holding the chicken. "So I slid on over there, you see, Lieutenant, figurin' that I'd catch them spies. But when I got there, there wasn't nothin' but this here chicken, just a-scratchin' around after bugs."

"I see," Stockard said. Cory could tell that he didn't believe Abner's story for a second. But the lieutenant nodded and continued, "Very well. Carry on, men." He turned to walk off but paused and looked over his shoulder. "I'll expect a drumstick from that Yankee spy you caught, Strayhorn."

"Yes sir, Lieutenant!"

Cory chuckled as Stockard left them. "You're lucky he didn't have you shot for abandoning your post."

"Naw, what's really lucky is catchin' this here chicken," Abner said with a grin. "The whole countryside's been picked so clean by foragin' parties that it's a pure-dee miracle this little fella was still roamin' around loose. We're gonna have us a fine meal tonight, yessirree."

The smell of cooking meat drew men to the campfire where Abner roasted the chicken that night. He shared the feast, such as it was, cheerfully and without begrudging his fellow soldiers. One man brought a banjo he had carried all the way from Chattanooga, and soon the sound of music and singing echoed through Allatoona Pass. It was no secret that the Confederates had fortified the pass, so they weren't giving away their position by singing. Besides, this was the best demonstration of high spirits on the part of the men for quite some time, and the officers didn't want to dampen it.

But over the next couple of days, as Johnston waited for Sherman to show up, it became obvious that the wily Union general had flanked the Southerners once again. Scouts brought in reports that Sherman had struck out cross-country and was swinging to the southwest. If he turned to the east, he could strike straight for Marietta.

It was like a dance, a delicate and deadly ballet executed by tens of thousands of weary soldiers through heavily forested hills slashed with deep ravines. The Confederate army hurried along narrow, winding roads, leaving the tracks of the Western and Atlantic behind just as Sherman had done earlier. The Federals had crossed the Etowah River already and were bearing down on a small settlement called Dallas. The Southerners reached the community first and set up a line at a crossroads near New Hope Church.

Sherman wasted no time in attacking after he reached the area and found the enemy waiting for him. To lead the attack, Sherman selected a division under the command of Gen. Joseph Hooker—"Fighting Joe," as he was known—who had commanded the Union army in its stunning defeat at Chancellorsville. Hooker was slow getting his men moving, positioned them badly, and threw them against a force under the fiery John Bell Hood who was ready and waiting for them. The assault was unsuccessful, and the Federals lost a large number of men. The casualties no doubt would have been even higher if a drenching rainstorm hadn't forced a premature end to the battle.

By the next morning, both sides had their full complement of men. The Confederate line stretched some six miles, and facing it was Sherman's entire army. The Federal commander's next move was an attempt to turn the Confederate right flank. Gen. Oliver O. Howard, one of the heroes of Gettysburg, was charged with this task. He proved not to be up to it, mistaking a bend in the Confederate line for its end. The forces sent forward by Howard found stronger resistance than expected but pushed ahead stubbornly, only to have their ranks shattered by artillery fire and close-range volleys from the Rebel riflemen. They were thrown back again and again, and as night fell, the Confederates launched a counterattack. Texas regiments commanded by Gen. Hiram P. Granbury charged down a ravine where a large number of Union troops had taken refuge. Fighting with rifle butts, bayonets, and bare hands in the darkness, the Confederates overwhelmed the ravine's defenders, capturing more than two hundred of them.

By the next morning, the reports of Confederate successes the past two days had Johnston optimistic. Hardee's corps stood ready at the left end of the line. Johnston ordered it to move forward and test the strength of the Union right flank, which Johnston suspected was the weakest part of the Yankee line. It was afternoon before the maneuver got under way.

Cory tramped along a wooded ridge with Abner beside him. A steady drizzle fell. Despite the fact that it was late spring, most of the trees were bare of leaves and had an odd nude appearance. Bullets had done that, ripping through the growth and cutting off leaves and sometimes entire branches. Some of the trees ended in broken trunks that had been split and shattered by artillery. In a way, the place reminded Cory of a graveyard. The broken trees were like tombstones, and the naked branches of the ones that still stood looked like the fingers of dead men reaching toward the wet gray heavens.

"I heard some news this mornin'," Abner said as they slogged through the mud. "There's been a bunch of fightin' up in Virginia."

"I know," Cory said. "I heard talk about it, too. They say there was a big battle in the Wilderness."

"I never been there. Is it as bad as it sounds?"

Cory had seen the stretch of thickly tangled woods west of Fredericksburg. He nodded, "It's worse. I don't hardly see how you could fight a battle there."

Abner waved his free hand at the thick growth around them. "Sort of like here?"

Cory chuckled, but the sound had a grim note to it. "That's right. This is pretty much a wilderness, too."

They marched on. Cory could see a few men to his right and left, but not many. The mist in the air and the clusters of trees made visibility poor. After a few moments, Abner said, "Did you hear about Stuart?"

"Jeb Stuart?" Cory asked in surprise. In one of the few letters he had gotten from home over the past few years, his sister Cordelia had told him that their brother Mac was riding with Stuart's cavalry.

"Yep."

"What happened to him?" Cory felt himself growing impatient with the way he sometimes had to drag information out of Abner.

"He got hisself killed at some place called Yellow Tavern. I never heard of it. Supposed to be close to Richmond."

Cory kept moving, but he was numb with shock at the news of the dashing cavalry leader's death. He knew where Yellow Tavern was; the Brannons always passed by the old roadway inn when they were going to Richmond for the annual fair and horse races every summer. He felt a pang of sorrow like a knife thrust as he thought about those long-ago days.

He hated to hear of Stuart's death—for one thing, that meant Mac had been in danger, too—but even more he mourned for what had been lost with the coming of the war. At the same time he could see that a way of life was ending, well on its way to destruction. He didn't necessarily agree with everything that had gone on in the South; the fiercely independent Brannon clan would never claim to own anyone or demand servitude. Slavery didn't mean anything to them, and if the government had decided to get rid of it, none of them would have blinked an eye at the decision. But the North seemed hell-bent on wiping out everything about the South, good and bad. Cory couldn't begin to understand that attitude. He didn't want to be told how to live, and he was damned if he was going to tell anybody else how he ought to.

An excited yell came from somewhere on the right, followed a second later by another on the left. Several shots spat out. The men around Cory and Abner began to run as best they could through the trees and undergrowth. The two followed suit, caught up in the excitement and anticipation of battle.

More shots sounded. Cory had his hand closed tightly around the lock on his rifle, shielding it from the dampness. He looked around for the Yankees, and suddenly they were there, charging through the woods toward the onrushing Confederate line. Cory stopped in his tracks and flung the rifle to his shoulder, cocking it as he did so. He found a target, an officer who was using his saber to wave his men forward. Cory fired.

For an instant, he thought his powder was too wet, that it was only going to fizzle at him. But then the rifle belched flame and lead and noise, and the butt kicked back hard at his shoulder. He lowered the rifle and saw the saber-wielding officer spin around slowly, dazed by the wound that was pumping dark red blood from his chest. After a moment, he slumped to the ground, either dead or dying.

Yelling, the Confederates surged forward. Cory reloaded and joined them. Abner had gotten ahead of him. Cory hurried to catch up, and the two men were almost side-by-side when they broke out of the brush and ran into an unexpectedly clear area.

A sheet of flame came from the other side of the clearing as the Yankees, crouched there behind fallen trees and other impromptu breastworks, opened fire. Billowing clouds of powder smoke rolled after the shots. Cory heard the ugly sound of bullets thudding into flesh, and all around him men began to fall. Abner was still on his feet, though, and he whooped in defiance.

"Get down!" Cory shouted as another volley smashed out from the Union line. He reached over, grabbed Abner's sleeve, and threw himself forward on the ground, pulling his friend down with him. Mud splashed up as they landed in a broad puddle. Lead scythed through the air over their heads.

Muddy water dripped off Abner's face as he lifted himself on his elbows and thrust the barrel of his rifle toward the Yankees. The hammer came down as he fired and the percussion cap snapped, but the charge in the barrel failed to ignite. The powder was too wet. The same thing happened when Cory tried to fire.

He tugged at Abner's ragged jacket. "We've got to get out of here!"

Abner turned his head and stared at Cory for a moment, looking as if he wanted to argue. Then he nodded and began scooting backward over the soggy ground toward the trees behind them. Cory did likewise. Even as they worked their way back, they heard a bugler somewhere behind them blowing retreat. The officers had realized this advance wasn't going well. The Confederates would fall back, regroup, and wait to see what they could be asked to do next.

When Cory and Abner reached the trees, they crawled behind several thick, bullet-battered trunks and pulled themselves into sitting positions. The rifle and artillery fire continued around them, creating a din that not even the rain and the mist could muffle. Abner's mud-streaked face grinned over at Cory. "This is sure enough a hellhole!" he called.

Cory had never heard a more apt description of any place in his life.

Chapter Three

A DRIVING RAINSTORM PELTED the men who marched eastward along the road to Marietta. After spending the last week of May 1864 skirmishing with the Yankees in the woods around New Hope Church, Pickett's Mill, and Dallas, Johnston was pulling back his army to a better defensive position northwest of the crossroads town of Marietta. Cavalry patrols had reported that Sherman was moving to the east, and Johnston had to block him. All during the long retreat from Dalton, Sherman had tried to flank the Confederates on the left. Now his movements represented a threat to the Confederate right. A quick shift of the army in that direction was the only answer.

"I swear, I'm growin' webs between my toes," Abner said as he and Cory splashed through the mud with the thousands of men in Hardee's corps. "Reckon before it's over I'm gonna have to grow me a set o' gills, too, or I'm liable to drown tryin' to breathe all the water in the air."

"It has to stop raining sometime," Cory said.

"You reckon? I thought so, too, but I'm about to change my mind. 'Round the next bend in the road, we're liable to come on an old feller with a long white beard who's buildin' him a big boat and loadin' animals on it."

Cory grinned and shook his head. Even under the worst of circumstances, Abner still made jokes. Cory was glad that he had befriended the lanky Tennessean.

The two of them had spent the past several days exchanging sporadic shots with the Yankees and turning back occasional patrols. Both armies had been unable to operate efficiently in the country that Abner had called the Hell Hole. Cory had not been surprised when the orders came to move out and head for Marietta. When one thing didn't work out—when it was too hard to kill the enemy—the generals tried something else.

41

Over the next few days the Confederates settled into a defensive line ten miles long that straddled the Western and Atlantic Railroad. Even for northwestern Georgia, this was particularly rugged country. Four brushy, good-sized mountains jutted up from the surrounding hilly terrain. To the north of the railroad stood Brush Mountain, to the south Pine Mountain and Lost Mountain. Behind those latter two elevations and also south of the railroad was a long ridge known as Kennesaw Mountain. Two knobs called Big Kennesaw and Little Kennesaw jutted up from the ridge. Cory was enough of a military tactician by now that as soon as he saw all this high ground, he knew the Confederate army would have to hold it in order to stop Sherman's advance toward Marietta and ultimately toward Atlanta.

Pine Mountain, which marked the approximate center of the Confederate line, stood a little farther north than the flanking Brush Mountain and Lost Mountain, making it a salient of sorts. A division from Hardee's corps was stationed atop it, so Cory, Abner, Lieutenant Stockard, and the other men of the division had a perfect view of the Yankee army as it maneuvered into place over the next few days. Sherman's men matched the Confederate line in length, stretching ten miles from northeast to southwest.

"We're right out in front," Abner said to Cory as they sat on a rock and watched the Yankees pitching their tents and struggling to erect earthworks out of the sticky clay. The sky was still overcast, with almost constant drizzle and intermittent downpours. Cory had just about forgotten what it was like to be dry and not covered with mud.

"Yes, we're out in front," Cory said when Abner fell silent. "What do you think that means?"

Abner spat into the mud. "Means the damnyanks'll come after us first. Leastways, that's the way it looks to me."

Cory nodded in agreement. Pine Mountain might as well have had a giant bull's-eye painted on it. This was where the next battle would start.

The Yankees were in no hurry, though. Slowly, large groups of men, artillery, and supplies were shifted toward the east, the Confederate right. To Cory's eyes, it seemed obvious that whichever general was commanding that part of the Federal forces, he intended to go around the mountain rather than up and over it. Cory couldn't fault the logic. Going around was better than charging uphill into the gun sights of a well-entrenched foe.

If the Yankees succeeded, the men on top of Pine Mountain would be trapped. Cory felt his tension growing as the days passed and the middle of June approached. Were they going to just perch up here like big dumb birds while the Yankees cut them off from the rest of the army?

Cory and Abner were standing under one of the pine trees that gave the mountain its name when they saw some officers approaching the crest on horseback. Cory felt a shock go through him when he recognized General Hardee. Next to him rode General Johnston himself, and trailing them slightly was the portly figure of Leonidas Polk. Officers from the staffs of all three commanders brought up the rear. The generals attracted a lot of attention from the enlisted men, several of whom began to follow them.

The generals rode almost to the point where Cory and Abner stood before reining in their mounts and swinging down from their saddles. They climbed to the top of an artillery redoubt. Hardee addressed Johnston: "You can see for yourself, General, how the Federals are moving around to the east of this height." He leveled an arm and pointed out the Union movement. "In another day, perhaps two, my men will be encircled."

Johnston nodded, weighing the situation. "Yes, this appears to be a perilous situation. Is there any way to block them?"

"Not from up here," Hardee said. "We would be forced to descend from the mountain in order to do so."

"Thus surrendering the high ground in the process." Johnston shook his head. "No, I think—" He stopped and lifted his head as somewhere down below, a cannon boomed.

Cory heard a distant whining sound grow higher in pitch as it approached. "The Yankees are shooting at the generals!" he said to Abner.

Even as he spoke, he realized that the Federal observers below couldn't have known who was up here. The distance was too great for that, even with the aid of field glasses. But the Yankees could see Confederates moving around on the crest of the mountain, and somebody down there had taken it in his head to lob a shell at them.

Cory and Abner dived for the ground as the artillery round whistled in. It exploded with a stunning force that made the earth shake under Cory. The shell had missed its target, though, bursting on open ground well away from the three generals.

The close shot made them realize the truth in the old saw about discretion being the better part of valor. "Come along, gentlemen," Johnston said as he hopped down from the redoubt and moved hurriedly away from the crest, heading for the shelter of the nearby trees. Hardee was right behind him.

Not so General Polk, Cory saw with wide eyes. The old churchman climbed down deliberately and walked after Johnston and Hardee, taking his time about it. He clasped his hands behind his back, the very picture of unruffled dignity.

Lying beside Cory, Abner exclaimed, "What the hell is the bishop doing?"

Cory didn't know. Maybe Polk was trying to put up a good front for the men who were watching. But in the next instant, whatever the general was doing ended tragically.

The whistle of another round cut through the air, and Cory wished he could tear his eyes away from the slowly strolling Polk. The general had almost reached the trees when the shell smashed into him from the left side. Cory couldn't see the shell itself, but he saw the gruesome result as the round failed to detonate and ripped a giant hole through Polk's body like a massive bullet. Only after passing completely through the general did the shell strike one of the nearby trees and explode.

Polk lay on the ground, smashed off his feet by the horrible impact. He had been dead when he fell; no one could have survived such a hideous wound. General Johnston darted out from the shelter of the trees, ignoring the threat of another Federal round that screamed in and burst close by. Johnston went to his knees and lifted Polk's lifeless form, resting the bishop's head in his lap.

Cory scrambled to his feet and ran over to the scene. Abner was right behind him. Lines of grief were etched into Johnston's haggard face as he looked up at the two of them. "Take General Polk away from here. Gently, lads, gently."

Cory and Abner bent and picked up the limp, blood-covered figure. As they straightened, Johnston came to his feet as well and reached into the pocket of Polk's coat.

"What are these?" he said as he pulled out three small, leather-covered books. He opened one and read the title in a hollow voice. "*Balm for the Weary and Wounded.* The volume is inscribed to me from General Polk." Johnston checked the title pages of the other two books, and his voice threatened to break as he said, "These volumes are the same, only inscribed to General Hardee and General Hood. General Polk must have meant them as gifts to the three of us, so that the words in them might serve as a comfort to us in this time of travail." Johnston snapped the books closed. "He was a beacon to us, but now that light has gone out."

He led the way to the horses as the artillery barrage from the Yankees died away. The targets were gone now, but the gunners down below didn't know just how much damage they had done, Cory thought as he and Abner carried Polk's lifeless body and lifted it over the saddle of the general's horse.

By nightfall, the Confederates had abandoned Pine Mountain and pulled back to strong positions on Kennesaw. Pine Mountain might have turned out to be a trap for the Southerners if they had stayed there, but the death of General Polk was a high enough price to pay. Too high, in the minds of many of the soldiers.

This was one more mark against General Sherman, one more wrong to be avenged when the final reckoning came with the man who had brought hell to Georgia.

OVER THE next week, as skirmishing continued between the two massive forces sprawled across the countryside, the Confederate line gradually contracted. Johnston placed Gen. William Wing Loring in command of the late General Polk's corps and ordered withdrawals from Brush Mountain and Lost Mountain. The Confederates would concentrate on holding Kennesaw Mountain itself.

Sherman, as always open to the idea of a flanking maneuver, tried to get around the Confederate line to the south. His goal for the time being was still the railroad, although the fact that Atlanta was only about thirty miles away could not have been far from his mind for very long. Johnston reacted to Sherman's move by shifting Hood's corps from the center of the line to the extreme left, replacing it in the center with dismounted troopers from Gen. Joseph Wheeler's cavalry.

Hood was waiting to block Sherman on the south, but he was not content to simply keep the Yankees from advancing. He had lost a leg at Chickamauga, and he was still as aggressive as ever and ordered an attack on the Federal forces.

This thrust proved to be disastrous and was repulsed by the Yankees with heavy Confederate losses. Once again, a stalemate settled in. Both sides dug trenches and crouched in them as rain-water collected. From time to time they fought artillery duels, and the lazy popping of rifle fire never ceased for long as pickets in the front lines took potshots at each other. Life for the soldiers atop and in front of Kennesaw Mountain became drudgery, pure and simple, boring yet still quite deadly at times.

During the night between Sunday, June 26, and Monday, the rains stopped.

"How long has it been?" Abner asked as he gazed up at the clear blue morning sky.

"How long since what?" Cory said.

"Since it wasn't raining."

"It hasn't been *that* long. A few weeks, maybe. And it didn't rain that whole time."

Abner waved a hand at the sky. "Maybe not, but it seems like it's been a year since we saw anything that looked like that."

Cory had to admit that it was nice to see that heavenly blue again, so different from the blue of the Yankees' uniforms. He would always despise that color. He had ever since the occupying Federal army had marched into Vicksburg and launched the chain of events that had ended with his separation from Lucille.

Abner and Cory sat behind a barricade of logs atop the crest of a small hill at the southern end of Kennesaw Mountain. Looking to the north, Cory could see the series of knobs that jutted up from the ridge: Pigeon Hill, Little Kennesaw, and Big Kennesaw. There was a small gap, a saddle, really, between Pigeon Hill and the place where Cory and Abner were posted along with two brigades commanded by Gen. Benjamin Franklin Cheatham. To the south were Hood's men, staying put after their failed foray a week earlier.

Cory stood and looked to the west and saw the Yankees milling around. Nothing unusual about that, he thought. The Yankees were always doing something, even when it didn't amount to anything. He thought they just liked to look busy, as if they were accomplishing some grand goal. They didn't know how to sit back and relax. Cory stifled a yawn.

A second later, he stiffened as an artillery bombardment began with a crash like the gates of Hades bursting open. Clouds of smoke billowed up from the Yankee batteries down below. Shells rocketed and whistled to the top of Kennesaw Mountain and its flanking heights. Along with thousands of other Confederates, Cory and Abner crouched behind breastworks and in trenches and held their breath as the hellish storm of lead and flame fell around them.

Then the Confederate batteries began returning the fire. The ground trembled under Cory's feet, dancing to the rhythm of the explosions. Thick clouds of smoke drifted overhead, blotting out the morning sunshine that had been so pleasant only moments earlier.

Sherman must have been waiting for the rain to stop, Cory thought. The Yankee general had been just biding his time, hoping for a clear day on which to attack.

Well, Sherman had his wish now.

The barrage continued for what seemed like hours but was only minutes. When the roaring finally died away, Cory and Abner stood up, tried to shake away some of the ringing in their heads, and peered carefully over their log breastworks. Musketry rattled to the north as waves of blue-clad troops surged forward toward Pigeon Hill and Little Kennesaw, but directly in front of the hill where Cory and Abner waited, no Yankees came toward them. The thick woods on the other side of a wide clearing at the base of the hill were quiet, seemingly deserted.

"How come they ain't attackin'?" Abner said. "Damn, I don't like this."

"You're worried because we're not in the middle of a fight for a change?" Cory tried to make light of the situation, but he knew what Abner meant. Anytime the Yankees behaved in some manner other than the expected one, it usually meant trouble.

"When they do come visitin', they'll be loaded for bear," Abner said. "Just you hide an' watch."

"I don't intend to hide," Cory said. "I'll be right here when the Yankees come."

That wasn't long in developing. About a half-hour after the assault on Little Kennesaw and Pigeon Hill began, a column of Federal infantrymen emerged from the trees opposite the lower hill where Cheatham's brigades were posted. Cory had figured that when the attack finally came, it would take its customary form—a long, loose line of men advancing first at a walk then speeding up to a run. Instead, these Yankees were packed more closely together than usual and came at a run right from the start.

Cory glanced to his right and knew that the object of the Union thrust had to be the gap between this knob and Pigeon Hill. If the narrow Yankee column could slash through there and reach the Confederate rear, Johnston's army would be divided. Dividing an army was the first step in defeating it.

Atop the hill, the Confederate line extended forward to the very brink then followed the crest by bending back sharply and forming an angle. The right side of the angle was manned by Gen. A. J. Vaughan's brigade; the left, where Cory and Abner were, by Gen. George Maney's brigade. These men, with a few scattered exceptions such as Cory, were Tennesseans, and they remembered all too well how they had been forced to retreat from their home state. That had been a bitter pill to swallow, and whenever they had a chance to strike back at the Yankees, such as now, they seized it. They poured fire down into the advancing Federal column, which split and came at the hill from both sides of the angle in the defensive line.

Cory rested his rifle on the topmost log and fired down into the mass of blue. Beside him, Abner's rifle roared. Cory dropped down to reload then stood up again and sent another bullet whistling toward the enemy. For long minutes, he and Abner kept up the fight, firing as quickly as they could reload, draw a bead, and press the trigger. Cory's eyes stung and watered from the powder smoke. He blinked them clear each time as he rammed another ball and charge down the barrel of his rifle.

The hillside below them had been mostly cleared of trees, giving the defenders an open field of fire. The Yankees, charging valiantly but blindly up the slope, fell in droves. Officers waved hats and sabers to exhort them on, but they fell themselves as Confederate lead ripped into them. Like so many battles Cory had witnessed and fought in, there was nothing fair about this combat. For the side entrenched and barricaded behind breastworks, killing the enemy was easy. For those soldiers caught in the open, it was pure slaughter, and nothing else. The only way for the attacking forces to win such a battle was to have such overwhelming numbers on their side that they could afford to suffer heavy losses on their way up the hill. The survivors would charge to victory on the backs of those who had already fallen, overrunning the defenders and forcing them to retreat.

That was the Federal strategy on this day, but the Yankee commanders had not reckoned on the devastating effect of the rifle fire that poured down from the top of the hill. Nor were rifles the only weapons employed by the hill's defenders. Pistols spat death at the Yankees, and men who ran out of ammunition hurled rocks at the enemy. Logs were plentiful. Some men picked them up and heaved them over the breastworks. The tree trunks tumbled wildly down the hill, breaking bones, crushing skulls, and sweeping men before them.

Still the Yankees came on, seemingly accepting of the death that was dealt out to them. Cory knelt to reload, and as he came up again, he was shocked to see a Union officer only a few yards away, bounding toward the breastworks, somehow untouched by the hail of bullets that filled the air.

With a wild look on his face, the Yankee waved his saber in the air and made an almost superhuman leap to the top of the log barrier. Several of his men were right behind him. "Surrender!" the officer shouted over the din of rifle and artillery fire as he hacked at the Confederates with his saber. "Surrender, you damned traitors!"

Cory was so stunned by the sight of the man that he forgot to fire his rifle. He stood there staring into the contorted face of the Yankee only a few feet away. The officer whipped the saber at him, and at the last instant he realized his danger. He ducked, but the flat of the blade struck him on the head anyway. Staggered by the blow, Cory went to a knee. Some of the Yankee's men were tugging at the officer's coat, trying to get him to come down from his exposed position, but he ignored them. The blade in his hand, dripping blood from the wounds it had inflicted already, started toward Cory again on the backswing.

Abner Strayhorn reached up, holding his rifle one-handed, jammed the muzzle against the Yankee officer's chest, and pulled the trigger. The blast blew the man off the breastworks. He dropped his saber, and his arms flung wide as he fell back onto the men behind him.

Cory struggled to his feet, still half-dazed by the blow to the head. He gave Abner a quick nod of thanks, then thrust the barrel of his rifle over the top of the logs and pulled the trigger. Without waiting to see if he had hit any of the Yankees—at that range, with so many right in front of him, he knew he must have—he dropped to a knee to reload yet again.

As the middle of the day approached, the Yankees began to fall back. It must have been clear by now, even to a commander as callous as Sherman evidently was, that the attacks on Kennesaw Mountain and the heights just south of it were serving no purpose. The Federals retreated only a short distance, however, before dropping to the ground and gouging out makeshift trenches of their own. They lay there with their rifles pointed up the hill and waited, just as the Confederates waited above, their own weapons poised to deliver more deadly volleys. For the moment, though, the battle waned, and both sides paused to take a deep breath.

It was a breath filled with the stench of death.

The ground between the front lines of the two armies was filled with bloody, mangled bodies. Most were dead, but some were still alive, screaming or moaning and begging for someone to help them. Cory had heard such lamentations over the years, and he wished he could close his ears to them now. There was no escaping the piteous wails, though.

Farther north along Kennesaw Mountain, fires had been started by the explosions among the brush at the foot of the ridge, and the Yankees who had fallen there began to be consumed by the flames, adding to the awful stink in the air. Taking pity on the men who were still alive out in that hell, Confederate commanders called a hurried truce and summoned the Yankees forward to rescue their fallen comrades. Some of the Confederates even climbed over the barricades and ran forward to help rather than stand by and watch as the wounded Yankees burned to death.

As the afternoon dragged by, an eerie calm descended over Kennesaw Mountain, the same sort of calm that could be found on many battlefields through the ages after great masses of men had struggled and died for their cause, whatever it might be. Death was no respecter of causes. Whether the body was dressed in blue or gray, a corpse was nothing more than carrion in the eyes of the world's eternal scavengers.

During that long afternoon, Cory leaned against the log breastworks with his rifle in his hands and waited to see what was going to happen next. Would the Yankees attack again? Surely not. Even as stubborn a general as "Uncle Billy" Sherman could see that the assault up the mountain had failed. Why spend the lives of his men for nothing?

"Thanks for what you did," Cory said to Abner.

"What do you mean?" the Tennessean sounded genuinely puzzled.

"When you shot that Yankee officer just before he was about to chop me to pieces with his saber."

"Oh." Abner shrugged. "It weren't nothin'. I just didn't want him standin' up there a-harpin' at us." He snorted. "Callin' us traitors. Hell, it was the damnyanks who up and decided that the ol' Constitution don't mean nothin'. We joined the Union of our own free will, and there ain't a blessed thing in any o' them old papers that says we can't leave the same way."

"Maybe not, but *they* say it." Cory nodded toward the Union lines. "And if they win, they're the ones who'll get to decide about that and everything else."

"Still don't make it right."

A lot of things weren't right on both sides of this conflict, Cory thought. But for now the firing had died away, and a breeze had carried off the worst of the smoke. When he looked up he saw blue sky overhead again, the same sort of beautiful blue sky that had arched over Kennesaw Mountain that morning, before all the dying started. Cory looked at the sky and wished he could just soar up into it like a bird. He wished he could fly away from the agonized screams, the crackle of flames, the mud that still sucked underfoot, the bright copper smell from the pools of blood . . .

But turning into a bird and flying away was a childish dream. He had to stay here. He was a man, not a bird, and he had to stay on the ground and kill and kill and kill.

Chapter Four

THE YANKEES STAYED WHERE they were, and so did the Confederates. Less than fifty yards separated them in some places. Soldiers from both sides called insults back and forth to each other. They were so close they could have chucked rocks into the others' trenches. Yet despite their proximity, the uneasy lull in the battle continued. Night fell with only scattered shots here and there. That continued the next day, and for several days after that. The bloody assault on Kennesaw Mountain had exhausted the Union army, and the Confederates, short on supplies as they were, were not in much better shape. Both sides were content to sit and wait and rest from their labors.

The stink of the rotting corpses between the lines could not be ignored forever, though. Cory was not surprised when the orders came down the line: a general truce had been called, and a strict cease-fire was to be observed while the Federals retrieved their dead. Those among the Confederates who wished to go out and help were given leave to do so.

When Abner heard that, he set his rifle aside. "I reckon I'll go lend a hand," he said.

Cory stared at him. "You're going to help the Yankees?"

"The sooner they get those poor boys buried, the sooner the air'll improve hereabouts." The Tennessean shook his head. "Besides, it ain't fittin' to just leave 'em out there. A fella who's passed on deserves a proper burial. Even a damnyank."

Cory couldn't argue with that, and he felt a little ashamed of his initial reaction. His mother had taught him better than to be so unfeeling, so unforgiving to others. As that thought went through his head, he uttered a grim chuckle at the memories it brought back. Abigail Brannon had never been the soul of forgiveness herself. Yet he knew that she would want him to help at a time like this.

Abner was already clambering over the breastworks. "Hold on," Cory said, putting his rifle down next to his friend's. "I'll come with you."

As he pulled himself to the top of the log barricade, he looked along the line and saw dozens of other Confederates climbing over similar breastworks and emerging from trenches. They walked out into the killing ground, gave curt nods to their blue-clad enemies, and bent to help the Yankees pick up the corpses.

Cory and Abner walked toward a group of Union soldiers. The men glared at them suspiciously, but then Abner nodded to them. "Howdy, boys. This is a mighty sad job, ain't it?"

"You're a fine one to talk," one of the Yankees said. He waved a hand at the scores of sprawled bodies carpeting the ground. "You Rebels are the ones who killed these poor boys!"

"A fella don't always like the chores he's got to do, like gatherin' up these gents and givin' 'em as close to a proper sendoff as you can manage with the way things are. We'd like to help, but if you don't want us to, we'll turn around and go back up the hill, no hard feelin's."

"There are plenty of hard feelings, you—"

One of the other Yankees put a hand on the speaker's arm. "Take it easy, Robert. This is a truce, remember?" He gave Cory and Abner a solemn smile and went on, "We'd be glad for you fellows to give us a hand. Where are you from?"

"Tennessee," Abner said as he bent to grasp the legs of a dead man, and the Yankee took the corpse's shoulders. "How about you?"

"Illinois." Together, they lifted the body and started carrying him toward the Federal lines.

"I'm from Virginia," Cory said to the Yankee who had been angry. "Where are you from?"

The man glared at him for a second then gave a grunt of resignation. "Michigan," he said. "Get his arms."

They lifted one of the corpses. Cory's skin crawled a little at the feeling of loose dead flesh in his hands. The sun had done its work well. The smell out here was unbelievably terrible. Ants and maggots already infested the raw wounds. This was as close to hell as Cory ever wanted to get.

To keep his mind off it, he breathed shallowly through his mouth. "My name's Cory Brannon."

"Robert Sloane."

"I'd say I'm pleased to meet you, Robert, but under the circumstances . . ."

"Yeah. I know what you mean." They reached the shallow trenches that had been scooped out of the earth by the Federals as they retreated from the attack several days earlier. Placing the corpse gently on the ground so that a burial detail could pick it up later, the two men started back out to get another one.

Sloane asked, "What do you do, back there in Virginia?"

"I haven't lived there for several years, but when I did, I was a farmer. My family has a place close to Culpeper. At least, they did. I don't now what's going on up there now."

"Neither do I. There have been a lot of battles—" Sloane broke off his words with a shake of his head. "I work in a mill. Worked in a mill, I should say, before this damned war came."

"Are you going to go back to that when the war's over?"

"Probably." The Yankee gave a harsh, bleak laugh. "If I live through it."

"I hope you do," Cory said, and he was surprised to realize that he meant it.

The two of them carried several bodies back to the Union lines in silence, then Sloane asked, "What about you? What are you going to do when it's over? Go back to that farm in Virginia?"

"No." The answer came without hesitation. "Oh, I'll go back and see my family, but I won't stay. I worked on a riverboat for a while, and I thought at the time I might like to keep on with that . . . but it didn't work out."

His mind went back for a moment to that awful winter day in February, two years earlier, when the *Missouri Zephyr* had exploded in the Tennessee River in front of Fort Henry, its boilers bursting and taking the boat to the bottom of the river. That terrible blast had killed the riverboat's pilot, Ike Judson, who had been Cory's friend, and everyone else on board. Only Cory and the boat's captain, Ezekiel Farrell, had escaped, and the cap'n had never been the same after that. Farrell had met his death at Fort Donelson, but not before Cory had promised him that he would look after Lucille.

He hadn't done such a good job of that, Cory thought bitterly. There had been long, painful separations between him and Lucille, although eventually they had been married during the siege of Vicksburg. Then had come the threat of Jason Gill, the abolitionist and Yankee agent who was more than a little mad with hatred of Cory. Lucille had had to go one way while Cory went the other, and again they were apart, with no way of knowing when—or if—they would ever be reunited again.

So saying that his ambition to someday be a riverboat pilot hadn't worked out was an understatement.

"You look like you're a million miles away, Brannon," the Yankee said.

Cory shook his head. "Sorry. Bad memories."

"I know what you mean. This damned war's got plenty of them and more coming."

"I'll be going to Texas after the war," Cory went on, for some reason unwilling to let the conversation die. "I once knew a fella from there. He said that the best land in the world was along a river called the Brazos. I thought I might claim some of it and settle there."

With Lucille, he added to himself. Texas was where he would find her and her Aunt Mildred, assuming they were still alive and safe.

"I hope you do," Sloane said. His earlier anger seemed to have dissipated. The grim task in which he and Cory were engaged must have drained it away. Cory knew that after talking to him for a while, Sloane found it difficult to hate a man just because of the color of the uniform he wore.

He wished the politicians in Washington and Richmond had felt the same way.

SEEING THAT he was not going to be able to dislodge the Confederates from Kennesaw Mountain without destroying his own army in the process, Sherman did what he had done since the beginning of this campaign: He tried to go around the enemy, moving to the south. Always south, bringing the Union army ever closer to Atlanta, even though the Federals were approaching at a tangent.

Johnston's reaction also was the same as always. He withdrew the army from Kennesaw Mountain, didn't even pause in Marietta, and pulled back all the way to the town of Smyrna, where the Confederates once again settled into a line atop a ridge.

Sherman had learned his lesson by now. Leaving only a small force in front of the Confederates to occupy them, he swung the rest of the army to the south and west once more. The grim dance continued with Johnston's moving all the way back to the Chattahoochee River, a scant five miles north of Atlanta. Sherman expected Johnston to retreat all the way across the Chattahoochee, figuring his opponent for too canny a commander to fight a battle with a river at his back. Over the past few weeks, however, slaves had been preparing especially sturdy fortifications along the north bank of the Chattahoochee. This line of thick redoubts and earthworks protected a railroad trestle and several pontoon bridges, so the Confederates could withdraw across the river in a hurry if they were forced to do so.

When Sherman saw the defenses set up along the Chattahoochee, he realized that once again he was blocked to such an extent that crashing through the Confederate line would be too costly. Although Atlanta was close now, with the losses he was bound to suffer in smashing Johnston's army, his own forces would be too weak to capture the city. Sherman had not come this far—within sight of the city—to fail in his objectives now. He issued orders for his men to circle, to the north and east this time, instead of south.

Sherman's goal was to get some of his men across the river so he could put pressure on the Confederate right flank and force Johnston to pull back to Atlanta. If he could accomplish that, then would come the ultimate battle, the struggle for the Gate City of the South itself. To Sherman's delight, the Union cavalry was able to reach the far side of the Chattahoochee at Roswell, and in early July, infantry under Gen. John M. Schofield forded the river at Sope Creek, only eight miles upriver from the Confederate fortifications. Schofield extended his hold on the south bank for more than a mile beyond the Chattahoochee. When scouts brought word of this development to Johnston, the Confederate commander knew that he could not withstand an assault by Sherman with such a dangerous threat on his right flank. Like it or not, the time had come to retreat yet again.

"I SWEAR, ALL we been doin' for the past couple o' months is runnin'," Abner said as he and Cory trudged across one of the pontoon bridges across the Chattahoochee. The army had waited until the middle of the night to move out, so that Yankee observers would not be able to see them. Under the feet of Cory and Abner and the thousands of other soldiers crossing the river with them, cornstalks rustled on the bridge. That was to muffle the sound of marching feet. It could prove disastrous if the Federals fell on them while they were retreating.

"Sherman keeps getting around us," Cory said in answer to Abner's complaint. "What we need is something to keep him occupied so he can't flank us all the time."

"Like a bunch o' cavalry makin' life miserable for him? I reckon that General Forrest might've made a difference if he'd been here."

Cory nodded glumly. Wherever Nathan Bedford Forrest was and whatever he was doing, Cory was sure it was bedeviling the Yankees. Yet he couldn't help but think that if Forrest had been on hand here, he would have found a way to turn back Sherman's dogged advance. And it would have been nice to ride with Forrest again, no doubt about that. The man was the best commander Cory had ever seen, a general who flat-out refused to lose and somehow found a way to win, even when the odds were against him.

They reached the south bank of the Chattahoochee, among the last groups of Confederates to do so. Behind them, the engineers moved in to take apart the pontoon bridges. There was no point in leaving them for the Yankees to use. Make it as difficult as possible for Sherman to get across the river, that was the idea. Once the pontoon bridges had been disassembled, then the railroad trestle would be set afire. When the flames started leaping high into the sky, the Yankees would know what was going on, but it would be too late then for them to do anything about it.

During the night, the army moved east. They camped on a ridge overlooking Peachtree Creek, which flowed west into the Chattahoochee. A few miles to the rear lay Atlanta itself. As Cory lay down to catch a nap while the sky turned gray with the approach of dawn, he wondered what it was like in the city. By now the population must have heard how close the Yankees were. They had to be terrified that Sherman—Uncle Billy, some in his own army called him, but to the Southerners he might as well have been called Satan—would overwhelm the defenders and come rampaging into Atlanta itself. Bitter though it was to admit, so far General Johnston had shown no signs of being able to stop the Yankees.

That feeling was just as strong in Richmond. Never a strong supporter of Joe Johnston, Jefferson Davis had even more doubts about him now. He dispatched a personal emissary, Gen. Braxton Bragg—his chief of staff and the former commander of the Army of Tennessee, which Johnston now led.

Cory and Abner were standing guard duty near Johnston's headquarters atop the ridge overlooking Peachtree Creek when Bragg arrived. Cory's eyes widened in surprise as he recognized the bushy eyebrows and dour expression of the army's former commander. Bragg stalked into Johnston's tent. Abner must have recognized Bragg, too, because he let out a low whistle.

"Never figured I'd see that fella again," he said, leaning closer to Cory and keeping his voice pitched low so he wouldn't be overheard. "Nobody's forgot how he dithered around whilst Grant sat in Chattanooga haulin' in supplies and gettin' stronger."

Cory nodded slowly in agreement. He had no liking for Bragg and had felt that way ever since the general had refused an appeal for aid from the besieged city of Vicksburg. Cory had carried a personal plea to Bragg from Gen. John C. Pemberton, the commander of Vicksburg's defenders, and Bragg's refusal to answer it ultimately had led to the city's downfall. His mishandling of the situation following the Confederate victory at Chickamauga had taken him down a few notches further in Cory's estimation.

But he was just a lowly private, Cory reminded himself, here to follow orders and not to pass judgment on generals. He rubbed his jaw. "I wonder what Bragg's doing here."

"Probably come to tell ol' General that he's bein' booted out," Abner said. "That'd be my guess."

Cory looked at his friend. "You really think General Johnston will be relieved of command?"

Abner shrugged. "Look at where we started out, and look at where we are now. It don't take a very smart fella to figure out that we been goin' backwards."

That was the truth, Cory thought. They had put up a good fight a few places along the way, but overall the campaign to stop Sherman's advance into Georgia had been a disaster. The bad part about it was that, try as he might, Cory couldn't think of anything Johnston could have done differently. It would have taken a Bedford Forrest or a Stonewall Jackson to come up with something daring enough to have a chance to stop Sherman. Cory's fervent hope was that General Bragg wasn't going to be placed in command of the army again. Bragg was a far cry from Forrest or Jackson.

A few days later, with reports coming in that all of Sherman's men were now on this side of the Chattahoochee, Abner's prediction came true. Joseph E. Johnston was relieved of command of what was left of the Army of Tennessee. His place was taken not by General Bragg but by the fiery John Bell Hood, who, although not from Texas himself, had risen to prominence commanding a brigade of Texans who had proven to be some of the fiercest fighters in the Confederate army.

With Hood's promotion on his mind, Cory dozed off that night as he thought of the Lone Star State. A part of him wanted to abandon this seemingly futile quest to save Atlanta and head west right now. He wanted to see that Brazos country he had heard so much about. Even more, he wanted to see Lucille. He wondered where she was tonight. When he and Colonel Thompson and Pie Jones had been running the supply line from Vicksburg, across northern Louisiana to the town of Marshall in the piney woods of eastern Texas, Lucille had gone along on the trip more than once. She knew the way there. Of course, the Yankees now controlled the railroad from Vicksburg to Shreveport, so Lucille and Mildred couldn't have gone by train. But they weren't traveling alone. Allen Carter, a Confederate veteran, was with them, along with Carter's son, Fred. At Manassas, Carter had lost a leg below the knee, but he got around pretty well on a peg leg and was about as tough and competent a man as Cory knew. And Fred, although he had the mind of a child, was courageous and devoted to Lucille. Cory suspected Allen Carter would have found a wagon for the four of them and headed toward Marshall. Once Cory got to Texas, that was the first place he would start to look for his wife.

But he couldn't go to Texas just yet, he realized. Once he might have been selfish enough to put his own desires above everything else and desert from the army. Lord knew, he still wanted to do just that and thought about it all the time. But something held him back. He supposed the hardships of the past couple of years, along with the friendships of men like Bedford Forrest and Col. Charles Thompson, had caused a conscience to sprout and grow in him. He had a sense of duty now, damn it, although he wouldn't have gone so far as to call himself an honorable man. Maybe he was getting there. Maybe if he lived long enough . . .

It would have helped if doing the right thing hadn't been so damned inconvenient.

He rolled over, trying to get more comfortable on the ground, wishing he could go to sleep, and he thought again about Texas. Lucille wasn't the only one waiting for him there. Pie Jones, that massive, harmonica-playing bear of a man, had gone west, too, rather than allowing the woman he loved to be taken back to a life of slavery. Rachel Hannah, with her fair skin and red hair, looked as white as anyone else, but she had black blood in her, and under the laws of the Confederacy, that made her a slave, nothing more than human chattel. The illegitimate daughter of a plantation owner and an octoroon house servant, Rachel had been sold to a tavern owner named Grat, who had treated her badly. Pie, Cory, and Colonel Thompson had rescued her from that life, and when Grat had tracked them down and threatened to use the power of the law to take Rachel back, Pie had taken her and fled, preferring a life as fugitives to the alternative. Pie had planned to strike out for the Brazos, having heard Cory talk about it. In a way, it bothered Cory a little to think that Pie had gotten the chance to see that country first, but he hoped that Pie and Rachel had made it. He really did.

He finally dozed off, not thinking of the air of desperation along the Confederate line or the massed thousands of the Union army only a few miles away, threatening not only the lives of the Southern soldiers but also the very existence of Atlanta itself. Instead, Cory's thoughts were hundreds of miles away to the west, in a land he had never seen, a land that he could only hope would one day be his own . . .

"DON'T MOVE," Pie hissed, his hamlike left hand resting lightly on his wife's shoulder. The fingers of his right hand were curled around the walnut grips of the revolver holstered on his hip.

A faint red line lay across the western horizon, a reminder of a vivid sunset. Overhead, the sky was shading from deep blue to black, and here and there stars were beginning to appear, faint pinpricks of light that grew more brilliant as the heavens darkened. Somewhere not far off, an owl hooted.

Or was it an owl? Pie had heard stories about how Comanche warriors signaled by hooting like that.

"Is it Indians?" Rachel whispered.

"Don't know." Pie pressed down a little harder on her shoulder. "Stay put. I'll take a look around."

She twisted where she lay on the ground and reached around to grab his thickly muscled arm. "No! If you go out there, they're liable to get you!"

Pie tried to peer through the darkness to spot whatever it was in the brush that had alarmed them. It had sounded like a man on horseback, and he was glad that he and Rachel had put out their campfire already. Whoever was roaming around out there, they would have been drawn to the flames had the fire still been burning. Of course, it was possible they could have seen it earlier. He shouldn't have made a fire, Pie thought. But from what he had heard, Comanches seldom if ever ventured this far east anymore, so he had thought it was safe.

He should have known better. He and Rachel had been in Texas for eighteen months. They knew by now that nothing and nowhere in this wild land called Texas was really safe.

They had been in Monroe, Louisiana, when Grat showed up and demanded Rachel's return. At that time, Monroe had been the western end of the railroad line the Yankees had since extended to Shreveport. For several months Pie had driven wagonloads of supplies between Monroe and Marshall, carrying badly needed provisions and equipment closer to Vicksburg. Pie knew the route well, and he and Rachel had had no trouble negotiating it on horseback.

As part of the Confederacy, Texas had fugitive slave laws, too, but no one there knew of Rachel's heritage. A Baptist minister in Marshall had been glad to perform the wedding ceremony, especially since he obviously figured that the big, bearded man and the pretty redheaded gal had been living together without benefit of clergy anyway. He was only too happy to save them from that life of iniquity. He probably would have dropped his teeth if he had known what he was really doing, Pie had thought more than once since then.

As for himself, Pie didn't give a damn. Rachel could have been black as the ace of spades, and he still would have loved her.

Because of his role in bringing the wagon trains to and from Marshall, quite a few people there knew Pie. If Grat came after them, he would have no trouble finding them if they stayed so close to Louisiana. Besides, Pie was curious about what Texas was like farther west. He had heard Cory talk about it so much, about the Brazos River in particular.

After a short stay in Marshall, Pie and Rachel had ridden out one night, telling no one where they were going. They rode to the town of Quitman, then made their way farther west to a little village called Dallas, on a branch of the Trinity River. They had to stay there longer than Pie wanted to, because Rachel came down with a fever. He had been afraid he was going to lose her, but the old woman who ran the boarding house where they stayed was able to nurse her back to health. Rachel's recuperation took several months, though.

During that time, Pie had been quite nervous at first, worried not only about Rachel's health but also that Grat might show up and try to take her away from him again. If that happened, the Confederate government would be on Grat's side. Feelings were divided in this part of Texas—a significant number of people supported the Union—but the Confederates tried to keep dissent under control. Pie heard about what had happened in a town called Gainesville, up by the Red River. There a mob had hanged a bunch of Unionists. Pie didn't know the details, but they didn't matter. What was important was that the farther west in Texas a person went, the less control the Confederate government had. A land without law and order had its dangers, of course, plenty of them, but Pie and Rachel were willing to risk that if it meant she would be safe from Grat.

In the meantime, despite Rachel's protests, Pie had to know who or what was approaching their campsite. If trouble was coming, he would have to deal with it.

"Stay put," he said again. "I'll be right back."

He came to his feet and slipped toward the screen of brush surrounding the clearing. For such a big man, he moved quietly when he had to. Their two saddle horses and a pack mule were picketed at the edge of the clearing. Pie had bought the mule with money he'd earned working for a freight company in Dallas while Rachel was getting over her illness. He had been able to load and unload twice as much freight in a day as anybody else. The wages had also bought the Henry repeating rifle that he picked up from the ground now.

Pie held his breath and listened. He didn't hear anything in the brush. But something was out there. He and Rachel both had heard it plainly only a couple of minutes earlier.

Maybe they should have stayed in Dallas, he thought, or in Fort Worth where they had lived for several months after that. Despite the settlement's name, there was no fort there now. The army had abandoned it years ago, before the war. Pie had worked as a blacksmith's helper, and Rachel had taken a job as a serving girl in a tavern. Pie hadn't liked her working there, not even a little bit, but she had plenty of experience from her days with Grat and knew how to handle herself. None of the men tried to bother her more than once. And the fugitive couple needed the money to buy supplies. Pie knew that. He learned from talking to the blacksmith that it would take them perhaps a week to reach the Brazos River, and once they got there, they couldn't be assured of finding a good place to settle right away. There were some farms and ranches along the river already, but they were few and far between.

Finally they had been ready to head west again. A few days' ride had taken them past the tiny settlement of Weatherford. There was nothing beyond it but open range all the way to the Brazos. Beyond the river was nothing except the former hunting grounds of the Comanches. The savages had been removed by the government to reservations in Indian Territory before the war, but most of them had slipped back across the Red River into Texas. Some of the wilder bands had never gone to Indian Territory at all but had hidden out instead. Some twenty years earlier, the Comanches had ruled the western two-thirds of Texas and had been a force to be reckoned with. Now their power and numbers had shrunk, but they were still dangerous.

Pie didn't think those were Comanches out in the brush. For one thing, the noise had come from east of the camp. Of course, it could still be Indians, coming back from a raid and heading west. Slowly, so as not to make too much noise, he worked the lever of the Henry and threw a round into the chamber. His hands tightened on the stock and breech of the rifle.

Suddenly, something exploded out of the brush in front of him. Pie let out an involuntary yell as the huge shape hurtled at him and flung himself to the side as the thing rushed past him like a freight train. Pie landed hard, knocking the wind out of himself. For a moment he couldn't speak as he rolled over and came to his knees, bringing up the rifle.

Off to the right, Rachel shouted, "Pie! Pie! What is it?"

"Stay back!" he called to her. In the last of the fading gray light, he saw the thing that had nearly trampled him swinging around. It lowered its head and pawed at the ground. The huge sweep of horns that jutted from its head extended a good five feet from one horn tip to the other. "It's just a cow!"

A longhorn, to give it the name the Texans used with good reason. These creatures were common sights all over this part of the country. Usually scrawny and tough, they seemed to thrive on poor grazing conditions, and as far as most people were concerned, they weren't good for a damned thing except providing hides and tallow. And they were mean, to boot, unafraid of humans and always looking to hook somebody with one of those long, wickedly curving horns.

Pie would shoot the thing if it charged him again, he decided. But he didn't want to kill the longhorn unless he had to. He waved the rifle at the beast. "Hyaaah! Get out o' here, you ugly brute! Git!"

"Pie?" Rachel called again. "Are you all right?"

"I'm fine, just tryin' to run off this ol' cow. Stay back and be quiet, darlin'. I don't want you drawin' its attention."

The longhorn stood there as if uncertain what to do. It snorted, blowing air angrily through its nose. Then, with a shake of its horns, it turned and trotted off, crashing through the brush on its way to wherever it was going. Pie lowered the Henry and heaved a sigh of relief.

Behind him, a cold, hard voice pierced the growing darkness: "Just go ahead and put that rifle on the ground, big boy, or I'll kill you right here and now."

Chapter Five

PIE DIDN'T MOVE, BUT in the back of his mind, he cursed bitterly. Nearly getting run over by the longhorn had shaken him and distracted him enough so that he hadn't noticed the approach of someone else, someone who, from the sound of that threat, was now holding a gun on him. He wished Rachel had kept quiet. The stranger, whoever he was, must have heard her and now knew there was a woman close by.

The stranger wasn't alone, either. Footsteps rustled around, and another man's voice said, "Go ahead and shoot him, Dave. Ain't no need to keep him alive."

"I'll decide that," the first voice said. "I want him to answer some questions first. Hell, we might even let him live."

Pie didn't believe that for a second. These men weren't Indians, and he supposed he should be thankful for that, but they might be something even worse. Like everywhere else in the Confederacy, Texas had its share of deserters and renegades roaming around. Pie had clashed with such men before, back when he and Cory had been together, and he knew how ruthless they could be. If they were deserters, they wouldn't hesitate to kill him and steal his animals and supplies, and if Rachel fell into their hands . . . He didn't want to think about that.

The only small consolation was that if the men tried to attack Rachel, they would be in for a surprise. She carried a pistol these days, and she knew how to use it. Pie had bought enough ammunition so that she could practice on a regular basis, and she had gotten fairly proficient with the .36 Navy Colt. If the men tried to grab her, she would make the sons of bitches pay a high price.

"You still ain't put down that rifle, big boy," the man called Dave said. "I don't plan to tell you again."

"Take it easy," Pie said. "I'm puttin' it down." He leaned over and placed the Henry on the ground at his feet.

"Now step away from it," Dave ordered.

Pie did as he was told, and then his spirits sank a little as a third man said, "Do we go roust out the girl now?" Pie had thought there were only two of the men. Now the odds had gotten even worse.

"Yeah, go ahead, Jenkins," Dave said offhandedly. "But don't you hurt her."

"I'll go with him," the third man said with such eagerness in his voice that it made Pie sick.

"You stay here, Avery," Dave said. "Jenkins doesn't need your help to round up one woman."

"Maybe there's more than one. Maybe there's a gal for each of us."

Dave chuckled at the suggestion. "I wouldn't count on it. But one will do for now."

It was dark, Pie thought, and the renegades probably could not see him any better than he could see them. If he turned and reached for the Colt on his hip, maybe he could get it out of the holster and get off a shot or two . . .

As if reading his mind, Dave said, "Don't you try anything, big boy. I've got a shotgun pointed right at you, and at this range, it'll blow you in two, no matter how big you are. Reach across your body with your left hand and take out that pistol, nice and slow and put it on the ground."

Pie hesitated. Shotgun or no shotgun, there was only so much he was going to take before he fought back. On the other hand, he couldn't throw away his life needlessly. He had to stay alive for Rachel's sake.

His nerves were stretched taut, and when a sudden shot blasted through the darkness, he couldn't help but jump. Somebody let out a yelp.

Pie's right hand started toward the Colt. He was liable to get shot anyway, so he might as well go down fighting.

A flurry of shots rattled out. The sharp cracks sounded like rifle fire to Pie. He threw himself forward in a rolling dive, hoping to get out of the way of as much of the shotgun blast as possible. Sure enough, both barrels of the weapon boomed, lighting up the night with the flame that blossomed from the twin muzzles. Pie felt the fiery rake of lead clawing at him as he landed hard on the ground and rolled over. The Colt came up in his hand and bucked against his palm as he triggered it, aiming toward the sound of the shotgun.

More shots and a sudden rush of hoofbeats filled the night. Pie had no idea what was going on. He surged to his feet. "Rachel! Rachel!"

"Pie!"

He ran toward the sound of her voice, but before he could reach her, a large shape loomed up out of the darkness beside him. For a second Pie thought the longhorn had returned. Then he realized the shape was a horse, an instant before the animal's shoulder caught him a hard but glancing blow and spun him off his feet.

The horse's rider reined in. "Don't move, dadgum it!" he ordered as he leaned over from the saddle and pointed a rifle at the supine Pie.

Looking up from the ground, Pie saw the man in silhouette against the starlight that filled the sky. The rider wore a wide-brimmed hat and sat the saddle like he was part of the horse. He went on, "Just hunker there till we get this all sorted out."

At least the shooting had stopped. Pie was desperate to know if Rachel was all right. He started to get up in spite of the rifle pointed at him. Nobody was going to hold him on the ground while his wife was in danger or maybe even hurt already.

A new voice pierced the air, strong and calm and carrying easily through the darkness. "Take it easy now, boys," the new voice coached. "I think we got all three of them. Looks like they were trying to rob these folks."

The man who was covering Pie with the rifle said, "I got one of 'em over here, Cap'n Jim. Either that, or a bear's wandered in from West Texas."

"Let's get some light," the one called Cap'n Jim said. A moment later, Pie smelled the sulfur stink of a lucifer being struck. Yellow light flared up as someone lit a lantern.

Pie looked around and saw that there were at least half a dozen men on horseback, plus several more who had dismounted and were moving around on the ground. One of the men on foot carried the lantern. He came toward Pie. The light revealed him to be tall, barrel-chested, and powerful-looking, with a face that might have been open and friendly at other times but was now set in hard, alert lines. He had a heavy Colt Dragoon revolver in his other hand and wore a broad-brimmed black hat. A leather vest over a faded homespun shirt, denim trousers, and high-topped black boots completed his outfit. The other men were dressed in similar fashion. They were typical Texans, hard-eyed men, some clean-shaven, some sporting bristly whiskers. The one who was covering Pie had a pronounced twang in his voice as he said, "See, Cap'n, I told you he was big as a bear."

"Who are you, mister?" the captain asked. He didn't look like any soldier Pie had ever seen, but clearly he was the commander of this group of men.

"Name's Pie Jones," Pie said. "Can I get up now?"

The captain nodded. "Just don't move too suddenlike. Curt there sometimes gets a mite jumpy."

The rawboned, lantern-jawed man called Curt grinned as he continued to point his rifle at Pie.

Pie climbed to his feet. "Three men jumped us," he said. "I reckon they were going to rob us and kill me. As for my missus—"

"Don't worry about her," the captain cut in. "She's fine." He turned and called, "Bring in the woman, Lacewell."

A moment later, Rachel entered the circle of light cast by the lantern, followed closely by one of the men. She cried out and rushed over to Pie, throwing her arms around his neck. She wasn't crying, but he could feel her trembling. He understood how she felt. He was a little shaky himself right now. Having Rachel in his arms again, safe and sound, helped a lot, though.

She caught her breath. "You're hurt!"

He could feel the wet spots on his back where some buck-shot had grazed him. "It don't amount to nothin'," he said. "Don't worry about it."

"You're sure?"

He nodded and pulled her closer to him again.

The man with the lantern said, "I'm Captain Jim Griffin. We're Texas Rangers. Been on the trail of three renegades for the past couple of days, ever since they raided a settler's cabin down by Thorp Springs and murdered him. I'd say the two we killed and that other one must be the men we were after."

Continuing to hold Rachel, Pie looked over her shoulder at Griffin. "The two you killed, you say?"

Griffin smiled faintly and nodded. "From the looks of things, you got the other one. That was a neat bit of greenhorn shooting, Mr. Jones."

Pie heaved a deep breath. "Good luck, more than anything. The good Lord must've took a likin' to me right about then."

"Never hurts to have the forces of righteousness on your side, along with plenty of powder and shot," Griffin said.

"You're Rangers, you say? Lawmen?"

Griffin shrugged broad shoulders. "Lawmen, soldiers, what-ever we need to be in order to keep Texas safe from Indians and from blackguards like these. With most of the menfolks gone off to war, the frontier's a more dangerous place than ever. And it never was what you'd call peaceful in the first place." A shrewd look came into Griffin's eyes. "You wouldn't by any chance be on the run from the law, would you, Mr. Jones?"

Without hesitation, Pie shook his head. "No sir. My wife and I, we're on our way to the Brazos River, lookin' for a likely spot to settle down."

Rachel turned her head to look at Griffin and nodded silently. Griffin touched a couple of fingers to the brim of his hat and said politely, "Ma'am." He looked at Pie again. "You're not a deserter yourself?"

"No sir. I was at Vicksburg when Pemberton surrendered to the Yankees and was mustered out there." That was another lie, of course, but Pie thought it was a convincing one and one that Griffin would not be able to disprove without having to go to a lot of trouble. "To tell you the truth," he continued, "the only reason I was worried about you bein' lawmen was because you said I killed that fella."

Griffin laughed lightly at that. "You won't be in any trouble for that, I reckon. The closest county seat is Weatherford, and the coroner there wouldn't be too happy with me if I hauled the bodies of three obvious criminals all the way back there for an inquest. No, we'll just plant 'em here and write up a report that says they met their Maker while resisting arrest."

"Thanks, Cap'n. Rachel and me just want to get on where we're goin' and find some good land to light on."

"Plenty o' that along the Brazos," the Ranger called Curt said. "Bet a hat on that. But the best of it's been gobbled up already by this fella who started a ranch there 'fore the war." He grinned at Griffin. "Ain't that right, Cap'n?"

"What this knothead is trying to say is that I've got a spread there myself," Griffin said as he jerked a thumb in Curt's direction. "The JG Connected. That's where we're headed now, in fact, as soon as we get these renegades in the ground. Would the two of you like to ride with us?"

Pie looked at Rachel and saw her eager nod. Although the risk involved with spending a lot of time with these rugged frontier lawmen made him a little nervous, he knew what Rachel was thinking. The same thought had gone through his mind. As long as they were riding with the Ranger patrol, they wouldn't have to worry much, if any, about running into Comanches or more deserters.

"We'd be much obliged for the company, Cap'n," he said in answer to the invitation.

"It's settled then." Griffin turned away and lifted the lantern. "All right, boys, some of you break out your shovels. We've got some digging to do."

WHILE SEVERAL of the Rangers dug a common grave for the three dead renegades, Griffin checked the wounds on Pie's back. As he had told Rachel, they didn't amount to much more than scratches. None of the pellets had embedded themselves. Griffin got a bottle of whiskey from Curt's saddlebags—"I just use it as medicine," Curt said with a grin—and gave it to Rachel along with a cloth.

"Clean the wounds with that," Griffin told her. "It'll keep them from festering."

"I know. I've patched up bullet holes before," she said.

Griffin looked at the two of them curiously as Rachel tended to Pie's wounds. "Where are you folks from?"

"Mississippi," Pie said.

"How about you, ma'am?"

"I'm from Mississippi, too," Rachel said. That wasn't true; she had been born and raised in Louisiana, on a plantation not far from Baton Rouge. But the Ranger didn't need to know that. She and Pie had discussed the need to keep their background vague, just in case Grat ever came searching for them.

"What made you decide to come to Texas?"

The question seemed innocent enough. Pie had the feeling that Griffin was just being friendly and making small talk. But the knowledge that the man was a lawman was still in the back of Pie's head, and he knew he wasn't going to forget it.

"A friend of mine in the army talked about it all the time," Pie said. That was almost true. Cory had been fascinated by Texas and the idea of coming here. He just hadn't been in the army, not officially. "He got me to thinkin' that I ought to see the place, too."

"There's nowhere better on earth," Griffin said. "I was born here myself. My folks came down here from Connecticut and were part of Stephen Austin's original colony. My pa was at Washington-on-the-Brazos when the old Texicans decided that they'd had enough of Mexico running things. He was at San Jacinto, too, when Sam Houston routed the Mexican army and grabbed old Santa Anna. I'm old enough to remember the Runaway Scrape before that, though, when families all over Texas had to pick up and leave their farms to keep the Mexicans from wiping them out. That was after the Alamo."

"Sounds like you or your folks were part of just about everything that made Texas what it is."

Griffin grinned. "That's true of nearly every man in this patrol. Us Texans haven't had time yet to grow really deep roots, but the ones that are there are strong, mighty strong."

"How do you feel about folks movin' in from other places?"

"It's just fine with me and most that I know. There's a saying some of the newcomers have: 'I wasn't born in Texas, but I got here as fast as I could.' You can't help but like somebody who feels like that."

Pie nodded. "Sounds good to me."

He winced as Rachel swabbed the bullet gashes on his back with the whiskey-soaked cloth, then he put his torn shirt back on. The burying was just about finished. When the last shovelful of earth had been patted down, one of the Rangers took off his hat and said a short prayer. Pie didn't feel much like praying for the souls of the departed, since they'd planned on killing him and raping Rachel before they murdered her as well, but out of respect for the Rangers he lowered his head. He didn't close his eyes, though, and he hoped the three renegades had wound up shaking hands with the devil in Hades.

"We'll be moving on for a while," Griffin said. "Probably make camp for the night a little farther west."

Pie nodded. "That's fine with us. I don't much want to stay here tonight anyway, after what happened."

He saddled their horses then helped Rachel mount. Taking the mule's reins, Pie swung up into his own saddle and heeled his horse into a walk. He and Rachel rode at the front of the group, next to Griffin and Curt.

The moon rose brightly behind them. The glowing orb was nearly full and cast plenty of silvery illumination over the rolling, tree-dotted landscape.

"They call that a Comanche moon," Griffin said. "War parties used to raid by its light. The Comanch', just like other Indians, don't cotton much to fighting at night, but they did plenty of it when the moon was that bright. Still do, sometimes."

Rachel asked, "We won't run into one of those war parties, will we, Captain?"

"Not very likely, ma'am. We haven't had any reports of raids in this part of the country for quite a while. One thing about Texas, though—anything is possible."

Pie could believe that. If anyone had asked him a few hours earlier what the likelihood was that he would be riding with a troop of Texas Rangers before the night was over, he would have said it was pretty damned unlikely.

After several miles, Griffin called a halt in a clump of trees atop a hill. In case of trouble, this place could be defended quite easily. The Rangers made a cold camp, eating a supper consisting of strips of jerky and biscuits left over from that morning's breakfast. They offered to share their food with Pie and Rachel, but Pie explained that they had already eaten.

At least two Rangers were on guard all night, but the hours passed peacefully, and the whole group was on its way again not long after sunrise the next morning, following a breakfast of bacon, freshly cooked biscuits, and roasted-grain coffee. The real thing seemed to be in short supply here in Texas, just like it was elsewhere in the Confederacy. Griffin said they would reach his ranch, the JG Connected, before the day was over.

Griffin's mount was a beautiful animal, Pie thought as he studied the horse. Powerfully built, the horse looked like he could run all day if need be. He had a sleek sorrel hide the color of burnt copper, a white face and legs, and an arrowhead-shaped white mark on the left side of his neck. There were also white markings on both sides of his belly.

"This is Sizzle," Griffin said with a smile as he noted Pie's interest. He reached forward and patted the horse's shoulder. "One of the best horses I ever had. The only one I ever saw who was his equal was called Yank." Griffin shook his head ruefully. "Not a good name for a horse in Texas, I know. But he was a mighty good horse. Died of old age a few years ago, not long after I started up the JG Connected."

"How can you run a ranch and ride with the Rangers at the same time?" Pie asked curiously.

"I leave a crew on the spread to keep an eye on things for me. My *segundo* is an old-timer who's smart as a whip and tough as whang-leather. He keeps things running just fine."

"Do you know of some good land out there where a fella could start a farm?"

Griffin rubbed his jaw. "The land around my ranch isn't really well suited for farming. Too rocky. And there are too many hills. But if you go south a ways, you'll find a lot of good bottom land on both sides of the river. There are quite a few creeks and smaller rivers that run into the Brazos, too, so there's plenty of water to be had. And you'll need those streams when the droughts come."

Rachel said, "You have droughts here?"

"Sometimes. It's worse out in West Texas, from what I hear. But sometimes months will go by without any rain to speak of, even around here. Luckily, a lot of the creeks are spring-fed, so they don't dry up completely."

"What about the winters?" Pie asked.

"Not too bad, except when a blue norther comes whistling down on us. It can be nice and warm, and then that norther blows through and the temperature drops 'way below freezing in a matter of an hour or two. Usually brings some snow and ice with it, too. But that only happens a few times every year. Like the sandstorms in the summer."

"Sandstorms?" Pie repeated.

"That's right. When the wind blows really hard out in West Texas, it picks up a lot of sand and carries it over here."

Curt said, "I've seen sandstorms so bad there's prairie dogs diggin' their holes thirty feet in the air."

Rachel stared at him.

"And you talk about dry," Curt went on with a grin. "I sure hope there's some rain again sometime. Not so much for my own sake, mind you, but for my ten-year-old nephew. *I've* seen rain."

"What?" Pie said with a frown and a shake of his head.

Griffin chuckled and said, "Don't pay Curt any mind. He's just joshin' you."

"No such thing!" Curt protested in mock innocence. "Next thing you know, cap'n, you'll be tellin' these here pilgrims that the story ain't true about the blue norther so cold it froze the birds' songs."

"That can't be!" Rachel said.

"Yes ma'am," Curt said with a solemn nod. "Why, the next spring when things finally thawed out, folks heard birds a-chirpin', but there weren't no birds there. The sounds were just left over from the winter, when they all froze."

Pie laughed. Obviously, the Rangers no longer suspected him and Rachel of any wrongdoing. It felt good to be accepted . . . even though they'd had to lie a little to gain that trust.

Late that afternoon, the group of riders topped a long, gentle rise and started down another slope that ran for several miles in front of them. Captain Griffin pointed to a thick line of trees that stretched across the terrain from north to south. "Those trees mark the river," he said. He swung his arm to indicate some rugged hills to the north. "See those hills? The river loops through them and makes a big bend. It doubles back on itself for a good ten miles, then turns right around and runs south again."

Pie looked to the horizon beyond the river and saw several larger hills jutting into the sky. From the top of them, he reckoned, a man would have a good, clear view of this entire stretch of the valley.

Griffin saw where Pie was looking and chuckled. "If you're thinking that seems a likely place for the Comanches to be watching us, you're right. In years past, that was one of their prime lookout spots. The Brazos was pretty much the border between them and the settlers. They raided some on this side of the river, but not as much. The Yankees had a fort west of here called Phantom Hill, and that went a long way toward pushing back the frontier. The fort's gone now, though, along with the Yankee army."

"The war seems a long ways off," Pie said.

Griffin nodded. "Yes, it does. That's because we've got our own worries back here, and whether or not somebody can have slaves isn't one of them. Once you get out of the piney woods over there in East Texas, nobody has slaves, anyway. You get a man to work for you on a ranch, you want him to be there of his own free will."

"Then you don't care if the Confederacy wins or not?"

"I didn't say that. The Yankees were wrong to try to take away the rights of the states." Griffin shrugged. "I'm just saying that however the war comes out, in the long run it's not going to matter that much here in Texas. We're used to making our own way. Shoot, we were our own country for a while, after we shook free of Mexico. Some folks will tell you we'd have been better off if we stayed that way, instead of joining the Union. I think becoming a state was in the back of most people's mind from the start, though. Shame it didn't work out."

"Maybe Texas should secede from the Confederacy and be its own country again," Rachel said.

"You might have something there, ma'am," Griffin said with a smile. "Don't reckon it'll ever happen, though. We've cast our lot with the South, and we'll rise or fall with the Confederacy."

Following Griffin's lead, the riders angled to the south before they reached the river. The terrain here along the Brazos was still rugged but not as hilly as it was farther north. Pie began to wonder if they were going to reach the ranch before night fell, but as the sun dipped toward the western horizon, they came within sight of several large cabins made of thick beams hewn from logs. They were built in the style that was so common here in Texas, a pair of rooms to each cabin with a covered area in between called a dogtrot. Pie also saw a good-sized barn and several corrals with split-rail fences, a squarish, sturdy structure that was probably a smokehouse, and a smithy. All the buildings were scattered around on a sprawling hilltop overlooking the river a hundred yards away. It was as pretty a place as he had seen in a long time, Pie thought.

Griffin reined in, pausing for a moment. "There it is," he said, pride in his voice. "The JG Connected. Most of it built with my own two hands. Well, mine and old Quirt's, I should say."

"Quirt?" Pie said.

"Quirt Coburn. That *segundo* I mentioned. That's a Spanish word, means *second*. He's my foreman, I guess you could say. Was right bower to Sam Houston, back in the days of the revolution. You'll meet him in a bit. Don't let him bother you. He's a crusty old sort, still got all the bark on him."

"Bet a hat on that," Curt said.

Several hounds loped out to greet the riders, baying loudly. A couple of men emerged from the barn, and another man came out of one of the cabins. He walked with a rolling, bowlegged gait and had long white hair and a white beard that jutted out fiercely. He glared up at Griffin. "It's about time you got back. You go gallivantin' off after redskins and highwaymen and leave me here to do all the real work."

Griffin grinned. "It's good to see you, too, Quirt."

The old man switched his gaze to Pie and Rachel. "Who's this? The gal's pretty easy on the eyes, but the fella looks like he's half bear."

"Some pilgrims who're looking for place to settle. Mr. and Mrs. Jones."

Pie nodded to the old-timer. "Call me Pie. This here's my wife, Rachel."

"Pie? What the hell kind of a name is Pie?"

"That's just what I've always been called. It's because I like to eat so much, I reckon."

Coburn squinted up at him. "Ever et any brazosberry cobbler?" he challenged more than asked.

"Can't say as I have," Pie said with a shake of his head.

"I got some cookin'. Light and set." Coburn looked over at Griffin again. "Welcome home, Jim."

Home, Pie thought. That sounded mighty good, even though this wasn't his home. But he would have one again someday, he vowed as he looked over at Rachel. And that day was going to be soon, too.

Chapter Six

P IE WAS A LITTLE confused when he woke up. He was lying on something soft, much softer than the ground on which he was accustomed to sleeping. It took him a moment to realize he was stretched out on an actual bed. Beside him, Rachel stirred slightly. They slept spoon-fashion, with his arms around her, and now she snuggled even closer to him. He felt desire for her growing and knew that she felt it, too, when she made a little noise of pleasure deep in her throat.

He wanted to make love to her, but now all the memories came back to him: the three renegades, Griffin and the Rangers, the ride to this ranch beside the Brazos River, the old man called Quirt . . .

Griffin had insisted that Pie and Rachel take his bedroom. "I'll bunk in with the rest of the boys," he'd said after supper the night before. "It's been a long time since there's been a lady out here on the JG Connected—"

"A long time!" Quirt had said. The old-timer snorted in derision. "Try never!"

"Well, yes, I reckon that's right," Griffin had said with a smile. "Anyway, ma'am, since you and Pie have been traveling for a while, I'd just feel better if you accepted our hospitality and slept in a real bed tonight."

Rachel hadn't been able to argue with that, and neither had Pie.

With sunlight slanting in the cabin's window, Pie knew the next morning had come. He stretched lazily, enjoying the feel of the sheets and the way the cornshuck-stuffed mattress cradled him. Rachel took hold of his hands and tugged on them to tighten his arms around her.

"My, this feels wonderful," she said.

"Yeah, but we oughta be ashamed of ourselves. Look how high the sun is. We've done slept half the day away."

"Oh, hush! It's not more than an hour after sunrise, Pie Jones, and you full well know it. Anyway, we deserve a little luxury. We've done without for such a long time." She rolled over in his embrace and kissed him. "Can we have a cabin like this on our ranch?"

"I don't see why not. All we got to do is find us a place and cut some trees. Cap'n Jim says there's plenty, all up and down the river."

"Are we going south?"

"That's where the best land is, according to the cap'n. We'll put in some crops and gather up some o' them wild cattle for beef and milk. Reckon we'll get along just fine."

"It sounds wonderful," Rachel whispered. "It's more than I ever dreamed of having. And so are you, Pie . . ." Her lips found his again.

He couldn't stop his hands from moving on her body. As he caressed her, the need within him grew even stronger, and he knew that whether it was proper and fitting to be romping in somebody else's cabin or not, he was going to have to make love to his wife.

That was when a shrill clatter came from somewhere outside, carrying with it an unmistakable sense of alarm.

Pie recognized the sound as somebody beating on an iron triangle. Such a racket usually meant the men were being summoned in from the fields for a meal. At this time of day, though, the ranch hands would have had breakfast already, and it was too early for dinner. That meant trouble.

He sat up and swung his legs out of the bunk. Behind him, Rachel said, "Pie . . ."

"I'll be right back," he told her as he stood up and pulled on his trousers. He shrugged into his shirt as he went to the door. Before stepping outside, he picked up the Henry rifle he had leaned against the wall the night before.

The iron triangle hung from a peg on the wall of the cabin on the other side of the dogtrot. Quirt Coburn stood there beating on it with the long handle of a ladle. He stopped as Pie came into the dogtrot. Pie saw several of the Rangers hurrying toward the cabin. He saw as well a stranger, a teenage boy in ragged shirt and trousers, sitting on a three-legged stool in front of the cabin. Captain Griffin was hunkered on his heels beside the boy, who had his hands over his face and was sobbing.

As Coburn finally stopped banging on the iron triangle, the Rangers gathered around Griffin and the boy. Pie joined the group, too. Curt asked, "Ain't that the Harrigan boy, Cap'n?"

"That's right," Griffin said. "There's been some trouble at his family's place." The captain's face was grim as he looked into the faces of the men gathering around him. "Comanches hit it early this morning."

"P-Pa and Juney never had a chance," the boy said in a choked voice. "They . . . they killed 'em both."

"How did you get away from them, son?" Griffin asked.

The boy sniffled and wiped the back of his hand across his nose. "I was down at the crick, fetchin' water. I heard all the yelpin' and hollerin', and then Pa's old shotgun went off, and I . . . I went to ground in the bushes. I couldn't see nothin' but the roof of the cabin from where I was. The Injuns hollered a bunch more, and Juney screamed, and then the Injuns rode off after settin' fire to the cabin."

"I didn't see no smoke," Coburn said. "And I keep a close eye for such."

"I had two buckets of water. I ran up there and flung them on the fire. It hadn't had a chance to get started good yet, so I was able to put it out." The boy's voice broke again. "There . . . there wasn't nothin' I could for Pa or Juney, though."

Pie glanced around the ring of Rangers and saw disapproving frowns on the faces of some of them. He knew why they looked that way. This boy had hidden in the brush while Comanches killed his father and some girl called Juney, probably the boy's sister. They thought he should have tried to help them, even though, armed with only a couple of buckets of water, there wasn't a thing he could have done except get himself killed, too. This was one of those horrible situations that came up sometimes on the frontier, when a man seemed to be damned no matter what he did.

Griffin patted the boy's knee. "You did the right thing, Tad," he said. "How long ago did this happen?"

"N-not long," the boy choked out. "The Comanch' ran off all our stock, 'cept for one old mule that's awful skittish. She lets me ride her, though, so I caught her and came right over here."

"Which way were the Indians headed when they left your place?"

"West. Across the river."

Griffin nodded. "I don't know how they slipped past us," he said to the other Rangers, "but they've probably been raiding over east of here. Now they've started home."

"We're goin' after them, ain't we?" Curt asked.

"Yes, I'd say we've got a good chance of catching them. They probably don't even know there's a Ranger patrol in the area." Griffin stood up and squeezed the boy's shoulder. He said to Coburn, "Quirt, take the wagon and some of the boys and go down to the Harrigan place to tend to things there." Tend to the burying, that was what he meant, Pie knew. "I want a few of the hands left here to keep an eye on the place," Griffin went on. "I don't think those Indians will double back, but there's always that chance. And we have visitors to look out for. The rest of us will ride after those Comanch'."

"Cap'n," Pie said, the words coming out of his mouth seemingly of their own volition, "I was thinkin' I might ride with you."

He hadn't known that Rachel had come up behind him until that moment. Now fully dressed, she put her hand on his arm and clutched it tightly. "Pie, no," she said in a low voice.

He turned to look at her. "Cap'n Griffin and the Rangers saved our bacon a couple of nights ago, Rachel. We'd have been goners if they hadn't come along when they did. Least I can do to repay 'em is give them a hand now."

Griffin said, "Your wife is right, Pie. This isn't your fight."

Pie looked at him. "Cap'n, remember what you told me about how some folks wasn't born in Texas but got here as fast as they could? Reckon that's the way I feel now. If this is where Rachel and me are goin' to make our home, then when trouble comes, it's our fight, too." He turned back to Rachel. "You understand that, don't you, darlin'?"

She didn't answer for a moment, but then she summoned up a faint smile. "I suppose I do. If you think something is the right thing to do, you have to go ahead with it, don't you?"

"Seems like it," Pie admitted with a smile.

Rachel moved over to the Harrigan boy, who was sobbing quietly again, and put her hands on his shoulders. "Go ahead," she said to Pie. "I'll help Mr. Coburn look after this poor boy."

Quirt nodded. "I'm obliged, ma'am." Pie could tell that the old-timer hadn't been looking forward to having to comfort the grieving, guilt-stricken youngster.

"That's settled then," Griffin said and turned to his men. "Saddle up. We'll get on the trail of those savages."

Preparations were made quickly. Pie pulled his boots on, strapped on the Colt, and stuffed extra shells for it and the Henry in his pockets. His horse was in the barn with the others. He threw the saddle on it and led it out.

Rachel came from the cabin that served as the cook shack and handed him a burlap sack. "It's some salt pork and biscuits," she said. "Mr. Coburn said for you to take it along, that you'd be liable to need provisions if it's a long chase." She touched Pie's arm. "Do you think it will be?"

All he could do was shake his head helplessly. "I honestly don't know. I never chased no Comanches before."

She came up on her toes and brushed her lips across his. "Be careful," she said in a half-whisper that was thick with emotion. "Please be careful, Pie."

"I will. You got my word on that."

"And good luck." She glanced over her shoulder at the still-sobbing Tad Harrigan. "I don't want to be crying over you, like that boy's crying over his family."

IN A very short amount of time, the Rangers were ready to ride. Griffin led the way on the big sorrel paint, Sizzle, flanked by Pie and Curt. The other men, nine in all, followed behind them, stretching out the line a little so they wouldn't be too bunched up in case of trouble.

The group rode south, following the eastern bank of the Brazos. "The Harrigan spread is about five miles this way," Griffin explained to Pie. "We'll cross the river there so we can pick up the tracks of the Comanches. It shouldn't be too hard."

"You really think we can catch them?" Pie asked.

"I think there's a good chance. They'll have a small herd of horses and cattle, and that will slow them down some. And they don't get in a hurry unless they know someone is after them." Griffin waved a hand toward the land on the other side of the river. "They still regard all of that as their own personal hunting grounds, all the way to New Mexico Territory. It would be undignified for them to run away while they're on their own land. That's the way their attitude strikes me, anyway."

"You've fought Indians before?"

"That's right. The state government has Rangers stationed in all the counties north and south of here, forming a sort of line all the way from the Red River to the Rio Grande. We're that line, and it's our job to keep the Indians to the west of it, so everything east will be safe for settlement." Griffin shook his head. "But there aren't enough of us, and you've seen for yourself that the line can be broken from time to time. When that happens, all we can do is try to chase down the raiders and make them pay for what they've done."

A short time later, they came in sight of a lonely cabin. The corner of one wall and part of the roof had been scorched by the flames that Tad Harrigan had extinguished before they could destroy the whole structure. Two shapes lay sprawled in front of the cabin.

"Damn it!" Griffin said as he caught sight of something moving around the bodies. "The buzzards are already at them. Come on!"

He heeled his horse into a run, with Pie and the Rangers following. Ugly black birds rose into the sky as the pounding hoofbeats approached, abandoning the corpses on which they had been feeding. As Pie reined in, he tore his horrified gaze away from what had been done to the faces of the man and the girl who had been killed by the Comanches.

"Tad lost his head," Griffin said in disgust. "He should have at least covered them up before he left. We'll do that now. It's all we have time for. Quirt can take care of the rest when he and the other boys get here."

A couple of the Rangers went into the cabin and came back out with their arms full of blankets. They spread the coverings over the two corpses, piling them thick so that the buzzards couldn't get at them again. Pie stayed in the saddle, knowing that there was nothing he could do to help here. The damage had been done already. As Griffin had said, all the Rangers could accomplish now was to try to settle the score for these murdered settlers and maybe hit the Comanche raiders hard enough to make the next war party think twice about venturing across the Brazos.

When the grim task of covering the bodies was completed, the Rangers rode down to the river, following a path that slanted down the bank to the water. The streambed was at least a hundred yards wide, but not all of it was covered with water. Several sandbars were visible.

"Follow me," Griffin said over his shoulder to Pie. "There's quicksand out there, so you have to know where you're going."

Pie nodded and kept his horse right behind the captain's mount. The rest of the group formed a line behind him. The water was shallow most of the way, but it grew deep enough in the main channel so that the horses were forced to swim. The men held their weapons and ammunition over their heads to keep the powder dry.

When the riders emerged from the river, water streaming from their clothes, the hot Texas sun began to dry them almost right away. They rode through the cottonwood trees on the west bank and emerged onto a grassy plain dotted with clumps of post oaks, cedars, and mesquites. It took only a few minutes of searching for the keen eyes of Griffin and the other Rangers to locate the tracks left behind by the Comanche raiding party and the stolen livestock they were driving before them.

Griffin set the pace, and it was a fast one. As Pie had expected, Sizzle seemed tireless. The large man was accustomed to riding, but not at such a swift gait. He hoped he would be able to keep up. The other men talked little amongst themselves. For the most part, they rode in a solemn silence. The task that had brought them here was serious business, and that responsibility weighed heavily on each one.

The morning passed, and the sun climbed until it was directly overhead and beating down with a brassy heat. There were large circles of sweat on Pie's shirt, and he wished he had one of those broad-brimmed hats like the Rangers wore. If he was going to stay here in Texas, he would have to get one of them, he thought. He tried to watch the tracks, but he couldn't always see them. Evidently the trail was plain as day to Griffin, though. The captain never slowed except occasionally, and that was just to give the horses a breather.

Griffin called a short halt early in the afternoon when the Rangers came to a small, winding creek. The horses drank from the stream and grazed a little while the men made a quick lunch from the salt pork and biscuits in the bag Pie carried on his saddle. Pie washed his food down with a long swig from his canteen then asked Griffin, "How much longer do you think it'll be before we catch up to them?"

"Those tracks aren't much more than an hour old," Griffin said, "and neither are the droppings the Indian ponies left. We'll push on as fast as we can, so we ought to spot them before dark."

"What happens when we do?"

"When they see us, most of them will turn back to fight while a few, usually the youngest ones, will keep pushing the horses and cattle on toward their home. It'll be up to us to brush past the defenders and take back the herd."

"That's what we're really after, then?" Pie said. "The stolen livestock?"

"Not entirely. We'll have to kill or at least wound some of the Indians to take back that stock. You have to understand how important it is to them, though, especially the horses. When a raiding party sets out to steal horses and comes back empty-handed, it's a shameful thing. That'll hurt their pride as much or more than killing some of them."

"That's important, hurting their pride?"

Griffin took off his hat and wiped sweat from the band inside it. "Think about it, Pie. The Comanches can't win, not in the long run. There are too few of them and too many of us. But they can make life miserable and dangerous for the settlers out here and delay the spread of civilization for a long time. Unless their spirit is broken. Unless they realize they're fighting a losing battle and give up. That's why we strike at their pride, to hasten the process and save lives on both sides."

Pie frowned and rubbed at his beard. "I reckon that makes sense," he said slowly. "Seems like sort of a shame to fight that way, though."

"You mean it's better to kill a man than to make him feel like a failure as a warrior?"

"Well, when you put it that way . . . Hell, I don't know, Cap'n. I'm the peaceable sort, myself. I'd just as soon not have to fight with anybody."

"You volunteered to come along with us."

"Yeah, because I stick by my friends, and you fellas have been good to me and Rachel. Don't worry, Cap'n. When push comes to shove, I'll do my part."

Griffin grinned and thumped a fist lightly on Pie's shoulder. "I wasn't worried, Pie. I know you're a fighting man. Rangers never let each other down."

Pie frowned and was about to ask what Griffin meant by that, but before he could, the captain turned away and called, "Mount up! We're riding!"

Again the group took up the trail, and now, after horses and men had rested for a short time, the pace once again was fast. Pie ignored the aches and pains caused by the hard riding and did his best to keep up.

Several more hours rolled by. The terrain grew more rugged the farther the Rangers went from the Brazos River. It was still flat for the most part, but hills and rocky ridges jutted up more often and were more thickly wooded. The ground under the hooves of the horses turned to hard red clay. Gullies choked with brush slashed the landscape and sometimes had to be gone around. It was harder for even the sharp eyes of Captain Griffin to follow the tracks left by the Comanches.

Then, abruptly, Curt called out, "Look yonder!" and pointed to a ridge about a mile ahead of them. Pie saw riders vanishing over the crest of the ridge.

"That's them," Griffin said. "Come on, boys!"

Now that their quarry was within sight, the Rangers poured on the speed. Pie knew it was asking a lot of his horse, but he urged the mount to keep up.

Instead of heading for the ridge where they had spotted the Indians, Griffin circled his men to the south and led the group along a narrow valley that flanked the route chosen by the Comanches. Pie figured he intended to hit the war party from the side, rather than coming at them directly from behind. He had never learned much about tactics during his time with the

Confederate army, but he remembered that a flank attack was usually a good idea.

The head of the valley loomed in front of them. As the Rangers galloped out onto a long stretch of flat land that ended in a sharp upthrust several miles ahead, Pie looked to his right and saw the Indians riding along behind a herd of at least fifty horses and cattle. Sharp yips of surprise floated through the air to his ears. The Comanches must have believed they had left any pursuit far behind, if indeed anyone had come after them.

Now they knew better, and several of the Indians immediately peeled away from the main group and raced toward the Rangers. Powder smoke jetted into the air from the muzzles of their rifles. But the range was too great, and it was impossible to aim from the back of a galloping pony. None of the bullets came anywhere near the Rangers, as far as Pie could tell.

Still the Indians came on, and after a moment Griffin yelled a command. The Rangers reined in, and three of them dropped from their saddles. They rested their rifles across those saddles as the well-trained horses stood absolutely still. The weapons began to crack.

A couple of the Comanches tumbled from the backs of their mounts. Another almost fell but managed to grab his pony's mane and hang on. The rest of the Indians turned and raced back toward the main group.

Griffin waved an arm and shouted, "Turn that herd!"

Several Rangers sent their horses springing ahead in a mad dash to head off the herd of stolen livestock. The others, including Pie, rode forward again, pressing the Comanches from the left flank. Pie guided his horse with his knees as he lifted the Henry rifle and peppered the raiders with lead, firing several rounds as fast as he could work the lever and squeeze the trigger. He didn't know if any of the bullets found their targets, but at least he was helping to harry the Comanches.

Curt was one of the men trying to head off the herd. Pie saw the lanky Ranger firing his revolver. One of the Indians with the herd raced out toward the Rangers, carrying a lance. Curt jerked his horse aside at the last instant as the Comanche warrior tried to ram the lance through his body. At almost point-blank range, Curt fired his Colt again, and the heavy ball smashed the Indian from his horse and sent him thudding lifelessly to the ground.

The main body of the war party suddenly wheeled around and charged the pursuing Rangers. Evidently, that was just what Griffin had been waiting for. "Dismount!" the captain bellowed at the top of his lungs.

With a precision to equal that of any well-trained regular cavalry unit, the Rangers reined in and swung down from their saddles. Some stood while others went to one knee. Rifles leaped to their shoulders. Flame blossomed from the muzzles of the weapons as a volley rang out. Pie joined in, cranking the Henry's lever and firing as fast as he could.

A veritable storm of lead whipped through the onrushing Comanches. Horses and men fell. Pandemonium reigned. The riders who survived the charge wheeled their ponies and raced toward the herd . . . but the other Rangers had reached the stampeding livestock and turned them back on themselves. Thick clouds of dust clogged the air. Shapes darted through the billowing clouds and sharp reports of gunfire speared through the confusion. The Rangers who had broken the Comanche charge hurried forward, snapping shots at any stragglers.

Pie was trotting along beside Griffin when a warrior on horseback loomed out of the dust in front of them. With a shrill cry, the Comanche swung an empty rifle at Griffin. The blow would have crushed the captain's skull if it had connected. But before the rifle touched him, Pie's shoulder slammed into Griffin and knocked him out of the way. Pie took the blow on his other shoulder. The rifle glanced off but still hit him hard enough to make his left arm go numb. With his right hand, Pie jabbed the barrel of his Henry under the chin of the Indian, flipping him off the horse as it raced past. The Comanche fell and slammed hard into the ground.

The impact didn't knock all the fight out of him, though. The warrior rolled over and started to come up with a knife in his hand. Pie stepped forward and kicked him in the jaw, sending him sprawling backward. The knife slipped out of the Indian's hand as he landed on his back and lay there with his head twisted at an odd angle. Pie felt his stomach lurch as he realized he had broken the Comanche's neck and killed him.

The feeling lasted only a second. Rifle fire erupted close beside him, and he turned to see Griffin shooting another warrior who dashed at them on foot, brandishing a lance. The Comanche went down, blood on his chest where the slugs ripped through him.

"Reckon we're even," Griffin said with a quick grin.

Pie nodded.

The swirling clouds of dust began to settle. A few more gunshots popped, but for the most part, the fight seemed to be over. As the air cleared, Pie saw three or four of the Comanches racing away over the plains as fast as their ponies would carry them. They were the only survivors from the raiding party, and Griffin called out an order to let them go.

"We want some of them to get back to their home," he said to Pie, "so they can tell the others who didn't go on the raid how bad we hurt them."

Curt and the other Rangers still on horseback had the herd of stolen livestock under control. The horses and cattle ambled back the way they had come. Griffin, Pie, and the other men checked the bodies of the Comanches lying scattered around on the ground. All of them were dead, and in a way, Pie was glad of that. Having seen what had happened at the Harrigan farm, he didn't think the grim-faced Rangers would have been in any mood to take any prisoners back with them.

Several of the Texans had suffered minor wounds in the battle, but none of them had been killed. They left the bodies of the Comanches where they had fallen. The warriors who had gotten away would return to claim the bodies of the slain, Griffin explained to Pie. The Rangers mounted up and headed east, driving the recovered horses and cattle before them.

"Some folks say that when you kill a Comanche like that, you ought to shoot his eyes out before you leave him," Griffin said to Pie. "That way, according to their beliefs, he can't find his way to the next world, so his spirit will be doomed to wander aimlessly for eternity."

"But you don't do that?"

Griffin shook his head. "Seems like too much, even after seeing the things I've seen out here, not just today but plenty of other times. They're dead and can't hurt anybody else. That's enough for me."

"I reckon it would be for me, too."

Griffin looked over at him. "You handled yourself just fine in that fight, Pie. I could tell you've seen combat before, even if you hadn't told us about being in the army. It strikes me that you'd make a good Ranger."

Pie's eyes widened in surprise. "Me? A Texas Ranger?" He shook his head. "I just came along today because I happened to be with you fellas and wanted to give you a hand. I never thought about bein' no Ranger."

"Sometimes our fate chooses us, instead of the other way around. Do me a favor, Pie, and think about it."

"Sure," Pie said, but he already knew what his answer would be. He had come to Texas so he could settle down with Rachel, not to be a Ranger and fight Indians and outlaws.

But it wasn't hardly safe out here on the frontier, he thought, and until it was, Rachel wouldn't be safe, either. No one would be. Without that thin line of men Captain Griffin had spoken of, that gunsmoke barrier between civilization and savagery, Texas would never be safe.

Sometimes fate chooses us, Griffin had said.

Pie suddenly had the uneasy feeling the captain was right.

Chapter Seven

U P TO HER ELBOWS in soapsuds and hot water, Lucille Farrell Brannon scrubbed the pots and pans in the bucket. She paused and lifted her arm, using the coarse sleeve of her homespun dress to wipe away the beads of perspiration on her forehead. Even here in the shade beneath the trees behind the inn, this was hot work on a summer day.

A faint smile tugged at the corners of her mouth as she went back to her chore. *Once upon a time*, the fairy stories started. Once upon a time, she had been the pampered daughter of a rich man, a riverboat owner who served as his own captain. She had worn fine lace and eaten at tables covered with fancy linen. In those days, never in her wildest dreams had she thought that someday she would be little more than a . . . a scullery maid!

It wasn't quite that bad, she told herself. She served customers in the inn's dining room and sometimes washed dishes, along with helping out on other household chores. It was honest work. There was nothing dishonorable about it. She and her aunt had to do something to earn their keep. They couldn't expect Bert Nowlin, the proprietor of the inn, to allow them to live there for free.

Besides, the existence she had led as the daughter of Capt. Zeke Farrell hadn't been all that luxurious in reality. The cabins and the salon on the *Missouri Zephyr* had been nicer than her quarters here, of course, but her father had never gone in for a lot of foofaraws and folderol. The *Zephyr* was a working boat, and it didn't ply the waters of the Mississippi on pleasure cruises. Everyone had pitched in from time to time, including the captain's daughter. Lucille had spent many days in boots, trousers, and a man's woolen shirt, with her long, honey-blonde hair tucked underneath a riverman's cap.

She remembered the way Cory had looked at her the first time he saw her dressed in those clothes. His eyes had grown wide, not with surprise but with admiration.

Lord, she missed him!

Nowlin came out the back door of the inn. Short, plump, and mostly bald with tufts of white hair behind his ears, he had a mild manner and a high-pitched voice. Although he might look soft, most people hereabouts knew that he had been at San Jacinto with Sam Houston and then later had fought the Mexicans again as a U.S. dragoon during the Mexican War.

"Come along inside when you finish that up," Nowlin told Lucille. "You've been working hard all day."

"There's always so much to do," she replied.

"Yes, but it doesn't all have to be done right now." he chuckled. "A pretty girl like you ought to rest a bit between jobs."

Lucille knew the innkeeper didn't mean anything improper by the comment. She and Mildred had been staying here at the inn for months, ever since they'd arrived in Marshall after fleeing Vicksburg with Allen and Fred Carter, and during that time Nowlin had not said or done anything to make her believe he was being forward with either of them. In fact, his chuckle and smile were positively avuncular, and that thought just made Lucille miss her Uncle Charles that much more. She wondered where he was and how he was doing.

And of course she wondered as well about her husband. About Cory . . .

The first time *she* had seen *him*, he had been nothing more than a starving, half-frozen wharf rat, eking out a miserable existence on the docks of New Madrid, Missouri. When he managed to earn a few coins by loading or unloading a boat, he usually spent them on rotgut whiskey in Red Mike's or some other squalid dram shop. He was as close to being an utter failure as a man could be while still drawing breath.

Yet there had been something about him even then, some indefinable quality proclaiming that under the right circumstances, he might amount to more. He had proven that when he'd helped save the *Zephyr* from fiery destruction at the hands of the mob led by the abolitionist and Yankee agent Jason Gill. Zeke Ferrell had taken Cory under his wing and intended to make a riverboat pilot out of him. He would have succeeded, too, if the war hadn't come along and taken away that chance.

Lucille hadn't taken Cory under her wing. She had taken him into her heart instead.

The romance between them had been tentative at first but grew ever stronger with the passing of each day. She had learned about his family back in Virginia, on the farm in Culpeper County. He had even admitted his full name to her— Coriolanus Troilus Brannon—and had explained his father's passion for the Bard and how John Brannon had named all of his children after either Shakespeare himself or characters from the man's plays. For her part, Lucille told Cory how she had grown up on the great river, raised by her father, never knowing her mother. The passion had been there in their relationship, of course, no doubt about that, but they were both friends and lovers, and Lucille had never known anything quite so fulfilling and wonderful.

Hardship had separated them, danger had dogged their wandering paths, and every time they were reunited, it seemed as if the war conspired to tear them apart again. At least, they had managed to be married during the siege of Vicksburg, so at last they could share fully the love they felt for each other.

Then Jason Gill had come into their lives again, bringing hatred and despair with him. Lucille and her aunt had been forced to flee to Texas while Charles Thompson rescued Cory from the jail cell where he had been languishing at Gill's orders. Circumstances must have sent them in different directions once again, because she hadn't seen Cory in months, and she knew he would have come to her as soon as he could.

She refused to even consider the possibility that Cory might be dead.

Before leaving Vicksburg, Lucille had heard that Gill was very sick and might not recover. She liked to think she was not a vengeful person. Yet a part of her could not help but hope that Gill's illness had proven fatal and that even now he was suffering the torments of the damned, as he so richly deserved.

"Lordy, girl, you look like you're a million miles away," Nowlin said. "And wherever you are ain't very pleasant."

Lucille gave a little shake of her head and forced a smile. "I was just remembering something."

"That husband of yours, I'll wager. Don't you worry, Lucy. He'll turn up one of these days. No man in his right mind would stay away from a girl like you any longer than he had to."

She knew he was trying to make her feel better, so she smiled again and nodded. She didn't even bother telling him she didn't like to be called Lucy. She and Mildred could never repay the kindness he had shown them.

They had come here to Marshall, Texas, from Vicksburg, following the same route the wagon trains had taken. Along the way over in Louisiana, Lucille had seen the tavern, deserted now, where Grat had kept Rachel a virtual prisoner. She didn't know what had become of Grat and didn't care, as long as he didn't show up to bother her and Mildred. It was difficult knowing what to do, whether to stay here or push on farther west. Cory knew the way to Marshall and had been here several times. He would be likely to think this was where his wife and her aunt would head after leaving Vicksburg. But Cory's ultimate goal was to move on west to the area along the Brazos River. He had a dream in his head that he would settle there someday. Lucille didn't know much about the Brazos, but she knew Cory. He might look for her there.

But if he did, chances were that he would come through Marshall first. For now, she decided, she and Mildred would bide their time. There was no way of knowing where Cory was, what he was doing, or how long it would take him and Uncle Charles to rejoin them.

She finished washing the pots and pans, setting them aside in a basket to drain. Then she dumped the bucket of water and carried it and the basket back into the inn's kitchen. Aunt Mildred did most of the cooking for Nowlin these days. She was at the big cast-iron stove, stirring a pot of stew. Lucille smelled fresh biscuits cooking in the oven. Supplies weren't as plentiful in Texas as they once had been, but compared to the rest of the South, the real hardships brought on by the war hadn't set in here.

"There are some gentlemen in the barroom who need tending to," Mildred said as she glanced over her shoulder at her niece.

"Where's Deborah?"

Mildred sniffed in disdain. "You don't think that girl can be bothered to actually do her job, do you?"

Lucille dried her hands on a cloth, frowning a little as she saw how red and rough they were. Life made few provisions for softness these days. "I'll take care of them," she said. She was used to serving drinks in the inn's barroom. Deborah Lassiter, the young woman hired by Nowlin to handle that job, was seldom where she was supposed to be, when she was supposed to be there, as Mildred had said.

Leaving the kitchen, Lucille went through the lobby and into the barroom. At this time of day, the place was usually empty. Not today, though. Four men sat around one of the tables, talking and laughing raucously.

Rather, three of the men were talking and laughing. The fourth man sat quietly, a reserved smile on his face as he gazed tolerantly at his rowdy companions. Lucille had never seen any of them before.

Behind the bar, Rollie Dewhurst stood polishing glasses. He was as thin and cadaverous looking as Bert Nowlin was round and friendly. Lucille didn't know all the details, but she was aware that Dewhurst had been Nowlin's partner in the establishment at one time. He had sold his share in the inn to Nowlin for some reason—Lucille suspected he had done so in order to pay off gambling debts, but she wasn't sure about that—and now only worked in the place.

Had she been in his shoes, Lucille wasn't sure she would have continued to work in a business she had once owned part of. But everyone had to walk his own path, and if Dewhurst was happy here, more power to him. Of course, he seldom looked happy, no matter where he was or what he was doing.

He shoved a tray across the bar at her. The tray had a bottle and four glasses on it. "Take this to the gentlemen," he said.

Lucille nodded, thinking that it would have been just as easy for him to deliver it to the table himself. Dewhurst had strict ways of doing things, though. In his world, bartenders poured drinks or put bottles and glasses on trays and serving girls carried them to the tables, and that was that.

Lucille walked over to the table and leaned forward slightly to place the tray on it. "Here you are, sirs," she said.

"Much obliged, gal," one of the men said. He spun a coin on the tabletop. "You're a pretty one, ain't you?"

"Thank you," Lucille said. She didn't flirt or banter with the customers. She rested her left hand on the edge of the table for a moment, so that the wedding band on her third finger was hard to miss. Even in a rough place like Texas, most men would never think of acting improperly toward a decent woman, and that wedding ring was a sign of decency.

The man spun the coin again. "Want to sit with us for a spell? We been on the trail a long time. Could use us some fancy company."

The man who had been sitting quietly now moved with the speed of a striking snake. His hand shot across the table and slapped the spinning coin flat. The sound of his hand striking the table was almost like a gunshot and made Lucille jump back a step in surprise.

"I truly don't feel like killing you today, Devers, so p'raps it would be best if you'd apologize to the young lady for your filthy insinuation."

The man had gone from a state of lazy, tolerant amusement to one of taut, deadly anger in the blink of an eye. His tone was still a quiet drawl, however, despite the cold fury burning in his eyes. His voice had a slight accent to it that Lucille recognized as British. She had met quite a few Englishmen on the *Zephyr*. They came to the United States on business, or for pleasure, or to escape some uncomfortable situation in their homeland. Lucille had heard some of them referred to as remittance men, usually the second or third sons from wealthy families. Under the British law of primogeniture they could not inherit the family estate, so to avoid embarrassment, they left England, either joining the army or simply traveling abroad, supported by payments from back home—remittances, in other words.

The man called Devers, who was obviously an American, flushed with some anger of his own. "Get your hand off me, Carnevan, or I'll cut it off."

The Englishman's other hand moved, coming out from under the table with a long, heavy, double-edged blade. "Speaking of cutting things off, this isn't the most propitious time to be giving a fellow ideas along those lines. If you know what I mean."

Devers swallowed and hesitated, torn between his anger and the desire to back down from Carnevan's implied threat.

"Gentlemen, stop it," Lucille said sharply. "There's no need for this."

"There's every need," Carnevan said. "This lout was being offensive. He should apologize to you, madam."

"That's not necessary—"

Carnevan drove the tip of the blade into the table so that the weapon stayed there, quivering slightly when he released it. The blade had passed between his fingers and between two of the fingers on Devers's hand underneath it. Devers stared at the knife, wide-eyed.

"I believe an apology *is* necessary," Carnevan said calmly.

Devers looked up. "I'm sorry, ma'am. I surely am."

"That's all right," Lucille said, doing some staring of her own. Carnevan's violent action had taken her by surprise, but she hadn't had a chance to react because his movements were almost too fast for the eye to follow.

Carnevan grasped the bowie knife and jerked it loose from the table. "I'll pay for the damage, of course," he said.

Devers yanked his hand back, clearly relieved and more than a little surprised that it was still whole and unpierced. "Forget it," he said. "I'll stand the cost. Hell, it was my fault."

"You're a good man at heart, Patrick Devers," Carnevan said with a smile. "You just get carried away from time to time by your Kaintuck heritage."

"You're right about that."

Carnevan came to his feet and slid the knife back in its sheath on his hip. He reached up and took off his broad-brimmed, flat-crowned brown hat, revealing a thatch of sandy hair. He was tall and broad across the shoulders, and most women would find him very handsome, Lucille thought as she looked up at him. Not her, of course, since she was married.

"Phineas Carnevan, madam, at your service," he said to her. "My friends call me Phin."

"I'm . . . Lucille." She had a little trouble getting the words out. Her heart was still pounding slightly from the tension of the encounter. "Lucille Brannon. Mrs. Lucille Brannon."

"I'm pleased to make your acquaintance, Mrs. Brannon." His smile was quite charming. Or, Lucille amended silently, it would be to an unmarried woman.

"Sit down, Phin," one of the other men said. "We've got some serious drinkin' to do before we start back to the Gulf."

Lucille took that as an excuse to leave the table. "If you gentlemen need anything else, just let me or Mr. Dewhurst know." She backed off a couple of steps then turned and walked quickly to the bar.

Dewhurst leaned over the hardwood and said in a low voice, "I thought for a second there was going to be trouble."

"So did I," Lucille said. She looked over her shoulder and saw that Phin Carnevan had resumed his seat. He had a glass of whiskey in his hand, like the other men. The glasses clinked together companionably. Clearly, the brief argument between Carnevan and Devers was already forgotten. "Do you know those men?"

Dewhurst shook his head. "No, but from what they were saying, I think they're smugglers."

"Smugglers?" Lucille whispered.

"Blockade-runners, I should say. They've got a boat, and they land supplies from England down around Galveston somewhere and bring them up here overland. That fella Carnevan, he's a foreigner of some sort."

"Yes, he is," Lucille said. Carnevan was a foreigner of the attractive sort.

But not to her, of course.

OVER THE next couple of months, Phin Carnevan showed up several times in Marshall. His ship was making regular trips back and forth from Texas to British ports in the Caribbean, where it took on supplies for the beleaguered Confederacy and delivered them to hidden coves along the Texas coast. But rather than turning over the cargoes to other men once they reached Texas, Carnevan stayed with the supplies he brought in until they reached Marshall. Lucille suspected that despite the air of camaraderie that existed between Carnevan and his partners—Devers and the other two men, Stokes and Hardy—the Englishman didn't fully trust them. Carnevan made a point of coming to the inn for a drink every time he was in Marshall. He was friendly with Lucille but never treated her with less than the proper respect. They became friends, nothing more, although after a while Lucille had to be honest with herself and admit that she did find him attractive. There was nothing wrong with that, though, she told herself. She would never be unfaithful to Cory, no matter what the temptation. She loved him too much for that to ever happen.

By mid-July, East Texas lay under a sultry blanket of heat that never lifted, not even at night. In the small upstairs room she shared with her aunt, Lucille tossed and turned in her night-dress, trying to sleep, willing a cool breeze to drift in through the open windows. But sleep would not come, and the thin curtains over the windows hung limp and motionless, unstirred by even the faintest breath of air. Mosquitoes buzzed around Lucille's ears, threatening to drive her mad. She couldn't slap at them or wave her arms to drive them away, because that might wake up Mildred, who somehow *was* able to sleep in these deplorable conditions. Finally giving up, Lucille slipped carefully out of bed and went to the window, pushing the curtains aside to peer out into the darkness.

Somewhere nearby, a dog barked furiously, disturbed by something. Lucille expected to smell a skunk, since there were plenty of them in the woods and they often caused the local dogs to raise a ruckus by wandering around the settlement after dark. But when she took a deep breath, there was no scent of polecat. Something else had stirred up that canine commotion.

She didn't think anything else of it, knowing how easily a dog could be prompted to bark. But then, a few moments later, movement below, in the inn's rear yard, caught her eye. She leaned forward, parting the curtains a little more.

A shape emerged from the shadows under the trees and started toward the inn, moving unsteadily. It was a man, she realized. His steps had something furtive about them, and Lucille wondered if he might be a thief who planned to break in the back door of the inn. The possibility made her breath catch in her throat. She thought she ought to go downstairs and warn Nowlin or Dewhurst. It was long after midnight; the inn was dark as everyone slept, or at least tried to sleep. A prowler might be able to get in and out without disturbing anyone.

Lucille hesitated a moment, trying to decide what to do, and in that moment, something happened to make up her mind. The figure crossing the yard stopped, wavered back and forth for a second, and then plunged forward on its face. Through the open window, Lucille heard him groan faintly. He wasn't a would-be robber at all, she realized. He was injured.

She turned and went to the door of the room, not hesitating now. Hurt as he was, the man outside posed no threat. She would go out and see if she could get him into the inn, then she could send Fred running for the doctor. Fred and Allen Carter shared a room just down the hall, paid for by the wages Allen earned working in a nearby livery stable. As Lucille hurried down the hall, she thought about stopping at the Carters' room and waking them so they could help her get the injured man inside. That could wait, though, until she determined his condition, she decided.

The siege of Vicksburg had given her some practical nursing experience. She could clean and bandage a bullet wound, set a broken bone, even sew up a bad cut if she had to. She might not even need to send for the doctor, she thought as she went down the stairs and through the kitchen to slip outside through the rear door.

She paused just outside the door, listening. No more sounds came from the man on the ground, who was a sprawled dark shape some ten yards from the inn's back door. He was either unconscious or dead, Lucille thought. She hoped he wasn't dead. She had seen corpses before, more than she liked to remember, but looking death in the face was never pleasant. She took a deep breath, gritted her teeth, and started forward across the yard.

She was about halfway to the fallen man when she realized she was wearing only her thin nightdress. She should have taken the time to put on a robe—although when dealing with a possibly badly injured man, a young woman's decorum was less important than usual.

When she reached his side, she went to one knee and put out a hand to touch his shoulder. He stirred a little when she did, telling her he wasn't dead after all. She was grateful for that. He was lying facedown. She grasped his shoulder with both hands and as gently as possible rolled him onto his back.

A three-quarter moon floated overhead. It gave enough light for Lucille to be able to recognize the features of Phin Carnevan. She gasped in surprise. A large dark stain spread across the right side of Carnevan's shirt. He was wounded, all right, not sick or drunk, which were other possibilities she had considered. She touched the shirt. The blood was still wet and warm. It hadn't been long since the injury was inflicted.

With him senseless like this, she would have to have help moving him. He was too big, weighed too much for her to lift him to his feet alone. She was about to straighten and turn to go back into the inn and fetch Allen Carter and Fred, when Carnevan groaned again. His eyes flickered open and tried to focus on her face.

Suddenly, his hand came up and gripped her wrist. "Miz . . . Brannon?" his voice choked with pain.

Lucille leaned closer over him. "Don't move, Mr. Carnevan," she told him, trying to keep her own voice level and calm so he wouldn't know how shaken she was. "Just lie there and rest. I'll get some help and send for the doctor." Judging by the amount of blood he had lost, his injury was beyond her ability to care for it.

"N-No! Get out of . . . here . . ."

"Yes, but I'll be right back. Don't worry."

"He's . . . behind me . . . the one who did this . . . close . . . behind me . . ."

Lucille's eyes widened as she realized what he meant. Until this moment, she hadn't even considered the fact that someone had done this to Carnevan, someone who obviously had been trying to kill him.

Someone who still posed a threat.

The rush of footsteps warned her. She reached down to Carnevan's waist as another shape lunged out of the shadows under the trees. Her fingers closed around the leather-wrapped grip of the bowie knife and pulled the weapon from its sheath as she came to her feet. She meant to wave the knife at the man rushing toward her and Carnevan and shout out a warning so he would stop and back off. But the man was too close, and he was in no mood to back off. Lucille heard a growled curse. Moonlight glinted off the blade as she thrust it out in front of her.

The attacker ran right into the blade. Lucille felt the razor-sharp tip shear through the man's shirt and penetrate the flesh beneath. It slid easily into the man's body, deep into his chest. The impact of the collision knocked Lucille back a step, but she managed to retain her grip on the knife. Something hot and wet trickled across the back of her hand.

The bearded face of Patrick Devers contorted in agony as he stared at Lucille from a distance of little more than a foot. "My God," he said hoarsely. "You've killed me, girl."

Then blood that was black in the moonlight gushed from his mouth, and he sagged forward, forcing Lucille to spring backward as he collapsed at her feet.

Chapter Eight

LUCILLE'S HEART POUNDED WILDLY, as if it were trying to burst out of her chest. All she could think about was that she hadn't meant to do it. Hadn't meant to kill Devers. Twice before, men had died by her hand, but those had been deliberate choices, made to save the life of the man she loved. This had been sheer happenstance.

Swallowing hard, she dropped to a knee beside Devers and put her hand to his throat to check for a pulse. Maybe he wasn't dead after all. She had to force herself not to recoil as his bristly beard brushed her hand. Touching his flesh made her shudder. His throat was still warm . . .

But there was no pulse to be found. That inadvertent thrust of the bowie knife must have found his heart.

Straightening, Lucille turned back to Carnevan. What had happened with Devers was over and done with; Carnevan was still alive, however, and in need of medical attention. She leaned over, touched his shoulder, and said, "I'll get help."

"D-Devers . . . ?"

"Don't worry about him. He can't hurt you again."

She didn't know if he understood what she meant by that. It didn't matter. She had to get Allen and Fred Carter. They could carry Carnevan inside.

"St-Stokes? Hardy?"

She had forgotten about them, Lucille realized. They were Carnevan's partners, too. And if Devers had double-crossed him and tried to kill him, Stokes and Hardy might represent just as much of a threat. What if they were following Devers and came along while she was inside? They would need only a second to finish off Carnevan. She couldn't leave him here. She would have to shout through the open window to Mildred and get her to bring help.

123

Before she could do so, however, Carnevan rolled onto his side with a groan of effort. "What are you doing?" she asked him, but he ignored her as he continued turning until he had his hands and knees under him.

"H-Help me," he said.

She wanted to tell him that he should lie still, that he was going to injure himself even more, but she saw that he wasn't going to be talked out of what he was doing. Hurriedly, she bent over and grasped his left arm to steady him as he pushed upright. He got to his feet, staggering heavily, and she was sure he would have fallen if she had not been there to help him. As it was, she needed all her strength to keep him on his feet.

"In the . . . building . . . ," he muttered.

She nodded. They started toward the inn, staggering so much that they must have resembled a pair of drunken sots. When they reached the back door, Carnevan had trouble negotiating the steps that led up to it. Lucille had to support most of his weight as they struggled up the steps. She gasped from the strain but somehow managed to keep him upright and get him into the kitchen.

He half-sat, half-fell into a chair. Lucille whirled back to the door and closed it, shooting home the bolt that normally was left unfastened. No one in these parts locked their doors at night. But evil was abroad on this night, and Lucille wanted to shut it out if she could.

She turned back toward the table where Carnevan was sitting. Although it was almost pitch-black in the room, she knew its layout so well she had no trouble getting around in it and finding a lamp. Matches were in the cabinet. She located them, struck one of the lucifers, and held the sulfurous flame to the lamp's wick. When it caught, she lowered the glass chimney and turned toward Carnevan. Another gasp escaped from her lips as she saw how pale and haggard his face was, how large the bloodstain on his shirt.

"Stokes," he whispered. "Hardy."

"They can't get in. I've locked the door."

"Have you . . . a pistol?"

Lucille shook her head. "No. Are they . . . are they trying to kill you, too?"

A hollow chuckle came from Carnevan's lips, which were thinned by pain. "Three wise men," he said. "Devers, Stokes, and Hardy. Bearing not gifts but treachery. But then I'm hardly . . . the Christ child, eh? More likely the . . . spawn of Satan."

He was out of his head from the pain and loss of blood, Lucille thought. She needed to see just how bad his wound really was. Trying not to think about Devers lying dead out there in the yard, she said, "Let me take your shirt off so I can help you."

He wasn't going to be able to make it easier for her. He slumped forward, his head rapping the table as he collapsed on top of it. She caught hold of him to keep him from slipping out of the chair and falling to the floor. When he seemed to be stabilized, she got a kitchen knife from one of the drawers and used it to slit the back of his shirt. Then she was able to peel the bloody garment off of him.

She had to get a cloth and clean off some of the blood before she could see the wound. It was a long, deep cut about midway up his right side, starting around on his back. From the looks of it, someone had attempted to plunge a knife into his back, but something had warned him, and he had tried to turn around to confront his attacker. He hadn't been able to avoid the thrust entirely, though.

The wound had bled freely, but the edges of it were clean, and it didn't seem deep enough for the steel to have reached any vital organs. If the injury was cleaned and bound up tightly, and if Carnevan would take it easy for a few weeks, Lucille had little doubt that he would recover. The problem was that Stokes and Hardy were still out there somewhere, eager to kill him.

Suddenly she thought about the front door of the inn. Like most of the other doors in town, it was unlocked. If Stokes and

Hardy found the rear entrance barred to them, they could easily go around and come in the front. They might be slipping through the lobby even now . . .

That thought sent her to the door between the kitchen and the hallway that led to the front of the building. Everything was quiet and dark and still along that short corridor. Nowlin slept in a room just off the lobby; Dewhurst's room was under the stairs. Only a few feet separated her from them, a distance that would take only seconds to cross. Still, Lucille couldn't bring herself to walk into that darkness.

She heard a step behind her. Her breath froze in her throat in horror. She didn't want to turn and look, but she had to. She saw the shadowy figure moving toward the table where Carnevan slumped unconscious, and without thinking about what she was doing, she threw herself at the man, hands clenched into fists that struck out in short, efficient punches.

"Ow!" Fred Carter said as he backed up hurriedly, lifting a hand to his nose. One of Lucille's blows had struck it solidly, jolting Fred's head back. He started to cry. "Miss Lucille, what are you doing? Why are you hitting me?"

She stopped short in her rush. "Fred!"

"I'm sorry, Miss Lucille," the young man said as he rubbed his sore nose. "I'm really, really sorry!"

"Oh, Fred, no! It's my fault. I'm sorry I hit you."

Fred blinked a few times, holding back tears. "You mean I didn't do anything wrong?"

"Of course not!"

"I thought since you were hitting me, I must've done something wrong."

Lucille's heart went out to this young man who, despite being in his midtwenties, had the mind of a child. An intelligent, compassionate child, to be sure, but a child nonetheless. She wanted to put her arms around him and comfort him, but there was no time for that. Not with a wounded, unconscious man on her hands.

Fred had seen Carnevan and knew something was wrong, too. He pointed a shaking finger at the Englishman. "Phin's all bloody. What's wrong with him? Is he hurt?"

Lucille nodded. "Yes, he is. He's been cut. Can you run upstairs and get your father and Aunt Mildred and tell them to come down here as quick as they can?"

"Can I have a drink of water first? I came down for a drink of water—"

"I'm sorry, Fred. You can have your water later. Right now, go get your father and Aunt Mildred."

His head bobbed up and down. "All right. I'm sorry Mr. Phin's hurt."

Fred had been introduced to Carnevan on a couple of occasions when the Englishman was visiting the inn. As always, Fred was ready to be friends with everyone as long as he wasn't mistreated, and he and Carnevan had gotten along well. Now, to help his friend, Fred turned and hurried up the rear stairs by which he had entered the kitchen.

Lucille went back to Carnevan's side and rested a hand lightly on his shoulder. He stirred a little. She pressed down harder, saying quietly, "It's all right. Just rest and don't move. It's all right."

She wished she could believe that. But the dead man lying out there in the rear yard said different.

A few minutes later, Mildred Thompson came down the rear stairs, hastily tying the belt of her robe around her waist. She was a small woman with streaks of gray in her still mostly dark hair. Usually that hair was braided and put up in coils around her head, but since she had gone to bed, it was loose and fell far down her back almost to her waist.

"My lands, child, what's all this?" she asked as she stared at Carnevan's bloody shape in the chair. "Fred said Mr. Phin had been hurt, and I can see that's true."

"He's been attacked. Someone tried to stab him in the back and wound up cutting him."

Mildred studied the wound and nodded. "That's what it looks like, all right. Who could have done such an awful thing?"

"One of his partners. The one called Devers."

"You're sure of that?"

Lucille thought about the corpse lying in the yard. "I'm sure," she said.

"Well, the first thing we have to do is get this wound cleaned and bandaged. Perhaps we should send for a doctor."

Carnevan was drifting in and out of consciousness. At the sound of Mildred's words, he stirred again and lifted his head. "N-no!" he gasped out. "No . . . doctor!"

Mildred leaned toward him. "But Mr. Carnevan, you're badly hurt—"

Carnevan pressed the palms of both hands against the table and pushed himself up so that he could look wildly around the kitchen. "No! Wouldn't be . . . safe!"

Lucille touched his shoulder again. "You're safe here, Mr. Carnevan." She hoped that was true. She felt better as she heard a thumping sound from the stairs. That would be Allen Carter making his way down.

He came into the kitchen with a worried look on his broad face. Fred trailed behind him. Carter stopped, balancing himself on his good leg. "What's happened here?"

Lucille was getting tired of having to make the same explanation, but she outlined the situation for Allen anyway. "One of Mr. Carnevan's partners tried to murder him. The other two may still be after him."

Carter glanced at the back door and saw that the bolt was thrown. "The front door?" he asked. He had been a sergeant in the Confederate army before losing his leg at Manassas. It was difficult to rattle his brisk efficiency.

"I haven't locked it," Lucille said.

"I'll take care of that while you and Mrs. Thompson tend to that wound." Carter swung toward the hallway. Over his shoulder, he asked, "Should I send Fred for the doctor?"

Carnevan had just subsided from his earlier protests. As he lifted his head again, Lucille said quickly, "That won't be necessary. We can take care of this, can't we, Aunt Mildred?"

"I expect so."

Lucille had no idea why Carnevan was so adamant about not summoning a doctor, but in his condition, Lucille thought it best not to upset him any more than necessary. "We can always send for the doctor and the sheriff later."

That innocent comment was enough to send Carnevan lurching to his feet. His face was as pale as milk, and his bloody shirt hung around him in tatters. "No! Not the . . . sheriff!"

Allen Carter frowned in suspicion. "Don't want the law, eh? Why not?"

Carnevan looked like he was about to pass out. Lucille wanted to reach out and take his arm to steady him, but the Englishman turned away from her to face Carter. He was holding himself together with a visible effort. Whatever he had to say must have been important, Lucille thought, in order to make him drive himself so hard.

"No . . . law," Carnevan grated out. "Devers and the other two . . . they made it look like . . . like I killed Pablo . . ."

"Who the devil is Pablo?" Carter asked, then glanced at Lucille and Mildred. "Beggin' your pardon for the language, ladies."

"One of our . . . drivers," Carnevan said. "They . . . murdered him . . . then tried to . . . kill me . . . tried to make it look like . . . we did for each other . . ."

With a gasp, Carnevan slumped back down into the chair, unable to stay on his feet any longer.

"If you're innocent, you don't have anything to worry about—" Carter began.

Lucille stopped him by putting a hand on his arm. "The law doesn't always believe the ones who are innocent, Allen. You know that. Let's just deal with the wound and let Mr. Carnevan rest. We can figure out the rest of it later."

Carter looked like he wanted to argue with her, but after a moment he shrugged instead. "I suppose the law can wait until morning. The shape Carnevan is in, he won't be going anywhere anytime soon."

"There's just one more problem . . ."

"What is it?"

Lucille's hand tightened on Carter's arm. She drew him over to the side of the kitchen and said in a half-whisper, "Devers is in the rear yard."

"What?"

Lucille grimaced and leaned closer to him, all too aware that Mildred and Fred were watching them curiously. "He's dead," she said in a whisper. "I killed him."

Her fingers dug in even harder on Carter's arm, urging him to silence. He stared at her for a long moment as if he didn't believe what he had just heard. After a few moments, he nodded. "Go ahead," he said.

"It was an accident. I didn't mean to do it. He ran into me while I was holding Mr. Carnevan's knife."

Carter was getting control of his surprise. He asked, "Where's the knife now?"

Lucille tried not to gulp. "Still in . . . in Devers."

Carter nodded. "All right, then. There's work to be done. You and Mrs. Thompson take care of Carnevan and get him upstairs. Put him in my bed. Fred and I will take care of the other."

"What are you going to do?"

Carter scrubbed a hand over his face. "I'm not sure yet. I'll have to think on it."

When it came to the matter of disposing of bodies, better him than her, Lucille thought. She went back to the table while Carter called Fred to his side, unbolted the door, and limped out into the rear yard with his son just behind him.

Clearly, Mildred was very curious about what Lucille had said to Carter, but she didn't ask any questions. Together the two women began the work of cleaning the wound.

"A doctor might take stitches to close this up," Mildred said as she looked at the long, deep gash. "I think it will heal without that, though, as long as we keep it clean and bind it tightly. I have bandages in my carpetbag that I cut from that old petticoat of mine. Can you run up and get them, Lucille?"

"Of course."

She hurried upstairs to the room they shared, found the bandages, and brought them down. In the meantime, Carnevan passed out again. Mildred swabbed the cut with a cloth soaked in whiskey. The fiery pain made Carnevan wince, even though he was unconscious.

When Mildred was satisfied the wound was clean, she pressed the edges of the cut together while Lucille wrapped bandages around Carnevan's torso and pulled them tight. He didn't wake up during the procedure, even when Lucille gave the bandages an extra tug and tied them.

"All right," Mildred said. "Let's get him upstairs."

She got on one side of Carnevan, and Lucille stood on the other. They grasped his arms and lifted him from the chair. He seemed even heavier now than he had earlier, Lucille thought. He roused slightly from his stupor as they wrestled him toward the stairs, coming awake enough to move his legs and feet. That helped. But getting him up the stairs was still difficult enough so that both women were drenched with sweat by the time they reached the upper landing.

Praying that none of the inn's other occupants would come out of their rooms, Lucille helped her aunt steer Carnevan down the hall to the room shared by Allen and Fred Carter. The door stood open a few inches. Lucille used her foot to push it back even more. She felt a surge of relief when they were inside the room, and she had kicked the door closed behind them.

No blood was showing through the bandages. Lucille hoped the crimson flow from the wound had stopped. She and Mildred carefully lowered Carnevan onto the bed, placing him on his uninjured side. A long sigh came from him.

"I'll go back downstairs and gather up what's left of his shirt," Lucille said. It wouldn't do to leave those bloody rags lying around.

Mildred nodded. "I'll keep an eye on the poor man. I don't think he's going anywhere, though."

Lucille hurried out of the room and back down to the kitchen. As she picked up the bloody, tattered shirt, the rear door opened. She took an involuntary step back, her eyes widening in fear. Then she relaxed as she saw Carter and Fred.

Carter had the bowie knife in his hand. Its blade was sticky with drying blood. He reached out and took the rags out of Lucille's hand. "Give me those," he said. "I'll clean this knife then get rid of them." He started industriously wiping away the blood from the blade.

Lucille felt a wave of sickness go through her. That was Devers's blood on the knife, she knew, and it was there because she had thrust the knife into the man's chest. She closed her eyes for a second. She was stronger than this, she told herself. She had once shot an evil man in what some would consider cold blood, and she had felt very little guilt over it afterward. Well, Devers had been an evil man, too; his attempt to murder Phin Carnevan was proof of that. And he had been just as responsible for his own death as Lucille had. Her back stiffened and her eyes opened. She was not going to lose control of her emotions over this.

"What did you do with the body?" she asked Carter.

"It's in the stable, under the biggest pile of straw we could heap on it," he said. "That's only a temporary solution, though. In a day or two, the smell will attract attention."

"But . . . but what else can you do?"

"Nothing. That's why we're leaving Marshall."

Lucille stared at him. "Leaving?"

Carter nodded. "Yes, tonight. Fred and I brought the wagon back. We'll load up and be a long way from here by morning."

"I . . . I don't understand."

"We're going out west," Fred said with a bright smile.

"You wanted to go on to the Brazos River country sooner or later," Carter said. "This is as good a time as any, I reckon. Carnevan's in danger from those other partners of his as long as he's around here, and you and him both might wind up in trouble with the law."

Lucille shook her head. "I don't understand," she said again.

"You heard him say that Devers and the others wanted to make it look like he and that Mex killed each other. Well, since that didn't work and Carnevan got away from them, the other two . . . what were their names again?"

"Stokes and Hardy," Lucille replied dully.

"They will try harder than ever now to get the law after Carnevan. They'll probably be in the sheriff's office first thing in the morning, telling him how Carnevan murdered the Mex and tried to kill them, too. When Devers turns up dead, Carnevan will get the blame—"

"But I killed him!"

"If that comes out, then Stokes and Hardy will just say you were in on the whole thing with Carnevan and knew he was going to double-cross them and try to kill them."

"That's a ridiculous story! No one would ever believe that, Allen."

"Stokes and Hardy have been working with the Confederate government, bringing in supplies from those British ports in the Caribbean," Carter pointed out. "They're crooks and killers, but they're important men, Lucille. It'd be their word against Carnevan's. The only others who know what really happened— Devers and that fella Pablo—are dead."

Lucille frowned in thought. What Carter was saying made some sense. Things *could* happen that way. She wasn't convinced they would, but she couldn't swear that he was wrong.

"So we just run away?" she said. "Then we'll be fugitives."

Carter shrugged. "From what I've heard, there's not much law out there on the frontier. The Texas Rangers are more concerned with Indian raids than anything else. Anyway, we'll get as far from here as we can before Devers's body is found. Even when he starts to stink, the old man who runs the stable will probably think it's just a dead rat or something. That's happened before. There won't be anything to connect Devers's death with the inn. If the law does come after Carnevan, they'll be looking for him alone. They won't suspect he's traveling with us."

Lucille closed her eyes and pressed clenched fists to her temples. It was true that she wanted to go farther west, but she had thought that would happen after the war was over, when Cory and Uncle Charles came to find them.

But if they weren't in Marshall, Cory would know to look along the Brazos River. They had talked enough about it that he would be sure that was where she had gone. She felt relatively certain about that. And if Carnevan was gone, Stokes and Hardy wouldn't be able to prove there was any connection between him and Devers's death. They could tell whatever story they wanted, but would the law believe them?

When you came right down to it, Lucille thought, there was no single best answer, no one course of action that was guaranteed to result in the right outcome. All they could do was head west and hope for the best, like so many other people had done over the years.

There was one other area of concern, though. "What about Carnevan's wound?" she said. "He's lost a lot of blood, and he's weak. I'm not sure he's up to a long ride in the back of a wagon."

"We'll make him as comfortable as we can," Carter said. "And I reckon it'll be better than staying here and maybe facing a rope."

Lucille couldn't argue with that. "I guess we're going then. I'll tell Aunt Mildred, and we'll start gathering our things."

Carter reached out as if he were going to pat her on the shoulder in encouragement, then stopped. He was a reticent man by nature, not one to demonstrate his emotions.

But Fred certainly didn't suffer from that condition. He stepped up to Lucille and gave her a hug. "You'll see, it'll be all right," he told her with a grin. "We're going west. It'll be fun!"

Lucille nodded and wiped away a brief tear. She didn't care whether or not the trip was fun. She just hoped they all survived it and survived on the frontier until Cory got there.

Then things would be all right. But only then.

Chapter Nine

CORY CAME TO A sudden halt, along with Abner Strayhorn and the other men marching along the road toward the new positions they would take up along Peachtree Creek. They were passing a two-story white frame house that served as the headquarters for the Army of Tennessee. The front door of the house opened, and a small, slight, gray-uniformed figure stepped out on the gallery. The man wore no hat, so that his balding head was visible. So was the neat gray goatee on his chin. Every one of the troops lined up along the road recognized Gen. Joseph Eggleston Johnston, the man who, until the previous night, had been their commander.

All along the line, the Confederate soldiers began to remove their hats. Cory did, too, although he had not served under Johnston for as long as some of these men. While it was true that Johnston had been unable to stop the Yankee advance into Georgia, he had fought stubbornly every step of the way and had retreated only when there was no other option remaining to him. The troops began walking again, slowly passing the house where Johnston stood watching them, a solemn expression on his face. No one cheered or rattled sabers or waved hats in the air. The demonstration was a quiet one, but there was no mistaking the admiration and affection these men felt for their former commander. Some of the officers walked over to the house and reached up to the gallery to shake the general's hand, then hurried on to catch up to their men. Johnston stood there until everyone had passed, lifting a hand just a little in farewell.

"Hood's a fighter, from what I hear tell," Abner said to Cory as they trudged on down the road. "Got his left arm tore up at Gettysburg and lost his right leg at Chickamauga but just keeps on agoin'. But I don't know if he'll ever be able to make the fellers feel about him the way they do about ol' General."

"I don't reckon that matters," Cory said, "as long as Hood can win the fight that's coming."

THERE WAS no doubt on either side that another battle was imminent. Sherman, hearing of the Confederate change of command and being advised by some of his generals who were personally acquainted with Hood from their days at West Point that Hood would strike quickly, moved to forestall such an attack. He cast his forces in a great arc north of Atlanta and struck first from the east, rather than coming in from the northwest where the Confederate line was strongest. Union troops led by Gen. James B. McPherson reached the railroad east of Atlanta and turned back to the west, tearing up the rails as they proceeded toward the city. Most of the civilians left in Atlanta fled when word of this Yankee thrust reached them.

Meanwhile, the blue-clad troops under Generals Schofield and Thomas maneuvered north of the city, trying to get in position to attack. When Hood's scouts brought him news of those movements, he seized on a plan to hit the Yankees—Thomas's command in particular—as they were crossing Peachtree Creek. Hardee's corps would lead the attack, falling on the Federals and driving them into an angle of ground formed where the creek flowed into the Chattahoochee River, where they could be destroyed.

That was Hood's plan, at any rate.

Cory knew only that he and Abner were moving up as part of Hardee's command, tramping through the woods and slogging across marshy fields as they moved north of the city. The mid-July sun beat down fiercely. It was a poor day for a battle, Cory thought as he sleeved sweat off his forehead . . . but then, any day was a poor day for a battle as far as he was concerned.

A little over a year had passed since the fall of Vicksburg, he thought. Up north, in Pennsylvania, Robert E. Lee had been defeated the day before at a place called Gettysburg. After that bleak day, many people in the South, if they were honest with themselves, wouldn't have given a hoot in hell for the chances of the Confederacy surviving for another year. But then had come Chickamauga, which showed that the Yankees weren't unbeatable after all, and the failed Federal campaign to take Richmond that had come to a bloody end with the slaughter at Cold Harbor back in May. Although embattled, the Confederacy was hanging on. It was still possible, with elections in the North coming up in the fall, that things could change. If that stubborn bastard Lincoln was voted out of office, whoever took his place might be more open to a reasonable settlement with the Confederacy. The South had paid the highest price in blood and death and destruction, but some folks up North were tired of the war, too. They just wanted it to come to an end, one way or another. Such sentiment was the Confederacy's last, best hope.

So putting up a fight still served a purpose, Cory told himself. Perhaps victory was no longer in the cards for the South, but with luck and dedication it might avoid an outright defeat.

His hands tightened on his rifle as a single shot barked out from somewhere up ahead. Following that report, a couple of seconds of silence ticked by, pregnant with anticipation. Then, with a sudden roar like the breaking of a thunderstorm, the battle was under way.

Shouting, Cory and Abner joined the surge forward. They emerged from a stretch of woods into an open field. A couple of hundred yards away on the other side of the field, a line of trees marked the course of the creek. The field was covered with Yankees who looked like they had been taken completely by surprise. Cory spotted a few tents, as if the Federals had started setting up camp.

Now, though, the Yankees found themselves with a desperate struggle on their hands. Howling and firing, hundreds of Confederates ran forward. In a matter of heartbeats, the Southerners found themselves amid the Federal troops. Hand-to-hand fighting broke out, with pistols, rifle butts, bayonets, even sticks and fists serving as the weapons of the moment.

Side by side, Cory and Abner bounded up to a group of Yankees. They had held off on firing until now. Knowing that they might get off only one shot each, they wanted it to be a sure thing. Cory leveled his rifle at one of the Yanks who turned a shocked face toward him. He pressed the trigger and felt the weapon kick hard against his shoulder. His hand stung from flecks of burning powder given off by the rifle's discharge. Through the smoke he saw his target stagger. Blood welled from the Yankee's mouth.

But that didn't stop the man from lifting the pistol in his hand and firing. Cory saw the flame from the gun's muzzle, felt more than heard the bullet slap the air beside his ear. Before the Union soldier could draw back the hammer to cock the pistol again, Cory lunged forward and buried his bayonet in the man's belly. The Federal screamed and slumped forward, almost pulling the rifle out of Cory's hand. He ripped the bayonet loose and used the butt of the rifle to knock the dying Yankee out of his way.

An officer slashed at him with a saber. Cory parried the blade with his bayonet then thrust the sharp tip at the man's face. The Yankee jerked back and whipped his saber around in a backhand. Cory tried to twist out of the way. The blade raked across his stomach, tearing open his shirt and leaving a shallow cut on the skin underneath. He smashed the Yankee's skull with the rifle butt, experiencing a fierce surge of satisfaction as he felt bone splinter and shatter under the blow.

The Yankees, not expecting the attack so soon even though they knew of Hood's aggressive nature, fell back to the creek. So fierce was the Confederate assault that many of the Federal troops jumped into the creek and risked drowning as they swam away rather than stand up to the attack.

Abner grabbed Cory's arm. "Come on!" he shouted over the din of battle. "We're goin' to take that bridge down yonder!"

They turned, along with quite a few of the other Confederates, and charged downstream to the spot where Peachtree Creek was spanned by a sturdy stone bridge. If they could capture the bridge, the Yankees on this side of the creek would have no way to escape except by swimming.

As the men approached the bridge, Federal artillery batteries hastily set up on the other side of the creek opened fire. Cory heard the deafening roar, saw the gush of smoke from the trees on the opposite bank, and watched men tumbling off their feet as shells ripped through the Confederate charge. Canister rounds exploded, shredding whatever human flesh was within reach of their deadly loads. Solid shot decapitated some men and tore others in half. It was grisly work, and Cory knew his life might end at any second with little or no warning.

He dropped to a knee and reloaded his rifle. Beside him, Abner did likewise. When they were finished, both men drew beads on the artillerymen across the creek. Cory fired, and Abner squeezed off his shot a second later. Two of the gunners were knocked away from their cannon.

Two more men, however, leaped forward to take their places. Always there were more Yankees. They were like sand fleas, Cory thought. It was impossible to squash all of them.

Not only that, but up ahead, on the bridge that the Confederates had sought to capture, more blue-uniformed troops poured across the creek. The Yankees had been surprised, but they had gathered their wits enough to launch a counterattack. Bullets whined around Cory's head. On both sides of him, men grunted under the impact of Yankee lead and fell bleeding and maimed to the ground. The hot day seemed hotter now, even though it was late in the afternoon and dusk would be approaching soon. Sweat bathed Cory's face and scored creases in the layer of powder grime that coated his features.

"Fall back! Fall back!" someone shouted. Cory didn't know where the order came from or who voiced it, but it was enough for him.

He tugged at Abner's sleeve. "Let's get out of here!"

Abner turned to agree and suddenly staggered. Cory thought he was hit and caught hold of his friend's arm to steady him. "Abner!"

"Go on!" Abner waved toward the rear. "Go on, Cory! Don't wait for me!"

"No, damn it! I'm not leaving you here!" Cory had known Abner for only a few months, but that didn't matter. He had seen too many friends die. The memory of leaving Lt. Hamilton Ryder under a tree as the Yankees closed in flashed through his mind. He wasn't going to leave Abner behind.

Abner gave him a hard shove. "Go on, dagnab it! I ain't hurt!" He grinned and pointed to his belt buckle, which was dented where a rifle round had struck it. "Just feel like I been kicked in the belly by a Missouri mule, that's all!"

To prove it, he broke into a run. Cory fell in alongside him. Bullets still sang through the air around them as they hurried toward the rear, along with the rest of the Confederates pulling back from Peachtree Creek. The timely, ferocious Federal counterattack had blunted the success of the Rebel advance and then broken it entirely.

Hardee's corps regrouped several hundred yards away from the creek. As Cory and Abner hunkered on their heels and tried to catch their breath, they heard talk swirling around them. Rumors, questions, curses . . . what it all amounted to was that another division that had been kept in reserve during the first part of the battle was coming up to reinforce them. General Hood wasn't giving up easily. No defensive maneuvers for him. Attack! Attack! Attack! Until the Yankees were vanquished.

For whatever reason, the reinforcements never appeared. As darkness fell, Cory knew that there would be no more combat on this day. Hood might not like it, but the attack along Peachtree Creek was a failure.

Just like Johnston had failed, time and again, to stop the Yankee advance.

CORY FOUND out the next morning what had happened to the reinforcements and why there had been no more fighting at Peachtree Creek. With the Yankees closing in on Atlanta from the east as well as the north, Hood had been forced to change plans and shift the reinforcing units to head off McPherson rather than continuing the tussle with Thomas. Still, McPherson's men were now close enough to the city to open up with their artillery. The evening before, the Yankees had set up their batteries and began to bombard the city. Cory had heard the distant, crashing explosions and knew they boded no good for the Southern cause.

The day was scalding hot. Since nothing was going on where Cory and Abner were, they sought out whatever shade they could find and spent the day sitting and sweating. More fighting took place to the southeast; the sounds of battle were audible even over the continued Federal barrage directed at the city. Clouds of smoke drifted across the sun, diluting its brassy glare. That brought no relief from the heat, however.

Late in the day, new orders arrived. The corps was moving. Cory wasn't sure where they were going, but he would have been willing to bet that it would be closer to the action. Probably much too close for comfort.

"They could've let us have some supper first afore we moved out," Abner complained as they marched south, toward Atlanta itself. It appeared to Cory that they were going to enter the city for the first time.

"You have any rations left for supper?" he asked.

"Well . . . naw, I don't reckon I do," Abner admitted with a grin. "Ate my last piece o' hardtack this mornin'. You got anything left?"

"Nary a thing. Looks like we're gonna have to fight on an empty stomach."

"Oh, well." Abner shrugged. "Won't be the first time. Prob'ly won't be the last."

Cory remembered times during his New Madrid days when he had thought he was going to starve to death. He had known hardship then and plenty of it, but looking back now at that time of his life, he realized it hadn't been quite as bad as he had thought. Sure, he had gone to sleep hungry on many a night, and during the winter the danger of freezing to death on the docks truly existed. But at least no one had been trying to kill him then. In a way, most of his troubles had been his own fault for being so damned stubborn, not to mention naive and gullible and weak. He could have pulled himself up out of that miserable existence if he had wanted badly enough to do so.

But it had taken Lucille coming into his life to finally give him the reason he needed.

The troops reached the outskirts of Atlanta in the dusk. Enough light remained in the sky for Cory to see the isolated patches of destruction, the occasional burned-out house, the streets pockmarked with shell holes. The damage grew worse as they drew nearer the center of town.

He had never been to Atlanta before. From what he could see, it must have been a nice place, he thought—before the Yankees came.

Cory would have expected that the town was abandoned except for the soldiers who were posted there. That wasn't the case, he soon discovered. Many of the buildings, even the undamaged ones, looked deserted, but in other places, civilians came out to line the street and give ragged cheers as the soldiers marched past.

"Give 'em what for, boys!" one old man shouted as he brandished a gnarled wooden walking stick over his head. Children waved Confederate flags. Women stepped out to press handkerchiefs and other keepsakes into the hands of men who had never seen them before.

It was a stirring sight, and Cory felt a tightness in his chest as he marched along and looked at the citizens of Atlanta who had turned out to offer their encouragement.

One young woman, blonde curls falling around her shoulders, ran up to him. "Take this, sir. Please take this and think of me!" she urged.

Without considering what he was doing, Cory reached out to take what she was holding up for him. He expected some scrap of linen and lace, but instead his fingers closed around a squarish hunk of something soft. He held it up before his eyes in the fading light and saw to his astonishment that the girl had given him a piece of bread. Supplies had to be scarce in Atlanta now; bread was as precious as bullets and much more precious than gold. And yet the young woman had given up what might be the only food she had.

Cory turned his head to try to look back at her. He had been forced to keep marching by the men behind him. He caught a glimpse of something pale in the gathering darkness. The girl's fair hair, perhaps. "Thank you!" he called back into the shadows. That was all he could do. "Thank you!"

Then he tore the piece of bread in half and turned to hold out part of it to Abner. "Here."

"What've you got—Son of a gun! Where'd you get that?"

"That girl back there gave it to me."

"What girl?"

Cory turned and looked again. There was no sign of her now. She was gone, vanished behind him in the darkness. "It doesn't matter," he said to Abner. "But maybe now we won't have to fight on a completely empty stomach after all."

Abner bit a small piece off the hunk of bread and made a sound of utter contentment as he chewed, taking his time about it. "That's right," he said after he had swallowed. "I never did cotton to the idea o' dying hungry. How do we know you don't go on to the hereafter that way?"

Cory took a bite of the bread, savoring its sweetness. He didn't want to think about dying or the hereafter. He wanted to think only about this moment in time and the gift given to him by a girl whom he had never seen before and likely would never see again, a girl who had placed her faith, her very future, in his hands along with that piece of bread.

He wouldn't let her down, he thought as he ate. He couldn't.

THE NIGHTLONG trek exhausted men who were already weary from months of fighting and marching. Many of them collapsed along the sides of the road and had to rest for a spell before joining the column once again. Some never made it.

Cory managed to stay on his feet and keep moving, as did Abner. By dawn the soldiers were well south of Atlanta and began to swing to the east. Cory wondered where they were. He knew McPherson's men had been advancing west toward Atlanta along the Georgia Railroad. Given that fact, and knowing how far they had marched, Cory thought it likely that they had flanked McPherson to the south, skirting all the way around the Union left. His guess was confirmed, at least to his satisfaction, when the column turned back to the north. They were going to hit McPherson's flank and rear.

By noon they had left the road and were cutting across country. Cory wondered if that was a mistake. The terrain was difficult, and the going was hard. The marshy ground underfoot sucked at a man's feet every time he went to take a step. Briars and brambles covered the landscape and clawed at the Confederates as they pushed their way through it. At this rate, they would be lucky to find the Federals by nightfall, let alone join in battle with them.

A sudden rattle of musketry up ahead took Cory by surprise. Clearly, the first ranks had found the Yankees after all. He pushed forward, slogging through the mud and using his rifle to make a path through the brush. Abner struggled along beside him. The firing up ahead grew more intense. They reached the edge of the tangle and broke out into another of the marshy fields that covered so much of the ground here east of Atlanta. A pall of smoke floated in the air, marking the line of battle.

Cory's heart pounded wildly in his chest, as it always did when he was going into battle. His mind had become hardened enough to combat over the years so that he was able to think clearly and calmly, but he had never been able to banish the fear entirely. No sane man could.

As he looked across the field, Cory saw regimental flags flying among the Union defenders. Cannons belched fire and smoke from the batteries that had been set up already when the attack started. It was almost like the Yankees had been waiting for them, Cory thought. Either they had great scouts, or they were the luckiest sons of bitches in Georgia today. Either way, this fight was going to be harder than Hood and the other commanders had envisioned.

Cory had been in the middle of the assaults on what came to be known as the Hornet's Nest at Shiloh. This was almost as bad. The Confederates charged into the face of withering rifle fire and a terrible artillery barrage. Cory dropped to a knee, fired, came up, and dashed forward, leaping over the bodies of fallen comrades to do so, and then went to a knee again to reload and fire. The pattern was repeated over and over. He couldn't see if his shots hit anything; the smoke was too thick for that. And he lost sight of Abner in the swirling clouds of gray. Bullets bored through the air around him and kicked up clods from the ground at his feet. Once a cannonball skidded past him, plowing a deep furrow in the dirt. Canister rounds burst like deadly fireworks. Cory stumbled forward, his mind numb to the dangers. If a man ever paused to think about what was going on around him in battle, to truly think about it, surely he would go mad.

On one knee, Cory finished reloading his rifle and brought it to his shoulder. As he did so, a Yankee loomed out of the smoke and charged toward him. Automatically, Cory aimed at the man's chest and fired. The man's torso jerked backward as the ball struck him, but his momentum kept his legs stumbling forward. The effect would have been comical if it had not been so ghastly. He lost his balance and toppled to the ground.

Four more Union infantrymen appeared right behind him, leaping over his body with savage grimaces on their faces.

The Federals were launching a counterattack, Cory thought. All around him, the Confederate line gave ground. He couldn't stand up to the Yankees alone. He came to his feet and backed away, loading on the move, his hands deft and sure from long practice. He fired again, sent one of the Yankees tumbling. Then Cory did the only thing he could. He turned and ran.

The Confederates regrouped in the trees around a large, stagnant pond. Cory leaned against one of the tree trunks for a moment, dragging in lungfuls of smoke-fouled air that choked him and made him cough. He wished he had some water, but the canteen on his hip was empty. He checked his ammunition pouch, saw that he had enough powder and shot for five more rounds. When that was gone, it would be bayonets and bare hands if need be.

"Cory!"

He swung around and saw Abner coming toward him. The lanky Tennessean had a scratch on his cheek, but that seemed to be his only injury. His powder-grimed face stretched in a grin.

"Damn, it's good to see you, ol' son! I was afraid them damnyanks'd got you when they come out after us."

Cory shook his head. "I managed to dodge enough times to stay alive."

"Well, we're about to hit 'em again, I hear tell, so they'll have more chances at us. But we'll have more chances at them, too."

No sooner were the words out of Abner's mouth than shouted orders came through the trees and sent the men stumbling forward again. To the rear, Confederate light artillery had been brought up and now peppered the Union lines, providing a diversion of sorts. The Federal gunners had to elevate their cannons and return the Confederate fire. Now, along the front, it would be infantry against infantry.

The wind whipped up for a moment, clearing some of the smoke from the air. Through the gaps in the clouds, Cory caught a glimpse of a treeless knob sticking up from the surrounding marshy plain. If the Confederates could push forward enough to capture that height, he thought, from up there they might be able to pour down enough artillery fire to win the day. With a sense of new urgency, he trotted forward along with Abner and the other men.

For the next two hours, it was push and shove, thrust and counterthrust, as Hardee's men tried to work their way toward the bald knob, and the Federals strove equally hard to keep them back. In the middle of the afternoon, Hood finally threw more reserves into the battle, sending in a division from the west, on what was now the Union right flank since the lines of battle had rotated ninety degrees. At the same time, Texas troops led by Gen. Patrick Cleburne circled the hill to the north and attacked the Federal rear. To Cory it was simply one long, smoky, dangerous fight. When he ran out of ammunition, he scavenged powder and shot and percussion caps from the pouches of dead men sprawled on the battlefield, Union and Confederate alike. Lead knew loyalty to no flag.

From time to time, he caught glimpses of the knob through rents in the smoke. The Southerners were drawing closer and closer to it. That hill had become the Holy Grail to these men. They would take it or die trying.

As the afternoon wore on, Cory found himself with a group of men rushing across a field toward a line of earthworks not far from the base of the hill. Flame spewed from the muzzles of rifles thrust over the earthworks. Bullets scythed through the onrushing Confederates. Cory tripped and stumbled over the bodies of men who had fallen already to the Federal fire. He kept going somehow. He knew he had one shot left in his rifle, and now, in the middle of a charge, there was no time to hunt for more ammunition among the corpses. He saved that round until he had crossed the fifty yards of the field and was right in front of the earthworks.

When the leading edge of the Confederate attack reached the Federal line, Yankees leaped on top of the earthworks to meet the charge head-on. Cory fired at last and sent one of the Yankees flying backward off the barrier. Then he reached the earthen wall and started scrambling up it, hands and feet slipping on the slick red clay.

As he neared the top, one of the Yankees hacked down at him with a saber. Cory jerked aside. The blade slithered down his left arm, ripping his sleeve. One-handed, he shoved his rifle up and out. The bayonet went into the belly of the Yankee with the saber. The man screamed and clutched his middle, then he folded up and collapsed as Cory pulled the bayonet free.

The fierce, hand-to-hand fight raged for seemingly endless minutes along the earthworks. A Yankee bayonet sliced Cory's calf open, but his return thrust found the throat of the Union soldier who had wounded him. After that, his leg didn't want to support him, and though he tried to retain his balance, he fell and slid down the earthworks, luckily on the Confederate side. If he had fallen among the Yankees, they would have made short work of him.

Using the rifle for a crutch, he pushed himself to his feet and looked up as more Yankees surged over the top of the earthworks in a counterattack. The Confederates broke as men turned to flee. Cory hobbled back toward the trees, too. Staying and getting himself killed wouldn't accomplish anything.

Although bullets flew all around him, he made it to shelter without getting hit. His leg was on fire and practically useless. He slumped to the ground under some trees and looked up at their bare, broken branches. Yankee bullets and artillery shells had stripped all the leaves from the trees and shattered many of the trunks and branches. In fact, as Cory pulled himself behind one of the trees, he felt the trunk shudder as bullets struck it. He hugged the ground, waiting for the hellish tempest to be over.

Finally the shooting died away. Cory looked around and saw that night was falling. He didn't know where Abner was or even if his friend was still alive. He didn't know how the battle had turned out for the Confederates, except that it hadn't seemed to be going all that well where he was. In fact, though they had gained some ground during the afternoon, in the end the Federals had pushed them back so that things stood just about as they had that morning. The Yankees were still in possession of that crucial height that commanded a view of the railroad and the turnpike leading into Atlanta from the east.

The generals could worry about such things, Cory told himself. What mattered to him at this moment was that he was still alive. He had survived another battle, made it through another long, bloody day. As the shadows gathered under the trees, exhaustion claimed him, and he slept.

TWICE IN the space of seventy-two hours, Gen. John Bell Hood had gone on the offensive, just as everyone in command on both sides of the great conflict expected. And twice, although the fighting had been ferocious, the battles had ended in stalemates. Sherman still menaced Atlanta from the north and east, just as he had before Hood sallied out to attack him.

The biggest difference was that now, after those three bloody days, the Confederate army had lost more than ten thousand men. Ten thousand men who could no longer help protect the Gate City of the South from the Yankees.

Now it seemed that God would have to have mercy on Atlanta . . . because William T. Sherman surely would not.

Chapter Ten

AHAND ON HIS SHOULDER shook Cory awake. He came up out of sleep ready to fight, his hands gripping the rifle as he looked around wildly for the enemy.

"Hold on there, son!" Abner Strayhorn said. The sharp words penetrated the fog in Cory's brain, and he realized it was his friend kneeling beside him, not some Yankee out to cut his throat.

His heart still pounding, Cory sat up and shuddered. Then he looked at Abner. "Are you all right?"

"I'm fine," Abner replied with a grin. "Not much more'n a scratch in all that fightin' yesterday." His expression became more serious. "Looks like you're hurt, though." He gestured toward Cory's leg.

Cory looked down at his calf and saw the dark stain that dried blood had left on his trousers. He tried to pull up the leg of the garment and winced in pain as it wouldn't come up. He realized to his horror that his calf was swollen to almost twice its normal size.

Fear made his heart race again. "Oh, my God," he said, his voice shaking. "They'll have to cut it off. The surgeons'll have to cut it off!"

Abner gripped his shoulder. His fingers pressed down hard. "Hold on," he said. "Ain't nobody cuttin' off nothin' until I've had a look at this here leg."

He took his bayonet off his rifle and used it to slice through the fabric of Cory's trousers. When Abner had laid bare the wounded calf, Cory gasped at how inflamed the flesh was around the black, ugly wound. He wanted to cry, and he felt himself on the verge of panic. He knew what the butchers in the field hospitals would do to him if they got hold of him while he was in this condition. Out would come the bone saw, and orderlies would

157

hold him down while the surgeons hacked off his leg at the knee. If he was lucky, he would get some laudanum to help ease the pain. He might not be that fortunate; he might have to stand the agony without anything to help him. And then, again only if fate smiled on him, he would live to be a cripple. Chances were, though, that the festering would still kill him.

Abner let out a low whistle. "One o' them damnyanks got you good. We'll have to tend to that."

"You can't . . . there's nothing . . ." Cory was too horror-stricken to go on.

"There's always somethin' you can do. Sometimes it don't work out, but you can always try." Abner stared solemnly at him. "You want me to fetch a surgeon, or would you rather I do what I can?"

"How . . . how can you . . . what can you do?"

The grin came back fleetingly on Abner's face. "You might not guess it to look at me, but I come from a family with a saw-bones or two in it. My grandpappy was a doctor, and so was his brother. I listened to them old-timers a lot when I was just a pup, so I know a thing or two about tendin' to ailments." Abner turned and delved into his pack. "I got somethin' in here I been savin' . . ."

He brought out a small silver flask.

Cory's eyes widened. "Is that whiskey?" he asked in a choked voice. He thought that over the years he had lost his craving for the stuff, but now it came back as strong as ever.

"Yeah, but you ain't goin' to drink it. Here, hang on to it for a second." Abner thrust the flask into Cory's hands.

Then, before Cory could ask him what he was about to do next, Abner slid his knife from its sheath on his hip and slashed the flesh of Cory's calf, cutting through the original wound.

Cory screamed as his head jerked back, the cords standing out on his neck. Agony flared through his leg and into the rest of his body. His back arched off the ground. A horrible stink assaulted his nostrils, and when he regained his senses enough to look down at his calf, he saw thick clots of gray-green pus welling from the wound, along with a steady stream of blood.

"What the hell—" An officer had come up behind Abner. "Private, what are you doing to that man?"

"Cleanin' out this wound, sir," Abner said. "It don't look or smell very pretty, but it's the best way."

"Damn it, you're not a surgeon. Get him to a field hospital right now."

"He says he don't want to go, Cap'n."

"I don't care what he says—"

Abner ignored the captain and grabbed Cory's leg, squeezing the calf so that more blood flooded from the wound. Cory gritted his teeth this time and held back the scream that wanted to come from his lips. Oddly enough, when Abner stopped putting pressure on his leg, he thought it felt a little better.

"Gimme that whiskey." Abner took the flask and shook it next to his ear. From the sound, the flask was about half full. He pulled the cork from its neck with his teeth and emptied the amber liquid over the raw opening in Cory's leg.

Cory couldn't hold back the scream this time.

His leg felt like it was on fire. But gradually the pain began to subside. Breathing hard from the effort, he propped himself up on his elbows and looked at his leg. The swelling had gone down some.

"Private, you disobeyed a direct order—"

Cory interrupted the captain this time. "Cap'n, I asked Private Strayhorn to tend to my leg. He comes from a family of doctors." That was stretching the truth a little, but not much.

"I don't care. Such insubordination must be dealt with." The officer hesitated then went on, "I order both of you to the rear. You'll help man the fortifications around Atlanta."

"Cap'n, the way I heard it, that's where the whole blamed army's goin' anyway," Abner said.

"That doesn't matter," the captain snapped. "That's the punishment I've decided upon, and it will be enforced."

"Yes sir. We'll be gettin' ourselves on into Atlanta, soon's I tie up this here leg."

The captain clapped a hand on Abner's shoulder for a second. "See to it, Private. Carry on."

"Ain't no such thing as clean bandages around here, so we'll do the best we can," Abner said after the officer had left. "I can cut some strips off my undershirt . . ."

"Use mine," Cory suggested. "It's cleaner."

Abner grinned. "Is that so? Well, it's your leg, so I reckon it's up to you what we use to bind it up."

Ten minutes later, with strips of cloth bound tightly around Cory's leg to slow the bleeding and protect the wound, Abner helped him to his feet. Cory used his rifle as a crutch, and Abner took hold of his arm to steady him as they started down the road to Atlanta with the thousands of other Confederate troops that were pulling back into the fortified city.

"How'd you find me, anyway?" Cory asked through clenched teeth against the pain.

"It warn't hard. Figured I'd find you sleepin' under a tree, lazy feller like you, and sure enough, there you were."

"Thanks, Abner."

"Don't thank me yet. I don't know that I did a damn bit of good for you."

"You didn't take me to the hospital. That would have been the end of me for sure."

"Might've been quicker that way," Abner muttered.

Cory limped along and pretended not to hear him.

IT WAS Vicksburg all over again, Cory thought countless times over the next few weeks. The Yankees menaced Atlanta on the north, west, and east, blocking the railroads that came in from those directions. They burned trestles and ties and pulled up the rails, heating them in bonfires so they could be twisted into unusable shapes known as "Sherman's hairpins." Only the Macon and Western Railroad to the south was still open, and Sherman wanted to cut it as well. He sent some units circling in that direction, obviously intent on destroying the city's one remaining source of supplies, forcing Hood to send four divisions to stop the maneuver. The Confederates clashed with the Federals near Ezra Church, west of the city, in sharp, bloody fighting that resulted in the loss of five thousand more Southerners. Hood was spending his human currency hand over fist, but this time, at least, he partially succeeded in blocking Sherman's advance on the Macon and Western. A second circling maneuver by Sherman was headed off with a smaller battle near Utoy Creek. Desperation gripped Atlanta, no doubt about that, but for now the city was holding its own.

Not without paying a price, however. For the past year, slaves and soldiers had been erecting a line of solid defenses around the city, a seemingly impenetrable barrier of earthworks and artillery batteries, trenches and redoubts, walls of felled trees and spiked logs. The only problem was that in places these fortifications were within a mile of downtown Atlanta, and nowhere were they out of range of the Federal artillery. The big guns pounded the city day and night. Shells fell whistling from the sky to wreak havoc and destruction. The civilians remaining in the city—of whom there were considerably more than Cory had thought at first—learned to hurry out of their houses at the first signs of a renewed bombardment and seek shelter in backyard "bomb-proofs": homemade shelters consisting of pits covered by roofs of planks and dirt. These were not actually bombproof; a shell falling directly on one of them usually destroyed it and killed the occupants. But by and large they provided a considerable amount of shelter from the storm of fire cast down from the heavens by the Yankees.

Yes, it was just like Vicksburg, Cory thought—but without Lucille and Charles and Mildred Thompson and Allen Carter and Fred . . .

At least he hadn't lost his leg. He gave thanks for that. The wound was healing, and after being laid up for several days at first, now he was able to get around again fairly well. It was going to leave an ugly scar on his leg, but he could live with that. He had no doubt that Abner had saved his life. Someday, he would repay that debt, Cory vowed.

July turned to August, and several more weeks dragged by. Cory and Abner spent most of their time in a rifle pit in the defensive line ringing the city. Cory had never experienced such trench warfare before: long, boring hours of doing nothing but waiting and watching, then fierce bursts of firing whenever someone was foolish or careless enough to expose himself to sniper fire from the other side. Cory estimated that he had fired hundreds of rounds. He didn't know if a one of them had hit anything except the dirt or log breastworks behind which the Yankees crouched fifty yards away.

One morning, Cory came out of a doze to hear an unusual sound—silence. He had grown so accustomed to the roar of the Federal artillery that not hearing it seemed wrong somehow. Abner slept beside him in the trench. Cory shook his shoulder. "Abner! Abner, wake up!"

"Huh?" Abner sat up, shaking his head groggily. "What is it?"

"Listen," Cory told him.

Abner frowned. "Listen to what? I don't hear nothin'."

"That's right. The Yankees aren't firing on the city."

Abner's eyes widened in surprise. "Son of a gun! You're right." He looked up at the clear blue sky. "No damnyank shells flyin' over our heads. That's a mighty nice change."

"Why do you think they've stopped?"

"Don't have no idea. I'm just glad they have, and I'll bet the folks in town are, too."

Cory didn't doubt that. For the battered civilians, any respite from the bombardment was a welcome one. He wondered how long this one would last. On occasion over the past few weeks, the Yankees had paused in their shelling, but never for very long.

As the morning passed and the shelling did not resume, it became obvious that there was something different about this lull. A lieutenant named Bean came along the trench and ordered Cory, Abner, and the other men manning this section to climb out and advance to the enemy trenches. Bean was the latest in a long line of junior officers commanding the company. Lieutenant Stockard and the half-dozen or so who had followed him had all been killed in battle over the summer.

"Lieutenant," Abner asked, "are we supposed to just waltz up to the Yankee lines like we're visitin'? They're liable to shoot us up on the way over there."

"Have you seen any sign of the enemy this morning, Private?" Bean asked. "The rumor is that Sherman has withdrawn. That's why the Federal guns have fallen silent."

"You mean given up, sir?" Cory said. "That doesn't sound like Sherman to me."

"Oh? I wasn't aware that you were personally acquainted with General Sherman, Private."

Cory flushed at the sarcasm. "I'll go," he said, using his rifle to brace himself as he started to climb up out of the trench.

"Me, too, I reckon," Abner said. He and the other men followed Cory's lead, clambering out of the trench and advancing into the no man's land between the Confederate and Union lines.

Cory held himself stiffly as he moved forward. He expected rifle fire to erupt at any second from the Yankee trenches. He tried to prepare for the shock of bullets striking his body. But no shots came from the enemy. Anticipation made Cory increase his pace, his gait a little awkward because he still limped slightly on his wounded leg. He trotted toward the Union lines, rifle held slanted across his chest.

Abner let out a loud whistle of surprise when he and Cory reached the first of the Yankee trenches. It was empty. Nothing remained to show that the Yankees had ever been there, not even a discarded ammunition pouch or canteen. Cory turned and shouted back to Bean, "They're gone, Lieutenant!"

Shading his eyes with a hand, Abner peered up and down the line of trenches. "Nary a damnyank to be seen," he said. "They're gone, sure enough."

Cory could barely believe it. After the battles along Peachtree Creek and then east of Atlanta, followed by the weeks of pounding from the Yankee guns, it was hard to accept the fact that Sherman had picked up and left without conquering the city. And yet he saw the evidence with his own eyes, heard the telltale silence of the big guns with his own ears.

They had won. Despite everything, against all odds, they had stood firm and denied the Yankees their goal. Cory suddenly felt weak, almost like he was going to pass out. He leaned on his rifle to steady himself as Abner tipped back his head and let out a howl of triumph. Other men echoed the cry, and soon the cheering began to spread. Slowly, as the realization that the Yankees were gone spread from trench to trench, battlement to battlement, the cheers followed, all the way around Atlanta.

Cory had never seen such a celebration as the one that took place over the next four days. The war-weary denizens of the city, soldiers and civilians alike, could hardly believe their good fortune. Church bells rang merrily for hours on end, and crowds thronged the streets, stepping around shell craters to shake hands with their neighbors and slap each other on the back in congratulations. They had outlasted the Yankees. Perhaps all was not lost after all. Parties were planned, including one giant victory ball to which everyone still in Atlanta would be invited.

Cory enjoyed the respite from the tension that had gripped him for weeks. Instead of catching catnaps whenever he could in the trenches, now he could sleep for long, uninterrupted stretches. Supplies were still scarce and hunger gnawed at his belly most of the time, but at least he could rest, and he could feel the rest restoring some of the strength he had lost while recuperating from the wound in his leg.

The only problem was that far in the back of his mind, a tiny voice warned him that all this was too good to be true . . .

It was the evening of the fourth day after the Yankees' apparent withdrawal that bad news reached Atlanta from scouts ranging south and west of the city. Instead of pulling back to the north, Sherman had shifted at least some of his army to the west. He was still after the Macon and Western Railroad—which meant that he was still after Atlanta, as well.

A bitter taste filled Cory's mouth when Lieutenant Bean came hurrying through the camp, calling out orders for the men to get ready to move. Cory perched on a stump while Abner sat cross-legged on the ground nearby, smoking his pipe. He knocked the bowl against a rock as he said, "Dagnab it, I don't like the sound of that."

"Neither do I," Cory said.

Abner looked at him through eyes narrowed with suspicion. "You don't reckon the Yankees have come back, do you?"

"I think there's an even better chance they were never really gone." Cory got to his feet and slung his ammunition pouch and canteen over his shoulder. "I told the lieutenant I didn't think Sherman would give up that easy."

Abner grinned. "Well, hell. Four days without fightin' is that much, I guess. Wish it could've been more, though."

So did Cory. It would have been all right with him if he never had to take up arms and do battle again. There had been a certain excitement and glamour in riding with Nathan Bedford Forrest, to go along with the undeniable danger of cavalry operations. But the past year spent experiencing combat as an infantryman had taught Cory the truth of war: It was a hard, bloody business with absolutely nothing to recommend it.

Except for the fact that sometimes a man had to fight for what he believed in. Fight to protect himself, his family, his home. Sometimes there was no other way.

Hardee's corps moved out that night, along with the corps commanded by Gen. Stephen Lee. They marched south from Atlanta, following the railroad. At tiny East Point Station, not far south of the city, the tracks split. The Atlanta and West Point, which reportedly was under attack already by the Federals, veered off to the southwest. The main line, the Macon and Western, headed southeast toward Macon and continued toward the sea, ultimately arriving at the coastal city of Savannah. Along the way it passed near the Confederate prison camp known as Andersonville, where as many as thirty thousand Yankee prisoners were being held. Cory had heard rumors that Sherman had sent some cavalry to free the prisoners at Andersonville, but the attempt had failed. That was good news. The last thing the Confederates in Georgia needed right now was thirty thousand more Yankees suddenly turned loose in their rear.

The marching troops followed the Macon and Western tracks to Jonesboro, about twenty miles south of Atlanta. They had tramped all night, and as dawn began to turn the sky gray, they moved wearily into position just west of the settlement. They established a line running north and south, facing the Flint River about half a mile away. Cory and Abner's company was at the far left end of the line.

Would the Yankees come to them, or would they go to the Yankees? That was always the question as the two sides maneuvered in preparation for battle. As the sun rose, Cory stared across an open field bordered on both sides by trees that ran all the way to the river. He didn't see any Yankees, but that didn't mean they weren't over there. Cory could tell from the way the Confederates were not erecting breastworks or other fortifications that Hardee planned to go on the attack, probably under direct orders from Hood to do so.

But if that were the case, why wait? Cory asked himself. They were just giving the Yankees more time to get ready. Noon came and went. Orders were passed down the line: An assault on the Federal positions would begin at three o'clock. That was six or seven hours too late, as far as Cory was concerned. On the other hand, he mused, all the men had been worn out from the all-night march when they got to Jonesboro. It was questionable how well they would have been able to fight if they had attacked the Yankees early that morning. Like so many other questions in war, there was no good answer, he decided.

He had a small piece of jerky in his pack. He fished it out and gnawed on it as he and Abner waited for the attack to begin.

The shooting started early. It wasn't much after two o'clock when musketry began to rattle. Moments later, the artillery joined in. Officers galloped along the line, waving their sabers and sending the men forward.

As Cory understood the plan of attack, the Confederate left was supposed to start toward the river then swing right to attack the Union flank where it turned back at a westward angle. Meanwhile, Lee's corps would hit the Yankees straight on from the front. But that was the area where the shooting had started, and Lee was supposed to wait until Hardee was engaged on the left.

Somebody had jumped the gun.

But it was too late to call back now. The dogs of war were already loose and howling. Cory ran forward with the others, feeling the ache in his calf where the muscles still were not as strong as the ones in the rest of his leg. Like Abner beside him, he shouted out his defiance at the Yankees. Something about combat made it almost impossible to enter into it quietly.

A man to Cory's left grunted and stumbled. He fell, blood pouring out a hole in his left side. Cory was barely aware of what had happened; his attention was fixed in front of him, not to the side. Then another man went down, and another, and as Cory looked to the left, he saw muzzle flashes. He wondered what was happening. There weren't supposed to be any Yankees along that stretch of the river. They were all farther north, about to be flanked by Hardee's corps.

But the Yankees *were* there, and a moment later Cory realized that the Confederates had been flanked, instead of the other way around. Even as they attacked, they were taking withering fire from their own left.

"Abner! Over here!" Cory shouted as he turned to the left and lifted his rifle. He saw the line of blue uniforms along the river and drew a bead on them. He pressed the trigger and felt the heavy recoil against his shoulder. Abner fired as Cory reloaded. More and more of their comrades broke off the charge and swung around to deal with the more immediate threat.

As the Confederate fire increased, the Yankees began to pull back. A bridge behind them spanned the stream. They stampeded over it. Whooping with excitement, what had been the left end of the Confederate line went after them.

Cory knew they were deviating from orders, but he was as caught up in the heat of battle as anyone else. Besides, Yankees were Yankees. Might as well kill these as any of the others.

The planks of the bridge thudded under the feet of the Confederates as they charged across. The bridge formed something of a bottleneck, and some of the men didn't want to wait to get across the river. They plunged into the stream and swam it, holding their rifles and ammunition pouches over their heads to keep their powder dry. Cory and Abner took the bridge, pushing across shoulder to shoulder with dozens of other eager fighters. When they got across, Cory saw that the number of blue uniforms up ahead seemed to have gotten larger. There was a bigger force on this side of the Flint River, and he worried that he and his companions had charged unwittingly into a trap.

That proved not to be the case. True, there were more Yankees down here who should've been farther north along the river, but they didn't seem to be expecting an attack. The Confederates hit them hard, pushing them back to the west, away from the stream. Cory and Abner were in the thick of it, staying together this time instead of getting separated. This side of the river was heavily wooded; the men fought from tree to tree, moving forward at a slow but steady pace.

Cory had no idea how the rest of the battle was going. It never entered his head to worry about it. He had plenty on his plate right here, firing at the Yankees, darting in and out of the trees, fighting hand to hand at times with bayonet and rifle butt. His mind retreated into the same faraway place it went every time he was in a battle. The detachment didn't mean he was less than alert, however; he was as sharp and watchful as ever, his thoughts crystal clear, his actions crisp. The young man who had failed at almost everything he had attempted in his life had now become, through necessity, a professional soldier, and a good one at that. Only when the battle was over would he feel slightly sick at what he had seen and done—if he survived it all.

The Yankee retreat threatened to turn into a rout. It would have, had not reinforcements arrived at almost the last moment. The Confederate thrust had penetrated several hundred yards across the river before the Federals stiffened and began to hold. As the afternoon waned, they did more than hold. They launched a counterattack of their own. Cory and Abner were kneeling behind a fallen tree when they saw a swarm of blue coming toward them. A cannon roared somewhere close by, sending a shell hurtling through the branches above their heads.

"That don't look good," Abner said as he reloaded.

Cory's rifle was ready to fire. He brought it to his shoulder, found a target, and squeezed the trigger. Thirty yards away, a saber-waving officer staggered and fell. "Maybe we'd better get out of here," Cory said as he lowered the rifle.

Abner fired. "That's just what I was thinkin'," he said over the din that surrounded them and pounded at their ears.

Both young men turned and ran toward the river. In a scattered, disorganized engagement like this, each man fought largely on his own and made his own decisions. Cory and Abner had decided to git while the gitting was good.

There was a lot of that going around, they discovered as they saw scores of other Confederates retreating toward the river. Once again, not everybody wanted to wait to use the bridge. In fact, now that they were retreating, even fewer men worried about that. Into the river they went, bullets kicking up spurts of water around them as they swam for safety.

Cory and Abner both risked drowning to get back on the right side of the river. Sputtering, they came up out of the water as they reached the east bank. Lieutenant Bean came up from somewhere, his face bloody from a gash on his forehead. "Fall back!" he shouted. "Regroup along the road!"

That was where they had started, Cory thought. He had a suspicion that the battle had not gone well for the Confederates, and he had to admit that he and his companions probably had not helped matters by haring off after those Yankees on their left flank. At the time, it had seemed like there was nothing else they could do; if they had kept on as planned, they risked being destroyed by enfilading fire. Now, having gotten a better look at the Federal forces, he knew there hadn't been enough Yankees to wipe them out or even slow them down much. They should have gone where they were supposed to go.

Firing continued up and down the Flint River until darkness fell, when it finally tapered off and eventually stopped altogether. Battered and exhausted, the Southerners licked their wounds and tried to catch their breath. Just as Cory suspected, the overall attack had failed. After several hours of bloody fighting, each side occupied about the same ground it had before the combat began.

The Confederates were still between the Yankees and the Macon and Western Railroad, though. That was the important thing. Atlanta's lifeline was still secure.

ONLY IT wasn't. That afternoon, while the fighting raged west of Jonesboro, Sherman had shifted still more men to the northeast and driven straight across the tracks between Jonesboro and Atlanta. The Macon and Western was cut, and down in Jonesboro, Hardee and Lee didn't even know it.

In Atlanta, Hood was informed of these developments and concluded that Sherman was about to launch a full-scale attack on the city from the south. Hurriedly, he sent word to Jonesboro, ordering Hardee to send Lee's corps back to Atlanta. Hardee was to remain where he was and hold Jonesboro. Thinking that Hood was underestimating the Union forces that still threatened Jonesboro, Hardee had no choice but to comply with Hood's orders anyway.

Now at half-strength, Hardee's men faced the bulk of Sherman's army. He stretched his line as thin as possible, running it along the western edge of the town and then turning back to the east and north, across the railroad tracks.

Not knowing that the Confederates had weakened themselves, the Yankees moved slowly during the day on September 1, 1864, the day after the battle along the Flint River. That gave the Southerners the opportunity to erect some breastworks of their own. Cory and Abner were a couple of hundred yards to the right of the spot where the Confederate line bent to cross the railroad. They knelt behind a barricade of logs and cotton bales. In front of their position and off to the left was a large cotton field. The railroad tracks were to their left as well.

"Wonder how many of the damnyanks are really over yonder," Abner said as he wiped sweat from his brow.

"No telling. Nobody's fared very well so far at predicting exactly what Sherman is going to do."

"He's a fightin' son of a gun, I'll give him that much. We should've knowed better when it looked like he'd turned tail and run. There don't seem to be much quit in him." Abner chuckled. "But there ain't much quit in us damn stubborn Rebs, neither."

A few skirmishes broke out around midafternoon as some Yankees probed toward the Confederate line. Then, a short time later, a full-scale assault began as the Federals advanced through the cotton fields that lined the railroad. The Southerners had had time to get ready. They fired from behind their hastily erected barriers, and each volley extracted a fearful toll from the charging Yankees. But no matter how many of the blue-clad soldiers fell, never to rise again, even more of them kept coming. Cory found himself following the mindless pattern of so many battles: load, aim, fire, load, aim, fire. Try not to think about the shoulder aching from countless recoils, or the nose and eyes seared by clouds of powder smoke, or the ears that rang from the constant din.

Frantic shouts from the left drew his attention. He glanced that way and saw that the line was collapsing at the spot where it bent into a right angle. Yankees poured through the gap, shooting and waving their battle flags. All Cory and his companions could do was hope that the reserves came up and plugged that hole, otherwise the Yankees would continue to split the line. They couldn't turn to repulse the Federals because they had to deal with the attack in front of them. The breakthrough threatened the entire line, however.

Once the Yankees had penetrated, there was no stopping them. An officer hurried along the line, shouting, "Retreat! Retreat!" until a Yankee bullet felled him. The Confederates pulled back, still fighting, their retreat an orderly one instead of a rout. But rout or not, they had failed to hold, and once again the Yankees were going to emerge triumphant from an engagement.

Reserves finally came up, along with the Confederate artillery, and stopped the Federal advance. The damage had been done already, however. The Macon and Western Railroad was firmly in Union hands between Atlanta and Jonesboro. The circle of Yankees around Atlanta was almost complete. That night, Hardee regrouped his men and pointed them south toward Lovejoy's Station. Stephen Lee's corps was somewhere between Jonesboro and Atlanta, not yet having reached the city after being summoned by Hood to help forestall an attack that had not come. And in Atlanta itself, Hood and the Confederates remaining there began the bitter task of evacuating the city. Time had run out. Hood's army was divided into three sections, and unless they reunited quickly, Sherman would be able to fall on each section in turn and utterly destroy it.

Cory and Abner were among thousands of dispirited men marching along the road to Lovejoy's Station that night, tramping through the darkness in retreat as they had so many times before.

"Where do you reckon we'll go now?" Abner asked.

Cory could only shake his head. "No telling. Macon, maybe. Or maybe we'll go all the way to Savannah. Now that Sherman's got Atlanta, what's going to stop him from pushing on all the way to the Atlantic?"

"We'll stop him," Abner said.

Cory didn't say anything. He didn't point out that in the end, they hadn't been able to stop Sherman from doing just about anything he wanted to.

Yes, time had run out on Atlanta, Cory thought. How much longer before it ran out on the Confederacy itself?

Chapter Eleven

THE SOUND OF HOOFBEATS made Henry Brannon look up from the chunk of wood he had just split. He rested the head of the ax on the stump and wiped sweat off his forehead. September it might be, but the sun was still hot, especially when a fella stood out in it and swung an ax for an hour or so.

A group of riders came along the lane toward the farmhouse. Henry wasn't surprised to see the blue uniforms. Cavalry patrols came by the farm pretty often. The Yankees still had some sort of headquarters in Culpeper. General Grant had been there for a while, but he had long since moved on south toward Richmond to capture the Confederate capital. That attempt had failed, but it had cost the lives of plenty of good Southern boys, including Capt. William Shakespeare Brannon, who had fallen and was buried at Cold Harbor. Not a day went by—not even an hour, hardly—when Henry didn't ache inside at the thought of his brother's death.

His hand tightened on the ax handle as the troopers rode closer. The ax was one of the few things on the farm that could be used as a weapon. The Yankees had confiscated all the rifles, pistols, and shotguns on the place. Henry supposed they feared an uprising against their occupying army. That wasn't likely to happen. Hard times—starvation, sickness, pure despair—had beaten down the inhabitants of Culpeper County until they didn't have any fight left in them, even if they had been foolish enough to think that a few civilians could accomplish anything against the Federal army. Still, the Yankees seldom missed a chance to grind folks down a little more.

The lieutenant leading the patrol signaled a halt as he reined in. He was young, probably in his early twenties, about the same age as Henry. He faced Henry and gave him what appeared to be a friendly nod. Henry didn't believe it for a second.

177

"Afternoon," the Yankee said in greeting.

Henry glanced at the sun. "Can't argue with that."

For a second, the Yankee looked annoyed but grinned. "I suppose not."

"If you're here to scavenge, you're out of luck," Henry said. "We don't have anything left except a couple of chickens and a milk cow."

The lieutenant shook his head. "We're not a foraging party. Supplies are coming in pretty regular now on the railroad. I'm looking for Henry Brannon."

Henry felt surprise go through him. If the Yankees were looking for him, it couldn't be for any good reason. But there wouldn't be any point in denying who he was.

"I'm Henry Brannon."

"Judge Darden in Culpeper tells me that you used to be the sheriff around here."

Apprehension grew inside Henry. Had these Yankees come to arrest him?

"I was the sheriff for a little while. Not very long, though."

"Would you mind riding back into town with us? My commanding officer wants to talk to you."

This was it, Henry thought. They were going to arrest him, all right. His muscles tensed. If he flung the ax at the lieutenant, that might distract the rest of the patrol for a second or two. He could turn and run into the barn—

And get himself shot in the back, he realized. He didn't stand a chance in hell of reaching the barn before those troopers could cut him down.

Before he could say or do anything, the front door of the farmhouse opened. The young lieutenant looked that way, as did the other cavalrymen. A couple of them shifted their hands closer to their pistols, Henry noted. He stiffened in alarm as his sister, Cordelia, a couple of years younger than he was, stepped out onto the porch. She stopped short in surprise at the sight of the blue-uniformed riders.

"Oh," she said. "I didn't know—"

The young officer jerked his campaign hat off his head and sat straighter in the saddle. "Lieutenant Joseph Keller, at your service, ma'am," he said. "Please don't be frightened. We're not here to cause trouble for you or your husband."

"Husband?" Not even the surprise and possible fear she felt could keep the word from coming out of her mouth. "You mean Henry? He's not my husband. He's my brother."

Keller blinked. "Oh. I see. Then you don't *have* a husband, ma'am?"

Henry stepped forward, still holding the ax. "That's none of your damned business, mister."

Now the troopers quickly turned their attention back to Henry, away from the pretty redheaded young woman on the porch. They didn't just move their hands toward their guns this time; they drew the weapons.

"Hold your fire!" Keller said. He was still holding his campaign cap in one hand. He flung out that arm to motion the others back. To Henry, he said, "It might be a good idea to put down that ax, Mr. Brannon."

For some reason, Henry didn't like being called *mister* by somebody who was about the same age as he was. Nevertheless, not wishing to appear threatening to the Yankees, he dropped the ax to the ground beside the wood-splitting stump. With Cordelia standing on the nearby porch, he couldn't afford to take any chances with having bullets flying around.

As for himself, he didn't much care whether the Yankees shot him. These days, he had to look long and hard to find a good reason to go on living. Taking care of what was left of his family was about the only thing he could come up with.

"Holster those weapons!" Keller ordered.

"Are you sure that's a good idea, Lieutenant?" a burly Yankee sergeant asked.

"I gave you an order, Sergeant McCafferty. I expect you to follow it."

"Yes sir," the sergeant answered, holstering his revolver and motioning for the other troopers to do likewise. Slowly, grudgingly, they put up their guns.

Keller turned back to Henry. "Now, Mr. Brannon, I'm asking you again to come along peaceably with us."

Bringing down more trouble on the head of the family was the last thing Henry wanted to do. He nodded his agreement to the man's request. "All right, Lieutenant. But you'll have to give me a ride. You see, we don't have any horses or mules left. You Yankees have taken them all."

Keller's mouth tightened in anger at Henry's scornful tone, but the young officer controlled his reaction. He held out a hand. "Come along. You can ride with me."

Henry reached up to clasp Keller's wrist and swung up behind him. As he did so, McCafferty commented, "Better you than me, Lieutenant. I ain't sure I could take the stink of a damned Reb so close to me."

"That'll be enough of that, Sergeant."

"Yes sir," McCafferty said. Henry heard the note of derision in his voice.

He couldn't let himself get mad, no matter what the Yankees said or did. If he flew off the handle, that would give them the excuse they needed to kill him or throw him in jail. He had to take whatever they wanted to dish out. He looked over at the porch, to Cordelia. "Tell Ma where I've gone." He was glad his mother and Louisa Abernathy were down at the creek searching for hickory nuts. Abigail Brannon had no use for Yankees of any sort, and she didn't mind saying so.

"Are you sure you'll be all right, Henry?" Cordelia called to him as Keller turned the horse around.

"Don't worry, Miss Brannon," the lieutenant said before Henry could reply to the question. "I'll see that your brother is taken care of."

"Perhaps that's what I'm worried about, Lieutenant," she responded tartly.

Keller just looked at her for a second. Henry could see the man's face only in profile, but he thought a smile tugged at his lips. All Cordelia gave back to him was a stony stare.

The lieutenant heeled his horse into a trot, heading down the lane away from the house. The rest of the patrol followed. Henry hung on. He didn't like being this close to a Yankee, just as the lieutenant probably didn't like having a Rebel riding with him. Neither of them seemed to have much choice in the matter.

After a while, the cavalrymen jogged their horses past the turnoff where the trail to Mountain Laurel left the Culpeper road. Henry felt his guts clench as he looked at the turnoff. There was nothing at the end of that winding road now, nothing except the burned-out shell of a once-great plantation house. Mountain Laurel, the home of planter Duncan Ebersole, had burned to the ground several weeks earlier, taking Ebersole with it. His was the only life lost in the blaze; none of the servants had been in the house when it caught fire. Henry supposed all the slaves had left the plantation since then, wandering off because they had no reason to stay. The fields lay fallow, the overseers were all gone, and no one cared anymore about fugitive slaves. Anyway, Lincoln had set them all free with his so-called Emancipation Proclamation, and if the Union won the war, as it seemed destined to do, soon slavery would be a thing of the past in the South.

Henry didn't care about that. What put the bitter lines on his face were the memories of Polly, Ebersole's daughter. She had married two of the Brannon boys, first Titus and then Henry after it appeared that Titus had been killed at Fredericksburg. None of them knew until later that Titus was still alive and in a Yankee prison camp in Illinois. Not until he had escaped and made his way back home had anyone been aware that he had survived the battle. Titus's homecoming had been a mixed blessing, though, and ultimately it had led to tragedy. Now Polly was gone and so was Titus—Polly dead and buried in the churchyard in Culpeper, Titus off fighting Yankees somewhere. He might be dead, too, as far as Henry knew. He had to work at it to make himself care anymore. He still thought Titus bore some of the blame for the death of Polly and the child she had been carrying. Henry's child . . .

He shoved those thoughts into the back of his head. Yes, there had been plenty of tragedy in his life these past few years. That was true of just about everybody in the South. He couldn't afford to dwell on it, not when he was a prisoner of the Yankees himself. He still wondered what they wanted of him.

Except for the Union troops around town, Culpeper resembled a ghost town. No fighting had taken place in the settlement itself, so the buildings had not been shattered by artillery fire or burned as buildings in so many other Southern towns had been. Some of the residents remained, but many had left, evacuating as the Yankees came in. They preferred taking to the roads as refugees to staying behind and placing themselves under the iron-fisted control of the invaders. Those civilians who had stayed in Culpeper seldom ventured out of their homes.

Henry felt another pang of regret as he and his captors rode by the abandoned store that had once been run by Michael Davis, an old friend of the Brannon family. Davis had left Culpeper even before the Yankees came. Henry had no idea where the man was now.

Keller brought the patrol to a halt in front of the courthouse. Henry slid down first from the back of the horse. The lieutenant and the other soldiers dismounted in military fashion, and one of the men led the lieutenant's horse away.

"My orders are to bring you straight to Colonel Avery," he told Henry. "Please come with me, Mr. Brannon."

Still feeling like a prisoner even though Keller seemed to be making an effort not to treat him that way, Henry followed the lieutenant into the courthouse. Those bad memories were everywhere these days, he reflected. For a while he had occupied the sheriff's office in this building. And before that, before the war, Will Brannon had been the sheriff of Culpeper County. There was no getting away from the reminders of everything the Brannons had lost.

Keller ushered Henry into an office that had once belonged to the county clerk. The chambers had been taken over by one of the Yankee officers. He looked up from a chair behind a scarred desk as the two men entered the room. Keller came to attention and snapped a salute. "Lieutenant Keller reporting, sir. I've brought Sheriff Brannon to see you, as you ordered."

"That's former Sheriff Brannon," Henry said. "You Yankees made me sort of obsolete."

The colonel returned Keller's salute. "At ease, Lieutenant." He looked at Henry and went on, "Perhaps it's time we changed that, Mr. Brannon. I'm Colonel Richard Avery, and I have a proposition for you."

Henry didn't like the sound of this. Any proposition put forward by a Yankee had to be a bad one.

Avery came to his feet. He was tall, broad-shouldered, and beefy. His florid face was topped by thinning gray hair and decorated by thick muttonchop whiskers. He extended a hand across the desk toward Henry, who ignored it. After a moment, Avery used the hand to gesture toward a chair in front of the desk. "Have a seat, Mr. Brannon."

"I'm fine where I am." Henry folded his arms across his chest.

The colonel looked irritated for a second, but then he chuckled. "Another stiff-necked Rebel, I see. Well, I can't say as I blame you. Losing a war must be a mighty hard thing."

"The war's not over yet."

"It might as well be." Avery caught himself. "But I'm not here to argue with you. Like I said, I have a proposition for you. We'd like for you to take your old job back, Mr. Brannon."

That took Henry by surprise, and he tried not to show it. "You want me to be sheriff again?"

"That's right. Culpeper and the rest of the county will remain under military jurisdiction, of course, but it's only a matter of time until the war ends. When it does, some sort of new government will have to be established that will be able to work with the army to maintain peace. We could bring in people from up north, of course, to run the civilian end of things, and I'm sure some of that will be done. But we'd like to have some of the natives from this area working with us, too."

"Traitors, you mean." Henry practically spat the words out.

"Not at all. Not traitors to the legally established and divinely ordained government of the United States of America. All you'd have to do is sign a loyalty oath—"

"Go to hell," Henry said.

Avery took a deep breath. His hand moved toward the flap of the holster on his hip. "How dare you!" he said through clenched teeth. "I could shoot you down right now, you damned Rebel, and no one would ever question me!"

Henry knew that was true. He heard feet shifting nervously behind him. The lieutenant cleared his throat. "Colonel, maybe this wasn't a good idea—"

"Shut up!" Avery roared. "I've tried to be polite to this god-damned peckerwood, but he won't have any of it."

"You're right about part of that anyway, Colonel," Henry said with a faint, bleak smile. "I don't want any of your damned federal government."

"You had your chance. Get out of my sight, Brannon, or I will kill you."

Henry didn't stand around and argue. He turned and stalked out of the office.

Keller hurried behind him, catching up with him in the corridor. "You shouldn't have done that," he said. He sounded genuinely concerned, not that Henry cared one way or the other whether he was. "The colonel isn't a good man to cross."

Henry stopped and turned to face the lieutenant. "You really think I'd turn on my own people like that? Would you, if the tables were turned?"

"I'd want to help my people," Keller said. "By working with us, you'd be in a position to do so."

Henry shook his head. "Sometimes there's some things a man just can't stomach."

"Keller!" Colonel Avery called from inside the office.

The lieutenant looked uncertain what to do next. Hurriedly, he said to Henry, "You'll have to get back to your farm as best you can, I'm afraid. I can't offer you a horse."

"Wouldn't take it if you did." Henry knew he was being a little hard on Joseph Keller, who seemed to want to be friendly. War didn't leave any room for such things as friendliness between enemies, though.

Keller went back into the colonel's office while Henry left the courthouse. Several Yankees loitered outside the building, including Sergeant McCafferty. The sergeant straightened as Henry came down the courthouse steps.

"Where's the lieutenant?"

"Inside." Henry jerked a thumb over his shoulder. "In the colonel's office."

"What are you doing running around loose, Reb?"

Henry looked coldly at McCafferty. "I'm going back to my farm. My business with the colonel is done." He started past the sergeant.

McCafferty reached out and stopped him by grabbing his arm. "Not so fast. We ain't in the habit of letting enemy spies run around behind our lines."

Henry wanted to jerk his arm out of McCafferty's grip. He wanted to smash a fist into the man's face. But what he did was stand there and force his voice to remain calm as he said, "I'm not a spy."

"I don't know about that." Some of the other soldiers began to crowd around the two of them. "Maybe we better take you down to the livery stable and question you for a while. What do you think of that idea, Reb?"

Henry knew that if he allowed McCafferty and the other Yankees to get him out of sight, they might beat him to death just for the fun of it. He said again, "I'm not a spy. Colonel Avery and Lieutenant Keller both said for me to go home." That wasn't quite true; Avery had just said for Henry to get out of his sight. He doubted the colonel would care if McCafferty and the others stomped the life out of him.

"Sergeant! Let go of that man!"

The sharp command came from the top of the courthouse steps. Without looking, Henry recognized Keller's voice. For a second, he thought McCafferty was going to ignore the order. Then the sergeant gave him an ugly grin and let go of his arm.

"Another day," McCafferty said under his breath. "Don't forget, Reb."

"I won't," Henry promised. He was beginning to understand why Titus felt that the only way to deal with all Yankees was to kill them on sight.

Keller came briskly down the steps and hustled Henry away from the group of soldiers. "I'm going to get a horse for you and ride back out to your farm with you," he said. "Otherwise, I'm afraid you won't reach there alive."

"I reckon you're probably right about that."

Keller looked over at him. "You don't seem too worried about the possibility."

Henry shrugged and shook his head. "When everything else has been taken away, a man's life doesn't seem to mean all that much anymore."

HER MOTHER was going to worry herself into a state if she wasn't careful, Cordelia thought as she watched Abigail Brannon fidget around the farmhouse kitchen. It was probably too late for that, she amended. Her mother was already in a state. She had been ever since she had returned to the house and found Henry gone, taken away by the Yankees.

Cordelia sat at the table with Louisa Abernathy. Louisa was a few years older, and though she had red hair like Cordelia, hers was several shades darker and more tightly curled. Raised a Quaker in the Midwest, Louisa had deserted her faith and family to help Titus escape from Camp Douglas and return home to Virginia. Even though Titus was gone now, the Brannon family had opened their home to her and welcomed her to stay as long as she wanted.

Cordelia knew from painful conversations she'd had with the older woman that Louisa considered what she'd done to be a betrayal of her beliefs. Louisa believed that her actions had condemned her to damnation. Cordelia had a hard time seeing things that way. As a good Baptist, she knew that God could be vengeful and terrible in His righteous wrath. But helping a man to escape from a hellish captivity and make his way back home to his family . . . Cordelia had a hard time seeing how that could be such an awful sin, even though things hadn't really turned out the way anyone would have liked.

Abigail turned away from the stove and said to Cordelia, "Why did you let him go? Why did you let them take him?"

Cordelia felt a flash of anger at her mother. "How could I have stopped them?" she asked.

"I'm sure there was nothing Cordelia could do," Louisa said. "Or Henry, either, for that matter. He had to go with them."

"They're going to kill him," Abigail fretted as she paced over to the table. "I just know they are. They're going to take him away from me, just like they did Will."

The death of her oldest son had devastated Abigail, Cordelia knew. Yet she couldn't help but remember when Abigail herself had driven Will away, telling him he was no longer a member of the family. They had patched things up before it was too late, thank goodness. But the grief over Will's death didn't belong to Abigail alone. Cordelia mourned for him, too, and she had to force herself not to resent her mother's attitude.

Abigail took a seat at the table. Louisa reached over to clasp her hand. "I'm sure Henry will be all right. From what Cordelia said, it sounds like the soldiers just wanted to talk to him."

"They didn't have to take him into town to do that. They're probably going to try to get him to sign a loyalty oath, since he was the sheriff. They did that before, and he refused. They'll put him in front of a firing squad this time, I just know it."

Cordelia and Louisa exchanged helpless glances. Nothing they could say was going to make any difference to Abigail until Henry returned.

The sound of hoofbeats made all three women look sharply toward the door. Abigail leaped up from her chair and rushed out of the kitchen. "Maybe he's come back!" she prayed. Cordelia and Louisa hurried after her.

Dusk was approaching. The sun had set not long before, dropping below the crest of the Blue Ridge Mountains to the west. But there was still enough light for Cordelia to see Henry dismounting from a horse in front of the house. The lieutenant who had led the patrol earlier was with him. The young officer touched gauntleted fingers to the brim of his campaign cap as Abigail, Cordelia, and Louisa came onto the porch. "Good evening, ladies," he said.

"Henry!" Abigail threw her arms around her son in a fierce hug that clearly made Henry uncomfortable. "Thank the Lord you're back! I was sure those devils had killed you."

Cordelia watched the lieutenant and saw the brief grimace that came over his face at Abigail's words. He didn't look devilish, she thought. In fact, he reminded her somewhat of a little boy with that friendly face and the shock of sandy hair under his cap. At the same time, he was definitely a grown man, and a rather handsome one at that.

Her eyes widened in shock as she realized what she was thinking. He was a *Yankee*, for heaven's sake! It didn't matter what he looked like, or even that he was trying to act polite.

"I'd advise you to stay close to home, Mr. Brannon," the lieutenant said to Henry. "As long as you do, you should be safe. We don't make war on civilians, and as you told me, you've never been in the Confederate army. Even if you had been, you would have had to give your parole before you were allowed to return home."

Henry gently disengaged himself from his mother's embrace and turned to face the Union officer. "Then you're convinced I'm not a spy?"

"Of course."

"Tell that to Sergeant McCafferty."

"I'll give McCafferty orders to stay away from this farm. Don't worry about that." Lieutenant Keller touched the brim of his cap again and nodded to the women. "Ladies." He wheeled his horse and rode away, leading the mount that Henry had ridden out from Culpeper.

"Are you all right, Henry?" Abigail asked, clutching his arm. "Those despicable Yankees didn't hurt you?"

"I'm fine," he assured her. "They just tried again to get me to sign a loyalty oath."

Cordelia knew her brother very well, and she had a feeling that something else had happened, something Henry didn't want to tell their mother. She didn't say anything, though. If there was no immediate threat, she preferred to let the matter drop. Abigail had worried enough already today.

The four of them started into the house. "That young lieutenant seemed almost nice," Louisa said.

"He's a Yankee," Henry said, clearly dismissing the very idea that Lt. Joseph Keller might be nice. Cordelia agreed. She would never have anything positive to say about a Yankee.

Never.

Chapter Twelve

LIEUTENANT KELLER HAD TOLD Henry during the ride back to the farm that Colonel Avery was convinced Henry was a spy. That seemed to be the Yankees' first reaction to any Confederate civilian. Avery had issued orders that the farm was to be watched for any signs of espionage or subversive activity.

Henry didn't say anything about that to his mother or to Cordelia and Louisa. No point in worrying them, he thought. Besides, he knew he wasn't a spy and didn't have anything to do with spies. The Yankees could watch the place all they wanted. They wouldn't see anything incriminating.

Over the next couple of weeks, Federal patrols rode by several times. Henry saw them in the distance. They didn't approach the farm but passed by the lane instead. He suspected there were watchers he *didn't* see.

But he had more important things to worry about. The situation on the farm was growing desperate. With autumn approaching, Henry had begun to lay in firewood for the winter, but he was worried there wouldn't be enough. If it was a particularly cold winter, they might be busting up the furniture and burning it before spring came. The food supply looked even worse. With only him, Cordelia, and Louisa to work the fields, the crops had been meager this year. They had some sweet potatoes and beans in the cellar, but not enough to last through the winter. The corn was all gone. With all the mills in the area either destroyed or taken over by the Yankees, there was no flour. No sugar. Very little salt. The pork from last year's butchering was gone. It was a wonder they still had a couple of chickens and a cow, Henry thought. The Yankees had confiscated almost all the livestock in the county. As long as the rooster kept doing his job and the hen continued laying, they would have a few eggs, and the cow provided milk. Looked at from that perspective, they were richer than most folks around here. So rich, Henry thought bitterly, that they might last an extra week or two before they starved to death.

But there was nothing he could do except to keep on working and preparing for fall and winter as best he could. That was all anyone could do.

Many of the settlers in the area had abandoned their farms and homes and headed farther south in hopes that conditions would be better there. More than once, Henry considered trying to talk his mother into leaving, only to discard the idea each time. He knew that Abigail Brannon would never leave the farm. It had been her home for more than three decades. She and her husband had cleared the land, planted the crops, built the cabin, and raised six children here. The roots were too deep, too strong. Not even war could pull them up, Henry thought. So the family would just have to make it through, one way or the other.

He came out of the barn one morning with a milk bucket in his hand, a frown on his face. The bucket was less than half full. The cow was giving less milk these days. If she dried up, they would be in worse straits than ever before.

The sound of an approaching rider made Henry pause and turn to look toward the lane. He saw one man trotting a horse toward the farm. The rider wore a blue uniform and black campaign cap, which came as no surprise. Hardly anyone moved around the countryside these days except the Yankees.

As the cavalryman came closer, Henry recognized Lt. Joseph Keller. This time Keller was alone, and Henry wondered what he wanted. Even though he doubted that Keller meant them any harm, Henry wished he had a weapon, a rifle or a pistol or anything else he could use to defend his family if he had to.

Judging by Keller's actions, that wouldn't be necessary. The lieutenant smiled and lifted a hand in greeting as he slowed his mount and walked it into the yard between the farmhouse and the barn. A canvas bag was tied onto the saddle.

"Good morning," Keller said.

"Come to check on the spy?" Henry's tone was caustic.

"Not at all. I never believed you were a spy, Brannon. That was all in Colonel Avery's head. I look at you and I see a man who's just doing his best to get by."

"That's the truth," Henry muttered. "Why are you here?"

"To give you this." Keller untied the short length of cord that held the bag to his saddle. He extended the bundle to Henry.

After a second or two of hesitation, Henry set the milk bucket on the ground and walked over to Keller's horse. He reached up and took the bag, a little surprised at the solid weight of it. "What is it?" he asked.

"A couple of hams. We received a shipment of provisions yesterday, and I thought you might be able to use them."

Henry's eyes widened. He could smell the aroma coming from the bag. He jerked it open and looked inside. Sure enough, two hams, just as Keller said. Henry's mouth began to water.

But then his lips thinned into a grim, hard line, and he shoved the bag at Keller. "Take 'em. We don't need them." His voice shook. "We don't want any damned Yankee charity."

Keller didn't take the bag. Instead, he edged his horse back a couple of steps. "It's not charity," he said. "It's compensation, due you for the inconvenience of being hauled into Culpeper and questioned a couple of weeks ago."

"Is that so? Do you Yankees *compensate* every innocent man you question? How about compensating the whole Confederacy for what you've done to it?" Henry knew his voice was rising in anger, but there was nothing he could do to stop it. "How do you make things right for all the killing you've done?"

"A state of war exists between the United States and its rebellious brethren," Keller said, sounding a little angry now himself. "Loss of life, though regrettable, is inevitable, and so is destruction. I don't like what we're doing down here any more than you do, Brannon—"

Henry snorted in contempt and disbelief.

"But if it's necessary to preserve the Union, then so be it," Keller went on. "That doesn't mean I can't attempt to redress what I see as a wrong. There was no need for what happened. Sergeant McCafferty and those other men might have killed you—"

"Henry!" The voice came from the barn, startling both men. "You didn't say anything about some Yankees threatening to kill you."

Henry turned his head and saw Cordelia emerge from the shadows of the barn. She had bunched up her apron and held it in front of her, carefully cradling a precious burden: While Henry tended to the milking, she had gathered eggs.

"Go on in the house, Cordelia," Henry told her. "This doesn't concern you."

"I think it does," she said as she came forward. "I hear yelling going on out here, and then I see we have a visitor—"

"This Yankee's not a visitor. He's a damned invader, just like the rest of his breed."

Keller took off his cap and inclined his head toward Cordelia. "Begging your pardon, ma'am. I didn't mean to disturb you."

"That's all right," Cordelia told him. "Now, what were you saying about someone wanting to kill my brother?"

Henry burst out, "For God's sake, leave it alone! It didn't amount to anything. Just some more typical Yankee bluster."

"I assure you that you have nothing to worry about, Miss Brannon," Keller said. "I've tended to the matter."

"Nothing to worry about," Henry repeated before Cordelia could say anything. "That's quite a joke, Lieutenant. How many eggs you got there, Cordelia?"

"Two," she said. "It's a good morning."

"Two eggs and less than half a bucket of milk. How well do you reckon four grown people can get by on that, Lieutenant?"

Keller allowed himself a brief glare at Henry before he turned a more pleasant expression back to Cordelia. "I know that times are hard here," he said to her. "That's one reason I brought your family a couple of hams. Your brother doesn't seem to want to accept them, however."

"Hams?" Cordelia's voice was hushed, as if she were repeating something sacred. "Really, Henry?"

"There are hams in here, all right," Henry said, hefting the bag Keller had given him. "But I told the lieutenant we don't need any Yankee charity."

"Charity, no." Cordelia came several steps closer and looked up at Keller. "But it wouldn't be hospitable if we turned down a gracious gift from a visitor."

"Damn it! I already told you he isn't a visitor—"

"I can't take the hams back," Keller broke in. "For one thing, the colonel wouldn't look kindly on this gesture if he found out about it. I'm afraid he would regard it as giving aid and comfort to the enemy. So do what you want with them, but don't try to give them back to me." He started to turn his horse.

Henry drew back the hand holding the bag, as if he intended to hurl it at the lieutenant. Cordelia came forward quickly and got between the two men. "Thank you, Lieutenant," she said. "I'm curious about one thing, though—why don't *you* regard this as giving aid and comfort to the enemy?"

Keller smiled. "That one's easy to answer, anyway. I don't think of you and your family and folks like you as the enemy, Miss Brannon. That's why."

With that, he put his cap on, wheeled his horse, and rode away without looking back.

Henry muttered a curse and acted again like he was going to throw the hams after Keller. Cordelia turned around, keeping the pair of eggs cradled carefully in her apron, and held out her other hand. "Give me that," she said.

"Blast it, Cordelia, they're Yankee hams!" Henry wondered why she couldn't seem to understand that.

"I think it's pretty likely they came from somewhere here in Virginia. That makes them Confederate hams, and we have more right to them than the Union soldiers do."

What she said made sense, Henry admitted grudgingly to himself. But he still didn't like the idea.

He knew someone else who wouldn't like it, either. As he gave the hams to Cordelia, he asked, "What are you going to tell Ma when she wants to know where these came from?"

Cordelia looked stricken, and he realized she hadn't thought of that. If Abigail Brannon knew they were eating food that came from a Yankee, there would be hell to pay.

As IT turned out, Cordelia had to do something she didn't like to do: She lied to her mother. But it was only a little lie, she tried to convince herself.

"The bag came untied and slipped off some Yankee cavalryman's horse while he was riding by, but he didn't notice," Cordelia explained that evening to her mother. "Henry and I went out and got it when he was gone."

She looked across the table at her brother. She couldn't read the expression on his face. He just sat there solemnly, neither confirming nor denying her story. He had agreed not to reveal where the hams came from.

Abigail and Louisa had been down in the root cellar that morning when Keller stopped by the farm, so they didn't know anything about his visit. When Cordelia spun her yarn about finding the hams, Abigail nodded in acceptance of the lie.

"If he was a Yankee, that means he stole these hams from some poor Southerner," she said. "It's only fitting that those thieving Northerners don't get to eat them. I feel sorry for whoever they were stolen from in the first place, though."

"I don't reckon we'll ever know," Henry said. That was his only comment on the matter.

They carved a little meat from one of the hams then hung the rest of it in the smokehouse with the other one. This unexpected bounty would have to last as long as possible.

Cordelia was hungry when she went to bed that night, but her pangs weren't quite as bad as usual. Drifting off to sleep, she thought of Lt. Joseph Keller with gratitude. She thought as well of how polite he was, and even handsome in a boyish, rough-hewn way. Those musings took her by surprise. She really hadn't given much consideration to any young man since Nathan Hatcher left Culpeper. Nathan had come close to breaking her heart with his refusal to embrace the Southern cause. Deserting the Confederacy to go and fight for the Union had been the final straw, the final nail in the coffin where their budding relationship was buried. Still, there were times when she missed him . . . the sound of his voice, the touch of his hand, the taste of the kisses they had shared so briefly. She was a healthy young woman, and she enjoyed the company of young men other than her brothers. These days, though, Henry was the only male around.

Damn Nathan anyway, she thought, then swiftly recanted. She knew from what Titus had said when he returned that Nathan had been in the Yankee prison camp with him. The Union authorities were convinced, for some unknown reason, that Nathan was a Rebel, not the Federal infantryman he claimed to be—and actually was, until he was captured by the Yankees while wearing Confederate gray at Fredericksburg. Cordelia had no way of knowing if Nathan was alive or dead now. She prayed that he was alive. He had been her friend, and for that reason he would always be special to her.

Joseph Keller, now, was another story. She didn't know what to make of him.

But she wished futilely that an image of his face had not been floating in her mind as she slipped into a thankfully dreamless slumber.

OVER THE next couple of weeks, Keller made several excuses to visit the Brannon farm. Considering the colonel's animosity toward Henry Brannon, Keller didn't really need an excuse. Avery had commanded that the family be watched; if anyone questioned Keller about his activities, he would answer that he was just following the colonel's orders.

It was quiet here behind the lines. That left Keller with mixed emotions. Elsewhere in Virginia, the Army of the Potomac was bogged down in the trenches in front of Petersburg, but at least those men were seeing some action on occasion. In the Shenandoah Valley, across the Blue Ridge Mountains, battles and skirmishes took place almost daily as Gen. Phil Sheridan tried to rid the valley of Confederate rangers. Down in Georgia, Gen. William Tecumseh Sherman had captured the vital city of Atlanta and had the Rebels on the run, some of them retreating northwestward into Tennessee while the rest of that part of the Confederate army fled toward the sea. It was only a matter of time until Sherman went after one group or the other, or both.

Nearly every day, Keller heard the other junior officers discussing these developments in the war. Eagerly, they debated strategy and laid out the glorious battle plans they would implement if *they* were in charge, instead of Grant, Meade, Sherman, and Sheridan. Flasks and bottles were passed around in the parlors of commandeered houses, and the confident laughter flowed as easily as did the whiskey. The Confederacy was beaten. That was the general consensus. Oh, the Rebels might hang on stubbornly for a while yet, but they had no real hope of winning. That had been gone for a long time. Now any thoughts the Confederate leaders might have had about negotiating a peace that would leave them with their new government intact were slipping away as well.

Still, much hinged on the upcoming presidential election. For a time, it had looked as if old Honest Abe might not be reelected. If that happened, the peace parties in both North and South would have the opening they hoped for: A chance to drive a wedge between the supporters of the war and present their own plans for a peace treaty. But if Lincoln won, the appeasers would be denied their chance. Only a total victory would satisfy the president and end the war.

Keller hoped that would be the case. A negotiated peace sounded wonderful—in theory. Many on both sides just wanted the killing to stop, no matter what the cost. But if that happened . . . if a treaty were put in place that would allow the Confederacy to continue to exist, even in an altered, weakened form . . . then they would just have to fight this war all over again in another ten or twenty years, Keller believed. And if that came about, the country might be so divided that it could never be reunited again, if that wasn't the case already.

Political theorizing aside, Keller shared his fellow officers' conviction that the war would be over soon, one way or another. So far, he had never been any closer to combat than hearing the dull roar of artillery in the distance. He had missed Antietam, missed Gettysburg, missed all the opportunities for a man to cover himself with military glory.

When he enlisted, he never would have dreamed that such a thing could ever be important to him. He wanted to do his part to help win the war for the Union, of course, but more than that, he wanted to get through it and return to the Ohio academy where he taught history and philosophy. He had been teaching for only a year when the Rebel guns fired on Fort Sumter. His career had barely begun, and he was anxious to resume it. Or so he had thought.

Now he considered the possibility that the great conflict would end before he had the chance to prove himself in battle, and he felt discomfort go through him. Discomfort, and even some unwarranted—he told himself—shame. He had nothing to be embarrassed about. He had been a good soldier, always following orders, always doing his best. But the real demands on him had been slight.

With all that weighing on his mind, it was a wonder he had any room in his brain for anything else, let alone for the thoughts he had been having since his first visit to the Brannon farm.

Since he had first laid eyes on a young woman with masses of red hair that tumbled about her shoulders, skin the color of cream that he knew would be incredibly smooth to the touch, and the most compelling green eyes he had ever seen . . .

In his tent at night, Keller felt himself growing warm with mingled embarrassment and desire when he thought about Cordelia Brannon. His parents had raised him to be a proper gentleman, so it bothered him when his more . . . human . . . nature asserted itself. Cordelia was a lady. Oh, not one of those Southern belles he had heard about, the ones who sat around the parlors in their great plantation houses fanning themselves languidly while they were waited on hand and foot by kowtowing darkies. Cordelia wasn't like that at all. For one thing, the Brannons didn't have a plantation house or any slaves, and for another, Cordelia was the sort of woman who was accustomed to hard work, yet she had never lost her gentle, beautiful spirit. Keller could tell that just by looking at her.

He was smitten, no doubt about that, but he told himself that wasn't the real reason he paid so many visits to the Brannon farm. Nor were his feelings for Cordelia what prompted him to bring them whatever supplies he could get his hands on without drawing attention to himself. He was just trying to be a fair, conscientious soldier.

The first time he went back to the farm, he brought a small pouch full of flour with him. It was barely enough to make a batch of biscuits, but he knew it was probably more than the Brannons had seen in a while.

From a distance, Keller watched until he saw the bright red of Cordelia's hair as she walked alone toward the creek. He circled, walking his horse so as not to make too much noise. The only reason he was approaching Cordelia alone like this, he told himself, was because of the hostility her brother had exhibited last time. After taking the chance of bringing the flour with him, he didn't want Henry refusing to accept it, the way he had tried to turn down the two hams.

As he neared the creek, he dismounted and led his horse closer. He stepped through a screen of brush and heard a gasp of surprise from Cordelia. Quickly, he held up his hand. "It's all right, Miss Brannon. I mean you no harm. It's Joseph Keller."

She carried a fishing pole in her hand and brought it in front of her as if she wouldn't hesitate to use it as a weapon if need be. Keller thought she looked utterly charming. In a voice that shook just slightly, she asked, "What are you doing here, Lieutenant?"

"I brought this for you." He held up the pouch. "It's flour. I thought you could use it."

"How did you get it? Did you steal it from your company's mess tent?"

That was exactly what he'd done, but he didn't want to admit that, even to her. So he said, "That doesn't matter. What's important is that I think you should have it."

"Why do we deserve it any more than any other family around here? We're hardly the only ones in Culpeper County who are having a hard time of it."

She was full of questions, Keller thought. Good questions, perhaps, but ones he did not want to answer. As he hesitated, she went on.

"And why do you come skulking around like this? You must have been watching the farm, or you wouldn't have known that I was down here."

"Your brother . . . The last time I was here, your brother wasn't pleased, and he didn't want to take what I brought." Keller took a deep breath. "I understand the way he feels, Miss Brannon. I'm sure I would feel the same way if the situation were reversed. But it's not, and we have to deal with things the way they are."

Cordelia came a step closer, but she kept the fishing pole between the two of them. "That doesn't answer my real question. Why are you trying to help us, Lieutenant? You may not consider us your enemies, but we are, you know. We're on opposite sides in this war, and there's nothing we can do about that."

"One day soon, this damned war will be over!" Keller burst out, startling himself with the vehemence of his reaction. For the moment, he had forgotten completely about the disappointment he felt that he had not experienced combat. "Then we'll all be countrymen again. I . . . I just want to help, Miss Brannon. I think you and your family are . . . are good, decent people."

She looked at him in silence for a long moment. He could tell she was considering what he had said. He saw as well that she didn't accept it completely. Maybe he needed to say more.

"And I believe . . . I believe you to be a very fine young lady, and I would be honored if you would allow me to . . . to . . ." His voice trailed off. He was stunned at what he was about to say, and he couldn't finish it.

Cordelia's eyes widened. She looked startled, too. She said, "Lieutenant Keller, were you about to ask me if you could come calling on me?"

His lips tightened, and he lifted his chin. "And if I was?"

"You realize that under the circumstances such behavior would be highly improper?"

Now that he had dug himself into this hole by revealing his true feelings, he could do nothing but press on. "As I said, the war will be over soon, God willing, and things will be different."

"Will they?"

She was maddening. Beautiful, but maddening.

"One can only hope."

Again, a moment of silence went by while Cordelia thought about what they had said. Then she held out her hand. "Give me the flour."

Keller handed it over. "Thank you."

"It's me who should be thanking you," she said, smiling and gesturing with the pole toward the creek behind her. "Dobie's Run is about fished out. I probably wouldn't have caught anything. For some reason I just can't stop trying, though. My brothers used to bring me down here to fish. Those were wonderful times."

"I'm sure they were."

"My brother Will was killed at Cold Harbor, you know."

"I didn't know. I'm sorry. I'm sure he was a fine man."

"Yes, he was." Cordelia gazed down at the ground for a moment, and when she lifted her head, tears glistened in her eyes as she looked at Keller. "I come down here to fish quite often, Lieutenant. If you'd care to join me on occasion, you would be welcome."

Keller's heart thudded heavily in his chest, and his throat felt as if a band had been drawn tight around it. For a moment, he was unable to speak. Then he swallowed a couple of times. "It would be my honor and privilege, Miss Brannon."

Cordelia smiled, and Keller thought he was going to die of happiness right there on the bank of the creek.

That was the start of it. A couple of times each week, he rode out to the farm and met her at the creek, away from the farmhouse and concealed from curious eyes by the trees and brush that grew along the stream. He brought food with him each time; not much, never more than a bit of flour or sugar or bacon, but it was all he could manage, and he was sure it helped sustain the Brannon family. He wanted to think so, anyway. As time passed, he and Cordelia became more comfortable with each other. She told him about her life, and he spoke of growing up in Ohio and teaching at the academy. Cordelia seemed especially interested in that. He sensed that she had a real thirst for education. She had attended school very little in her life. Perhaps when the war was over, he could do something to help her . . .

When those thoughts went through his head, he did his best to stifle them. It wouldn't do to think too much about what might happen after the war. The fighting was still going on. There was still plenty of dying to be done. He might still find himself in battle, and if that happened . . . if he had to kill some of Cordelia's countrymen . . . she might not feel the same way about him as she did now. Their friendship might be over before it had the opportunity to grow into something else.

For now, they had to live in the present and let the future take care of itself. And as the season edged toward autumn, the happiness he felt increased each time he saw her.

THIEVIN', SNEAKIN' *son of a bitch.* The lieutenant was taking food to the Rebels, Vernon McCafferty thought as he sat his horse on the crest of a rolling hill near the Brannon farm.

He knew that Lieutenant Keller had disappeared from time to time over the past few weeks, and he had wondered where the young officer was going. Keller never vanished when he was on duty; whatever errands he was carrying out, he did them when he wouldn't be missed. Finally, McCafferty's curiosity had gotten the better of him, and today he had followed the lieutenant.

Almost as soon as Keller rode out of Culpeper, McCafferty figured out where he was going.

The sergeant lifted a spyglass to his eye and squinted. Keller's figure appeared in the glass, seemingly brought closer. McCafferty watched him ride past the trees to the creek. Through the screen of brush and tree trunks, McCafferty kept his gaze fixed on the blue of Keller's uniform. A moment later, he saw a flash of reddish gold as well.

The Brannon girl had red hair. McCafferty remembered it well from the one time he had seen her, when the patrol picked up her brother. The girl was well worth noticing, he thought. She had a pretty face and big eyes and all that thick red hair. McCafferty's tongue came out and touched his lips as he remembered the curves of her body and the proud way her bosom filled the front of her dress. Yeah, she was a looker. He was willing to bet she would be a mighty sweet lover, too.

A fresh-faced kid like Keller didn't deserve anything that sweet, McCafferty told himself. The Brannon girl needed somebody older, somebody who could appreciate how truly fine she was. Somebody with some experience. Like him. A spitfire like that would need some taming, and Vernon McCafferty was just the man to give it to her.

He watched the play of movement through the trees, unable to tell exactly what they were doing over there. He could hazard a guess, though, and the images that possibility called up in his brain made him even more determined that he would have Cordelia Brannon for himself. He already had plans, big plans, and while Cordelia wasn't part of them, he saw no reason why he couldn't delay things long enough to pay her a visit. If she was impressed with Lieutenant Keller, just wait until she had herself a *real* man, McCafferty thought.

He grinned, closed the spyglass and stowed it away, then turned his horse and rode back toward Culpeper, his brain filled with visions of Cordelia Brannon and all the things he was going to do to her.

Chapter Thirteen

ENRY THOUGHT HE MUST be losing his mind. The smile on his sister's face looked like the smile of a woman in love. And that was impossible.

Yet he had seen a similar expression before—on Polly's face.

He had to believe that Polly had honestly loved him; otherwise nothing in his life had ever had any meaning and he might as well go mad. During those dark days when Titus's return from the dead had turned all their lives upside-down, Titus had hinted that Polly had had other reasons for marrying Henry, more disturbing reasons. There had been the baby, of course; Polly didn't want their child to be born out of wedlock. But she must have loved him, Henry thought, otherwise she never would have made love with him in the first place.

His own life was a thicket of emotion and tragedy, too tangled and dense for him to even try to make sense of it now. But one thing shone through: He had seen the smile of a woman in love often enough to recognize it, and he saw it on Cordelia's face now.

A chilly wind blew out of the northeast as Henry stood just inside the barn and watched her walk toward the creek. She had been spending more and more time down there lately. Sometimes she came back with a fish dangling from a stringer, and on those occasions, the Brannons and Louisa Abernathy had a decent meal for a change. Cordelia had been doing more of the cooking lately, along with Louisa, and it was amazing how they were able to make something out of nothing. But Cordelia wasn't catching enough fish to justify all the time she spent at Dobie's Run. Something odd was going on.

Henry decided he was going to find out what it was.

He let Cordelia get well away from the house before he started after her. Then he walked toward the creek, knowing she would head for the place where the stream made a bend and

211

formed a deep hole where fish liked to congregate. That is, he corrected himself, that's where she would go if fishing were really all she had in mind.

The sky was overcast. It would rain later, Henry thought as he glanced up at the clouds. Summer was over at last, and he was happy to see it go. Atlanta had fallen, Richmond was still threatened by the Yankees, and nothing good had happened for the Confederacy since the foe had been turned back at Cold Harbor. Even that victory had come at a high price. Before it had taken place, Gen. Jeb Stuart, the dashing cavalry commander who once had seemed invincible, had fallen at the battle of Yellow Tavern. Stuart's death mattered to the entire Confederate army, especially the cavalry, of which Henry's brother Mac was a member. The death of one infantry captain named Brannon hadn't been nearly as important in the great scheme of things . . . except to the people who had loved Will.

Henry shook those gloomy thoughts out of his head. He was faced with a mystery now in Cordelia's behavior, and he was determined to get to the bottom of it.

As a child, Henry had idolized his older brothers and wanted to be just like them. He wanted to be as tough as Will, as good with animals as Mac, as fine a shot as Titus, and as big a dreamer as Cory. It had taken a long time for Henry to accept the realization that he would never equal his brothers at any of those things, although he was better than average at most of them. Mac and Titus both had been able to move through the woods with the silent stealth of an Indian. Henry was almost as quiet as he slipped through the brush and trees along the bank of the creek. He paused from time to time to listen. He was rewarded when he heard the sound of voices up ahead.

He had been right, he told himself. Cordelia *was* meeting someone here at the stream. Henry couldn't figure out who it might be, though. Nearly all the eligible young men in the county had gone off to fight in the war. Of the ones who had come back, most were badly wounded or permanently crippled. The mere fact that Cordelia might have a beau didn't surprise Henry; she was a normal young woman, at least as far as he knew, and he recalled that she had been sweet on Nathan Hatcher at one time, before Nathan had turned out to be a Yankee-loving traitor.

Henry paused and debated furiously with himself. Though he couldn't make out the words, that was definitely his sister's voice he heard. Cordelia was talking to a man. Henry told himself that he had no right to interrupt them. A sudden merry laugh from Cordelia convinced him more than ever that she was in no trouble and that there was no real reason for him to interfere.

No reason other than the fact that she was his sister, and as her big brother he had a right . . . no, a responsibility . . . to keep an eye on her and make sure she was conducting herself as a proper young lady from Virginia should.

He slipped forward in a crouch, parting the bushes a little so he could peer through the tiny gap he had created.

What he saw shocked him to his depths. Cordelia was sitting on a fallen tree, smiling and talking and laughing with a young man who sat beside her.

And that young man wore the blue uniform of a *Yankee*.

As Henry watched, transfixed by surprise and anger, the Yankee turned his head to say something to Cordelia. Henry recognized the profile of Lt. Joseph Keller. That *wasn't* a surprise. He understood now why Keller had brought them the hams and why the lieutenant had taken such an interest in the Brannon family. It wasn't the rest of them Keller was interested in, just Cordelia. More than likely he had been smitten by her the first time he saw her. Putting aside the fact that she was his sister, Henry knew how pretty Cordelia was, and smart and compassionate to boot. A young man would have to be both blind and a fool not to take an interest in her.

But a *Yankee*, for God's sake! And from the looks of things, Cordelia was encouraging him. Henry's jaw tightened in anger as he saw her rest a hand lightly on Keller's arm while they talked. The intimacy of the gesture infuriated him.

He had to do something about this. He had to put a stop to it—now.

CORDELIA WASN'T sure exactly when things had changed between her and Joseph Keller. At first she didn't even know why she agreed to meet him at the creek several times a week. There were the supplies to consider, of course; the family really needed the provisions that Keller brought to them. And although she hated to think she was currying favor with the enemy, it might not hurt to have a friend in the Union camp in case of bad trouble. Cordelia didn't believe for an instant that Keller would betray his fellow soldiers or go against the commands of his superior officers in order to help the Brannon family, if it ever came down to that. He was too honorable for such behavior. But if he could do something to help them without compromising his principles, Cordelia thought that he would.

Above all else, she found that she enjoyed his company, enjoyed having a friend again. She and Louisa had become close during the time the older woman had spent on the farm, but that wasn't the same. Though she might have liked to deny it, if Cordelia was going to be honest with herself she had to admit that she liked Keller. She was even attracted to him.

And that attraction was returned. He made that clear by the way he looked at her and spoke to her in his kind, gentle voice. He had never done anything improper. In fact, the first time she had touched his arm as they talked, he had looked as if he wanted to pull away for fear of offending her. But he hadn't, and on subsequent visits she had been able to tell that he was growing more comfortable with her. She was certainly more relaxed around him. In fact, today she had thought that it might be time for her to take the initiative, to be daring and kiss him. He might think she was terribly forward, but she was ready to risk it. The only thing holding her back was the knowledge, ever present in the back of her mind, that he was a Yankee, a member of the army that had invaded her homeland and killed her brother. But not all Northerners were evil. She had never believed that, no matter what the firebrands and the staunch Confederates like her mother claimed. And she knew as well from the things Joseph had told her that he had never been in combat, had never been responsible for the deaths of any Southern boys.

The way she felt was an awful dilemma, and Cordelia didn't know what the answer was. Maybe Joseph could help her figure it out. She leaned closer to him, tipping her head back slightly so she could look up into his face. They had been laughing over something one of them had said—Cordelia didn't even remember what it was—but now they both grew solemn.

"Joseph . . ." she said, her voice barely above a whisper.

That was when her brother Henry burst out of the bushes nearby, shouting, "Cordelia! Get away from that Yankee!"

With a shocked gasp, she sprang to her feet and turned to face Henry. One of her hands went to her breast. Joseph stood up as well, his hand moving toward the flap of the holster at his waist.

"Henry!" Cordelia said. "What in the world—"

"I said get away from that Yankee!" Henry pointed a finger at Joseph. "Leave her alone, you bastard!"

"Hold on, Brannon," Joseph said, his voice shaking with barely repressed anger. "You can't talk to me like that."

"I'll talk to you any way I damned well please. This is still Brannon land."

"And it's under martial law and Federal jurisdiction."

Cordelia said, "Stop it, both of you!" She moved to place herself between them. "Henry, go on back to the house. There's no need for you to be here."

"The hell there's not. From what I saw, it looked like this damned Yankee was about to molest you!"

"That's not true at all!" Now her anger got the best of her, made her careless about what she was saying. "I'll have you know that *I* was about to kiss *him!*"

"What!" Henry said, outraged, while Joseph just stared. "You were?"

She turned briefly and swatted a hand against his broad chest. "Don't be such a . . . a dolt! Of course I was." Facing Henry again, she went on, "Lieutenant Keller is a gentleman. He would never take advantage of a woman."

Henry's fists were still clenched, and Keller still rested a hand on his holstered pistol. The air was thick with impending violence. Cordelia knew that if she budged from her position between them, something terrible might happen. So she stayed where she was and fixed a stern glare on her brother. Right now, she was more afraid of what he might do than she was of Joseph's possible reaction.

Henry had gone through a time of terrible tragedy and strain ever since Titus had returned the previous Christmas. He had seen his world torn apart and had lost both his wife and their unborn child. Cordelia feared that he might snap, and if he did, there was no telling what he might do.

Finally, Henry said, "This has been going on for weeks, hasn't it?"

"Nothing is going on," Cordelia said. "Lieutenant Keller and I are friends, that's all. He's been kind enough to bring us some more supplies whenever he could—"

"So that's how you've been doing it. I wondered where all that food came from." Henry's face was cold, merciless. "I never figured you were consorting with the enemy to get it."

"Henry Brannon, I've never consorted with anybody!"

"Be careful what you say, Brannon," Joseph put in. "I won't have you insulting Cordelia."

"You're the insult, just being here on our land," Henry said.

"Then perhaps I'd better go."

Cordelia turned toward Joseph. "No!" she said, but Henry nodded.

"That's a damned fine idea. Get the hell out of here and don't come back."

With his jaw tight, Joseph returned Henry's stare for a long moment then turned to Cordelia. "I regret any of my actions that may cause any trouble for you, Miss Brannon. I think you know that such was never my intention."

"Oh! Lieutenant Keller . . . Joseph . . . you don't have to go . . ." She clutched at his arm.

Gently, he disengaged her fingers from the sleeve of his uniform. "It's for the best." His eyes met hers. "You know that."

The worst of it was that she did know. Yes, it had been nice spending time with him. She had enjoyed talking to him. For the first time in months, perhaps even years, she felt truly alive again when she was around him. But there were things that could not be avoided forever, obstacles that could never be gotten around. The spectre of what the Yankees had done to Virginia, to the rest of the South, would always be between them. Maybe someday, long after the war was over, things would be different. But not now, certainly not now, and probably not for a long time to come.

"I'm sorry," she whispered.

"So am I." His hand found hers and squeezed it briefly. The touch was fleeting, but Cordelia knew she would never forget it. Joseph turned away and walked toward his horse. He jerked the reins loose from the bush where they were tied, swung up into the saddle, and gave Cordelia one last regretful glance before he turned his mount and rode away.

"Damned good riddance," Henry said.

"Oh!" Cordelia exclaimed again. She turned toward her brother and struck out at him, swinging a tightly clenched fist that caught him in the chest with enough force to make him take a backward step. He looked at her in surprise and anger.

"What in blazes was that for?"

"You had no right . . ." Cordelia tried hard not to cry, but a single sob escaped. "You had no right to do that."

"You can't be that upset because I ran him off. He's a Yankee, for God's sake!"

"He's a fine young man, and he was kind to us. You've been eating the food he brought, too."

"Don't think I don't know that." Henry grimaced. "Just the thought of it makes me sick."

"You'd rather starve to death?"

"Than take charity from a Yankee? You're damned right I would!"

Cordelia shook her head. She was wasting time, energy, and breath arguing with Henry. He would never understand. He had too much bitterness now, filling him up until there wasn't room for anything else. He couldn't admit that there might be good in anyone, especially a Yankee. She saw it in his eyes. He was just like Titus now, cold and hard and lifeless inside. The pang of regret she felt from the double loss she was suffering stabbed deep inside her.

She had lost a friend in Joseph and a brother as well. Henry had been claimed by the pain that consumed his soul.

And there was nothing Cordelia could do about either one.

LIEUTENANT KELLER looked like he was ready to cloud up and rain all over somebody when he got back to Culpeper, McCafferty thought. Things must not have gone well out at the Brannon farm. That was just too damned bad, he told himself with a sly smile. Keller wasn't going to get any more chances at the girl, not after today. McCafferty would see to that. The time had come for him to put his plan into action. He had modified it somewhat, because the more he thought about it, the less reason he could see why he couldn't just take Cordelia Brannon with him. Wherever he wound up going, she would sure as hell make the journey more enjoyable. And if she slowed him down too much . . .

Well, once he'd taken his pleasure with her, a knife across her throat would dispose of that problem in a hurry.

Like Keller, McCafferty was from Ohio, but unlike the studious lieutenant, the sergeant had grown up in Cleveland, orphaned at an early age and living on his own. In his youth he had earned a living unloading iron ore from the boats coming down from Lake Superior, through Lake Huron, and on to Lake Erie. The iron was bound for the blast furnaces in the Flats along the Cuyahoga River. That occupation had hardened McCafferty's muscles and also taught him that life was hard, as hard as the iron that came from those furnaces. If a man wanted something, he had to take it for himself, because sure as Hades nobody was going to give it to him.

The war had been a way for him to get away from the docks, and besides, he hated those damned Rebels. Bunch of lazy, no-good peckerwoods who sat around doing nothing all day while they made their darky slaves do all the work. The filthy bastards deserved whatever they got, according to McCafferty's way of thinking.

The problem was that he didn't like the army any more than he had been satisfied with his life in Cleveland. He still had to put up with being bossed around all the time; only now the ones giving him orders were a bunch of soft-handed sons of bitches who had the authority to do so only because somebody had decided to call them officers. They weren't like the hard-fisted bosses back on the docks who had earned the right to command because they knew how to stand up to life and smash it in the face. McCafferty could never respect a man like Keller, with his book-learning and his even-handed treatment of the Rebels.

So it was time to leave. Simple as that.

There was a chance the army wouldn't even bother coming after him. Washington had more to worry about than one deserter. They had all those Rebels to take care of. And today they would be even more distracted than usual, because the paymaster was coming in on the afternoon train. McCafferty hated to leave without collecting what was coming to him, but his best chance to slip away unnoticed would be when the men lined up to receive their pay. They wouldn't be thinking about much of anything else.

Keller went to his tent without saying anything to the sergeant, probably to brood about the Brannon girl. McCafferty saddled his horse and ambled down toward the depot, leading the animal.

The tracks of the Orange and Alexandria Railroad ran down to Culpeper from Manassas Junction. Now that the Federals controlled this entire area of Virginia, the trains were running regularly again, bringing supplies to Culpeper. The railroad brought the paymaster as well. McCafferty was at the station when the train rolled in on schedule and a colonel stepped down from one of the cars carrying a heavy leather pouch, followed by two guards. They were met by more soldiers, who escorted the paymaster and his guards to the big, red-brick house that had been commandeered to serve as army headquarters.

McCafferty watched them start down the street. He wasn't the only one. All the troops who were out and about turned to let their eyes follow the man who brought their money.

McCafferty swung up into the saddle and rode out of town without anyone paying the least bit of attention to him. Even the pickets were distracted and careless, as men usually were when they were posted behind the lines and in no real danger. That was exactly what McCafferty had been counting on. He should have gotten away clean.

"Sergeant! Sergeant McCafferty!"

With a curse, McCafferty reined in and hipped around in the saddle to see who was hailing him. He thought he recognized the voice, and as he saw the lieutenant galloping after him, he knew he was right. Why hadn't Keller stayed in his tent?

"Sergeant, where do you think you're going?" Keller asked as he rode up alongside McCafferty.

McCafferty gestured vaguely. "Just out for a short ride, Lieutenant. It's been awhile, and I figured this horse o' mine needed to stretch his legs a bit."

"You shouldn't be leaving town without authorization."

McCafferty held in a contemptuous snort. Keller was a fine one to talk about leaving without authorization. The lieutenant slipped away from headquarters several times a week to spark that Brannon gal and sneak food to her family. A family of Rebs, at that. But he didn't want to argue with Keller. That would just take up valuable time, and now that McCafferty had decided to make his move, he didn't want to waste a single minute.

He glanced around. The settlement was behind them, but some of the buildings were still visible about a quarter of a mile away. No patrols were in sight. In fact, McCafferty didn't see a soul anywhere. His hand dropped to the bayonet that was sheathed at his waist. Lowering his voice to a conspiratorial tone, he said, "You see, Lieutenant, the truth of it is . . ."

Frowning, Keller leaned closer to hear what he had to say.

McCafferty leaned toward Keller, too, and casually slipped the bayonet from its sheath. Taking the lieutenant completely by surprise, he lashed out, sinking the blade into his mid-section. Keller opened his mouth to yell, but before he could make a sound, McCafferty released the bayonet and back-handed him across the face, knocking him out of the saddle. Keller toppled off his horse and fell heavily on the ground. The animal shied away.

McCafferty was off his own horse in a heartbeat. He dropped to his knees beside Keller, intending to rip the lieutenant's belly open with the cold steel. Before he could do so, the sound of rapid hoofbeats came to his ears. He jerked his head up, eyes wide and frantic. He caught a glimpse of movement through some trees to the south.

That would be a routine patrol riding in, he thought. They weren't looking for him—yet. But in a matter of seconds, they would emerge from behind those trees and might see him. He leaped up, grabbed his horse's reins, and mounted hurriedly. Catching up the reins of Keller's horse, he kicked his mount into a trot. Keller lay on his back in some tall, dead grass that partially concealed him. It was possible no one in the patrol would notice him, at least not right away.

McCafferty cast one final glance at the lieutenant. Keller was unconscious, and his face was deathly pale. The front of his uniform was sodden with blood. He might even be dead already, McCafferty thought. If not, he would be soon.

The fleeing sergeant didn't waste any time getting away from there. He didn't rush, though, because he didn't want to draw attention to himself. If anyone in the patrol saw him, he wanted them to think he was just a trooper leading a spare horse, bound on some innocent errand, no doubt carrying out orders. That was the impression he wanted to give.

It must have worked, because no one came after him. He rode at least half a mile before pausing to look back. No pursuit was in sight. Now he could risk a gallop, and he urged his horse into a run that took him toward the Brannon farm.

Now to get that redheaded girl and put this part of the country—and the damned war—behind him forever.

ABIGAIL AND Louisa must have wondered what had happened when Henry and Cordelia came back to the house with such grim, angry looks on their faces. Neither of them volunteered to explain, however, and for once Abigail suppressed her curiosity and didn't demand to know what was going on. Cordelia was grateful for that much, anyway. She was in no mood to tell her mother about Lt. Joseph Keller. Abigail would never understand. To her, all Yankees were alike: enemies to be hated and despised. And Louisa was too meek to pry into something that didn't concern her.

As the afternoon went on, Cordelia found herself wishing she could talk to someone. Louisa already knew about Joseph's clandestine visits to the farm; Cordelia had had to tell her so she would have an ally in concealing the secret from Abigail and

Henry. So when she saw Louisa going to the barn late that afternoon, Cordelia gathered up her courage and went after her.

Abigail was in the kitchen. Cordelia didn't know where Henry was. He had spent a couple of hours splitting wood, probably to work off some of his anger and frustration by swinging the ax as hard as he could. Now he didn't seem to be anywhere around, though. Cordelia suspected he was walking in the fields or the woods, trying to calm down. She understood the feeling. Right now, she wasn't sure if she would ever be calm again.

She stepped into the barn, feeling a chill go through her as she moved into the shadows. The air was cool even on sunny days now, and soon there would be frost on the ground in the mornings. The seasons were changing, as change they must. Nothing ever stayed the same. That was a bittersweet inevitability when times were good, but in times of trouble, change sometimes brought relief.

"Louisa?" Cordelia said, not seeing the older woman. "Are you still in here?" She supposed Louisa could have gone out the back of the barn.

She stopped short as she saw something on the ground in front of her. Her eyes were still adjusting to the difference in light, and at first she couldn't make it out. Then, with a startled gasp, she realized the huddled shape was Louisa, lying unconscious on the dirt in the aisle that divided the barn. Cordelia hurried toward her friend.

She had taken only a couple of steps when someone grabbed her from behind, an arm looping across her chest so hard she couldn't breathe as a hand clamped roughly over her mouth to stifle any outcry. She felt herself pulled against a broad, muscular body as a voice hissed in her ear, "Take it easy, gal. You and me, we're goin' for a little ride."

Chapter Fourteen

As IF HE WERE a child half his age, Henry picked up a broken branch that had fallen from a tree and heaved it as hard as he could, letting out an explosive grunt of effort as he did so. He watched the branch spin through the air but took no satisfaction in how far he had thrown it. In earlier years, he probably would have grabbed up another branch and thrown it, too, just to see if he could beat the first toss. Now, though, he was just letting off steam. Trying to, rather, because it wasn't working. He was just as upset now as he had been when he left the house to take this walk.

How could Cordelia have done such a thing? Keller was a Yankee. The enemy. One of the invaders who were devastating the South. If things had been different . . . if he had met some Northern girl, say . . . he wouldn't have fallen for her, no matter how pretty she was or how lonely he was. And Lord knew he was lonely these days. But he wouldn't have let himself feel anything except contempt for a Yankee. He couldn't. He was too loyal to the Confederacy.

So why had she done it? he asked himself again. Why had Cordelia betrayed her homeland and her family?

It wasn't for the supplies Keller had been bringing, Henry was sure of that. The family could have made do without those. It was true that all of them had lost weight and were starting to look a little gaunt, but they were still a long way from starving. It hadn't been a matter of life and death.

Could it have been solely because Cordelia was, well, smitten with the Yankee? Henry supposed it was possible. As a male, he knew it was impossible for him to comprehend fully how any woman's mind worked, even a member of his own family. The question was, did that make it better or worse? What was the biggest betrayal?

And what gave him the right to pass judgment on his sister in the first place? A nagging voice in the back of his head asked that question, and he wished it would just go away.

He had to admit to some truth in the implied accusation. His own life was hardly perfect, his own behavior far from exemplary. He had gotten his brother's wife pregnant, after all, and then married her, making her a bigamist. True, none of them had known that at the time, but still . . .

Then he had allowed things to spiral out of control until Polly wound up dead. Again, that hadn't been his fault, at least not directly, but he couldn't help but think that if he had done things differently, she might still be alive. By now they would be the parents of a beautiful baby, a son or daughter who would have been a proud addition to the Brannon family.

Henry shuddered and put his hands over his face. He felt the tears coming and could do nothing to hold them back. The power of his sobs shook him to the very depths of his being.

He would have thought he was cried out months before, but that proved not to be the case. All the grief he had buried came welling back up. A part of him wondered if he would ever put it behind him for good.

At first he barely heard the screams. They were faint but still audible, drifting through the crisp autumn air from the house and the barn. Henry lowered his hands and felt the cold bite of the wind on cheeks wet with tears. Something was wrong. The screams were cut short with a frightening abruptness. Henry took a step, then another, then broke into a run.

The sudden crack of a shot made him go even faster. He was seized by an awful fear that whatever was wrong, he was going to be too late . . .

CORDELIA DIDN'T recognize the voice of the man who had her in an iron grip, and for the moment, she was too frightened to worry about such things. She just wanted to get *loose*. Panic raced through her veins. She struggled, but he was too strong for her. She was afraid for herself and afraid for Louisa as well. What had the man done to her?

She felt herself dragged across the barn and heard the stamping sound of horses moving around nervously. "Quit fightin'!" the man ordered her. "I'll wallop you if I have to. I will, and don't you forget it!"

Cordelia thought she had heard the voice before, but she still had no idea who it belonged to. The man whirled her around and thrust her toward one of the horses. From the corner of her eye, she caught a glimpse of Louisa stirring slightly on the ground. At least she was still alive, Cordelia thought in relief. The man hadn't killed her.

The callused hand went away from her mouth, but before she could cry out, the man stuffed a rag between her lips. It tasted horrible, and she gagged on it, trying to spit it out. The man cuffed her on the back of the head, stunning her.

"Get up there," he said. He shoved and lifted, and Cordelia found herself being thrown across a saddle.

Behind her, Louisa sat up and screamed.

The attacker couldn't be in two places at once. If he went to silence Louisa, Cordelia could slip down from the horse and run away. Clearly, he didn't want that to happen, because he stayed at Cordelia's side, shoving her forward and using a cord to lash her wrists together around the neck of the horse. Now she couldn't dismount.

Wildly, Cordelia twisted her head toward the man, and for the first time got a good look at him. She recognized the burly shape and the heavy-jawed face, and after a second she knew where she had seen him before. He was the Yankee sergeant who had been with the patrol Joseph led to the Brannon farm, back when Henry had been summoned to town. She didn't recall his name, but she remembered that he seemed to have an intense dislike of the people he considered Rebels. Now his face wore a murderous glare, and she knew he wouldn't hesitate to kill anyone who got in his way.

Still screaming, Louisa pushed herself to her feet and ran unsteadily toward them. In the dimming light, Cordelia could make out the bloody welt and lump on Louisa's forehead where the sergeant must have struck her earlier, knocking her unconscious as she came into the barn. Now she flailed at the burly sergeant, her fists bouncing futilely off his chest. He shoved her away, sending her tumbling off her feet again.

He swung around and grabbed the reins of the second horse. Cordelia knew that if he rode off, leading the horse with her on it, no one would be able to catch them. There were no other mounts on the Brannon farm. She pulled desperately at the cord binding her wrists but was unable to loosen it.

The sergeant mounted up and started toward the open doors of the barn, leading the horse Cordelia was on. Louisa scrambled to her feet and came after them, clutching at the harness of the sergeant's mount. She shrieked for help. Cordelia wondered where her mother and Henry were. Surely they had heard the screams by now.

Cursing, the sergeant drew his foot out of the stirrup and kicked Louisa in the chest, sending her flying backward. He drew his pistol and twisted in the saddle, firing across his body at her. Cordelia screamed against the filthy rag in her mouth as she saw blood fly through the air, but the only sound that came out was a muffled squeak.

Tears welled from Cordelia's eyes, tears of terror and sorrow. Again, she didn't know if Louisa was alive or dead, only that her friend was hurt.

The sergeant urged both horses out of the barn and into the yard. Cordelia saw Abigail burst out of the house onto the porch. She tried to scream a warning, but no words came past the rag. Seeing movement, the sergeant threw a hurried shot toward the house. Cordelia flinched at the sound of the blast. Splinters exploded from the porch railing as the bullet struck it. Abigail ducked back through the still-open door, evidently unhurt by the shot.

Please, God, don't let him hurt my mother! Cordelia prayed. She didn't care about herself anymore. She just wanted the sergeant to get away from here without harming anyone else. If that meant she had to go with him and submit to whatever he meant to do to her, then so be it.

He kicked his horse into a run and headed past the barn, dragging the other mount behind him. Cordelia was hanging on for dear life now. Her position on the back of the horse was none too stable, and she knew that if she fell, being tied on as she was, she would wind up being dragged under the slashing hooves of the animal.

As they galloped past the corner of the barn, Henry suddenly appeared, sprinting in from the fields. He leaped to the top of the stump that was used for splitting wood, hitting it with one foot as he launched himself in a flying tackle toward the sergeant. His arms went around the man as he crashed into him, driving him out of the saddle and off the horse.

Loose now, Cordelia's horse raced on by. She tugged up on its neck as hard as she could, trying to get it to stop. The horse slowed then came to a halt, but it wasn't motionless. It still danced around skittishly. Cordelia struggled to bring the animal under control.

Finally, she made the horse turn so that she could see what was happening. Henry and the sergeant rolled on the ground, locked in a grim, desperate battle. The sergeant had dropped his pistol when Henry knocked him off the horse, thank goodness, but now he was trying to get his hands around Henry's throat and choke the life out of him. Henry fended off the attack as best he could, but the sergeant was heavier and stronger than him. The man's knee came up and smashed into Henry's groin, making him cry out in agony and curl up on the ground. The sergeant straightened him by smashing a fist to his jaw. With a decided advantage now, the man locked his hands around Henry's throat.

Acting purely on instinct, Cordelia banged her heels against the sides of her mount and sent the horse leaping forward. She guided it as best she could toward the two men lying on the ground. The sergeant heard the thunder of hoofbeats and looked up to see the horse bearing down on him. With an inarticulate yell, he threw himself to the side, out of the way.

Henry was alert enough to roll the other direction. The horse passed between him and the sergeant. Again Cordelia fought to bring the animal under control and turn it around. As she succeeded in doing so, she saw Henry on his hands and knees, scrambling toward the gun the sergeant had dropped. It lay in the dirt several yards from him.

But behind him, the sergeant had regained his feet and snatched up the ax that had been leaning against the stump. Raising the sharp-bladed tool above his head, he hurled himself toward Henry.

Finally, Cordelia managed to spit out the awful-tasting rag jammed in her mouth. "Henry! Behind you!" she called out.

Henry's extended hand slapped down on the gun butt. He rolled over, bringing up the weapon as his thumb looped over the hammer and pulled it back. The revolver roared. Flame geysered from its barrel, followed by billowing smoke. The sergeant loomed over Henry, about to bring the ax sweeping down in a killing blow, but he jerked backward as the bullet smashed into his chest. It looked like he had been snatched away from Henry by a giant, invisible hand, Cordelia thought. The ax slipped from his fingers and went spinning away. He landed on his back, staring up at the late afternoon sky with eyes that were turning glassy already. A dark pool of blood spread from underneath him.

The echoes of the shot faded gradually away, leaving behind a tense, eerie silence. Cordelia could hear only her own breath rasping in her throat. She leaned against the horse's neck and felt faint.

Henry climbed to his feet and walked slowly over to the sergeant's sprawled body. He cocked the gun again and kept it trained on the man until he seemed sure the sergeant was dead. Then he turned to his sister.

"Cordelia! Cordelia, are you all right?"

Before she could answer, her mother ran out of the house, crying her name. Abigail came down the steps from the porch and hurried toward the horse.

Cordelia's throat was raw, and she had trouble speaking, but she managed. "Louisa's in the barn. She . . . she's hurt!"

Henry turned and rushed inside the barn. Abigail reached the horse and started plucking futilely at Cordelia's bonds. "Are you all right?" she asked.

"I . . . I'm fine," Cordelia said. Other than being shaken from the ordeal, that was the truth. She hadn't been hurt. But she couldn't say the same for Louisa, who had been hit by the shot the sergeant had fired inside the barn.

"Ma, you're going to have to get the ax to cut that cord," Cordelia told her mother. "The knot's too tight to untie."

Abigail nodded and turned away from the horse. She started toward the ax, which was lying on the ground nearby, then stopped short as she realized she would have to walk toward the dead Yankee sprawled in the yard. Cordelia watched as her mother glared at the man for a long moment, and then Abigail did something that shocked Cordelia, even after everything that had happened already.

She spat on the corpse.

Then she picked up the ax and released her daughter. It was a delicate operation, and Abigail had to be careful not to cut her as well. But after a moment, the cord fell away from Cordelia's wrists, and she was free.

She slipped off the horse but clutched at its mane and leaned against the animal for a moment as her strength deserted her. Her mother put an arm around her shoulders. "Come in the house," Abigail said. "You need to lie down."

Cordelia turned her head and looked toward the barn. "I can't . . . Louisa was hurt. That . . . that man shot her . . ."

She slid out of her mother's embrace and started toward the barn. Abigail hurried after her. Before they could reach the barn, Henry came through the open doors, carrying Louisa. She looked small and helpless, cradled in his arms that way.

"I think she'll be all right," Henry said. "The bullet hit her in the arm. I'm not sure if any of the bones are broken."

Abigail's natural strength came to the fore. "Take her in the house," she ordered briskly. "Put her on the sofa in the parlor. Cordelia, do you feel up to heating some water on the stove?"

"Of course, Ma."

"Go do that, then. We'll clean the wound and get it bandaged." Abigail reached out and pushed back some of the curly, dark red hair that had fallen over Louisa's face. "Poor dear. Knowing this family has brought her nothing but trouble."

Henry carried the unconscious woman into the house. His mother and sister followed, leaving the dead man behind without so much as a backward glance.

DUSK WAS settling over the Virginia countryside as Henry emerged from the house later. He had the pistol tucked behind his belt. He went down the steps and walked over to the body of the Yankee sergeant.

McCafferty, that was his name, Henry recalled as he looked down at the dead man. Other than that, Henry didn't know a blessed thing about the man except that he had hated Confederates. In fact, McCafferty had struck him as the sort of man who hated just about everybody. Even in death, his face looked truculent and full of rage.

He was the only man Henry had ever killed. A feeling of sickness clenched Henry's insides. He would have killed the man who had taken Polly's life if he'd had the chance, but fate had denied him that opportunity. Instead he had been forced to cross that threshold of taking another life in the heat of combat, when he had acted without thinking, firing to save his own life and the lives of his loved ones.

Henry knew that under the same circumstances, he would have done exactly the same thing again. He wouldn't lose any sleep over McCafferty's death. Still, a fella couldn't just step back from something this big, this portentous, without stopping to reflect for a minute. He dragged the back of his hand across his mouth and took a deep breath.

The worst of it was, the son of a bitch was a Yankee. The others would come looking for the sergeant, and when they found his body, they wouldn't be interested in what had happened or how it had happened. They wouldn't listen to reason, wouldn't let anyone explain. They would just arrest the man responsible for McCafferty's death and either hang him or put him in front of a firing squad.

Henry thought furiously. They could drag McCafferty's body into the woods and bury it, but that might not do any good. The sergeant might have told someone before he left Culpeper that he would be coming to the farm. Even if he hadn't, some of the soldiers might have seen him coming in this direction. Henry couldn't imagine Colonel Avery letting the sergeant's disappearance go without an investigation. Sooner or later, the Yankees would find the corpse. Even if they didn't, they were likely to blame him anyway.

As far as Henry could see, there was only one thing he could do that would avoid retaliation.

A few minutes later, Cordelia came out of the house and found him in the barn. He had led both horses in there and tied them to a post. Now he brought a pair of saddlebags out of the tack room and slung them over the back of one of the mounts.

"How's Louisa?" Henry asked before his sister could demand to know what he was doing.

"She's awake now." Her voice was hoarse from screaming and from being gagged. "Ma says she'll be all right if she doesn't come down with blood poisoning."

"Don't reckon there's too much chance of that, not as clean as Ma keeps everything, including bullet holes."

"Henry . . ." Cordelia put a hand on his arm. "What are you doing? Are you going somewhere?"

He had known he couldn't keep her from asking any questions, but that didn't mean he had to answer them. "Did she say anything about what happened when McCafferty jumped her the first time?"

"McCafferty," Cordelia repeated. "That was his name. I remember it now." She shook her head. "No, Louisa couldn't really tell us what happened. She didn't even know he was there until he hit her and knocked her out."

"He must have been hiding in the barn, waiting for one of us to come out here." Henry checked the cinch on the saddle.

"But why? What did he want?"

Henry shrugged. "Who knows? Yankees don't have to have a good reason for the hell they put us through. Just look around, Cordelia. Look at what they've done all over the South."

"This didn't have anything to do with the war."

He looked sharply at her. "You sound mighty sure of that."

It was hard to tell in the shadows, but he thought Cordelia blushed. "McCafferty wanted me. He came here to kidnap me and . . . and . . ."

"Well, he won't ever bother any other girls anywhere," Henry cut in, his voice hard. "I'm glad he's dead, and not just because he's a Yankee."

For a moment, Cordelia couldn't say anything. Then she realized what her brother was about to do. "You still haven't told me what you're doing or where you're planning to go, Henry."

He nodded. "As far away from here as I can get."

Her hand tightened on his arm. "No!"

"It's the only thing we can do, Cordelia," he said with a sigh. "I thought about trying to hide McCafferty's body, but the Yankees are sure to come looking for him, and they're likely to find him, no matter what we do. When they do, they won't care what

he did to Louisa or what he tried to do to you. They'll just exe-
cute me for killing him. Probably call me a guerrilla, like those
rangers of Mosby's over in the Shenandoah. The only way to protect you and Ma and Louisa is for me not to be here when they
come. That way maybe they'll go after me and leave you alone."

She shook her head. "No, Henry. Please—"

"Tell them that I'd got hold of a gun somewhere and I shot
McCafferty as soon as he rode up. You and Ma and Louisa didn't
have any part of it. It was all my doing." He turned slightly and
put his hands on Cordelia's shoulders, holding tightly to her.
"You hear that? *It was all my doing.*"

Tears began to roll down her face. "But Henry, if you go, we
. . . we'll be alone here . . ."

"I know it. Don't think I haven't thought about that. But
you'll be safer in the long run this way. Just like . . . just like
when Will had to leave, so that the Fogartys wouldn't come after
the rest of us."

"And we were all mad at Ma for running him off when that
happened, remember?" A note of desperation crept into her
voice. "Henry, we're a family. God knows we've gotten scattered
over the past few years, but there are still a few of us here. This is
Brannon land. We belong here. You belong here."

A sad smile touched his face. "You're right. Maybe after the
war, I can come back. It can't last too much longer, not the way
it's going now." He pulled Cordelia to him, hugging her fiercely.
"I'm sorry," he whispered. "This is the only way."

She clutched at him, shuddery sobs running through her
body. Henry held her for a long moment, then gently pushed her
back. "I'm taking both horses," he said. "Reckon I'll probably
have to switch out to stay ahead of the Yankees."

"Wh-where are you planning to go? To find Mac and join the
cavalry?"

"I thought about that. But you know how Mac is. He'd pitch
a fit and tell me that my place was here at the farm. Leaving here
is hard enough without that. I hear that General Hood is down in

Tennessee now. I thought I might see if I can get over there and join up with him."

"The last of the Brannons to join the army," Cordelia said almost wistfully.

"We don't know that. We don't know where Cory is or what he's doing."

"No, but if he's still alive, I'll bet he's fighting the Yankees. Sooner or later, this damnable war draws everyone into it."

Henry couldn't argue with that. For years, ever since the fighting had begun, a part of him had felt like he was letting down his country and his fellow countrymen by not serving. Now that the time had come when that appeared to be his only option, he suddenly wished he didn't have to go.

He leaned forward and kissed Cordelia on the forehead. "Don't tell Ma until after I'm gone."

"She'll be mad as an old wet hen."

Henry gave a hollow laugh. "I reckon you're right. You're getting the worst of it, though. All I have to do is dodge some patrols and go off to fight Yankees. You have to deal with Ma."

She hugged him again, hard. "You be careful, hear?"

"I will. And I'll be back. That's a promise. When the war's over, you look for me, because I'll be coming up the road to home and you and Ma."

"I'll look," Cordelia whispered, and minutes later, as Henry rode slowly away from the farm into the gathering darkness, the words lingered in his mind like a sad, fading breeze.

THE SWIFT rataplan of hoofbeats drew Cordelia and Abigail out of the house and onto the porch. Light from the open door spilled around them. Behind them in the parlor, Louisa Abernathy slept peacefully on the divan, her wounded arm bandaged. Later, after she had rested some, they would move her upstairs to her bedroom.

For now, though, they had Yankees to deal with.

The group of riders swept up to the house, reining in as an officer called out a command to halt. Cordelia saw a man she didn't recognize, but the colonel's rank was easy enough to make out. He had to be Colonel Avery, she suspected, the area commander who thought every Southerner he encountered was a Confederate spy.

Without greeting the two women on the porch, the colonel issued orders to his men. "Break out those torches and search the house, the barn, and any of the outbuildings. If McCafferty's here, I will find him!"

"You won't have to look very far, Colonel," Abigail called from the front step. She pointed. "He's right over there."

The officer turned a stony expression toward the women. "Good evening, madam," he said stiffly. "Do I understand you correctly? Sergeant McCafferty is here?"

"He's here, and he's not going anywhere."

"Colonel!" a trooper shouted. "The sarge is dead!"

"Dead!" Avery repeated in surprise.

Abigail placed an arm around Cordelia's shoulders. "That man attacked and almost killed a friend of ours who's staying with us. And he tried to kidnap my daughter. We had no choice but to defend ourselves."

Avery leaned forward in the saddle. "You're saying that *you* killed Sergeant McCafferty, madam?"

Cordelia had argued up one way and down the other with her mother, explaining to her what Henry had said and what he wanted them to tell the Yankees. Although she had not discussed it specifically with Henry before he rode out, she intended to tell the Yankees that he would be going down to Petersburg to see about joining up with Robert E. Lee and what was left of the Army of Northern Virginia, rather than heading for Tennessee and Gen. John Bell Hood. She didn't think the Yankees would be able to catch Henry, but at the least, she wanted to put them onto the wrong trail anyway.

Abigail, on the other hand, had insisted on telling whoever came looking for McCafferty that she had killed the sergeant. "They won't do anything to me," she had insisted. "A mother protecting her child has a right to do whatever is necessary. Even a Yankee can see that."

Cordelia wasn't so sure. She had heard stories about how some Southern women had been thrown in jail for spying and other crimes against the Yankees. She didn't like to think about how her mother would fare if she was taken away and put in some Northern prison.

But once Abigail had made up her mind, it was almost impossible to persuade her to do otherwise. Now she said in answer to Avery's question, "Yes, I did. The man deserved to be shot like an animal."

Cordelia flinched a little at the proud defiance in her mother's voice. Abigail wasn't making it easy for the Yankees to let her get away with this. The colonel might think he had to make an example of this feisty Southern woman.

But Avery just nodded, as if he were agreeing with her. "I truly regret this man's actions, madam."

Cordelia tried not to stare. A Yankee apologizing? To a Confederate? It was almost unthinkable.

An even bigger surprise was in store for her. One of the other men edged his horse forward. Cordelia saw that he was hunched over in the saddle, and men on either side of him held his arms to support him, like he was hurt. As he lifted his face, Cordelia gasped at the sight of Lt. Joseph Keller's strained features.

"Cordelia," Keller asked. "Are you all right?"

She ignored the soldiers, ignored her mother as well, and hurried down the steps to go to his side. She caught hold of his hand and looked up at him. "What happened to you?"

"McCafferty stabbed me when he deserted."

"Oh, my God!"

Joseph squeezed her hand. "Don't worry. The surgeons say I was lucky. The blade didn't hit anything vital. I'll be all right."

"You ought to be in a hospital!"

"That's what the surgeons told me," Joseph said with a smile. "But I made them bandage me up so tight I can hardly breathe instead. I knew McCafferty was heading this way, so I had to be sure you were all right."

Colonel Avery announced, "We'll take charge of the, ah, corpus. Again, Mrs. Brannon, my apologies for this incident. Though you perhaps won't believe it, my men are not barbarians. War or no war, I demand civilized behavior."

For one of the few times in Cordelia's life, she saw that her mother didn't seem to know what to say. Finally, Abigail nodded grudgingly. "Thank you," she replied. That must have cost her, Cordelia thought, expressing gratitude that way to a Yankee.

Cordelia looked up at Joseph. "You should go back and rest, so you can recover from that wound."

"Yes, I will. Thank you for your concern, Miss Brannon."

Anyone who had been watching and listening to them a few moments earlier would realize what a sham the lieutenant's sudden formality was. But neither he nor Cordelia wanted to flaunt what was between them, so Cordelia squeezed his hand again then stepped back. Several of the soldiers slung McCafferty's body over the back of a horse and tied it there. The Yankees turned their mounts and rode away from the farm. Cordelia stood at the bottom of the steps and watched them go.

From the porch, Abigail said, "You seemed awfully friendly with that young man, Cordelia."

She didn't want to have that argument with her mother right now. Instead, she said, "You know what this means, about that man McCafferty being a deserter, don't you, Ma?"

"It means your brother didn't have to leave," she answered. "The Yankees weren't after him at all. But how can we tell him the news? How can we bring him back now? We don't even know for sure where he was going."

Cordelia stared into the darkness and knew her mother was right. Henry was out there somewhere, riding through the night and thinking he was a fugitive. They had no way to find him, no way to catch up to him and tell him the truth. He was gone. The last of the Brannon boys, off to war at last.

And all they could do was pray that the Lord would watch over Henry and bring him home safely.

Chapter Fifteen

TO SOMEONE RAISED IN the heaven that was Virginia, this Dakota Territory had the appearance of pure hell, Nathan Hatcher thought as he trudged along, dust swirling around him that had been kicked up by the marching feet of the regiment, the weight of a carbine painfully heavy on his shoulder. The afternoon sun beat down on the column with an uncomfortable heat. Beads of sweat trickled through the layer of dust coating his face. Swelter in the day, freeze at night. Except when the big sky opened up and poured down pelting sheets of rain, as it had the day before. That was what these soldiers had to put up with. But in a few more months, after they had reached their destination, Fort Rice, winter would set in, and for months there would be nothing but cold and snow and ice. At least, that was what Nathan had heard.

He didn't care. Anything was better than wasting away in a Yankee prison camp. Better to die on the plains than in some dank, dark hole of a prison cell.

He wore the blue woolen uniform of the First U.S. Volunteer Regiment. This wasn't the first time Nathan had worn the blue. Back in the early days of the war, he had left his home in Culpeper County, Virginia, to go north and enlist in the Union army. That decision had cost him a great deal, most notably the friendship of Cordelia Brannon. In private moments, Nathan had dared to hope that someday there might be more than friendship between them . . . but that hope had died when he told her that because of his loathing for slavery he could not support the Confederacy.

The Brannons were not slaveholders and had no great fondness for the practice, Nathan knew. But they *were* Virginians, and they would fight to the death to protect their home from what they saw as an unwarranted invasion. Nathan could almost bring himself to see the matter from their point of view. Almost, but not quite.

So he had left and joined the enemy, and his Southern drawl had caused him much grief during his time among the Northerners. But he had been willing to put up with that in order to do his part for what he believed to be the noblest of causes. Then, in a freakish twist of fate, an encounter with a Confederate deserter during the battle of Fredericksburg had resulted in the man's changing uniforms with Nathan. Back in Confederate gray, with the distinctive accent of the South dripping from his every word, Nathan had been unable to convince a group of Yankee captors that he was really one of them. With no papers to prove otherwise, he had been deemed a Confederate prisoner of war and sent to the infamous Camp Douglas, a sprawling piece of hellish ground just outside Chicago, Illinois. It was there he had been reunited with an acquaintance from back home, none other than Cordelia's brother Titus. Eventually, after months of suffering the torments of the damned, Nathan and Titus had escaped from the camp with the help of a young Quaker woman, Louisa Abernathy. During the arduous journey back to Virginia, however, Nathan had been recaptured.

Convinced that he was going to die in captivity, Nathan had been on the verge of giving up any hope when fate intervened once again. The U.S. Army began to recruit prisoners who were willing to renounce their allegiance to the Confederacy and swear an oath of loyalty to the Union. Though Nathan no longer believed in the high-minded self-righteousness with which the Federals cloaked themselves, he jumped at the chance to get out of prison any way he could. He had been one of the first prisoners to swear the oath, and now he was a member of the First U.S. Volunteers. All the regiment's enlisted men had been drawn from Yankee prisoner of war camps, though the officers were all regular army. They had spent six months training at Union-held Norfolk, Virginia, under the watchful eyes of the Yankee officers, who were alert for any signs of preparation for desertion.

Being that close to home had been painful for Nathan. Despite all reason, despite knowing that she now hated him, he wanted to see Cordelia again. He wondered if Titus had made it back safely to the Brannon farm. But he had sworn an oath and knew he had to be true to it.

Then the orders everyone had been waiting for finally came. The regiment was going west to fight Indians. Given the fact that the country was at war, the savages on the western frontier had become bolder than ever in their raids and depredations. The U.S. Volunteers were to put a stop to such things.

From Virginia they had been taken by transport ship to New York, where they boarded a train bound for Chicago. At Chicago, the regiment was split; four of the companies were to be posted to Milwaukee, Wisconsin, while the other six companies were bound for St. Louis and from there to their ultimate destination, an isolated outpost in the Dakota Territory known as Fort Rice.

They had left St. Louis on the riverboat *Effie Deans*, chugging the short distance up the Mississippi to the point where the Missouri River joined the Father of Waters. The *Effie Deans* veered into the channel of the Missouri and began making its laborious way upstream. The going was slow because of low water; the boat had to follow carefully the twists and turns of the river's channel. After a full month of traveling, the riverboat had gone as far as it could go. Sandbars that were impassable because of the low level of the river barred the way. The men of the regiment had to disembark and prepare for a march upriver to Fort Rice. The distance was a little more than 270 miles, over terrain that was flat, almost totally devoid of trees, and lacking good water.

Grass grew out here, but little else. To Nathan, who had grown up in a land covered with trees and shrubs and flowers, Dakota looked particularly barren and unappealing. But he was alive, and the air he drew into his lungs, though dust-laden, was free air. Months of having regular rations had restored the strength to his wasted body that had been sapped away by the ordeal in prison.

So, all in all, he was glad to be in the Dakota Territory. He just wished they would get where they were going.

The regiment had been marching for three days since leaving the riverboat. From what Nathan had heard speculated by the sergeants, they ought to be nearing the Crow Creek Agency, a small outpost where peaceful Indians congregated. Nathan had never seen an Indian before, and he had mixed emotions about the prospect. On the one hand, he firmly believed that they were God's creatures, too. But on the other hand, he had heard all the stories about how vicious and bloodthirsty they could be. He knew the U.S. Volunteers had been sent to Dakota to fight and subdue the savages. Violence and danger were inevitable. But that didn't mean he had to look forward to it.

Despite those feelings, he experienced a surge of relief when he and several other members of the column spotted tendrils of smoke in the air several miles ahead of them.

"That'll be Crow Creek," Patrick Cardwell said to Nathan.

Cardwell and Nathan had become friends, since both were Virginians. Cardwell had been raised on a small farm much like the one owned by the Brannons.

One thing set Cardwell apart from the rest of the regiment, however: His wife had come west with him.

Elizabeth Cardwell was a petite, pretty young woman who had come to Norfolk to visit her husband after receiving the news that Patrick had enlisted in the U.S. Volunteers and would be training there. Through sheer determination and her ability to charm the regiment's officers, she had talked her way into accompanying the soldiers to New York on the transport ship. Then she had insinuated herself on the train carrying them to Chicago. At each step of the journey, unlikely though it seemed, Elizabeth had been able to convince the regimental commanders to let her come along, until now she was marching alongside her husband through this desolate territory. Nathan would not have believed such a thing possible if he had not seen it with his own eyes.

"I hope there's another woman there," Elizabeth said. "It would be quite pleasant to see a female face and hear a female voice after being surrounded by you men for so long."

Patrick laughed. "I wouldn't wager on that. I daresay there aren't many women anywhere in this Godforsaken territory except the redskinned ones. What do you think, Nathan?"

"I don't have any idea," Nathan said with a shake of his head. "Everything about this place is new to me."

"Aye. That's the truth."

A short time later they came within sight of the agency itself: a compound surrounded by a stockade fence made of cedar pickets that must have been hauled in by wagon from elsewhere, since trees were in such short supply here. Sprawled around the stockade was an Indian settlement, a scattering of conical dwellings that appeared to be made of some sort of animal hide. Many of them had crude, garish symbols and drawings daubed on them. Dirty-faced children and scrawny dogs ran around frantically, for no apparent reason, while the adults of the village stood and stared at the marching soldiers. Men and women alike wore buckskin clothing and had blankets draped around them. Their thick black hair had been greased down with animal tallow and shone in the sunlight. Some of the men wore feathers in their hair as adornments. Their faces were solemn, their eyes so dark they seemed to be bottomless pits. Nathan had never seen anything like them.

Col. Charles Augustus Dimon, the commander of the regiment, called a halt and then strode forward to greet the post commander, who came out of the crude fort at the head of a small detail of soldiers. Elizabeth Cardwell was thrilled when a woman emerged from the fort as well, arm in arm with a man dressed in civilian clothes rather than a uniform. Elizabeth hurried forward, and the two women embraced, even though they had never seen each other before this moment. Nathan learned later from Patrick that the civilian couple ran a school here at the agency, where they endeavored to teach English and the ways of the white man's civilization to the children of the Crow tribe. The regiment wasn't there long enough for Nathan to be able to form an opinion on how successful their efforts were. Looking at the filthy, screeching Indian children, however, it seemed to Nathan that civilizing them would be an impossible task.

After resting at the agency for three days, the column started north along the river again, taking with them some oxen, wagons, and supplies borrowed from the outpost. With each mile, the landscape became more barren. Grass was sparse. The most common vegetation was in the form of clumps of low, prickly cactus. The men quickly learned to avoid getting anywhere near these plants, as the stickers they bore seemed almost to leap from them and pierce the clothing and flesh of anyone who ventured close to them.

The Missouri River made a good landmark; as long as the soldiers marched alongside it, they couldn't miss the outposts to the north. But that was just about all it was good for. The water was so muddy it was undrinkable, more like a thick soup than actual water. Small ponds of rainwater had collected here and there on the plains, but they were stagnant, and drinking from them meant risking a bout of severe stomach cramps and diarrhea. The men did without as long as they could, but thirst eventually forced them to drink from the ponds. Sickness was rampant.

Somehow, Nathan avoided the illness, as did Patrick and Elizabeth Cardwell. Elizabeth continued to march beside her husband, even though Colonel Dimon told her that she could ride in one of the wagons if she wished. She just smiled at him. "I've gone through a great deal to remain with Patrick, Colonel, so with your permission I'll walk with him awhile longer."

Dimon was a disciplinarian, almost a martinet. On the riverboat, he had had one of the soldiers executed by a firing squad for attempting to desert. But not even he was going to argue with the strong-willed Elizabeth. She was allowed to stay with Patrick.

The next outpost was Fort Sully, named for the commander of the troops in the entire territory, Gen. Alfred Sully. When the

USV arrived at Fort Sully, they found the old warhorse himself, out on patrol with a force of soldiers from Fort Rice. Colonel Dimon introduced himself to Sully and presented his men. It was still 170 miles to Fort Rice, and with the experienced eye of a veteran commander, Sully saw that the Volunteers weren't in very good shape. He gave them what supplies he could spare, and after a short rest the column again moved on.

A few days later, the raging dysentery claimed its first victim, a young private from Kentucky who had to be buried alongside the river. As a member of the burial detail, Nathan patted down the mound of freshly turned dirt with his shovel and wondered if he would live to see Fort Rice. Had he left that hellhole of a Yankee prison only to die out here on the prairie?

He stepped away from the grave and wiped the back of his hand across his mouth. Even if he did die out here, it was better this way, he told himself. Better to die in the open, in the sunlight, than in a cell.

A couple of days later, the column was still marching alongside the river when word of possible trouble flew back from the scouts in front. "Indians! Indians!" the soldiers told each other. A group of possible hostiles had been sighted up ahead. Nathan unslung his carbine and tightened his grip on the weapon. Sergeants hurried along the column, arranging the troops in ranks, lining them up to fight. Patrick Cardwell sent Elizabeth hurriedly to the rear, where the supply wagons were grouped together for defense.

She touched his arm for a moment before leaving. "Be careful, Patrick," she said in a low, urgent voice.

A few feet away, Nathan watched and felt a twinge of jealousy. Though he could barely imagine Cordelia Brannon being here with him the way Elizabeth was with Patrick, just the thought was enough to make something ache deep inside him for a moment.

He and Patrick moved up with the other men. Looking across the plains that bordered the river, Nathan saw the Indians, at least threescore of them. They were mounted on small but sturdy ponies. If the Indians attacked, they would stand little chance against six companies of infantry. But they could do some damage before being wiped out, Nathan thought. If there was a fight, some of the soldiers would die today, too.

One of the Indians rode out in front of the others. He walked his pony slowly toward the soldiers. Unlike the Indians back at the Crow Creek Agency, he wore not just a feather or two in his hair but sported instead a large, flowing headdress made up of hundreds of feathers. Nathan thought he looked both magnificent and barbaric.

"That must be their chief," Colonel Dimon said. "Perhaps he wants to talk. A parley, yes, that must be it." The colonel turned and made a curt motion with his hand at the nearest non-com. "Sergeant, you and half a dozen of your men, follow me."

The sergeant, a stocky, black-haired Irishman named O'Malley nodded. "Yes sir," he answered and turned to bellow, "Burke, Henderson, Hatcher, Johnson, Fox, Wall! Fall in!"

Nathan's breath seemed to freeze in his throat. He moved ahead with the others, knowing that he had to follow orders. Along with Sergeant O'Malley, they marched forward, trailing a few feet behind Colonel Dimon, who walked with his back held stiff and straight and his hands clasped behind his back.

The Indian chief halted his pony when the soldiers were within twenty feet of him. Dimon gestured for the men behind him to halt as well then walked ahead another ten feet by himself. The colonel was an unpleasant man most of the time, but Nathan had to give him credit for the courage he displayed at this moment.

Dimon came to attention and snapped a brisk, respectful salute. The Indian watched impassively.

"Good day, sir. I am Colonel C. A. R. Dimon, in command of the First United States Volunteer Regiment."

He waited for the Indian to say something. The Indian sat silently on his pony.

After a moment, Dimon cleared his throat and went on, "We are under orders to proceed to Fort Rice on the Missouri River and relieve the Thirtieth Wisconsin presently stationed there. We wish only peace with the native tribes, but we will brook no hostilities. According to General Sully—"

The Indian smiled and spoke for the first time. "Sully," he said. "Two Bears knows the warrior called Sully." His English was guttural but understandable.

Dimon drew a deep breath and took the opening the Indian gave him. "General Sully is a great warrior. Am I to assume that you are Two Bears?"

The chief inclined his head just enough to answer the question in the affirmative. At least, Nathan thought that was what he was doing.

"Two Bears is a great warrior, too," Dimon went on. "And great warriors do not need to make war."

"The Yanktonai do not make war," Two Bears responded. Slowly, gravely, he swept his arm toward the mounted Indians behind him. "Many moons we fought with Sully and his bluecoats, but now Two Bears has signed the paper and there is peace. Two Bears and Sully are friends. The Yantonai and the bluecoats are friends."

Dimon nodded eagerly. "Will you come to Fort Rice and be my guest, Two Bears?"

"Two Bears will do this."

"And perhaps you will bring other chiefs who wish to sign the paper and be friends with the army?"

"This will be done," Two Bears said.

Dimon struggled to contain his self-satisfaction and enthusiasm, Nathan saw. Clearly, the colonel was quite pleased with himself for arranging a parley with the other chiefs in the area. Perhaps he saw himself bringing peace to the entire Great Plains and being hailed as a hero.

Nathan was just glad the Indians and the soldiers weren't shooting at each other.

Two Bears said, "We go now," and turned his horse to ride back to his warriors. When he rejoined them, they urged their ponies into a run, and they raced off whooping and shouting.

"What a superb beginning to our efforts here!" Dimon said as he turned back to the soldiers. "Just superb!"

THAT WAS the only thing superb about the trek to Fort Rice, Nathan thought. Several more men died of dysentery before the regiment reached the fort. When they finally spotted the buildings on top of a bluff on the west bank of the river, a ragged cheer went up from the companies. No one knew exactly how their lives here would work out, but everyone hoped that at least it would be better than the seemingly endless march it had taken to get here.

Fort Rice had been in existence only a few months. The men of the Thirtieth Wisconsin had arrived there back in the summer when there was nothing. Cottonwood trees grew along this stretch of the river, making it a good location for a fort. The soldiers had set to work right away felling the trees and using the logs to construct the buildings of the post. Many of the buildings were still unfinished when the former Confederates arrived. The First USV were not reinforcements for the Thirtieth Wisconsin; they were replacements. The regular army troops moved out almost immediately, heading back downstream with the wagons the Volunteers had brought. They were bound for the battlefields of the east, where they would take the place of men who had fallen in the charnel houses of the Wilderness, Spotsylvania, and Cold Harbor.

The already completed barracks would house only four companies of the six that had come to Fort Rice. With winter approaching, the most important task was to complete the other buildings so everyone would have adequate shelter. Though it must have gone against his grain, Colonel Dimon dispensed with drilling. All the efforts of the men would go toward construction and resupplying the fort's larder. Some details were assigned to building, others concentrated on cutting down the trees along the river, and still others were sent out as hunting parties to look for elk, antelope, and deer.

The soldiers had not seen any Indians since the encounter with Two Bears and the Yanktonai several weeks earlier. With his head still filled with hopes of achieving peace, Dimon issued strict orders to the hunting parties. They were to keep an eye out for Indians but not to initiate hostilities with them. The only way the soldiers could fire their weapons was if they were fired upon first.

All vestiges of summer were gone by the time the soldiers reached Fort Rice. Now the sky was a heavy, leaden gray most of the time, and a cold wind blew constantly from the north. The men were grateful for the work details. At least they felt a little warmer when they were moving around.

Hunting details didn't have that luxury. The wind seemed to cut right through them as they tramped across the prairie in search of game. Such patrols usually consisted of six men with a sergeant in charge.

In mid-November, not long before Thanksgiving, Nathan was with one of the hunting parties on a day when the sky promised snow. There had been several snowfalls already, light dustings that turned the ground white for a day or two before melting. As Nathan walked along, he glanced up at the sky and wondered if this would be the time when one of the dreaded Dakota blizzards came blowing in from Canada. He had seen snow in Virginia, of course, but only occasionally. He had trouble imagining a snowfall so heavy that the powdery stuff piled up a few feet deep on the plains.

The men were about a mile west of the fort. The colonel didn't like for them to go much farther than that, but sometimes it was necessary in order to locate any game. The elk and antelope and buffalo were learning to avoid the buildings on the bluff above the river. Their animal cunning told them that man was dangerous.

Sergeant O'Malley was in charge of the detail. The other men were Privates Kaye, Butler, Napier, Denton, and Durham. Nathan wasn't a close friend to any of them, but he knew and liked all of them. They fanned out, walking about twenty yards apart with their rifles held ready. Sergeant O'Malley had told them that if they saw anything in the way of game, even a ground squirrel or prairie chicken, to take a shot at it. Meat was meat.

Off to Nathan's right, Durham fired. Nathan turned to look and saw an antelope bounding away, apparently unhit. Immediately, several of the other soldiers blazed away at the animal. The antelope veered back and forth, guided by instinct, and with a flick of its tail disappeared over a small rise. O'Malley cursed.

"Got away, the damn-blasted thing did! But maybe where there's one, there are more just over that hill. Come on, lads!"

The soldiers broke into a trot that carried them up the long, gentle rise. There were no real hills out here, just rolling undulations in the land that could conceal more than it would appear they should. Maybe there was a whole herd of antelope just over that rise, Nathan thought as he ran along, his rifle clutched in his right hand as it dangled at his side.

Then he crested the height and saw what was on the other side: not antelope, but Indians.

All seven members of the patrol came to an abrupt halt. "Sergeant . . . ?" Kaye said.

"I see 'em, laddie. Maybe they're peaceful, like those other red devils we saw down south o' the fort."

There were perhaps a dozen of the Indians sitting their ponies about fifty yards away. They wore heavy buckskin garments stained with grease and decorated with beads and fringe. None of them sported a feather headdress like the one Two Bears had worn. Maybe none of them was a chief, Nathan thought. Or maybe they belonged to a different tribe and didn't wear such things, even the chiefs. He didn't know. All he was sure of was that he wished they would turn around and ride away. They made him nervous, just sitting there like that.

"Maybe we better back up, boyos," O'Malley said warily. "Out o' sight, out o' mind, and all that. Come along now, back over the hill."

But before the soldiers could retreat, the Indians started forward. Their ponies moved at a slow, deliberate walk at first. Maybe they wanted to parley like Two Bears, Nathan thought.

Then, with no warning, after they had closed the distance somewhat, the Indians suddenly sent their mounts leaping forward at a dead run, straight toward the startled soldiers. Savage whoops filled the air.

Nathan wanted to turn and run, but he knew they couldn't get away from the Indians on foot. Fleeing would just give the savages the chance to ride them down from behind. O'Malley's voice boomed out, giving orders.

"Steady, lads! Kneel and fire at will!"

Nathan dropped to one knee and brought the rifle to his shoulder. He hoped the men who had fired at the antelope a few minutes earlier had reloaded. He saw that some of the Indians had rifles, old trade muskets from the look of them. The guns boomed, but they were wildly inaccurate. Firing from the backs of galloping ponies that way, the odds were heavily against the Indians hitting anything.

Others had bows and arrows, though, and they were much more accustomed to those weapons. As they closed in, arrows began to whip through the air around the kneeling soldiers.

A ragged volley came from the troops, and the echoes of the shots hadn't died away when Durham cried out in pain and fell backward, an arrow lodged in his left shoulder. Nathan felt sorry for the wounded man, but there was no time now to care for him. Every second was precious. Nathan reloaded, his hands moving in jerky, automatic motions. A couple of years earlier, he had gotten his first taste of combat near the town of Sharpsburg, Maryland, along Antietam Creek. He had panicked that day and been unable to fight. Fredericksburg had been almost as bad. But his experiences at Camp Douglas and afterward, when he and Titus and Louisa Abernathy were on the run from the Yankees, had toughened him both physically and mentally. He knew now that a man's fate in battle might be largely in the hands of whatever bloodstained god watched over such things, but at least a small portion of each man's destiny remained in his own hands. He had to seize what opportunities he could to save his own life, and that meant killing the enemy instead. Many men died for a cause. To survive, a man had to be willing to kill for it.

Nathan brought the rifle up again and squeezed the trigger as soon as he had settled the sights on one of the attacking Indians. The savage jerked back as the bullet smashed into his chest. He managed somehow to stay on his horse, clutching the animal's mane as he sagged forward.

The Indians turned and raced away on their ponies. None of them had fallen during the skirmish, but Nathan was sure several of them were badly wounded. He thought they might be planning to regroup and launch a second charge at the soldiers, but instead, the riders kept moving, vanishing in the distance on their swift ponies.

"A couple of you men grab Durham and get him on his feet," O'Malley said. "Head for the fort, fast as your feet will carry you, lads. Hatcher, you and Butler are rear guard. Keep an eye out for them bloody savages. Everybody, double time!"

The patrol headed for Fort Rice, Nathan and Private Butler bringing up the rear. Nathan cast frequent worried glances over his shoulder, but he didn't see the Indians anywhere. Perhaps the resistance put up by the soldiers had been stiffer than they expected. Maybe they'd just had enough of the fight. Nathan knew that he'd had plenty. Durham was the only one wounded and his injury didn't appear to be too bad, but Nathan knew just how lucky he and his companions had been. If the Indians had been determined, the soldiers could have been overrun and wiped out today.

But despite the fear that still coursed through his veins, despite the dangers and the brush with death just past, Nathan found that he was still glad to be here. Dakota Territory was a harsh, ugly, brutal land. But go back to a prison cell? Never. Even if he were not facing the threat of prison, the idea of going back east to a place where soldiers who should have been fellow countrymen were slaughtering each other was more than Nathan could stand.

The Yanks and the Rebs could have their damned war. For better or worse, the frontier was now Nathan Hatcher's home.

Chapter Sixteen

LOVEJOY'S STATION WAS SOME thirty miles south of Atlanta, and it was a bedraggled, dispirited bunch of Confederates who marched into the small settlement in early September 1864. Fresh from their defeat by the Yankees at Jonesboro, Gen. William J. Hardee's corps was reunited at Lovejoy's Station with the command of Gen. Stephen D. Lee as well as Gen. John Bell Hood's troops that had been evacuated from Atlanta. To a man, they all knew that Atlanta had fallen and that the hated Sherman had ridden into the Gate City of the South and covered himself with the glory of their defeat. The knowledge was a bitter pill to swallow after fighting so long and hard to keep the city out of Sherman's bloodstained hands.

Cory and Abner bedded down on the depot platform along with all the other men who could crowd onto it. At least they would have a little protection from the elements if it started to rain. They curled up in threadbare blankets and slept restlessly, then woke up to face another day of short rations and a seeming helplessness to deny the Yankees anything they wanted.

As usual, they spent some of the time talking about what they were going to do after the war. Cory still had his sights set on Texas, where he hoped to be reunited with Lucille. Such thoughts consumed most of his waking hours and even intruded on his dreams.

"I was thinkin' I might just up and go with you," Abner said. "I recollect how another ol' boy from Tennessee went off to Texas awhile back. Name of Crockett."

"Davy Crockett, you mean?" Cory asked.

"That's right. Him and me, we're from the same part of the state. No reason I can't sort of follow in his footsteps."

"If I remember right, he was killed fighting the Mexicans," Cory pointed out.

"That's what they'd like you to believe," Abner said with a grin. "I read some o' them Crockett Almanacks, though, that say he really lived through the battle there at the Alamo and went on to have a bunch more adventures. Fought Injuns and tamed whirlwinds and suchlike."

Cory shook his head. "Those are just stories."

Abner frowned. "You mean somebody just made 'em up?"

"That would be my guess."

Abner sighed in disgust. "Why in tarnation would anybody want to do that? Just sit around all day and make up stories that ain't even true, and then folks read 'em and believe 'em. It ain't fittin', if you ask me."

It seemed like a pretty ridiculous notion to Cory, too.

Several days passed quietly, and he was grateful for the chance to rest all the bumps, bruises, and scrapes that had come from months of fighting. No one knew for sure where the army was going next or what General Hood had planned for them. Given Hood's history, Cory thought it likely that the general would find some way to get them mixed up in a battle with the Yankees again. The next such conflict might be the one that destroyed what was left of the Confederate army. Cory told himself not to be so pessimistic, but after everything that had happened, it was hard to look for anything good to come out of whatever occurred next.

Rumors flew around the camp. Hood was going to try to retake Atlanta. No, he was going to strike out for Charleston or Savannah. Or perhaps he would circle Atlanta, leave it in Union hands, and head north to attack the Federal rear in Tennessee or North Carolina.

Whatever Hood did, he would do it without Gen. William J. Hardee. The two generals had never liked or fully trusted each other, and Hood, probably unfairly, placed much of the blame for the series of defeats around Atlanta on Hardee's shoulders. He even requested that President Davis assign Hardee elsewhere, and about the same time, Hardee asked for a transfer to another command. Davis satisfied both of them by sending Hardee to Charleston, South Carolina, to take over the Department of South Carolina, Georgia, and Florida.

The first Cory knew of this was when Abner came hurrying up to him.

"Grab your possibles. We're pullin' out," he announced.

Cory was sitting with his back against the wall of the station building. He looked up in surprise. "What are you talking about, Abner?"

"Gen'ral Hardee's been reassigned. He's headin' for South Carolina, and we're goin' with him as his escort."

Cory laughed humorlessly. "Just you and me?"

"Naw, the whole comp'ny. I just run into Lieutenant Bean, and he told me to gather the boys an' get 'em ready to travel. We'll be takin' us a train ride."

Cory pushed himself to his feet, using his rifle to brace himself. Even though he had rested for several days, a great weariness still filled him. It was a weariness more of the spirit than of the body, he thought, but wherever it was centered, it still made him reluctant to move.

Especially when that movement would take him even farther from Lucille. How had it worked out that while she had headed west, he found himself shuffling farther and farther east? Charleston, for God's sake! That was on the Atlantic coast.

At least he couldn't go any farther east than that, he told himself with a grim smile. Not without getting on a boat, anyway.

And as he gathered his few belongings, he wished that thought had not occurred to him. After everything that had happened to him already, there was no point in tempting fate.

A RATTLING old train carried them from Lovejoy's Station to Macon to Savannah on the Georgia coast. They passed through there in the middle of the night, changing trains for Charleston.

Once they had arrived, General Hardee settled into command, and the men who had accompanied him became his headquarters company. As such, they had little to do, which meant Cory and Abner had time to take in some sights that were new to both of them.

Cory had never seen the ocean before, although the Mississippi River at New Orleans was so big it had seemed like an ocean to him the first time he laid eyes on it. He stood on one of the waterfront streets and looked out across the harbor to where a rock fortress rose grimly from the gentle waves.

Standing equally entranced beside him, Abner said, "So that's where it all started, huh? Fort Sumter. Don't look like much, does it?"

A red flag flew over the fort, flapping idly in the ocean breeze. At this distance, Cory couldn't make out many details, but he knew that banner was the flag of his country. He swallowed hard and couldn't speak for a moment. "The Yankees should have left that rock when we asked them to." After a moment's pause, he added, "If they had, maybe all the rest of it wouldn't have happened."

"Don't you believe it. Them damnyanks was bound and determined there was gonna be a war. They figured that was the only way they could make us lick their boots."

But it wasn't all the Yankees' doing, Cory knew. The Southern firebrands had been just as determined to force things along until a war was inevitable. No matter how long he lived, Cory thought, he would never understand it. Some things were worth fighting for, even dying for, and a man's home was one of them. The leaders of the Confederacy had practically invited the Yankees to invade, and sure enough, the arrogant, know-it-all Northerners had been glad to oblige. Cory remembered a line from one of Shakespeare's plays, a line that hadn't been one of his father's particular favorites but one that John Brannon had quoted often enough so that Cory thought of it now.

A pox on both their houses.

GEN. P. G. T. Beauregard, one of the heroes of the victory at Manassas—just a little more than three years earlier, but now it seemed like an eternity—was in overall command of all Confederate forces except the Army of Northern Virginia, which was still led by Robert E. Lee. Beauregard had much to occupy him. Sherman was still ensconced in Atlanta, but he might move at any time and threaten some other part of Georgia. And Hood was determined to remain on the aggressive, which in this case meant swinging around Atlanta to the west and striking northward to destroy the railroad and cut Sherman's supply line.

By October 1, Hood was on the move, his men tearing up the tracks of the Western and Atlantic Railroad north of Atlanta. Hood's objective was to go right back up the Federal supply line to Chattanooga and perhaps on into Tennessee. This led to an ironic reversal of events from the previous spring. Now the Confederates began advancing to the north, into enemy-held territory, while the Yankees fought defensive actions in an attempt to hold them back.

A particularly bloody clash at Allatoona in early October, though inconclusive, emboldened Hood and convinced him his plan would work. He intended to draw Sherman after him until he was in the right position to turn around and smash the Union army. Beauregard was less enamored of the scheme, but after traveling to northern Georgia for a face-to-face meeting with Hood, he gave his approval for the operation. Hood's men fought all the way up the railroad to Tunnel Hill, capturing it in what had to be a moral victory for the Confederates, since that was where Sherman had begun his Atlanta campaign.

The only problem was that Sherman was not cooperating. He had pursued only halfheartedly, leading Hood to shift farther west into Alabama before turning north again, still with designs on Tennessee. Gen. George H. Thomas, the Rock of

Chickamauga, was already in Nashville with orders from Sherman to deal with not only Hood but also Nathan Bedford Forrest, whose cavalry had been raising hell in middle and western Tennessee for the past several months. Truth be told, Sherman was glad that Hood had launched an invasion of Tennessee. That would keep Hood busy while Sherman continued on to his real objective: the long-planned march across Georgia to the sea, with the port city of Savannah squarely in his sights.

The time had come for a new sort of campaign, a campaign that would, according to Sherman, teach the Southerners to rue forever their folly in provoking a war. Sherman would cut a swath of utter destruction across the heart of the Confederacy and in the process ensure Abraham Lincoln's reelection as president. The capture of Atlanta already had improved Lincoln's chances for victory over Gen. George B. McClellan, the Democratic candidate and former commander of the Army of the Potomac. Little Mac was still highly regarded by those men who had served under him, but more than soldiers would vote in this election.

Sherman set off in the middle of November to teach the Rebels his bloody lesson. To the northwest, in Tuscumbia, Alabama, Hood was getting ready to move as well, aiming to march through Tennessee to Nashville. He was waiting to be joined by thirty-five hundred hard-riding, hard-fighting horsemen led by the hardest-riding, hardest-fighting of them all: Forrest.

THE RAIN pounded at Henry as he rode along a narrow, twisting, mud-choked trail. Although he suspected it was only midafternoon, the overcast was so thick that a darkness almost as impenetrable as night had begun to settle over the soggy landscape already. It had been raining for days now, long enough for Henry to start wondering if he would ever see the sun again. And since he avoided settlements and even farms for fear of running into

Yankees, he wondered as well if he would ever again be warm and dry.

He had been angling southwest for several weeks, ever since leaving the farm near Culpeper. Paralleling the Blue Ridge, finally crossing it down in the corner of North Carolina, tracking over into Tennessee. The last rumor he'd heard was that General Hood was somewhere in the southern part of the state, either that or just across the border in northern Alabama. Henry had found a newspaper in an abandoned farmhouse with an article about a speech President Davis had made, telling how General Hood was going to capture Nashville. The paper had been dated only a few weeks earlier, so the farm hadn't been deserted for long. Henry had stayed there for a couple of days, resting his pair of horses and wondering how things were going at home. He hoped the women were all right. As far as he could tell, the Yankees hadn't come after him to punish him for McCafferty's death. Maybe Cordelia had sent them in the wrong direction. She was smart as a whip; it might have occurred to her to do something like that.

Henry considered waiting out the rest of the war on the abandoned farm, but in the end, he decided not to risk it. For one thing, he would probably starve to death. For another, there were strong Federal forces in both Nashville and Knoxville; patrols probably went out from both towns on a regular basis. He decided to swing south of both those settlements and continue on westward, knowing that the odds were he would find General Hood's army sooner or later. Then the skies had opened up and the rains came, and Henry was able to travel only a few miles each day over the muddy roads.

Besides slowing him down, the mud also muffled the sound of hoofbeats, which was a mixed blessing, Henry decided as several riders suddenly loomed up out of the gloom in front of him. He hadn't heard them coming at all. He stiffened in the saddle and reached under his coat for the pistol that had belonged to the dead Yankee sergeant. He doubted that it would fire; the damp likely had gotten to the powder. But he wasn't going to be captured without at least attempting to put up a fight.

"Hold it there, boy!" a man shouted over the noise of the rain. "Who be you?"

The accent was undoubtedly Southern. Henry heaved a sigh of relief. These riders weren't Yankees after all.

"I'm a friend," he said as he reined his mount to a halt. "I'm looking for General Hood's army."

"Not a spy, are you?"

Henry felt a flash of annoyance. Back home in Virginia, he had been accused of spying. Now, here in Tennessee, his own countrymen distrusted him. "No, damn it, I'm not a spy."

He faintly heard a chuckle. "Feisty one, ain't you? You a soldier? Got separated from your comp'ny?"

"No, that's why I'm looking for General Hood. I want to join up with him and help fight the Yankees."

"Well, that can prob'ly be arranged. Come along with us, if you're of a mind to."

Henry moved his horse forward. "You men are with General Hood?"

"We're with General Forrest, and he's with General Hood. Reckon that makes us all part of the same bunch."

"You mean Bedford Forrest?" The family hadn't gotten many letters from Cory over the past few years, but the ones they had received had mentioned the Confederate cavalry leader with great admiration. Cory had ridden with Forrest during several campaigns.

"There ain't any other Forrest to speak of," the spokesman for the group of cavalry troopers replied. "Are you comin' or not?"

"Yes, I'm coming. Are you on your way to join Forrest now?"

"That's right. We're on our way back from a scout along Shoal Creek. Had a little skirmish with the Yankees there a couple of days ago." A note of pride entered the man's voice. "We sent 'em runnin'. That'll teach 'em to stand betwixt us and home. Most of us are Tennessee boys, and we're ready to send all them damn Yankees back where they come from."

For the first time in days, a smile touched Henry's haggard, unshaven face. "Up in Virginia, we feel pretty much the same way."

As he turned his horses to fall in with the Confederate horsemen, he realized he had gotten mixed up at the last crossroads he'd come to. He had been riding northwest instead of southeast. In the pouring rain, it was hard to know which direction was which. But if he had kept going that way, Henry thought, sooner or later he would have ridden right into the middle of the Yankee army. This chance encounter with the Confederate patrol had been a lucky one indeed.

Full night had fallen by the time Henry and his companions reached the place where Hood's army was camped. The rain had stopped by then, but a raw, chilly wind was still blowing. The leader of the patrol, who had introduced himself to Henry as Ernie Murrell, explained that this was really just part of the army. Three columns were on the move northward into Tennessee, their ultimate destination being Nashville. This was the right column, led by Gen. Alexander Stewart. The middle column was commanded by Gen. Stephen D. Lee, while the left, westernmost column was under the command of Gen. Benjamin Franklin Cheatham. Fine officers, all three of them, according to Murrell. General Forrest was in overall command of the cavalry accompanying all three columns; his command was attached to Stewart's column and was charged with screening the advance on the right flank.

Murrell led Henry toward a tent where a man sat by a small fire; he was perched on a stump and smoking a pipe. He didn't stand up as Murrell approached, but if he had, Henry suspected he would be tall and lean. He had that look about him. Dark hair swept back behind his ears and topped a high forehead. A beard jutted fiercely from his chin. His hollow-cheeked face was dominated by a pair of deep-set, piercing dark eyes. Just from the air of intensity and command that seemed to surround the man, Henry assumed he was looking at Forrest.

"No sign of the Yanks along Shoal Creek, General," Murrell reported.

"Good." Forrest didn't waste words. He looked at Henry and went on, "Who's this?"

"Fella we ran into on the trail. Says he's been lookin' for General Hood and aims to join up and fight Yankees." Murrell paused for a second then added meaningfully, "He's got a couple of pretty fair mounts with him, General."

"Is that so? Are you interested in joining us?" Forrest inquired. "If you're looking for action, there should be plenty to suit you."

Henry hadn't given much thought to joining the cavalry, but as he looked at Forrest in the firelight, he knew he would prefer to do his fighting on horseback rather than slogging through the mud with the infantry. He nodded. "That would suit me just fine, General."

"Have you got a name?"

"Yes sir. It's Brannon. Henry Brannon."

Forrest looked like the sort of man who was seldom surprised. But at the mention of Henry's name, his eyes sparked with interest. "I knew a young fella name of Brannon. Rode with me on several occasions."

"Yes sir, that was my brother Cory. He didn't write many letters, but he spoke of you often in the ones he did."

Forrest stood up and extended a hand. "I'm glad to meet you, Henry. That brother of yours was a good man to have around."

Henry shook hands with the general and ventured a question. "Do you happen to know where Cory is now, sir?" He halfway dreaded the answer. Given Cory's reckless nature, he might have fallen in battle. Hell, Henry thought, in this war even the men who were careful died in droves sometimes.

Forrest shook his head. "I'm afraid I don't. When I parted ways with General Bragg after our victory at Chickamauga

Creek—a victory that Bragg utterly wasted, I might add—Cory stayed behind. His wife's uncle, a Colonel Thompson, was wounded, and your brother felt that he needed to look after him." Forrest puffed on the pipe for a moment. "Haven't seen him since. He's quite a resourceful young fella, though. I expect wherever he is, he's all right."

That made Henry feel a little better. So did the warmth coming from the fire. It helped dry his sodden clothes somewhat. He extended his hands toward the flames. "Thanks, General. For the hospitality, and for the news about Cory."

"Are you the fighting devil your brother is?" Forrest asked with a grin.

"I don't know, sir," Henry answered honestly. "But if you let me ride with you, I figure I'll have plenty of chances to find out."

HENRY SHARED a tent with Murrell and two other men, Wade Foreman and Jeb Carruthers. There had been a fourth man in the tent until a few days earlier, Murrell explained. "He come down with the grippe and died, most likely because of all this rain and chilly weather we been havin'. Damned shame. He was a good feller."

"I'll try to live up to that," Henry said.

Murrell clapped him on the shoulder. "You'll do fine. The general liked you, and he's a pretty good judge o' character."

Although the ground was soggy inside the tent, it was better than having no protection at all. After Henry had taken care of his horses, he crawled into his blankets and fell into a deep sleep. The exhaustion brought on by the strain of the past few weeks kept him from dreaming.

He awoke to hear Murrell exclaim, "Lordy, would you look at that!"

Henry unwrapped himself from his covers and crawled out into a world that was still gray and overcast, but at least it wasn't raining this morning. It was snowing instead, a thick curtain of flakes that swirled and danced in the light wind that was blowing. Henry's breath fogged in front of his face. The temperature had fallen below freezing during the night, and the snow was piling up already. The scene would have been beautiful under normal circumstances. As it was, though, the snow might just slow down the Confederate advance that much more.

After a skimpy breakfast of hardtack and grain coffee, the men mounted up and moved out through the snow. As Henry rode along with Murrell, Foreman, and Carruthers, it occurred to him that he had not sworn any oath of enlistment or been enrolled in any regimental records, as far as he knew. That didn't seem to make any difference to his companions. They regarded him as one of them. Nor had the quartermaster wasted any time in taking Henry's second horse and giving it to one of the other troopers. The horses he had brought were just as important, if not more so, than he was, he sensed.

Murrell filled him in on all the gossip surrounding the campaign in which they were engaged. "Some Yankee general name of Schofield is holed up at a place called Pulaski. We're tryin' to get betwixt him and the rest of the Yankees up at Columbia. If we can do that, we can hit ol' Schofield, then grab control of the Duck River crossin' at Columbia. Thomas is up at Nashville, but he won't be able to stop us if we can keep Schofield from linkin' up with him." Murrell leaned over in the saddle and spat. "The Rock of Chickamauga," he said scornfully. "That's what the Yankees call Thomas. We see what they call him when we've busted him up into little bitty pebbles."

Despite the cold weather, the short rations, and the threadbare uniforms worn by many of the men, spirits were high. Henry could understand that. Most of these men were Tennesseans. They were going home, riding to liberate their state from the grip of the Yankees. Henry didn't blame them for being excited. He would have been, too, if he'd been on his way to drive the invaders out of Virginia.

Around midday, a spate of gunfire broke out up ahead and to the right of where Henry rode with his three tentmates. "Come on, boys!" Murrell said and kicked his horse into a run. The animal's hooves threw a spray of snowflakes into the air. Henry, Foreman, and Carruthers followed. Henry held the reins with one hand and slipped the other inside his coat. His fingers curled around the smooth wooden grips of the pistol. He had cleaned and dried it that morning before the troopers broke camp, and it had been protected inside his coat ever since. He thought there was a good chance it would work if he needed it.

The snow was still falling, but not as heavily as it had been earlier. The gunshots grew louder. Henry caught a glimpse of muzzle flashes through the gloom. A line of trees bordered the road on the right, and up ahead, several Confederate cavalrymen were firing carbines and pistols at something on the other side of those trees. Return fire came from the enemy. Henry saw flashes of blue uniforms through the swirling white of the snow.

He and his new friends closed in on the skirmish. He pulled the pistol from behind his belt. He had never fired from the back of a running horse before and didn't know if he would be able to hit anything. He would give it a try, though. That was all he could do.

Murrell suddenly swerved his mount through a narrow gap in the trees. "We'll get 'em in a crossfire!" he shouted back over his shoulder. Foreman and Carruthers hit the gap behind him. Henry brought up the rear, fighting the reins a little. He thought of himself as a good rider, but he realized now what a difference there was between cantering along on a decent road and galloping cross-country into combat. He had to concentrate on staying in the saddle.

More gunfire sounded, closer than ever now. Henry looked ahead and saw Murrell and the others moving in on a group of at least a dozen Federal cavalrymen. If the Confederates realized they were outnumbered, they didn't seem to care. High-pitched Rebel yells split the air.

Henry swallowed hard. He had come down here to Tennessee to fight the hated Yankees. Here was his chance. He lifted the pistol and pulled back the hammer.

The gun went off before he was ready, the rough pace jarring his finger against the trigger. He yelled in surprise as the weapon blasted and bucked against his palm. He had no idea where the bullet went. He knew he had to calm down if he was going to survive his first battle. As he cocked the pistol again, he pulled the horse back into a slower run. Now he could level the revolver and at least aim a little before he fired again.

This time when he squeezed off a shot, he was confident that the bullet went in the right direction. He couldn't tell if he hit any of the Yankees, though. A haze of smoke filled the air. Combined with the still-falling snow, it made it almost impossible to see anything.

But Henry saw the Union cavalryman coming toward him only a few yards away. The man loomed up seemingly out of nowhere. He brandished a saber over his head and sent his horse lunging toward Henry.

Henry swung the pistol around and pressed the trigger, but nothing happened. To his horror, he realized that in the excitement and confusion of the moment, he had forgotten to cock the gun. He jerked on the reins and leaned far to the side in an effort to avoid the blade. The saber sliced through the air near his head, missing him. But he was off-balance now, and so was the horse. With a shrill whinny, the animal fell. As the horse toppled over, Henry had the presence of mind to kick his feet free from the stirrups. He sailed through the air as he was thrown from the saddle.

Landing so hard that the breath was knocked out of him, Henry rolled over in the snow. The Yankee was practically on top of him. The man leaned over to thrust his saber at Henry, obviously planning to skewer him and pin him to the ground.

Before the thrust could find its target, another shape on horseback appeared beside the Yankee. Henry recognized Jeb

Carruthers. A muzzle flash split the snowstorm as the Confederate fired into the Yankee's side at point-blank range, blowing the Northerner out of the saddle. The man crashed to the ground a few feet away from Henry, close enough for Henry to see his face contort in agony as he died from the bullet that had ripped through his vitals. A few flames flickered around the hole in his uniform, which had been set on fire by sparks from the barrel of Carruthers's gun. The flames went out as snowflakes settled gently on them. The flakes hissed as they melted.

Henry looked into the dead man's open, staring eyes, then rolled in the other direction and retched, though there was not much in his stomach to come up. The closeness of his own brush with death, on top of watching the Yankee die at such close range, was too much for him. Sickness roiled his insides.

But there was still a fight going on. A calm, icy voice somewhere deep inside his brain reminded him of that fact. He got his hands and knees under him and pushed himself to his feet. Somehow he had held on to the pistol when he fell. And his horse was dancing around skittishly only a few feet away. Henry grabbed the reins, spoke soothingly to the animal, and swung up into the saddle. The skirmish had turned into a saber-swinging melee as Confederate cavalry pinched in from both flanks against the Federal troopers. Henry didn't have a sword, but he rode up close behind one of the Yankees and yelled, "Hey, Yank!"

The man turned, and Henry saw he was carrying a carbine. The Yankee tried to lift the weapon, but Henry was too fast for him, firing into his chest from a distance of five or six feet. The Yankee's eyes widened in shock as he went over backward, falling off his horse.

Henry desperately wanted to be sick again, but there was no time for that. He had one more round in his pistol. He fired that at another Yankee and was rewarded by the sight of blood splashing from the man's shoulder. The Union trooper sagged in the saddle but didn't fall. He galloped off into the snow.

The rest of the Yankees who were still mounted followed his example. They turned tail and ran, racing away from the scene of the battle. Some of the Confederate horsemen went after them. The popping of gunshots receded into the distance.

Henry tried to reload as he sat on his horse, but his fingers were cold and clumsy. Carruthers, Murrell, and Foreman rode up alongside him. Henry looked at Carruthers and nodded. "Thanks."

Carruthers grinned. "Figure you'll do the same for me, happen you ever get the chance."

Henry nodded, knowing the man was right. Now that he had ridden into battle with these troopers, a bond existed between them, a bond of a sort that Henry had never experienced before. It wasn't like they were brothers, but in some ways it was almost that close.

"You done all right, Brannon," Murrell said. "I thought you would. You got the look of a fighter. Reckon that's what the general seen in you, too." He prodded his horse toward the north. "Come on. Let's go nip at the heels o' them Yanks."

Henry finally finished reloading his pistol. He closed it and tucked it under his coat again. Then he fell in with the others as they rode in pursuit of the enemy.

Chapter Seventeen

Chapter Seventy

FOR THE NEXT FEW days, the cavalry was mounted and on the move from before dawn until it was too dark to see each night. Even though Henry had spent weeks in the saddle as he traveled from Virginia to Tennessee, he had never in his life done so much hard riding, and sore muscles announced that fact to him every morning when he crawled out of his blankets and got ready for another day of skirmishing with the Yankees.

It had been Hood's plan to get around the Yankees while Schofield was still in the village of Pulaski. However, Schofield's scouts must have brought him word of the Confederate movements, because the Federals had pulled out and were heading north toward the town of Columbia as fast as they could go. Hood wanted the pair of bridges over the Duck River at Columbia, and his columns were in good position to get them if only Schofield could be delayed. Unfortunately, the Federal cavalry did a good job of keeping Forrest occupied so that the Confederate troopers were unable to range as far ahead as they would have liked. Still, Forrest's men made it as far as the outskirts of Columbia before they were forced back. Much to Forrest's disgust, Schofield's infantry was able to march into the town and start erecting fortifications along its southern edge. Hood had lost the first leg of this desperate race.

But the objectives could still be won. Facing the possibility of crossings by the Confederates either upstream or down—or both—Schofield decided to abandon the newly built breastworks and withdraw to the northern bank of the river. He did so, and the last of his men to cross set fire to the bridges behind them. Hood's infantry moved into Columbia, occupying the town without a shot being fired. That wasn't going to do them much good, however, with the Yankees now safely on the other side of the river.

On November 28, Henry found himself, along with his new friends and the rest of Forrest's cavalry, riding east along the Duck River, looking for a crossing so they could ford and establish a foothold from which an attack on Schofield's rear could be launched. The heavens were still cloaked with clouds and spat down snow intermittently. At times during the past few days, the weather had warmed above freezing, but any thawing of the roads just made the mud worse. These were terrible conditions for fighting a war, Henry thought . . . though even with his limited military experience, he wondered if there was such a thing as good weather for a war.

He had not seen Forrest himself since that first night. Today Henry and his companions rode near the front of the cavalry column. He could see Forrest taking the lead with several trusted subordinates. Murrell and the others had been with Forrest for quite a while, and they remembered Cory, although they had not known him personally. From what they said, Cory had served as a scout for Forrest and had been something of a protégé to the general. Henry didn't figure he would ever command that sort of trust and respect from Forrest, but that was all right. All he wanted was to do his part against the Yankees and make it through the rest of the war alive so he could go home one of these days.

Another thing he had discovered was that the strain of almost constant skirmishing with the Federals made it difficult to dwell on the past. Thoughts of Polly still came to him, of course; he knew he would never lose the memories of what they had had together, or the regrets for what they had been denied. But the pain within him had dulled to a bearable level now. He didn't know if that was because of the circumstances or the simple passage of time or a combination of the two. But he was grateful for it, regardless of the cause.

Late in the afternoon the riders came to a spot where the river looked shallow enough to ford. Forrest sent some of the men across, waiting just long enough to see that they were going

to make it, then rode on with the others. Again, a few miles farther on, they found another ford, and again Forrest split his
party. Henry and his tentmates were with the final group that
rode on. The sound of gunshots drifted through the cold air, following them.

"Reckon the boys north of the river have run into the
Yanks," Murrell said. "Schofield's prob'ly got cavalry strung out
all along here, keepin' an eye out for us."

It was nearly dusk when the last group of Confederate riders
crossed the river with Forrest himself at their head. Henry shivered as cold water rose over the tops of his boots. The horses had
to swim for a short distance. Hood's infantry would not be able
to cross here without a bridge of some sort. Luckily, the engineers were skilled at their job and could lay down a pontoon
bridge over a stream this size in less than a day.

The Yankees, however, didn't wait until everyone was out of
the water. Carbines began to spit fire from the trees on the northern bank of the Duck. With his famous twin long-barreled pistols
in his hands, Forrest led the charge against them. His guns
barked wickedly as he swept into the trees with a large group of
men thundering along right behind him.

Henry had picked up a seven-shot Spencer carbine and some
ammunition from a dead Yankee trooper a couple of days earlier.
The Spencer was quite a prize and was envied by his friends. He
was a little surprised none of the officers tried to claim it, but they
just congratulated him on his find. Now he held the weapon and
ammo pouch well out of the water as he guided the horse the last
few feet. The horse came out onto the bank and wanted to pause
and shake, but Henry didn't give the animal the chance to do so.
Instead he sent the horse leaping forward after Forrest. Beside
him, Foreman let out an eager yip that was echoed by Murrell
and Carruthers. They were impatient to get into the fight that
was going on up ahead.

The Spencer was fully loaded. Henry held it in one hand
and used the other on the reins as he guided his mount through

the trees. He hoped to grow comfortable enough on horseback so that someday he could use just his knees to guide the horse in battle, leaving both hands free for the carbine. Now, though, he was still worried about falling off or having the horse run away with him.

The Yankees were running already before Forrest's sharp onslaught, Henry saw. He brought the horse to a stop and drew a bead on one of the fleeing troopers. For a second, he hesitated, knowing that he was about to shoot a man in the back. Then he pressed the Spencer's trigger and felt the recoil against his shoulder. He saw the man topple off his horse.

The sight brought a twinge of guilt, but Henry suppressed it. This was war, after all. Killing Yankees was why he was here. Ever since the beginning of the war, he had wanted to get in on the fighting and thought it was unfair that Will and Mac pressured him to stay home. Now that he was in the thick of it, now that his hands had blood on them, he wished more than anything else that he was back home in Virginia. He supposed that until the time came, a man never knew how the killing was going to affect him.

But it was easier now than it had been a few days earlier. That probably meant something, but Henry didn't know if he liked it or not.

Hood's engineers were right on Forrest's tail. Even as the cavalry was clearing out the Yankees on the north side of the river, the engineers moved in to start work on the bridges they were charged with building. At each of the three fords, the pontoons went down and planks were hammered onto them. The bridges took shape with amazing swiftness, so that by midnight, infantrymen were tramping over them, crossing the Duck River.

There was no time to rest. After spending most of the night in the saddle, the Confederate horsemen were on the move again early the next morning, November 29. The Union cavalry, which had been strung out along the river, had congregated in response to the crossings made by Forrest's men the day before, and now they were all together again, forming a formidable force. To Forrest, however, the concentration of the Yankees just meant they would be easier to drive before him. That was what happened that morning.

Time and again, Henry and the men with him rode up on a lagging bunch of Federal troopers and prodded them north with an exchange of gunfire. Clearly, the Yankees had no interest in standing and fighting on this day.

It was around midday when Forrest turned away from the pursuit. Leaving only a small group of men to continue harassing the Yankees, Forrest swung to the west with the rest of the cavalry and headed for the settlement of Spring Hill. Henry would not have known that, being unfamiliar with Tennessee, if Murrell hadn't told him. All these troopers knew the area intimately.

"Spring Hill's on the turnpike betwixt Columbia and Franklin," Murrell explained. "And past Franklin, the road runs on up right into Nashville. Schofield must be runnin' up that turnpike as fast as his stubby little legs'll carry him."

Henry didn't know anything about the Yankee general, didn't know if Schofield had stubby legs or not. He didn't care, either. He was growing numb from the constant riding and fighting. Some Yankee general had called Forrest "that devil," and Henry could understand why. Forrest and the men with him rode like the devil, and they fought like the devil, too.

They were on a road called the Rally Hill pike and had just passed an old tollgate when Forrest sent a large group of cavalry sweeping forward toward a stand of trees. For the past little while, guns had been popping up ahead as Confederate scouts ran into Yankee skirmishers. Most of the Federal cavalry was northeast of here, Henry knew, but he supposed some of the blue-clad troopers could have worked their way back toward Spring Hill. He charged forward along with Murrell, Carruthers, Foreman, and several dozen more riders.

A volley ripped out from the trees. Bullets sang through the air and thudded into the horses and men racing over the snowy landscape. Henry's eyes widened in surprise as he heard the roll of gunfire and saw men and horses falling before it. That was no handful of skirmishers or cavalrymen up there in the trees; that was the damned Yankee infantry, dug in and waiting for the Confederates to come to them. Even with his limited experience, Henry could figure out that much. Combat was a very efficient teacher if a man lived through it.

Blunted by the volleys from the trees, the charge broke up and the men turned to ride back up the hill. Henry hadn't fired a shot. Things had fallen apart before he could do so. But Forrest wasted no time in rallying his men and ordering them to attack again. "I figured they was in there, boys," he called out. "Now we know it!"

This time the cavalrymen started firing sooner. They spread out farther, too, not giving the Yankees so many good targets, and several small groups reached the trees before being forced to retreat by the heavy fire from the Federal infantry. Henry emptied the Spencer from the back of his horse then turned and headed back up the hill, knowing that if he stopped to reload out there in the open, he would be cut down.

Since horseback charges didn't seem to be working, Forrest dismounted his men and sent them at the Union right. As they worked forward, Murrell said between shots, "Schofield's got some of his men into Spring Hill ahead of us, dadgum him! He's tryin' to keep us from reachin' the Franklin pike and blockin' it."

That made sense to Henry. He didn't spend a lot of time mulling over the strategy, though. He was more concerned with staying alive. He used every hump of ground, every pile of rocks, every log fence he could find for cover as he advanced toward the Federal lines. Even though he had one of the prized repeaters, his ammunition was limited, so he tried to make every shot count. The Yankees were well hidden in the trees, though. Finally, the Confederates had to pull back yet again.

Henry knew that Hood's infantry was coming up somewhere behind them. The cavalry might not have to overwhelm the enemy by itself; it might be enough for them to keep the Yankees occupied until Hood was in position to strike. The afternoon was waning, though, despite the fact that the overcast finally had broken and sunlight slanted down through gaps in the clouds. Given the time of year, Hood would have to hurry if he wanted to launch an attack before nightfall.

Advance brigades of the Confederate infantry arrived not long afterward. The general in charge rode up for a quick conference with Forrest, and then both cavalry and infantry moved out in a concerted charge, with their respective generals riding in the forefront, sabers drawn. Not too far back, Ernie Murrell said, "That other general's Pat Cleburne, from Ireland by way o' Arkansas. Hell of a fighter, from what I hear."

Henry hoped that was true. They needed all the fighters they could get on their side.

The infantry swung to the side to take the enemy on the flank while Forrest and the cavalry continued to charge head-on. For several minutes, the Yankees put up a stiff fight, but now they were outnumbered and finally had no choice but to pull back. As they retreated toward Spring Hill and the Franklin turnpike, about a mile behind them, the Confederates kept up the pressure. Henry used the last of his ammunition for the Spencer and had to switch to the pistol. The Yankees were close in front of them, turning to fight a futile rear-guard action. Close beside Henry, Wade Foreman let out a whoop and yelled, "Give it up, you Yankee sons o' bitches!"

At that instant, Henry heard a horrifying sound, the likes of which he had never heard before. It was a loud roar, followed instantly by a high-pitched whistle and then another blast that seemed to be right on top of them. Henry's horse staggered heavily, and he had to hold on tightly to keep from being thrown. He glanced over beside him, where Foreman had been riding only a second earlier and saw that the man was gone. Twisting in the saddle, Henry looked back and saw a mangled heap of bloody flesh that had been Foreman and his mount. A canister round from a Federal cannon had exploded right in Foreman's lap.

Henry tasted bile in his mouth and swallowed the sickness that threatened to overwhelm him. No matter how shocked and horrified he was, he couldn't give in to those emotions now. The Yankee artillery continued to thunder, the big guns entering the fray now where they had been silent earlier.

Hood's forces, moving quickly, had outpaced their own artillery and so had nothing with which to counter the Yankee bombardment. Forrest and Cleburne had no choice but to call a halt to the attack, at least for the time being. But they had pushed the enemy back almost to the turnpike. After a short breather to rest and regroup, as well as to give their own big guns a chance to come up, they could hit the Yankees again. The smell of victory was in the air. Everyone could sense it, even a novice like Henry.

In the meantime, Henry found Murrell and Carruthers, who had gotten separated from the others during the charge, and told them about Foreman.

Murrell grated out a curse. "Wade and me been friends for a long time, since before this damn war. I hope the Yankee gunner who fired that shot burns in hell."

A lot of the Yankees were probably thinking the same thing about their Confederate counterparts tonight, Henry thought. If everyone got his wish, hell was going to be busting at the seams before this fight was over.

EVERYONE EXPECTED the order to charge again to come at any moment. But that didn't happen, and as the last light of day faded and night settled down, a courier arrived from General Cheatham with a message that Forrest and Cleburne were not to attack the Yankees again without further orders. Henry was standing near enough to the general to see the anger and bafflement on Forrest's face as he was given the message.

Left with nothing to do but make the best of a muddled situation, Forrest ordered his men to feed and care for their horses. Meanwhile, the infantry began to make camp for the night, pitching tents and starting cooking fires. The frantic action of the day seemed to have fizzled to a halt.

A short time later, Gen. Alexander Stewart came up to the front, expecting an attack to begin momentarily. Finding that such was not the case, he conferred with Forrest, and then both generals set off to find Hood and discover what the plan really was . . . if, indeed, there was a plan.

Henry knew nothing of the meeting between the generals or its outcome until orders came for the men to saddle and ride. They were going to swing around to the north of Spring Hill in one last attempt to cut the turnpike and hold it against the Union retreat to Franklin.

Murrell and Carruthers reminisced about Foreman. Henry mourned the man's death, even though he had known him for only a short time. But a lot of good men had died already, and a lot more would soon meet their Maker, Henry figured. Tonight it might be his turn.

The cavalry rode through the darkness. A few lights in the distance marked the position of the settlement. As the riders neared the turnpike, Henry saw more lights up ahead. When they got closer, he saw that the glow came from lanterns hung on the Yankee supply wagons rolling along the road. He had time to check his pistol, then the orders came to charge. Several hundred horsemen galloped forward, their job to stop the advance of tens of thousands of Yankees.

The outcome was a foregone conclusion. A few minutes of skirmishing, and the cavalry withdrew, desperately low on ammunition. They had never had a chance, Henry realized. Hood had ordered Forrest to send them up here in a last-ditch effort that signified nothing and had no chance of succeeding. At least he and Murrell and Carruthers hadn't been killed or wounded, he thought bitterly as they rode back toward the Confederate camp.

By morning of November 30, everyone knew what had happened. Through indecision, confusion, and just plain bad judgment, the Yankees had been allowed to escape from what should have been a deadly trap. All through the night, Schofield's forces had streamed up the turnpike toward Franklin. Every time it had appeared that the Confederate army had the enemy where they wanted—first at Pulaski, then at Columbia, and now at Spring Hill—the Yankees had slipped away somehow. The scattered camps buzzed with angry speculation about just what had gone wrong.

"Hood's blamin' it on Cheatham and Cleburne and Bate," Murrell reported as he squatted next to a tiny fire with Henry and Carruthers, referring to the three divisional commanders of the army. "I heard 'bout it from one of the boys who was up at the big house with the general this mornin' when they rode over to Rippa Villa where Hood's been stayin'. Them generals thought they'd be sittin' down to a nice breakfast, but then old Hood lit into 'em."

Carruthers looked down at the small piece of pone in his hand. "This is all we got for breakfast."

"Well, Forrest and them other officers got hell for breakfast. Hood told 'em it was all their fault the Yankees slipped past us last night."

Henry frowned in confusion. "I don't understand. When the infantry moved up, General Hood never ordered them to block the road, did he? That was the cavalry's job, and there just weren't enough of us."

"That's what General Forrest pointed out to him. Old Forrest didn't take too well to bein' chewed out that way. From what I heard, he had some words of his own with Hood. Said that if Hood were a whole man instead of a cripple, he'd whup him good."

Hood's disabilities included a useless left arm, a reminder of Gettysburg, and an amputated right leg, incurred at Chickamauga. As a result of these wounds, the general had to be tied into his saddle whenever the army moved. The general's constant agony fueled a rumor that Hood used so much laudanum to dull his pain that his mind was muddled more often than not. That was just the sort of commander a fighting force needed, Henry thought bitterly.

"We should've had them bastards," Murrell said in conclusion. "I tell you, boys, I sure do hate to think that ol' Wade died for nothin'."

"We'll get 'em today," Carruthers said. "But if we don't . . . hell, we'll just chase 'em all the way to Nashville." He laughed, but it had a hollow sound.

The army was on the move early. Now that the Yankees had gone on, there was nothing to stop the Confederates from using the turnpike. Again the advance was split into three columns, one flanking the road on each side, the third staying on the turnpike itself. Forrest and the cavalry ranged out ahead of this central column as the infantry marched north toward the town of Franklin, which lay in a bend of the Big Harpeth River.

By midmorning, the cavalry caught up with Schofield's rear guard. Henry heard the firing and within minutes joined the fight himself, riding ahead with Murrell and Carruthers to harass the Yankee stragglers with pistol fire. He wished he could get his hands on some more ammunition for the Spencer; during the short time he had used the repeater, he had grown quite fond of the weapon.

Henry and his friends were close to the front as they came within sight of a small hill rising in the distance. Between them and the hill lay at least two miles of open fields. Henry had a sinking feeling when he saw the terrain. His misgivings were shared by Murrell.

"Damn it," Murrell observed, "if the Yanks are on top of that hill, they can make things mighty hot for us if we try to take it."

"I know that place," Carruthers said. "Franklin's not far on the other side of it. There's a bunch of old breastworks along there, too. I'll bet the Yankees got to work on them as soon as they got there this mornin'. By now they've had a chance to build 'em up some."

Henry had never charged an enemy entrenched behind breastworks, but he could tell from the way Murrell and Carruthers were talking that it wasn't a good thing. "Maybe what we should do is go around them," he suggested.

Murrell grinned. "Now you're thinkin' like General Forrest. I'll bet that's just what he has us do. We can cross that river somewheres else and hit the Yankees from behind. Hell, if we can get around 'em, there ain't no reason why we can't go right on to Nashville. It ain't but a little ways on up the road."

That idea appealed to Henry. Forrest's force wasn't big enough to capture the city by itself, but the cavalry could wreak havoc and soften the place up for when Hood's infantry got there, not to mention playing hell with the Yankee supply and communication lines.

It seemed like a good idea to Henry, but obviously, someone else didn't think so. The cavalry halted again as the infantry came up. Not the artillery, though. The big guns were still far to the rear, unable to keep up with the rest of the army on the muddy roads.

Scouts went out, probing at the hill blocking the path of the Confederate advance. Henry expected the Yankees to be dug in up there, but reports filtered back that the enemy had retreated even farther, to the breastworks on the outskirts of Franklin itself. The Confederates moved up, cresting the rise, and Henry saw to his dismay that the terrain on the far side was even worse for a frontal assault: another two miles of wide open, almost treeless plain, the ground rolling gently with no place to hide, no cover to shield them from what was sure to be a rain of fire from the Federal guns.

The cavalry was divided then, some of it going to each flank. Henry and his friends were on the right. He could see the blue water of the Big Harpeth River in the distance. After so many days and weeks of rain and snow and chill and gloom, this afternoon was almost pleasant with its warming sunshine. The wind was still cold, though.

An officer rode by and ordered the men to dismount. "We won't be fighting from horseback today, boys," he said.

Murrell grimaced as he swung down from the saddle. Henry understood. Although he was still far from an expert rider, Henry would have felt better about going into battle mounted. A good horse could carry a man out of trouble in little more than the blink of an eye. A foot soldier, though, could do nothing but slog forward, even though he might be marching straight into the mouth of Hades itself.

Henry left the Spencer on the saddle and checked his pistol. The cylinder was fully loaded, but he didn't have much spare ammunition. He could reload once, maybe twice, and that was it. He glanced up at the sun with its weak, late autumn glow. There was only about an hour of daylight left. Maybe General Hood would decide to wait until the next morning to attack. In that time, he could change his mind, decide to let Forrest try flanking the Yankees instead.

"Move out! Straight ahead, boys!"

The shouted order made Henry draw a deep breath. There would be no delay. The attack was beginning now.

Henry moved forward, the pistol at his side. Somewhere behind him, a band began to play "Dixie." He looked to his left. From where he was at the far right end of the line, he could see the whole sweep of the Confederate advance. Rank after rank of men in tattered gray and butternut, many of them without head-gear, some without shoes. But they stepped out briskly in the dimming light. Brightly colored battle flags, now somewhat faded, snapped in the breeze above them. It was a spectacle the likes of which Henry had never imagined. He had experienced combat, but never before had he witnessed an entire army going into battle at the same time. His heart swelled with pride. Surely on this day the Confederate army would prove to be invincible. How could these soldiers not be, looking like they did?

Yankee artillery began to boom. Shells smashed into the line, canister rounds burst and spewed their deadly fruit. Still the soldiers pressed on. Their pace increased until their determined walk became a run and then, as had happened so many times in the past, fierce shouts welled from thousands of throats. On across the long, open field they surged.

Henry yelled, too, without even thinking about it. Most of the Union artillery fire was concentrated on the turnpike, where the attack was centered. Out here on the flanks only a few shells burst. Henry held his fire, knowing he was a long way from pistol range. Time stretched out, slowed down. Eerily, the charge across the fields seemed to take hours. Smoke rose into the sky from the artillery and from the rifles and carbines of the Federal troops crouched behind the hurriedly fortified breastworks. More and more of the running men stumbled and fell as lead ripped through them, but the others kept going, bounding over the bodies of their fallen comrades. And now they were close enough to start firing, too.

An artillery round exploded to Henry's right, throwing him off stride. He caught his balance and continued to run, glancing around to make sure that Murrell and Carruthers were all right. They were still with him, firing their carbines as they charged toward the Yankee defensive lines. Henry waited. He would save his bullets for the last minute, when he was close enough to the enemy that he couldn't miss. Those shots might make the difference, he thought. They might allow the Confederates to break through the Federal line.

At the same time, fear hammered through him, and he had to force his muscles to keep working, carrying him forward. He tried to make his mind and his feelings numb so he would not be overwhelmed by panic. Maybe some men could go into battle without being afraid, but he wasn't one of them. He wanted to turn and run the other direction.

In the end, his devotion to duty, the bond he felt with the other men, and his hatred of the Yankees and everything they had done to the South carried him ahead. Clouds of powder smoke rolled across the battlefield, choking and blinding him, but he pressed on, fighting his way through some thick brush, until he saw the Union breastworks no more than fifty yards in front of him. All was chaos around him now, the air filled with the hum of flying lead and the rattle of musketry and the screams of hurt and dying men.

Henry fired once, twice, as he ran forward. He was blinded for a second by the smoke, then it cleared and revealed to him the Yankees firing over the barriers of earth and stone and logs. The leading edge of the Confederate attack reached the breastworks and surged up and over them. Flags from both sides waved above the mass of fighting and dying humanity, bits of cloth darting back and forth, weaving around each other as if they were doing battle along with the men who carried them. Henry screamed incoherently as he reached the breastworks and started to clamber up them.

He thrust the pistol toward the blue-clad shapes that swam before his eyes and pulled the trigger. The gun bucked in his hand. He pulled the hammer back and fired again, repeating the near-mindless action until the pistol was empty. The hammer may have clicked harmlessly on an empty chamber several times before Henry realized what was happening; he never knew for certain about that. But he knew in this bloody madness that he would never have a chance to reload. He jammed the empty gun behind his belt and reached for a saber some officer had dropped. Union, Confederate, it didn't matter. All that was important was that the blade was sharp enough to hack the life out of the enemy, to cut through flesh and spill blood . . .

Henry's hand had just closed over the saber's grip when something smashed into his head and sent him tumbling backward into darkness.

FARTHER TO the west, in the center of the Union line, the vast column of gray- and butternut-clad men smashed into the Federal earthworks. The left side of the Confederate advance had farther to go before reaching the Union defenses, but as the light faded and dusk settled over the landscape, that part of the advance closed with the enemy as well. The line of battle stretched for miles.

It was desperate fighting, hand-to-hand clashes in the shadows. At first, as the charge began, it seemed to the defenders that the Southerners could not possibly cross so much open ground to reach them. Surely the artillery and rifle fire would break the back of the charge and repel the Rebels back to the southern hills from which they advanced. But the attackers swarmed over the advance Union position and followed the retreating Federals into heart of the Union line, their high-pitched yells providing a counterpoint to the crash of cannons and the crackle of rifles. Clouds of smoke roiled over the ground, concealing the Confederates for long moments, but when the wind cleared away those clouds, each time the line of gray was closer. With a crash like that of some primeval earthquake, the two sides were butted together.

The attacking Rebels at the center of the line were already in the midst of the Yankee earthworks, firing and stabbing and clubbing the defenders at close range. The Federals pulled back momentarily, then reinforcements came up, and the Union line stiffened. The Confederates fell back and charged again.

The mass of men charged and charged again. Hood was ensconced at a command post atop a nearby hill, but the clouds of powder smoke and the gathering darkness prevented him from seeing how the battle was going. All he could see were distant spurts of flame from the discharge of Union guns and the fireflies of combat in the gloom. Obviously, the Yankees were putting up a heavy resistance. They would have to be swept before the victorious Army of Tennessee in order for Hood to achieve the glorious success that he so obviously—in his own mind—deserved. The attack would continue, despite the fall of darkness, just like it had two years ago, when Hood broke through the Union defenses at the beginning of the Seven Days' battles. The key to success then—and now—was to attack and attack and attack. That was how Lee had defeated McClellan and Pope and Burnside and Hooker. That was how Hood would defeat Schofield and then Thomas.

Again and again the Confederates charged over the hotly disputed ground. The fighting was the heaviest at the center of the line, but it was pure hell from one end to the other. At the very center, where the turnpike followed by Cheatham's division cut through a farm belonging to a family named Carter, Patrick Cleburne urged his men forward, fighting side by side with them like a common soldier rather than a divisional commander. A Yankee bullet struck him just below the heart, killing him instantly. Not far away, Gen. Hiram Granbury fell dead, shot in the head. Off on the Confederate left, Gen. Otho F. Strahl was wounded while passing reloaded rifles forward to the front. His aides sprang up to carry him to the rear, but before they could do so, Strahl was hit again, mortally this time. Brig. Gen. John Adams fell in the fighting, as did Brig. Gen. States Rights Gist. Brig. Gen. John C. Carter suffered a wound that would take his life several days later. Another brigadier, George W. Gordon, was captured by the Yankees. Few men realized until later that, in this battle, the commanders seemed to be in as much danger as the lowliest private or drummer boy.

Many more command-grade officers fell during the bloody afternoon and early evening. Colonels fell as well, as did majors and captains and lieutenants. Field command fell sometimes all the way to sergeants. Still the battle continued. Men fought blindly, unable to see much of anything because of the darkness and the smoke. But it didn't take being able to see much to thrust the barrel of a rifle over the top of the breastworks and pull a trigger. Yankees and Rebels were packed so tightly it wasn't even necessary to aim. Nearly every shot shredded flesh and smashed through bone.

Before the fighting finally dwindled toward midnight, more than seventeen hundred men from John Bell Hood's Army of Tennessee lay dead or wounded on the plains just south of Franklin. The firing fell to sporadic exchanges between pickets, and Schofield withdrew his exhausted army to the northern bank of the Harpeth River and silently marched on to Nashville. The battle was over, but the cost for whatever Hood had won was tremendous.

It was a price these gallant Southerners could scarcely afford to pay.

Chapter Eighteen

F LAMES FLICKERED BEFORE HENRY'S eyes. The fires of hell, he supposed they were, because he was suffering the torments of the damned.

Other than the flames, pain was all he knew when he regained his senses. Great hammers wielded by gleefully chortling imps smote the inside of his skull. The vicious pounding sent wracking shudders all through his body. To move was sheer torture. His lips were as dry as paper, his tongue as coarse as a rasp. His throat was on fire. Convulsions made his muscles twitch and jerk. He wasn't dead after all, he decided. Death was supposed to be peaceful, not filled with all this fury and clamor and misery. Unless he really was in hell . . .

"Here you go, old son. Have some water."

The booming voice assaulted his ears, but the next instant brought heavenly relief. Something cool and smooth touched his cracked lips, and cold fire poured into his mouth and down his throat, easing the parched flesh. Henry tried to lift his head to suck harder on the cup.

The movement made his insides twist. He choked as the water he had swallowed came back up. He tried to turn onto his side but was too weak. Strong hands grasped him and rolled him over so he wouldn't choke. Then, as the spasm passed, he was eased onto his back again.

"Not so fast this time."

When the voice first spoke it had seemed so loud that it might as well have been the voice of God. Now it seemed to be at a more reasonable volume. Henry even recognized it. The voice belonged to Ernie Murrell. Slowly, as more of the blessed water dribbled into his mouth, he figured out that he was lying on the ground with his head in Murrell's lap.

A face moved into Henry's field of view. Jeb Carruther's raw-boned visage peered down at him. "Is he all right?" he asked.

"Reckon he'll be fine," Murrell said. The words were still painfully loud to Henry's ears. He was reminded of the one time in his life he had been hung over. Before the war, when he was still a boy, he'd filched a bottle of Titus's whiskey and drank the whole thing to see what it was like. He had been so sick the next day that he had hardly touched liquor since then. He figured his mother had known what was wrong with him, but for once Abigail Brannon had held her tongue and at least pretended to accept the fiction that Henry had come down with some sort of stomach grippe.

Murrell took the cup away from his mouth. Henry wanted to clutch at it and drink more, but he knew Murrell was right to limit him. Whatever had happened to him, he had to recover from it slowly.

The muscles in his throat worked and his lips moved. No words came out. He tried again, forcing himself to say, "Wh . . . what happened?"

"You got shot in the head, that's what happened," Murrell said matter of factly.

Henry closed his eyes. *Shot in the head.* So he was dying, and Murrell was just trying to make him comfortable so that he could spend his last few minutes in peace. It wasn't working.

"My . . . mother," Henry whispered. "Abigail Brannon . . . Culpeper County . . . Virginia . . . send word to . . . to her—"

"Whatever you got to tell your ma, you can do it your own-self," Murrell said. "You ain't dyin', Brannon. That Yankee bullet just parted your hair, creased your scalp, and maybe barked your skull a mite. Knocked you colder'n a mackerel, though. Jeb and me, when we saw you fall, we each grabbed an arm and hauled you out of there, back here. If we'd have left you there, the Yanks would've bayoneted you for sure."

Henry slowly reopened his eyes. "You . . . fell back from the . . . breastworks?"

Carruthers hunkered on his heels next to Henry and Murrell. "That's what the officers was yellin' for us to do," he said. "There was no way we could bust through that Yankee line. They was dug in too good. The officers knew it, too." Carruthers shook his head solemnly. "Not that there was a whole lot of 'em left by the time the fightin' was over."

"It was bad, mighty bad," Murrell said. "Pat Cleburne's dead. So's his right bower, General Granbury. And States Rights Gist, and Strahl, and God knows how many more generals. Never saw a battle like this before, where the generals were droppin' almost as fast as the men."

"We almost broke through for a minute." Carruthers's words were wistful as he spoke of the missed opportunity. "But then the Yankees plugged the gap, and that was all she wrote." His voice broke in sorrow. "This here army is wrecked, plumb wrecked. Hood threw us at the Yankees and threw us at the Yankees until there . . . there ain't hardly nothin' left."

"Then we're going to . . . retreat?" Henry asked.

"Nobody knows what we're goin' to do," Murrell said. "We're just sittin' here, waitin' for mornin'."

Henry was able to turn his head this time without feeling as if his skull was about to explode. He looked out into a vast darkness dotted with campfires. The night was filled with the moans and screams of the wounded and dying, pleading for water or release from pain. The sounds formed a terrible harmony, one of the worst things Henry had ever heard.

Now that his wits had returned to him somewhat, he looked again at Murrell and Carruthers. After studying them for a moment, he asked, "You boys . . . hurt?"

"A scratch here and there, but we was damned lucky," Carruthers said. "'Course, if we hadn't pulled back when we did, I reckon we'd all be dead now, a-layin' out there in that ditch in front of the Yankee lines with all the other dead men piled up like cordwood."

"What about . . . General Forrest?"

"The general's all right, I suppose. Mad as hell, prob'ly. He took some of the boys downriver and forded the Harpeth, tried to get at the Yankee rear that way, like we talked about. But the Yankee cavalry was waitin' for him, and they beat him." Murrell sounded like he could hardly believe what he was saying. "Made him hightail it back across the river. First time I ever heard of such a thing. If your brother was here, he could tell you that Forrest ain't one to throw away the lives of his men for nothin'. Never has been."

"Not like some other generals we could all name," Carruthers said in a voice edged with bitterness and pain.

Henry closed his eyes again as a tide of weariness swept over him. "Then it's over," he said. "There's nothing else we can do."

"I reckon we'll see," Murrell said, "come mornin'."

BUT IT wasn't over, unbelievable as that was to the men who had survived the five hours of pure hell that became known as the battle of Franklin. The toll taken by the battle was enormous: More than seven thousand men killed, wounded, or captured. Six generals dead: Cleburne, Granbury, Gist, Carter, Strahl, Adams. The bodies of Cleburne, Granbury, and Strahl were laid out on the veranda of the Carnton plantation house, which was being used as a field hospital. Henry sat not far away on a stump, nursing his head and watching a line of men pass by the house to pay their respects to the fallen commanders.

Several more generals had been wounded or captured. Fifty-three regimental commanders were killed, wounded, or captured. The loss in leadership was so staggering that it was difficult for the mind to grasp.

Gen. John Bell Hood certainly had trouble grasping it. He was up and about early on the morning of December 1, preparing for yet another attack on the Federal fortifications, when scouts brought word that the Yankees had abandoned Franklin during the night. Schofield had pulled out and no doubt was even now hustling up the turnpike toward Nashville, less than twenty miles away.

Hood immediately ordered his army to go after them. He rode into Franklin, tied onto his saddle, laudanum coursing through his veins, and congratulated his men on the great victory they had won by forcing the Yankees to retreat to Nashville.

Forrest was getting ready to move already, splitting his force to ford the Big Harpeth River to both east and west of Franklin. Once across the river, the two groups would converge on the settlement at Brentwood, about halfway between Franklin and Nashville. The plan was for the cavalry, after reuniting at Brentwood, to block Schofield's retreat if possible or to harass the Yankees if not.

Henry was still dizzy, but as he sat on his stump at the Carnton house, he was able to swallow some grain coffee and gnaw on a small square of hardtack without getting sick. The food settled his stomach somewhat. When he felt strong enough, he went to saddle his horse.

Next to him, Murrell was getting his own mount ready to ride. He looked over at Henry. "You was wounded, Brannon. You don't have to go with us."

Henry grunted in dismissal of that idea. "There are men who were hurt a lot worse than I am who are riding with you this morning. I'll do my part."

"Suit yourself."

A rag was bound around Henry's head, covering the narrow, blood-crusted furrow where the Yankee bullet had clipped him just above the left ear. The injury was painful enough that he couldn't wear a hat, but he wasn't worried about that. He supposed he looked a little like a pirate with that rag around his head like that. He didn't feel the least bit piratical, however.

Forrest's riders set off as the sky began to turn gray. They were accompanied by the horse artillery, commanded by Lt. John Morton, the brilliant young artillery officer who had been with Forrest since the autumn of 1862. Henry, Murrell, and Carruthers were with the men who forded the river east of Franklin. As soon as they were on the other side of the stream, they galloped northward.

Henry's head ached, but not intolerably. The pace of the horse and the pounding of hooves increased the ache, as did the growing light as the sun rose. He wished he could just lie still in a dark room somewhere, but such peaceful havens were nowhere to be found on this day.

Around midmorning, as the riders approached Brentwood, shots suddenly rang out. A small force of Union cavalry dashed from behind a barn and attacked the flank of the Confederates. Outnumbered, the Yankees could do no more than hit and run. Yelling and whooping, some of Forrest's men pursued them toward some trees. As he watched, Henry felt a sudden misgiving. He had seen something like this before. Sure enough, a moment later Federal artillery hidden in the trees roared forth with a volley that tore through the charging Confederate line.

This time, the Southerners had the means to fight back effectively. Morton's guns came up quickly and roared back at the Yankees. Opposing salvos filled the air for several long, deafening minutes. Then the Yankees, outgunned now as well as outnumbered, retreated.

"Hate to see that damned Yank cavalry," Murrell said. "That means Schofield's gone on up the road and sent back the horsemen to be his rear guard. That wily little sumbitch didn't waste any time."

"He'll be in Nashville by noon," Carruthers predicted, a gloomy expression on his face.

The cavalry rode into Brentwood and rendezvoused with the group that had skirted Franklin to the west. With Forrest at their head, the horsemen rode on north toward Nashville during the afternoon. Early dusk was falling as they made camp within sight of the city. Henry saw the spire of the capital building in the distance.

He felt nothing special about Nashville. He had never been there, and besides, he was a Virginian, not a Tennessean. To him the city was only a Yankee stronghold. But he knew that it had been the army's objective for the last month, and his pulse quickened a bit as he looked toward the city now disappearing in the fading shadows. This was as close as the Confederates had been to Nashville in a long time. The moment probably would have meant more to him if he hadn't been so blasted woozy from his wound.

Even after being in the saddle all day and not eating, Henry wasn't hungry. Murrell badgered him to eat anyway. Henry managed to get down a cup of thin soup. The men sat around the fire and talked about the difficulties ahead.

"The Yankees have been sittin' there in Nashville for years, just gettin' ready for this," Carruthers said. "With the Cumberland loopin' around the city like it does, they got some natural defenses workin' for 'em."

Murrell nodded solemnly. "I hear tell they got trenches and breastworks, and more trenches and breastworks behind them. And now Thomas has got Schofield and his men added to what he already had. I'm tellin' you, boys, it's gonna be a hell of a tough nut to crack."

Henry didn't know anything about the city or the fortified landscape surrounding it. But he knew that if the Yankees had mustered any sort of sizable force, Hood's battered and weakened army could not hope to defeat them. He said as much then added, "No disrespect to General Hood."

Moisture sizzled as Murrell spat into the fire. "Show all the disrespect you want," he said. "General or not, he didn't have no right to do what he done to us yesterday. I'll fight them Yanks up one way and down t'other *as long as we got a chance of winnin'.*" Murrell shook his head. "But I'm startin' to think it's time to give up and go home."

Carruthers lowered his voice to little more than a whisper. "You mean we ought to desert?"

Henry frowned. As bad as it was to talk about deserting the army, it would be even worse for him. He had no home to go to right now. It wouldn't be safe for him to return to Virginia until the war was over, one way or the other.

Murrell hesitated before answering Carruthers. "Naw," he finally said. "I don't reckon we could do that. It'd always stick in my craw if I knew we'd run from the Yanks. But it sure does look to me like we gone out of our way to lose that fight yesterday, and if we attack again as soon as the infantry comes up, we'll lose that one, too."

Henry knew Murrell was right about that. Battered, bloodied, outnumbered, if Hood's Army of Tennessee mounted a full-fledged assault on the defenses around Nashville, disaster would be the only possible outcome.

But that attack was not to come right away. As the infantry marched up the turnpike from Franklin and arrived in the hills around Brentwood, overlooking the valley of Brown's Creek that separated them from Nashville, Hood formed them into a line that stretched four miles and spanned the four major roads that entered the city from the south. A week passed while the two armies sat there and glared across the valley at each other.

Stuck there as they were, men on both sides could only speculate about what was going to happen next. Judging by appearances, Hood seemed to want to lay siege to the city. Such tactics had worked for the Yankees at Vicksburg and Atlanta, but for the life of him, Henry couldn't see how Hood hoped to manage such a thing here. Plenty of supplies were still flowing into Nashville from the north and east, and Hood's skimpy forces had no hope of cutting those supply lines. Not even Forrest, the most skillful cavalry raider on the Southern side, could accomplish that with the number of men at his command.

By laying siege to Nashville, it seemed to Henry that the Confederates really would be holding themselves prisoner, and if anyone was going to be starved into submission in such a situation, it was them, not the Yankees.

Whatever happened at Nashville, it seemed unlikely that Henry was going to be there to see it, because after several days of waiting, orders came for the cavalry to mount up and ride.

As he saddled his horse, Henry asked Murrell, "Where do you think we're going?"

"From what I hear, General Hood's sendin' the cavalry down to take Murfreesboro. That's about thirty miles southeast o' here, on Stones River. We had us a big fight there a couple of years ago, but the Yankees have a sizable garrison there now."

"What's that got to do with taking Nashville?"

Murrell shook his head. "Beats the hell outta me."

Puzzled or not, there was nothing for the men to do except mount up and set off toward Murfreesboro, following the Chattanooga Railroad. Henry, Murrell, and Carruthers rode near the front of the column, where they could see the tall, lean Forrest on a fine horse.

The delay in front of the lines at Nashville had given Henry time to get over his wound, at least somewhat. His head had pounded viciously for several days, and a blurriness came and went over his eyes. Those problems had grown better. At times his head still ached, but his vision no longer bothered him and he hadn't been sick at his stomach for several days.

The cavalry paused at every bridge they came to along the railroad and set fire to the spans. Some of the trestles were protected by Yankee guardhouses, but the few men who were stationed at those posts took one look at the Confederate cavalry and surrendered. The general had several thousand men in his command and was being followed closely by a division of infantry, so that his total force numbered around sixty-five hundred men. The Federal garrison at Murfreesboro consisted of approximately eight thousand men. The Southerners would be outnumbered, but the odds were close enough for Forrest.

After two days of burning bridges and tearing up track, the cavalry closed in on Murfreesboro. Forrest led a smaller group forward to get an idea of what challenges awaited them. Henry and his two companions were among the men selected for that reconnaissance.

As they rode alongside the railroad tracks, Forrest looked over at Henry. "Brannon, isn't it?" The general hadn't spoken to him since the night Henry joined the cavalry.

"That's right, sir."

"How are you enjoyin' life in our little band?" the general asked with a wry smile. Without waiting for an answer, he gestured toward the rag still tied around Henry's head. "You look a little like an old mammy. What happened to you?"

"A minor wound at Franklin, General. I thought it made me look like a pirate."

Forrest threw back his head and laughed. "Then a pirate you shall be, Mr. Brannon. I recall that your father had a fondness for Shakespeare?"

"That's right. He named all of us after characters in the plays, except for my brother Will. His name was William Shakespeare Brannon."

"Was?" Forrest repeated.

"Yes sir. He fell at Cold Harbor."

A solemn expression replaced the rakish grin on Forrest's face. "My sympathies. Too many good men have fallen."

"Yes sir."

They rode on, and a short time later Forrest called a halt. Using field glasses, he studied a slight rise about a mile away. "The Yankees have got themselves a damned fortress up there," he said under his breath. "The fortifications go right across the railroad. I can see the snouts of quite a few big guns pokin' over those walls, too."

For several minutes, Forrest conferred with his staff. Henry and the others sat nearby, waiting. This was a scouting mission only; they would not be attacking the Yankee garrison with such a small force. From Forrest's reaction, it seemed that they wouldn't be attacking, period. Henry didn't have any field glasses, but with the naked eye he could see the line of thick earthworks that had been thrown up by the Yankees on top of that rise. They looked mighty formidable to him.

The advance group stayed where it was and let the rest of the cavalry and the infantry come up to them. Unless the Yankees were blind, they had to see the Confederates moving into position northwest of the fortress. "What do you think we're going to do?" Henry asked Murrell and Carruthers.

"Cavalry's no good for chargin' a fort," Carruthers said. "We'll have to draw them Yankees out somehow."

Murrell nodded. "That's right. General Forrest won't go to them. He'll make the Yankees come to him."

That night, as the Confederates made camp, they kept their fires smaller and less numerous than usual. Let the Yankees sit up there in their fort and grow confident, Henry thought. Make them think Forrest's force was smaller than it really was. That was the idea. Henry knew how arrogant those Northerners were. They might grow irritated at the idea of a relatively few Rebels keeping them bottled up. If that happened, they were liable to come out to brush away what they considered to be nothing more than an annoying handful of Confederates. Just like swatting at a bug.

But this bug had a stinger in its tail.

In the morning, just as Forrest must have hoped, a Federal column marched out of the fort and started toward the Confederate camp. Quickly, Forrest moved up the infantry to meet the attack head-on, while the cavalrymen swung up into the saddles and galloped toward the flanks. As soon as the two columns of infantry were engaged, the cavalry would pinch in on the Federals from the sides.

Henry rode through the cold morning next to Murrell and Carruthers, along with hundreds of other troopers who veered to the left, around the end of the Confederate line. Cannons began to thunder in the distance as the artillery on both sides opened the battle. The rattle of rifles and muskets followed hard on the heels of the big guns. Henry stayed alert, expecting to see Union cavalry riding out to meet them at any moment, but there was no sign of blue-clad horsemen. The Yankees seemed to be intent on fighting this engagement with foot soldiers alone.

The troopers closed in, galloping over the fields and aiming toward the clouds of smoke that rose into the sky and marked the position of the fighting. As they thundered toward the Federal right flank, Murrell snatched off his hat, waved it over his head, and let out a defiant howl. Carruthers followed suit. Henry would have, too—had he had a hat. He settled for a furious Rebel yell of his own.

They could see the battlefield now, and Henry's yell died abruptly as he realized what was happening. The Confederate infantry was retreating, falling back under the assault of the Federal charge. Through gaps in the roiling smoke, Henry caught glimpses of a tall figure on horseback waving a sword as he tried to rally the men around him. That was Forrest, and Henry could imagine the general's rage as the infantrymen broke and fled in the face of the enemy.

As Henry watched, Forrest threw his sword aside and leaned from his saddle to snatch a battle flag from a color-bearer as the man scooted past him. With the worn flagstaff in one hand and his reins in the other, the general wheeled his horse in a tight circle and lashed out at the retreating soldiers, using the tattered crimson colors of the Confederacy to drive them back toward the front. It was an awe-inspiring sight, but Forrest's valor would prove futile if the cavalry didn't act quickly to stem the tide of the Union attack.

Henry jammed his heels into the flanks of his horse and sent the animal surging forward. The line of cavalrymen hit the Yankees from the side, driving in among them. Bllue-clad men fell screaming under the hooves of Henry's horse as he drew his pistol and fired. Again and again he saw Yankees falling as his gun blasted. Powder smoke blinded and choked him, but he kept fighting until the pistol's hammer fell on an empty chamber. Then he reversed the weapon and used the butt to smash the skull of a Yankee who was trying to draw a bead on another Confederate cavalryman.

The chaos continued for long minutes. Unable to reload, Henry used his mount as a weapon, riding down as many of the Yankees as he could. He continued clubbing the ones he could reach with the pistol. He was going to have to get himself another pistol or two, maybe a saber, the cool, collected part of his mind thought. The rest of him kept on fighting with a mad frenzy that gripped him.

Finally, the Yankees broke and ran. They streamed back across the fields and up the hill toward the fort. The Confederate cavalry harried them on their way and didn't fall back until the cannons mounted on the earthen walls of the fortress began to belch fire and smoke. Several men laughed defiantly as they turned and raced away from the artillery barrage.

As the cavalry regrouped, Forrest rode among the men, shaking hands with them and offering quiet words of congratulations. Anger warred with pride in his expression. The enemy had been defeated today at the last minute by the efforts of his gallant horsemen, but the situation would never have grown so desperate if the infantry had not crumbled so quickly. Whoever commanded that division of foot soldiers would be in for a tongue-lashing from Forrest, Henry thought.

Forrest paused and shook hands with him. As usual, the general had come through the battle unscathed. He said, "A hot bit of business there for a while, wasn't it, Brannon?"

"Yes sir." Henry ventured a question. "What are we going to do now, sir?"

"Well, since we sent those Yankees runnin' back into their hole, we'll just let them stay there for a while. If they come out again, we'll whip 'em again. In the meantime, there are bridges to burn and tracks to tear up. We'll wreck every railroad in this part of Tennessee, by God! The Yankees ain't bringin' in any more supplies this way."

Henry nodded. "Sounds like a good idea to me."

"Mighty glad you approve," Forrest said, his voice dry with humor. The day could have been disastrous, but it had turned out well for the Confederacy, at least here at Murfreesboro.

But as he rode back to the Confederate lines with Murrell and Carruthers, Henry couldn't help but wonder how things were going elsewhere.

Chapter Nineteen

THIS PART OF THE world had never seen anything like it: total war. Destruction and confiscation of private property and terror waged against civilians as well as soldiers. Since the middle of November, Gen. William Tecumseh Sherman's armies had been sweeping through Georgia, destroying everything in its path like a horde of ravening locusts. The destruction started before that, though. Before leaving Atlanta, Sherman ordered that the business and industrial sections be put to the torch. He might be leaving Atlanta behind, but he didn't intend for the Confederacy to be able to get any use out of the place again.

Despite Sherman's orders that the residential areas of the city were to be spared, the fires set by his engineers quickly spread. Exploding shells left in a former arsenal made things even worse, and then when the flames reached an oil refinery, all hell broke loose. Huge pillars of flames leaped into the sky, topped by roiling clouds of black smoke that were visible for scores of miles. With the city already ablaze, the Yankees could no longer be controlled. They tore through Atlanta in an orgy of looting and wanton destruction. No civilian was safe. All the citizens could do was hunker in their homes and hope that they would be spared from the inferno and from the rampaging troops.

Sherman and his men left little behind them but desolation when they pulled out. Ahead of them lay a country ripe for even more destruction.

The goal was Savannah, Georgia's major port city on the Atlantic coast. Rations for Sherman's army were running low, but the general didn't see that as a problem. His men would live off the land, taking what they needed and ruining everything else. Sherman's goal was more than strategic: He wanted to capture Savannah, but more than anything else, he wanted to teach the Southerners a lesson. Blaming them for the war in the first place, it was now time for them to reap the whirlwind, as Sherman saw it.

Besides, up in Washington City, Abraham Lincoln was sitting in the White House with an election victory behind him. Little Mac McClellan had gone down to defeat in the voting. There would be no treaty, no negotiated peace between the United States and the renegade Confederacy. Only a total victory that meant the end of the rebellion would end the war now. When it was over, the Confederacy would be no more, forever and ever, amen. If it took waging war on civilians to bring about that end, then so be it, Sherman decided.

For four weeks in November and December, hell was let loose across the midsection of Georgia. In two columns, Sherman's army marched toward the sea. As they came to the farms and plantations of the Georgians, they slaughtered livestock, looted houses, and set fire to the dwellings and barns when they were ready to move on. With nearly all the men gone, there was no one to protect these places. Women, children, and the elderly had to stand by and watch helplessly as their homes were wrecked and then put to the torch. To resist would be to risk injury or worse, because the officers' control over their men was tenuous at best.

The Northerners saw their wrath as righteous and firmly believed that whatever they dished out, the Rebels had it coming. In their march, they encountered escapees from the infamous prison camp called Andersonville. These former prisoners, ragged scarecrows all, told horrifying stories of the camp's crude shebangs and mass graves, of starvation and torment and death. Then Sherman's men reached the town of Millen, where many of the prisoners relocated from Andersonville had been housed for a time at Camp Lawton, and as they saw more evidence there of horror and deprivation, the desire for vengeance grew even stronger in the soldiers. How dare those filthy, no-good Rebs treat our boys like that? they asked themselves.

It was doubtful that many of them had ever heard of a place in Illinois, on the outskirts of Chicago, called Camp Douglas or New York's Elmira or Fort Delaware . . .

On they marched, scavenging and burning what they couldn't carry away. Wherever they found slaves, they set them free. The blacks welcomed the Yankees as saviors, hardly able to believe that their days of bondage were finally over. Many followed the armies across the countryside, intent on forging new lives for themselves in the North, which they saw as a Garden of Eden, a place where they believed they would be welcomed with open arms. After all, they told themselves, the Yankees had freed them. Surely they would encounter no prejudice in the land those saviors called home.

Still the troops moved on, and as they did, gangs of what came to be known as "bummers" traveled with them. These renegades, mostly poor white Georgians with their ranks bolstered by deserters from the Confederate army, turned on their own people and joined in the destruction. They were out for whatever they could get and cared nothing for whoever got hurt. Though preachers shouted about the heights the human soul can obtain, the bummers were living proof that there are no depths to which the human soul cannot sink.

Here and there, skirmishes broke out as the Confederates tried to muster some opposition to the relentless Union advance. More than once, a wavering line of gray-clad soldiers appeared ahead of the columns, and smoke spurted from the muzzles of ancient muskets. A few volleys of rifle fire scythed through the defenders and swept them out of the way. When the soldiers marched past the sprawled, bloody corpses, they saw the grizzled faces of men as old as ninety and the unshaven cheeks of boys as young as twelve. Old men and cubs . . . they were the only ones remaining to fight the invaders. Well, they were Rebels, the Yankees told themselves. No matter how old or how young, they deserved to die, didn't they? They were Rebels, just Rebels, who had gotten what was coming to them.

November turned to December, and the march continued. Soon, it would be Christmas.

CORY WALKED up the steps to the porch and paused to look down the street toward the harbor at the mouth of the Savannah River. This gracious old house that had been opened to General Hardee and his staff commanded a fine view of the water. At times like this, Cory thought how nice it would be to sail away over those waves, leaving all his troubles behind him. He could only do that, though, if he had Lucille with him, and God knew where she was these days.

And he wouldn't sail off anyway, Cory told himself with a faint, grim smile. Although he had become fond of the sound and sight and smell of the ocean during the months he had spent in Charleston and now here in Savannah, he was a landlubber at heart, and he knew it. He would never be happy without solid ground under his feet. Maybe that was a sign that he was growing up at last.

Of course, once the Yankees got here, he might not have a chance to get much older. Reports had streamed into Hardee's headquarters about the devastation being wreaked by Sherman's army between here and Atlanta. The newspapers might not be reporting it—they were still trying to paint a rosy picture—but the soldiers knew. They were aware of what Sherman was doing, and they knew he was barreling right toward them.

The door of the house opened behind Cory. "Good morning, Lieutenant Brannon," a female voice greeted him. "Come in and have some breakfast."

Cory turned with a smile for his hostess. "Thank you, Mrs. Heaphy. That sounds mighty good."

Betty Heaphy was the epitome of Southern graciousness. An attractive woman with red hair and a scattering of freckles, she ushered Cory into the house. She was a widow and had been more than happy to have Hardee and his staff quartered here. The big, whitewashed house had been built more than 120 years earlier, not long after Savannah was founded in 1733 as Georgia's first permanent colonial settlement. Cory had heard a great deal about the city's history while he was here. Savannah's citizens were quite proud of their home.

General Hardee was at the table in the dining room, enjoying breakfast with several members of his staff as well as the dapper General Beauregard, recently arrived in the city. Hardee looked up as Cory entered the room with Betty Heaphy.

"What news from our scouts, Lieutenant?" he asked.

"Nothing good, sir," Cory said. "Some of the Yankees appear to be headed for Fort McAllister."

Beauregard leaned forward and gestured with his fork. "That rascal Sherman wants to link up with his navy. I'll wager there are Yankee ships waiting just offshore for him to capture one of the ports."

Hardee sighed and nodded. "I expect you're right, General."

The city of Savannah lay on a twenty-mile-wide tongue of land between the Savannah River to the north and the Ogeechee to the south. The mile-wide Savannah served as the border between Georgia and South Carolina. Earlier the Yankees had tried to capture the railroad terminal on the South Carolina shore just across from the city. Such a maneuver would have cut off any escape to Charleston and would have meant that the ten thousand defenders of Savannah would be bottled up in the city once Sherman arrived.

This Federal advance, however, had been beaten back by the Georgia militia, which had just arrived in Savannah after skirmishing unsuccessfully with Sherman's juggernaut. It had been quite a valiant effort, from everything that Cory had heard, and for now at least, the Charleston and Savannah Railroad was still in the hands of the Confederates.

The question was whether Hardee would use it to evacuate his men or stay and fight to a bitter end.

Hardee waved Cory into an empty chair. "Sit down and have a bite, Lieutenant. Where's that sergeant of yours?"

"Sergeant Strayhorn has ridden out to check on the defenses, sir," Cory replied as he lowered himself into the chair. With his fork he speared a couple of hotcakes from a platter in the middle of the table. The food was better here in Savannah; that was one thing you could say for the place. Blockade-runners had been quite successful in bringing in supplies past the Yankee ships that patrolled the coast; however, Cory knew that situation was not going to last much longer. Already some provisions were beginning to run low. If Sherman laid siege to the city, it wouldn't be long until it was Vicksburg all over again, he thought glumly. He would never forget those grueling days and the illness, starvation, and deprivation. The only good thing about the siege of Vicksburg was that he and Lucille had gotten married while it was going on, in a cave dug out for shelter from the endless Federal bombardment.

He hated to think that the same thing could happen to this beautiful city by the sea. It was going to happen, unless some miracle occurred to divert Sherman from his chosen course.

Sometimes, Cory thought, it was better to be a simple foot soldier, unaware of what was happening on a broader scale until the shooting started and the enemy was right in your face.

He and Abner Strayhorn had come to Charleston in that role, infantrymen as part of Hardee's headquarters company. But the general had found out that Cory had served as a scout and aide to Bedford Forrest and had promoted him to sergeant, making him an orderly. By the time Hardee had come down the coast to Savannah to supervise its defense, Cory had been promoted again, this time to lieutenant, and was serving as an aide to the general. His rise through the ranks had been swift, but in a war there was little time to waste. Men who had the ability to handle a job had to be placed in a position to do that job. Cory had been able to bring Abner up through the ranks with him, although one rung lower on the ladder. Abner didn't mind. He was perfectly content to be a sergeant, claiming that officers, even junior ones like Cory, had too damned many responsibilities.

Betty Heaphy brought more hotcakes from the kitchen. Cory ate his fill, having learned the soldier's lesson that no matter how much food was in front of him now, the odds were that soon he would be hungry again. The generals continued to discuss the situation as Cory ate.

"I think you had best get the engineers to work on a pontoon bridge across the Savannah," Beauregard suggested. "You'll want to be able to get your men across to the railroad in a hurry if such becomes necessary."

Hardee frowned at the idea. "That would mean abandoning the city, General."

Beauregard inclined his head. "Indeed it would. Better that than the utter destruction of your army, General."

"I do not plan for my army to be on the verge of utter destruction, sir," Hardee said stiffly.

If Beauregard took any offense at Hardee's tone, he gave no sign of it. "Of course not. Our defenses are sound and well manned. Sherman will never reach Savannah. But I'd give some thought to that bridge anyway."

"Yes sir, I'll do that," Hardee said. Beauregard was his superior, the only officer of higher rank in this part of the Confederacy, and although Beauregard had stopped short of giving Hardee a direct order to build a bridge across the Savannah, Cory knew the result would be the same. The bridge would be built.

On several occasions, he had ridden out of the city with General Hardee on inspection tours of the city defenses to the south and west. The fortifications were formidable: breastworks, trenches, rifle pits, artillery emplacements, all fronted by a barrier of fallen trees that had been sharpened and interlaced to form a deadly obstacle. No commander could have asked for a stouter line from which to repel the enemy. The problem was that even counting all the regular army soldiers and militiamen in Savannah combined, there were hardly enough to man the defenses. The line of breastworks was solid; the line of men behind them was much more fragile.

After breakfast, the generals and the senior officers withdrew to the parlor, where they had spread out maps and odd bits of information. The endless discussion of strategy and preparation and contingencies went on all day. Cory remained in the parlor most of the time, but late in the afternoon he went out on the porch again and sat in a rocking chair, close enough so that Hardee could summon him easily enough if he was needed. Cory was an officer now, but at heart he was still a civilian. He did his best, but he would never be the sort of military man the others were.

The day was warm, especially for December. Here on the coast, the weather was always mild, he supposed. He gazed across the harbor toward the South Carolina shore. When he had left home in Virginia years earlier, his ambition had been to travel, to satisfy his restless nature. He had certainly done plenty of that, he thought. He had been all over the place . . . everywhere that men were killing each other over their politics.

"Cory!"

The shout from the street made him turn his head and start up out of the chair. He saw Abner hurrying along the road toward headquarters. The sergeant turned in at the gate in the white picket fence and came up the walk almost at a run.

Cory met him at the top of the steps. "What is it, Abner? What's wrong?"

"Beggin' your pardon, Lieutenant. I didn't mean to call you—"

"Don't worry about that," Cory cut in. "Just tell me what's happened."

"Fort McAllister's fallen. The damnyanks took it a little while ago. We just got word."

Cory's heart sank. Fort McAllister was the main link in the defensive line to the south. It was considered virtually impregnable from the sea.

"How could they do that?" Cory asked, his voice little more than a whisper. "It must have taken the whole Yankee fleet."

Abner shook his head. "Sherman struck from the weak side, from the land."

That seemed almost as unlikely to Cory as an attack from the sea. When he had been with the general during his first inspection of the fort, he had seen with his own eyes the impassable trench that surrounded the strongpoint. At least fifteen feet deep and seven feet wide, the bottom of the trench was packed with fallen timbers that had been sharpened to wicked points and imbedded in the ground at an angle that threatened to impale anyone who tried to clamber over them.

"How? How could they . . ."

"Don't know. The report said it didn't take the damnyanks no more'n fifteen minutes to get through the trench and overrun the place. Not many of them got themselves killed, neither." The strain in Abner's voice showed that he understood the gravity of the news just as well as Cory did. "I reckon there'll be a courier showin' up soon with an official report for the generals. I come on ahead when I heard about it. Figured I'd give you the lowdown first. Maybe you can sort of get the general ready for the bad news."

No amount of preparation could soften this blow, Cory admitted to himself. Without the garrison at Fort McAllister to protect Savannah from the south, Sherman would be able to resupply his army from the ships that could now come ashore without having to worry about McAllister's guns. And as soon as Sherman was ready, he could turn north and bear down on Savannah. This wasn't the very end, Cory thought, but it was damned close.

"I'd better let General Hardee and General Beauregard know about this," he said dully.

"What do you reckon we're gonna do?"

Cory could only shake his head. "Fight or run," he said. "That's all that's left."

SOMEWHERE IT was probably warm, Henry thought, but sure as hell not here in Tennessee. For several days, Forrest's cavalry had been pinned down near Murfreesboro, not by the enemy but by the elements.

Another storm had blown in on December 7 and lasted for more than a week, bringing not snow this time but rather sleet. It came down hard, almost as thick as a pouring rain, accompanied by high winds and the bitterest cold of the season. When the ice storm finally stopped, it left an inch-thick layer of the frozen, slippery stuff on everything—ground, trees, bushes, buildings, anything that was out in the open. A man risked a fall and a broken arm or leg every time he tried to walk ten feet. As for riding the horses, that was out of the question.

So since they couldn't fight or continue the destruction of the railroads in the area, Forrest's men pitched their tents to wait out the storm and groused about the weather and John Bell Hood. The weather was more popular.

Hood had made his headquarters at a nearby plantation home known as Traveler's Rest, and rumors ran through the ranks that the big house was living up to its name. Hood hosted several elaborate dinners there for his officers, basking in the warmth of a massive fireplace and enjoying lavishly prepared food while his troops, many of them lacking shoes, coats, and blankets, shivered and made do with meager rations.

Henry, Murrell, and Carruthers sat around a small fire, trying to draw some warmth from the meager flames.

"I reckon it's goin' to warm up today," Murrell said while gnawing a tiny shard of hardtack. "I can feel it in my bones."

"I can't even feel my bones anymore, it's so damn cold," Carruthers said, "let alone tell what the weather's gonna do."

Murrell looked over at Henry. "Does it ever get this cold up where you come from?"

"It gets cold in Virginia," Henry replied. "Some places up in the mountains get quite a bit of snow. Where my family lives, it's not that common, but I've still seen snow plenty of times in my life."

"What about ice like this?"

"Not so much. A few times, that's all."

"Well, I'll be damned glad when it starts to melt off here, that's all I can say."

True to Murrell's prediction, the temperature warmed during the day. The sun came out for a while, and that made the ice begin to melt. Soon there was a steady *drip-drip-drip* from the coating of the cold stuff that had sheathed the trees. Henry hoped that by the next day, the roads would be fit to travel, even though they would no doubt be quite muddy.

Late that afternoon, it became obvious that the cavalry would have to travel, regardless of the weather. A courier arrived from General Hood and brought bad news with him. George H. Thomas, often criticized for being slow to move, had finally taken action, sending part of his army venturing out from Nashville to launch a probing attack at the right of the Confederate line before ordering an even heavier assault against the Confederate center. Hood was pulling back to form a new defensive line, but he needed Forrest to return to Nashville as soon as possible.

Henry halfway expected Forrest to order a night ride, but given the weather, that would have proven disastrous. Instead, the general decided that they would pull out the next morning. The men were able to get one more night's cold, restless sleep in their tents, but they were up well before dawn, saddling their horses and preparing to ride out. Forrest always liked to get an early start, Murrell told Henry. They left with empty stomachs, having practically exhausted their rations.

A day's hard riding over the muddy roads brought them closer to Nashville, close enough to hear the seemingly constant rumble of artillery in the distance. But night found them still separated from Hood's army, and again a courier brought unwanted news. The Yankees had smashed the line, forcing Hood to retreat. That retreat had become a rout, as men poured pell-mell over the Brentwood hills, heading south as they tried to put as much distance as possible between themselves and their blue-clad pursuers.

When Henry heard the report, he felt almost as sick as he had after a bullet had barked his skull. Hood was a fool, and his grandiose plan to recapture Nashville and push on to the Ohio River had come to nothing, its only result being the decimation of the Army of Tennessee. The defeat was a terrible one, and now, as Hood tried to pull back, the Yankees followed, determined to utterly crush their foes.

Henry figured that since the cavalry had missed the fight at Nashville, now the job of forming a rear guard would fall to Forrest. The next day, December 17, that was what happened. Forrest sent a large segment of his cavalry galloping across country to rendezvous with Hood's retreating army. Henry and his two companions were among those riding to protect the infantry.

Their destination was Franklin, site of the battle that had doomed Hood's invasion of Tennessee, although the general hadn't accepted that fact at the time. Henry and the other hard-riding horsemen came within sight of the Harpeth River during the afternoon. Units of Hood's army were already fording the river east of Franklin, going back the way they had come over the same pontoon bridges. The cavalry turned north, moving to block the Federal cavalry from descending on the hapless Confederates hurrying toward home.

Henry, Murrell, and Carruthers had ridden only a short distance when a unit of Union cavalry burst out of some trees ahead of them. The Yankees' Spencer repeaters cracked spitefully as they opened fire. With bullets whipping around them, Henry and his companions charged. Henry emptied his pistol at the foe. Something tugged at his left sleeve. He knew it was a bullet. Another cut through the tail of his coat as it flapped behind him. Murrell and Carruthers yowled and fired their carbines. One of the Yankees went down, tumbling out of the saddle and off his horse. But Carruthers cried out in pain as he jerked back and almost fell. Henry twisted to look at him, saw the blood on his left shoulder. Carruthers had been hit and couldn't defend himself—and one of the Yankees was riding right at him, swinging a saber.

Henry hauled his horse around in a sharp turn and sent the animal lunging toward the Yankee closing on Carruthers. The horses tried to shy away from each other, but their momentum was too great. They came together with a crash, and both went down in a melee of flailing hooves.

Henry threw himself out of the saddle as his mount fell. Landing hard on the ground, he rolled over and came up in a crouch, holding an empty pistol. He saw a flicker of movement in front of him and realized that the unhorsed Federal cavalryman was hurling himself toward him. The man hacked at him with his saber. Henry's reflexes were the only thing that saved him. He blocked the blow with the pistol. The blade slid off the barrel of the gun. The Yankee stumbled forward, right into the backhanded blow that Henry struck across his face with the revolver. The man grunted in pain and flinched back, dropping the saber to clasp his shattered jaw with both hands.

Henry grabbed the saber and rammed it into the Yankee's belly. Blood gushed hotly over his hands. He twisted the blade, ripping through the man's guts. The Yankee let out a garbled scream as he folded over and collapsed on top of him, showering him with gore. Henry thrust the dying man aside in revulsion and pulled the saber free. He climbed to his feet, weariness flooding through him.

The rest of the fight was over, he saw. One Yankee was left alive, and he was riding away hellbent for leather as Murrell sent a carbine shot after him. The other Federals were sprawled on the ground, dead or dying. Carruthers still sat on his horse, but he was hunched over in the saddle, clutching his injured shoulder.

Murrell rode hurriedly over to check on his friend's wound while Henry stripped the ammunition pouch from the dead Federal. When he checked it, he found several dozen rounds for the Spencer and nodded in grim satisfaction. Now he had ammunition again for the repeater and a saber as well. This had been a good day's work.

And it was just getting started.

FOR THE rest of the day, Forrest's men screened the retreat across the Harpeth River by what was left of Hood's army. George H. Thomas's infantry was still a good distance to the north, so Forrest's command had to contend only with the Union cavalry. The day was filled with sharp little skirmishes, but by nightfall the Confederates had crossed the river, destroyed the bridges behind them, and made camp between Thompson's Station and Spring Hill.

Wounded badly enough that he was out of action, Carruthers had been turned over to the surgeons in the retreating Confederate column, although he had insisted to Henry and Murrell that he was still fit enough to go on fighting. They knew that wasn't the case. Carruthers had passed out twice from loss of blood and was so weak he had to be tied into the saddle in order to stay on his horse.

All of Forrest's cavalry had regrouped by now, and these men formed the nucleus of the army's rear guard. Even though the Yankees were still in pursuit several days later, Forrest's determined efforts prevented the Federals from closing in on the ragged remnants of the decimated Army of Tennessee.

Henry spent every day in the saddle, riding and fighting alongside Ernie Murrell. The brief respite from the cold was over, and the skies were now thick with gray clouds. Freezing rain pelted the retreating soldiers. The roads were little better than quagmires.

The army trudged through the mud and the ice and the snow with far less enthusiasm than the men had shown a month earlier. Back then they were returning to the land that was the home state for many of them. Now the land was a cemetery for those who would never leave again.

And although few of the freezing, starving, ragged men gave any thought to the season other than to curse Tennessee's worst winter in anyone's memory, Christmas was less than a week away.

Chapter Twenty

IN SAVANNAH, THERE WOULD be little if any celebrating during this holiday season. Not with the Yankee invaders on the city's very doorstep.

Cory stood on the rear second-floor balcony of the Heaphy home and trained a pair of field glasses to the south of the city. Although he couldn't actually see any of the Yankees, he saw smoke rising into the sky from their campfires. They were taking life easy down there, he thought, taking their own sweet time about getting ready to move on the city. So far there had been no attacks. The only communication from the enemy had been a message from Sherman to Hardee demanding that Savannah be surrendered without delay. If not, Sherman wrote, he would "feel justified in resorting to the harshest measures." Cory had seen the message himself, and when he read it, he felt like crumpling the paper into a ball or ripping it into shreds. Neither action would change a damned thing, he knew. Like the gentleman he was, Hardee had been restrained in his response to Sherman's blunt ultimatum. He had declined to surrender, of course, and had subtly chided Sherman for his bluster. That might put a bee in the Yankee's bonnet, Cory thought, but it seemed unlikely that Hardee's refusal to surrender could make the situation any worse than it already was.

Hardee sat behind Cory in a wicker armchair. "Any news of the enemy's movements?" he asked in a voice little more than a murmur.

"No sir. We have good scouts posted to keep a watch on the Yankees. I'm sure we'll hear mighty quick if they start to move against us."

"I imagine they'll make an announcement when they commence action, probably to the accompaniment of their artillery."

335

Cory lowered the glasses. "Yes sir, I expect so." A continual bombardment had worked at Vicksburg. It would work here just as well.

Footsteps clattered inside the house. The door to the balcony opened, and Abner stepped out. "General Hardee, sir—" but he was interrupted by a man pushing impatiently past him.

Cory turned to see General Beauregard striding onto the balcony. Beauregard's face was dark with anger.

"General," he said to Hardee, "I see that the pontoon bridges across the river are still not completed."

As Cory had expected, Hardee had ordered the engineers to build a bridge across the Savannah River. The work had barely gotten started, however.

"General, my men have begun the construction work—" Hardee began.

"Not good enough. They must be done and done quickly."

Cory had gotten to know Hardee fairly well. He could tell that Beauregard's snappish tone angered the general. But good soldier that he was, Hardee merely nodded. "Of course, sir."

"I intend to speak to the engineers myself."

"As you wish." Hardee looked at Cory. "Lieutenant Brannon, accompany General Beauregard and provide him any assistance he may require."

Cory snapped to attention and saluted. He suspected that Hardee was sending him along so the engineers would know that the general was acceding to Beauregard's wishes.

The real reason Hardee had dragged his feet about the bridges, Cory thought, was because at heart the general was a fighting man. Building those bridges meant that the city's defenders were going to evacuate Savannah, give it up without a fight. That stuck in Hardee's craw. Cory understood completely. He didn't like the idea, either.

Yet from a strategic point of view, Beauregard was right. If the Confederates stayed where they were, they faced a battle that was unwinnable. It was all right to hope for a miracle; sometimes miracles actually happened. But with Robert E. Lee's army pinned down at Petersburg and Hood off somewhere in Tennessee, no one was left to deliver such a miracle. Hardee was on his own here at Savannah, facing a strong, well-fed, well-supplied foe. Outnumbered six to one, ultimately the defenders had no chance. They might fight to the last man, but in the end every one of them would either die or be captured.

Beauregard stalked off the balcony. Cory followed, jerking his head at Abner to indicate that the sergeant was to accompany him. Along with members of Beauregard's staff, they walked down to the riverfront with the general.

When they got there, Beauregard lit into the engineers, barking orders, striding back and forth, and making suggestions to speed up the process of bridge building. Cory observed, somewhat in awe, as the pace of the work increased. Details of soldiers were sent to the plantations upriver with orders to bring back as many rice boats as they could lay their hands on. These small, flat-bottomed boats, commonly used by workers in the flooded rice fields, were given an extra layer of caulking then positioned to serve as makeshift pontoons. Heavy wheels from railroad cars were attached to them to serve as anchors and keep them in place. Meanwhile, more gangs of slaves and laborers were charged with tearing down warehouses and other buildings along the river. The lumber obtained by this demolition was brought to the site and laid across the pontoons. Before Cory's eyes, the bridges began to take shape.

"They ain't much for looks," Abner said, "but as long as they'll float and hold up a fella's weight, I reckon they'll do."

The bridges would have to support more than just a man's weight. They would have to hold up to the burden of thousands of men marching across them as they fled the city.

The mile-wide span of the Savannah River was broken by two long, narrow islands that divided the river into channels. Hutchinson's Island was closest to the city, so the first pontoon bridge was built to it from the foot of West Broad Street. Upon reaching Hutchinson's Island, the troops would march across the sandy ground and then use another bridge to get to Pennyworth Island. The third bridge would reach from Pennyworth Island to the South Carolina shore. Using the islands as steppingstones, the engineers were able to complete the bridges in three days, under the nearly continual prodding of Beauregard.

Meanwhile, in order to mask the evacuation plans and to induce Sherman to believe that the defenders intended to make a fight of it, Hardee ordered the big guns around the city to open a bombardment on the Union lines. The Yankees answered in kind, sending shells whistling into the city. None of them did much damage, however. Yankee skirmishers approached the defensive line and traded rifle shots with the Confederate pickets. No real battles broke out, but there was a constant racket in the air as cannons boomed and riflemen on both sides sniped at each other.

By the morning of December 20, the bridges across the river were ready. Cory and Abner looked on as a weary Hardee issued orders for the men along the defensive line to begin pulling back and concentrating along the riverfront. The troops that were already in town started moving down to the river first. The retreat across the river would not take place until that night so that it would be covered by darkness.

At dusk that evening, Hardee climbed to the balcony of the Heaphy house and leaned his hands on the railing as he stared out at the campfires of the Yankees in the distance. The fires were becoming visible in the gathering shadows, although they wouldn't be for long as fog rolled in from the ocean.

Cory followed in time to hear the general murmur, "I would have liked to give that man a tussle. But that will have to wait for another day."

Cory nodded. "Yes sir. And I anticipate that day will come soon enough."

Hardee smiled faintly. He was carrying his hat. Now he settled it on his head. "I expect you're right, Lieutenant."

He left the balcony, intending to go to the riverfront to supervise the evacuation of the troops. Cory would have followed on Hardee's heels, but Betty Heaphy stepped out to block his path with a worried expression on her face.

"Lieutenant Brannon," she asked, "what's to become of us here in Savannah?"

Cory tried to sound reassuring. "The Yankees have no reason to do anything against the city. I believe they will treat you all decently, Mrs. Heaphy."

"But . . . but that man Sherman . . ."

Cory knew what she meant. As the various companies of Georgia militia had been driven back to Savannah by the relentless Federal advance, they had brought with them stories of the horrible devastation wreaked by Sherman's men. Across a swath of Georgia sixty miles wide, hardly a building was left standing. They had all been burned, as had the fields on every farm and plantation. The cattle that had not been slaughtered to feed Sherman's troops had been murdered out of sheer spite, along with all the horses, mules, and pigs. By and large, the soldiers had spared the lives of the civilians they encountered, but that was all they spared. Everything else was gone, destroyed.

So Betty Heaphy had every right to worry, Cory thought. But he was convinced that Sherman would not lay waste to Savannah as he had to the rest of Georgia.

"You don't have to worry," he told her. "The Yankees want this port. They won't destroy it. They'll just occupy Savannah, like they did Vicksburg. I was there, you know, after the city was surrendered. It wasn't that bad."

Physically, it hadn't been that bad; that much was true. U. S. Grant had moved into Vicksburg with a minimum of fuss and no looting. He had even ordered that the starving townspeople be fed from his army's rations. But with the coming of the Yankees, the soul of the city and its inhabitants had been ripped out. Hope was dead, and nothing was left except a dreary existence under the heels of the conquerors.

That was what Savannah had to look forward to.

But telling that to his former hostess would do no good, Cory thought. Instead, he gave her a hug. "Don't worry. Everything will be all right."

He could hardly remember a time when that hadn't been a lie, he reflected as he left the house, found Abner, and started down to the riverfront.

Straw had been spread over the planks of the bridges to muffle the sound of marching feet—an old tactic but an effective one. The troops shouldered their weapons and picked up their packs then moved out without a backward glance at the city they were leaving behind. Along the defensive line, the Confederate bombardment continued, carried out by skeleton crews of gunners who would pull out as well once the evacuation was well under way.

Hardee remained almost until the last, his staff and aides waiting with him. The big guns fell silent as the last men abandoned the fortifications. In the navy yard, a short distance downriver, flames suddenly spurted into the night sky as the ships were set ablaze. The buildings on shore were torched as well. The Yankees would get no use from them.

File after file, rank after rank marched through the streets of Savannah to the river and then across the bridge to Hutchinson's Island. It seemed to Cory that the men would never stop coming. But he knew that no matter how many of them there seemed to be tonight, if that same number of men were spread out around the city to defend it from the marauding Yankees, they wouldn't be enough.

Abner watched the blazing shipyard and the seemingly endless ranks of soldiers. "It'd all be a mighty impressive sight if it wasn't so damned sad."

"Yes," Cory agreed. "It's damned sad, all right."

Finally, it was their turn to leave. They walked across, following the general. Behind them, engineers brought up the rear. As they crossed, these last men chopped holes in the hulls of the boats that had served as pontoons. As the boats began to sink, the ropes that held the bridge in place on shore were cut as well. The engineers hustled toward the South Carolina side of the river as the bridge began to sink behind them and drift seaward on the current.

It was almost dawn on December 21 by the time the last of the troops were safely across the river. The Confederate ram *Savannah*, the only ship that hadn't been set afire earlier in the night so that it could serve as a guard in case the Yankees started downriver, was at the end of its usefulness as well. The vessel's captain touched off a long fuse leading to a keg of gunpowder in the magazine and then rowed away in a small boat with the last of his crew. A few minutes later, a huge explosion rocked the *Savannah* and sent more flames shooting high into the air.

On the South Carolina shore, as the men were preparing to march northward, Cory heard the explosion and felt the ground tremble under his feet. He looked back, saw the burning boat upon the river, and stared at the flames for a long moment as they leaped and cavorted and eagerly consumed all they touched, sparing nothing.

Then Abner touched his shoulder, and he turned and joined the others, tramping off into a damp gray dawn cloaked in mist.

LATER THAT day, cautious Union scouts advanced to the Confederate defensive line and found it deserted. More troops poured forward in response to this news, and a delegation of officials from the city came out to meet them, bearing the word that the Confederate army was gone. Civilians were all that remained in Savannah.

By nightfall, the city was occupied by Federal troops, and American flags flew from several of the buildings. Gen. William Tecumseh Sherman entered Savannah the next day, December 22, pleased with what he found. Other than the burned navy yard and some slight damage from the artillery, the city was in fine shape—although the same could not be said of the hearts of its dispirited inhabitants. Sherman himself was ecstatic, reveling in his victory. Some of his officers regretted that Hardee's army had slipped away and had not been destroyed, but not Sherman.

The March to the Sea had been executed with only a few casualties to his army—a fact that was widely reported in the Northern newspapers when word reached the anxious Federal leaders in Washington. That overwhelming success would have been spoiled had Sherman's army been forced to fight street to street, house to house to capture Savannah. That his men would have triumphed in the end, Sherman had no doubt—but it would have been a costly victory in blood and lives.

That day of reckoning for the rebellious Southerners was still to come, but before that, he would have the chance to deal out still more punishment to the Confederacy. Well satisfied, he sat down and composed a telegram to be sent to President Lincoln in Washington:

> I beg to present you, as a Christmas gift, the city of Savannah, with one hundred and fifty heavy guns and plenty of ammunition, and also about twenty-five thousand bales of cotton.

It was a rare gift indeed, this destruction of a nation.